Until Us

Carmen Rosales

Hillside Kings Series

Hidden Scars

Hidden Lies

Hidden Secrets

Hidden Truths

Cartel Kings

Cartel Kings Book One

Steamy Romance Standalone's

The Sweat Box

Love or Honor

Changing the Game

The Prey Series

Thirst

Lust

Appetite

Forgive Me For I Have Sinned

Forbidden Flesh

Dark Romance

Dirty little Secrets

Sugar Coated Secrets

Like A Moth To A Flame

Giselle

Author's Note

I want to thank all the constant readers for purchasing my book and taking a chance on me. If it weren't for you, I wouldn't be able to keep writing and sharing my stories.

This is not as dark as my usual books, but I wanted to share Aura's story. It had some very dark moments. Death is dark, and when it happens to someone you love, it's one of the darkest moments of your life. I think Aura's loss was just as dark as any dark romance you might have read.

It was previously published as a duet Until Her and Until Now. I felt Aura's story needed a few touches. I didn't feel like I was done. To be honest, I think a book can evolve just like our lives. It can change. It can be better.

Aura's story became Until Us because it wasn't only about her. It was about everyone that was part of her journey. The people she loved and lost, but ultimately, she found happiness. In her heart, they live on forever.

Thank you, reader, for being part of my journey.

—Carmen Rosales

"Love isn't soft, like those poets say. Love has teeth
which bite and the wounds never close."
    — Stephen King, *The Body*

Kalum

It is my last year in high school, and I plan to sail through my senior year with the hottest girl on my arm. But when a new girl moves into my house, school, and life, I'm determined not to let her presence dim my spotlight. But as I grow closer to her, I feel an attraction I can't resist. I have to decide between the girl I thought I wanted and the one I can't live without. They say first loves don't last forever, but nothing prepared me for her, until...
it was too late.

Aura

Still reeling from the death of both my parents, I'm left without options except moving in with another family for room and board in exchange for a job as their new housekeeper after I graduate. Attending Elite Spencer Academy as a senior in the richest part of town, I have to navigate through the labyrinth of emotions and find myself torn between two captivating worlds. Until I meet Kalum. He was perfect. He was beautiful. Until... he spoke.

When my world crumbles, I meet Lane. Lane offers me refuge from a broken heart and a passion as intense as the engines he rebuilds. My heart has to navigate the treacherous waters of life's most profound emotions, and my choice would shape the destiny of not one but two loves.

My name is Aura Rayne, and this is our story.

Chapter 1

Aura

I sit in the back of a black Rolls-Royce as the driver pulls through a gate that leads to a sprawling mansion. My jaw almost hits the floor. I have never seen a house so big up close before. These people are insanely rich. The lawns are manicured and have hedges made into figures. The house looks like a celebrity mansion with acres of secluded real estate.

This is nothing compared to how I was raised. My parents lived on the other side of town, where the working-class people live.

The driver opens the back passenger door and gets my three suitcases out of the trunk. It's everything I own—basically the clothes on my back.

My parents were out for a night on the town when they were sideswiped by a semi-truck and died instantly. Thinking about them brings a sting to the back of my eyes. Since my parents had loans on practically everything they owned, the bank sold the house, and anything left was paid to creditors. I was left with nothing at seventeen. No money, no house, and no place to live.

My mother's neighbor heard of an opening for a housekeeper nearby where she worked on this side of town. When the family learned of my situation, they spoke to the social worker, and rather than being sent to foster care, the judge granted them temporary custody for four months until I turned eighteen. The stipulation is that I work the maximum number of hours a seventeen-year-old can work after school, and they'll provide room and board to include paid tuition to Spencer Academy for my senior year.

The double doors open, and a butler greets me.

"You must be Aura."

I give him a nervous smile. "Yes."

"I will have your belongings brought to the maid's quarters so you can get settled in."

The loss of my parents devastated me. I went to therapy and grieved for two months until the doctors were sure I was mentally stable. My friends back home promised they would be there when I returned, but I was closed off. Marcus promised he would call me and assured me our relationship wasn't over, but that has faded too.

"Thank you."

"Mrs. St. Claire will be down in a minute to give you a tour and tell you her expectations while you're here."

As I nod, I hear the click-clacking of heels on the pristine cream marble floors.

"There she is."

A woman in her late forties with an elegant chignon approaches, making my shift dress paired with my Converse feel out of place.

"Hello, Mrs. St. Claire. My name is Aura."

"Yes, yes, I know, dear. Miss Locke, your neighbor, told me so much about you. I trust her judgment, and she only said great things. I met with the social worker, who assured me everything had gone smoothly with the paperwork. I have taken the liberty to enroll you at Spencer Academy. Mr. St. Claire donates a hefty sum to the school every year, so the principal was considerate enough to grant us an exception to have you enrolled." She looks down at my worn sneakers, and I can tell by her expression she doesn't approve. She tries to play it off when I catch her scrutiny by giving me a dry smile. "I hope the trip over was easy."

"Oh yes, ma'am. Everything was perfect. I had no issues on the drive over."

"Please call me Diana. Ma'am makes me feel so... so old."

"Okay, Diana."

Looking at her closely, I notice her perfect bone structure and flawless complexion, which could only come from Botox and a good dermatologist.

She leads me toward a staircase to the second floor. Once we reach the landing from the marble staircase that leads to a hallway, there is a room next to the laundry room. She opens the door, and at the foot of the full-size bed are my three suitcases.

"This is your room. The rest of the house staff stay in the downstairs wing. I put you in this room next to the laundry room for convenience and the fact that you're younger. After school, I will need you to work for four hours cleaning the second floor and laundry. When you graduate, the head housekeeper, Miss Jean, will give you a detailed schedule. For now, I just need the second floor, including Kalum's room, cleaned, and when his friends are over, you'll tidy the mess they make. Miss Jean has had it with their messes."

She points at a wall-to-wall closet with four neatly pressed school uniforms hanging. "These are the school uniforms we picked up from the cleaners. The dry cleaner comes for pickup every Thursday before you head to school, and delivery is every

Saturday in the afternoon. Since there is no bus transportation, you will ride with Kalum to and from school."

Camila told me the St. Claires had a son the same age as me. She said that Mr. St. Claire was an equity investor tycoon and that I was in good hands.

The St. Claires will also give me a weekly two-hundred-dollar allowance as a perk for agreeing to stay with them and take the job after graduation.

When Mrs. St. Claire leaves the room, I sit on the bed and look around. It's more luxurious than any room I've ever had. The room has a mini-fridge and flat-screen TV mounted on the wall. Everything is nice and fancy, but it isn't home, and my parents aren't here. My mother was a loan officer, and my father worked as an assistant manager at a lumber store. My parents met in college, and my mother fell pregnant. She finished school, but my father had to drop out and get a job to support us.

It was rough sometimes because they lived paycheck to paycheck and could only afford the necessities. I went to public school my whole life, but my parents' love made up for my lack of luxury at home. I couldn't have asked for better parents. I take in my surroundings with a heavy heart. No more home-cooked meals or nightly talks with Mom and Dad on the front porch. They are gone, and now it's just me.

Chapter 2

Aura

I head downstairs dressed in the school uniform and light makeup to make a good first impression. I'm in the kitchen looking inside the massive fridge stocked like a grocery store and decide on yogurt for breakfast. When I close the door, I jolt.

"You scared me!"

Gray eyes belonging to the most beautiful face I have ever seen are attached to the body leaning against the granite counter. He tilts his head, raking his eyes over me in my uniform.

"Who the fuck are you?"

Well, there goes first impressions. I notice he is wearing the same colors as my uniform with a Spencer Academy logo on his blazer. This must be Kalum.

My gaze follows his tailored jacket—the guy is massive. He has broad shoulders with straight brown hair you want to sink your fingers into. The only thing that makes him a turnoff is his scowl as he looks at me with disgust.

Standing to his full height, he easily towers over me. He

must be like six foot three to my five foot one. When he crosses his arms, the jacket stretches at the seams.

"I asked you a question."

I snap myself out of it and hope he doesn't think I was ogling him. Well, I kind of was. Marcus is five-eleven and lean. This guy is muscular and huge.

"I-I'm sorry. My name is Aura, and you must be Kalum. I'm supposed to ride with you to school." I wince when he raises his eyebrows. "I'm the new housekeeper."

I open the yogurt, then grab the spoon to dip it and bring it to my mouth. I swallow, feeling the cool, creamy sensation slide down my throat that feels like heaven.

"I don't care for my mother's charity projects, and let's get one thing straight. I'm not taking you with me to school."

My eyes widen at the harshness of his tone. Why is he such an ass? How am I supposed to get there on time or there at all? My appetite vanishes, and I toss the half-eaten yogurt in the trash and quickly wash my spoon.

"Your mother told me you would give me a ride to school."

He raises his fingers and pinches his nose. "Maybe you'll understand this way. I. Do. Not. Give. A. Fuck. I'm not giving you a ride to school, ever."

I place my hands on my hips. "Why not?"

"I don't want to be seen with you."

"You don't even know me."

He claps his hands together sarcastically. "Exactly. I don't know you, and I don't want to know you. When you see me, don't look at me, don't talk to me. To me, you are just like everyone who cleans this house. The hired help. It doesn't include free rides to school. Figure that shit out on your own."

This guy may be good-looking, but he's an asshole.

"You know what? Forget it." I grab my backpack and head out the front door.

I walk down the long driveway and pull up the map on my phone. Great, three miles. I blow a puff of air out of my mouth and take a deep breath and start walking. After walking for ten minutes, I feel the ground trembling under my feet and hear the roar of an engine. I look over my shoulder to the sound coming from down the road and see a matte-black sports car zoom by me.

I give a loud shriek and run toward the grass on the side of the road as the wind blows my skirt up, but I catch it in time, making sure I don't flash anyone. When I look up for a brief second, I can see the red taillights. I make out the license plate, and it reads KALUM.

What a rude, rich prick. What is his deal?

After the three-mile hike on the road passing huge, gated estates, I see an imposing gate with the Spencer Academy crest on it. The school looks like an old church they made into a private school. Whatever it is, it screams wealth and high-privileged snobs. This is nothing compared to Spencer Public High School.

I'm sweaty and hot. My hair sticks to the back of my neck, and I pull the long tresses and smell. I love for my hair to smell like shampoo or body spray, but right now, it smells like outside. If I have to walk every morning to school, I'll have to figure something out. There is no bus, and I cannot afford an Uber every day. I will have to make some extra money for rainy and snowy days when walking is not an option.

When I pass the gate, I scan the student parking lot. There are rows of expensive cars normal teenagers do not drive. These people are insanely rich, but I'll have a tough senior year if they're all like Kalum.

I walk into the admission office and retrieve my schedule and locker number. People pass by me, giving me curious stares. Most likely because they've never seen me before.

After closing my locker with the click of the lock, I see a girl with short black hair and expressive dark eyes smiling at me. I look nervously behind me to see if she is smiling at me or someone behind me. When I turn back around, she gives me a smirk.

"Hi, I'm Exie, and you must be Aura."

Confused, I pinch my brows together. "How do you know my name?"

"That's easy, silly. Kalum already told everyone that you are the hired help in his house. The new housekeeper and his mom's new pet project."

I flinch at how cruel Kalum is by telling everyone my business. Now everyone will know I'm the charity case on top of being the new girl.

Her eyes soften. "It's okay. He's a dick to everyone. Well, except the bitch crew."

"Who's the—"

Three girls wearing their uniform skirts shorter than customary, paired with thigh-high stockings and heels, walk down the hallway in unison. Girls look with envy, and guys turn around to check them out. Two brunettes flank the blonde in the middle.

"Wait," the blonde demands, and the other two stop and turn around with raised eyebrows. The blonde looks at me from head to toe. "Yep, that's her. The maid Kalum told me about staying at his house."

I cross my hands over my chest and remember that the shirt is too snug on my breasts. Thanks to my mother, I have medium-sized breasts and a plump backside that makes it diffi-cult finding clothes that properly fit, leaving three inches of room on my waist. It wouldn't be a problem if I wasn't short and petite everywhere else. I had to quickly pin and sew the sides with a sewing kit because the skirt fit funny when I tried it on. These girls don't have that problem. They just hike the skirt to make it shorter. I'm the opposite. I'm trying to make it longer so I don't flash my ass to the world.

"Don't get any ideas with Kalum, bitch. He's taken."

I snort and walk up to her. "You know, insecurity is a real turnoff."

The hallway becomes quiet as students stand and watch. I guess no one talks down to this prissy bitch.

She glares at me, and four guys looking like Greek gods walk down the hallway. My eyes are trained on a particular one. Kalum sidles up to the blond prissy skank, and I watch as he slides his hand around her waist. She leans into him with familiarity. Come to think of it, it looks like a match made in heaven.

"What's up, baby?" he says in a sultry voice.

He turns to me with a sarcastic smirk. "How was your walk?"

Before I can answer, wanting nothing more than to wipe that smug grin off his face, the blonde speaks up.

"I was just warning your maid here when it comes to you." She purses her lips as she looks up. "You know how these common skanks hired to work get ideas."

Rolling my eyes, I avert my gaze, and it lands on honey-brown eyes. It's one of his friends standing to his left. His eyes soften, and then he looks at Kalum and who I'm assuming is Kalum's girlfriend with the way she took her claws out, ready to attack. I can't decipher his expression, but it looks to me like annoyance.

The other three eye me with amusement.

One of them is brave enough and says, "Hey, I'm Jimmy. Aura, right?"

I nod. "Yeah."

When the bell rings, signaling the start of first period,

everyone walks away like a bunch of ants on an ant farm. Once I find my assigned English class, I slide into an empty seat.

I notice the people who go here all act like Kalum. Rich snobs who haven't had a hard day in their lives. I take out the string I have been braiding, place my book on top to hold it in place, and begin braiding the strings together to make a friendship bracelet.

When I was twelve, my mother taught me how to make them. When I started high school, I kept growing out of my clothes, and things were expensive. She showed me how to braid the different colors and make different lengths with letters inside the bracelets to sell at school. Then I opened an Etsy account and began to take custom orders and turn a profit. It wasn't much at first, but now I'm making a little bit of money. That was when I didn't have to worry about being on my own so soon with no support. There is no mom or dad to give me more life lessons or guidance. I bite down on my lower lip to keep it from trembling from the grief that consumes me when I think about them being gone so soon.

I begin braiding when I feel eyes boring into me. When I turn my head, intense gray eyes narrow. The hairs on the back of my neck stand in awareness. Kalum stares at me from across the room, and I would give anything to know what's on his mind. Our gazes connect, but I keep threading. The teacher doesn't even notice. Mr. Krupp is busy writing notes on the smart board. When he finishes, I pull out my phone and snap a picture when he isn't looking.

It's the best way to take notes. Why write everything down in a rush when all you have to do is snap a picture and have all the notes saved instantly.

It's lunchtime, and I enter the cafeteria. It's fancy, with tables and actual wood chairs instead of the custom picnic tables you see in public high schools. Thinking about my old school, I miss Gina and Marcus. I tried texting Marcus this morning, but he didn't answer.

At first, I was mad he didn't respond right away. My fear was that he would find someone else and forget about me. I accepted that he would, but I didn't think he would ghost me so soon. It stings, and I guess it hurts more because I have no one. I'm all alone, and even Gina will find new friends to hang out with. They will all move on.

Getting over feeling sorry for myself, I push all my doubts aside and scroll through my phone to my bank app and calculate how much I will need to save for an Uber for rainy days, snow days, and lunch at school. I quickly figured out that from now on, I would have to bring a homemade lunch to save enough.

My plan is to graduate and leave. I have no intention of staying on with the St. Claires as their housekeeper. I know I kind of led Mrs. St. Claire on by agreeing to this arrangement, but what choice did I have? *None at the moment.*

I get up from the empty table and make my way to the line to grab something to eat. I grab a small portion and calculate how much they charge for food. The guy with the soft brown eyes the color of honey stands next to me while I contemplate buying the water or the iced tea. I quickly scan the area to find the price, and he slides his tray closer.

"Which one do you prefer?" he asks.

I chew on the corner of my lip. He probably would laugh because I need to buy the cheaper one. How do you tell a guy who lives in wealth you're worried about the price of a can of iced tea or a bottle of water?

"Take both," he says, grabbing them.

He places them on my tray. I look up, and his eyes soften, caressing my face.

"That's not necessary. I'll just take the water. I'm gonna need it to hydrate for my walk home," I tell him, placing the iced tea back.

He frowns. "Kalum didn't drive you?"

"Do you really need me to answer that? I'm the hired help and the maid. I don't get free rides to school."

"I'm Ca—"

I quickly walk away, knowing I'm being rude. He's friends with Kalum. Let him laugh it up with his friends. I don't care.

When I reach the register, the lady in a Spencer Academy staff uniform begins to ring me up.

"That'll be eleven dollars and seventy-five cents."

Jesus, that's about two hundred and thirty-five dollars a month if I eat the same thing every day. I reach for my wallet, my long hair sliding forward. A large arm towers over me and hands her a black credit card. My eyes widen, and my head tilts up when I see it's the guy with the brown eyes who I was so rude to earlier.

"Can you charge five hundred and put it on her account, please?"

My head snaps to the lunch lady as she places the card in the card reader.

"What is your name and student account number?"

"No. I-I can't take it."

He sighs behind me, handing her the iced tea. "If you could, please add this and swipe my card," he commands.

The lunch lady's eyes widen, and then she looks at me, giving me a grin.

"I can't pay you back."

"I don't want you to pay me back. It's no big deal."

"It's five hundred dollars," I deadpan.

He chuckles and shrugs. "So?"

Knowing I have no choice, I rattle off my information to the lunch lady.

He places the iced tea I wanted on my tray and grins.

"Like I was saying, my name is Cason."

"Nice to meet you. You didn't have to do that. I'm sorry I was rude to you earlier. It's just that not everyone has been very nice to me here."

"I want to be the first. If you'll let me?"

I bite my bottom lip nervously, standing by the empty table I was sitting at earlier.

His smile widens. Taking the time to get a good look at him, I notice he has straight teeth when he smiles and a nice face. He's nice to look at and seems harmless. He is tall and fills out his uniform in all the right places, but I don't trust him. I can't trust anyone here.

"Yo, Cason." We both turn to see one of his friends waving at him. "Stop slumming it with the help and come over here. We need to go over plays for our next game."

I stiffen at his remark.

Cason shakes his head, clearly pissed off, and gives him a hard glare. My eyes scan the rest of the table, and gray eyes find mine, sporting a scowl.

Rolling my eyes, I turn to Cason. "I don't think this is a good idea. You should go."

I plop myself on the chair, relieved when he walks away. Even if he paid to add money for lunch to my school account, I decide to still bring my lunch. I'm sure at the end of the year they can reimburse the card he paid with, or I can give him the money if they give it back in a check.

The three girls dubbed the bitch crew enter the cafeteria like they own the place and sit near who I can now assume are the football jocks. The blonde all over Kalum in the hallway sits next to him, practically on his lap. I catch Cason's gaze, but he looks away, acting like he's paying attention to his friends. I keep my eyes on my tray and begin to eat, but then something hits me, like tiny pebbles against my back.

I turn around and notice peanuts bouncing off me all over the floor. I look up and notice Jimmy and everyone laughing with their hands covering their mouths, trying not to attract attention from the cafeteria staff.

I take a deep breath. "These rich pricks are dumb and immature," I mumble.

I notice Cason looks at his friends with a frown, but he doesn't stop them. My eyes find Kalum and watch him laughing along with the bitch crew, and I give him a glare.

Another peanut flies and lands in my hair. I slam the tray on the table, and it draws curious glances from the other students. They begin to laugh when they realize what's happening. I slide the peanuts out of my long hair. I move to empty my tray in the trash, needing to leave, not having touched my lunch.

I'm not one to throw away food usually, but students are not allowed to take the trays out of the cafeteria, so I'm fucked. I can't stay here when it's everyone against me, so I grab the water, my gaze trained on the jock table, and notice Cason following my movements. He frowns when he sees I threw away my food, and I purposely throw the iced tea, letting it plant inside the trash bin with a big thud and make my way to stop by their table looking right at Jimmy.

He gives me a smirk. "What's wrong, Aura? Don't you like peanuts? They can taste good if you spread them."

I cross my arms over my chest. "You really need to stop being so careless and pick your nuts up from the floor. They're so tiny, they are scattering all over the place."

Kalum chuckles, and Cason grins. I lower my voice. "And

just so you know. You're the last person I would ever spread my legs for, you nasty prick."

Jimmy snickers, but I can tell by the twitch of his right eye that I hit a nerve by calling him nasty and announcing I would never give him the time of day. He's attractive in a boyish, immature way, but so not my type. None of them are. I can't stand them, and the bitch crew is even lower on my list.

I give Kalum one last glare before Jimmy says, "I hope you enjoyed your lunch."

I raise my middle finger high enough in the air so he can see as I walk toward my next class.

Chapter 3

Kalum

I watch her retreat out the cafeteria door, admiring the way her skirt hugs her small waist and the fabric moves up her ass. The girl must have a huge ass for her uniform to bunch up like that. I see her trying to lower it so she doesn't flash everyone, and just thinking about it makes my cock strain in my uniform trousers. Fuck, she's hot. When I saw her this morning in my kitchen bent over looking in the refrigerator, I leaned on the counter to admire the view, hoping to get a glimpse.

When she straightened, I could tell the top was too tight over her chest, telling me she has a big rack. My eyes lingered over her until I reached beautifully shaped brows, a slender nose, and the most kissable mouth I have ever seen. I couldn't believe this was the seventeen-year-old my parents hired as our new housekeeper. I don't know the details, but I do know that she turns eighteen in a couple of months.

When she asked me for a ride, I knew I couldn't be that close to her in the confinement of my car. I wouldn't make it the three-mile drive to school with her right next to me. I don't know what the hell is wrong with me. I never lose my mind over a girl. I'm Kalum St. Claire, starting linebacker for Spencer Academy, and I can fuck any chick I want.

All I have to do is snap my fingers, and one appears. It's most likely why Sarah is on my dick. She is always trying to get me to have sex with her. Sarah is your typical snooty rich girl with blond hair and classical features, but she is no Aura.

"That's fucked up, Jimmy," Cason says disappointedly.

I look up to see what he's complaining about.

Jimmy shrugs. "I think I'm in love."

I give him a glare because Jimmy saying that means he wants to stick his dick in her.

He smirks at me. "What? Who cares. Besides, Kalum, you said she is just the help. Who gives three fucks about her anyway?"

"She didn't even get to eat," Cason chides.

"Aw. Catching feelings already from slumming it."

"Fuck you, Jimmy," Cason snaps.

Wanting to know what he said to her, I take the opportunity and ask, "Yo, Case. What were you telling her in the line?"

He swipes his hand over his face. "Nothing."

Why is he evading the question? Alarm bells go off in my head. What am I missing here?

"She lives in my house, asshole. I need to know what you told her and what she said."

"Nothing, Kalum. It's no big deal. She didn't do anything."

I give him a hard stare, and he sighs. "I paid for her lunch, alright?" he confesses.

What the fuck? He paid for her lunch. My stomach sinks. I know I was a total dick to her this morning, but another guy paying for Aura's anything just doesn't sit well with me.

"Why?" I ask with a hard edge to my voice.

He gives me a hard stare, and I raise a brow. He knows I'm pissed, and he looks

nervous.

"I didn't think it was cool for her to worry if the price of water or iced tea was too high. She obviously can't afford to pay for her own lunch. She hardly had anything on her plate." He

points at Jimmy. "And asswipe over here made sure she felt uncomfortable enough that she ended up throwing it all away. I put five hundred on her lunch account so she

didn't have to worry. I was trying to be nice."

"How noble of you. I hope you don't think this means you get to fuck Kalum's maid now," Jimmy says sarcastically.

"Shut the fuck up, Jimmy," I snap. Jimmy shuts his mouth, clearly realizing I'm not fucking around. I'm bigger, and I have more size than they do, and everyone knows I have a bad temper, so they tread carefully around me.

My head spins as I imagine Cason with her. I just met her hours ago, but here I am playing with my emotions. I take out my phone, using the opportunity not to allow Cason or anyone to buy Aura anything. I send Cason five hundred dollars through the Pay app.

His phone vibrates, and he scowls when he opens the notification. "I don't want the money back. I didn't tell you to send it to me."

"I don't need my parents breathing down my neck about you covering her lunch," I say

with a bite in my tone. "It's bad enough she's living with me."

"I hope you talk them into forgetting about the whole thing," Sarah chimes in.

I push Sarah off me to give me distance. The perfume she wears is starting to get to me. *Liar.* What really bothers me is the way Cason is acting about Aura.

"You should start worrying about her three-mile hike to and from school every day. The poor girl said she needed water so she could hydrate. You are such an asshole, Kalum. I'm

positive she didn't do anything to you for you to treat her like shit."

"Stay away from her. She's my problem, not yours," I growl.

Sarah whips her hair around and faces me. "Why are you so bothered about it, Kalum?"

I give her a hard stare. "Stay out of it, Sarah."

She pouts and turns around with a huff. Good. I don't need her jealousy crap right now. Aura is a pain in my ass. I didn't ask to babysit a chick who will eventually clean my underwear. Fuck. Just thinking about her touching anything that encases my dick on a

daily basis turns me the fuck on. I flew right past her while she was walking, hoping her skirt

would lift to get a glimpse, but I was disappointed. I'm dying to get a glimpse of her plump ass. My mind wonders if she is wearing boy shorts, a thong, or regular panties. I never would have thought my mother would agree to have someone who looked like her living in my house.

Cason was eye-fucking her. At first, I thought he was curious about Aura, but the way he acts when I'm giving him shit about her tells me all that I need to know. Cason likes her.

Brian glanced briefly at her, and I know it's because of Wendy that he didn't full-blown

gawk at her. When Aura walks into a room, she is totally unaware of the effect she has on guys.

Chapter 4

Aura

I t's the end of the day, and I dread the three-mile walk to the St. Claire's house. I can't say it's home because I don't have a home. After my long walk-through mansion road, as I call it, I have to work for four hours cleaning the second floor, which includes Kalum's room and bathroom. I wonder if he is messy or a clean freak.

I'm lost in my thoughts when I swing the metal door of my locker open and do a double take. There, sitting in all its glory, is a cold can of iced tea and a warm sandwich. I lean back slightly over the locker door to see if anyone is watching me or to give me a hint of who could have placed the food there but come up empty. It's just people trying to get their stuff and leave for the day.

I check the lock on the door. Whoever placed the food inside knows how to get into my locker without the code. When I grab the warm sandwich, the melted Swiss and turkey sub makes my stomach growl in protest. It smells so good my mouth waters.

Looking at the wrapper, I notice that it's from a sub place

and not the cafeteria, and I wonder if it was Cason. He figured I liked the iced tea, and I remember him frowning when I had to throw away my lunch because of Jimmy and his immature bullshit.

Closing the locker with a thud, I make my way with the sandwich and iced tea in hand, quickly opening the wrapper and taking the first bite. I outwardly groan at how good and perfect it tastes. It was exactly what I needed.

When I make it out of the parking lot, I see a familiar black Rolls-Royce parked in the student parking lot. The driver quickly exits and gives me a grin.

"Miss Rayne?" he drawls.

I slow my steps and swallow the bite of food I had in my mouth. "Yes."

"I'm here to take you home." He opens the back passenger door and waits for me to enter the vehicle.

"Oh, I think you're mistaken. I wasn't waiting to be driven anywhere."

Who could have called for a driver? I place the can of iced tea under my arm and retrieve my phone to see if I have any missed messages.

When I see there aren't any, I look up. "I'm sorry, but no one has let me know that they sent you to pick me up."

He smiles. "I can assure you the St. Claires have requested me to take you home."

I recognized him from the first time I was taken to the St. Claire's house, and since the ride is requested from them, I don't want to argue or give cause for Mr. and Mrs. St. Claire to be upset with me. I slide inside the luxury cabin of the car, and like the first time, the smell of fresh, expensive leather assaults me.

I have never been in a luxurious car before meeting the St. Claires and quickly wrap my sandwich up to avoid making a mess in such a beautiful car. My parents always had one car, and it was a used Honda with no leather or any luxury this vehicle offers. The driver takes us out onto the road, and the ride is short since it's only three miles.

<hr>

I enter the pristine home so over the top with marble floors and expensive vases with an iron-accented spiral grand staircase like you see in celebrity houses on TV.

I walk up the staircase and enter my room to get ready to clean the second floor like Mrs. St. Claire instructed me to.

After cleaning the hallway bathroom and making sure everything is in place, I look over to a closed door that must be Kalum's room. Taking a deep breath, I close my eyes briefly and turn the intricate knob, watching the door slowly swing open. My eyes scan the football trophies lining the wall of the massive bedroom.

Looking around, I realize his king-size four-poster bed is unmade. There is a pile of clothes in one corner and a huge mess on a wooden desk that must be where he does his homework.

Walking farther inside, I inhale the scent of his cologne mixed with a scent that is all male. This is what he must smell like up close, and if I'm being honest, it's attractive. If I compared the scent of Kalum to Marcus, there is just no comparison. Kalum smells expensive and dangerous. Marcus is just, well, Marcus. Typical teenage football player and the star quarterback of Spencer Public High School.

I begin to work stripping the sheets of Kalum's bed, hoping I don't find something that will scar me for the rest of my life like a used condom, and place the comforter with sheets in separate piles. Placing my headphones in my ears, I play

"24/7" featuring Ella Mai and start singing along as I get to the pillows next.

Swaying my hips, I grab the caddy just outside the door and begin to wipe his nightstand. My brows furrow when I notice a cell phone plugged into the charger. Awareness snakes down my spine, and I realize I'm not alone.

The air in the room has changed, and it's charged with an energy I can't place. The smell of clean body wash that matches the scent of cologne assaults me. I turn my head and jolt, dropping the rag in my hand.

I place my hand over my chest and take my headphones off. "You scared me," I say breathlessly.

Standing in all his shirtless glory with a white towel wrapped around his waist is Kalum leaning against the door-jamb, tilting his head with a brow raised. Are those tattoos all over his arms and chest?

Come on, Aura, get a grip.

"I-I'm so sorry. I didn't know you were home." I lower my gaze so he doesn't notice I'm staring at him.

He pushes off the doorway and walks farther into the room, and my eyes move, looking at the floor. I have never seen a man naked in person before, but Kalum St. Claire is all man, and the lower half of me recognizes it. The man is gorgeous—everywhere—with a chiseled body, but he has the worst attitude when he speaks.

My cheeks heat. I bend my knees, lowering slowly to pick up the rag, and turn to keep wiping down the furniture, hoping he will go back and change in the bathroom, preferably with the door closed.

"What are you doing in here?"

I freeze and angle my head toward him, and he is still clad in the towel.

"What does it look like? I'm cleaning your room. Your

mother instructed me to do it when I came home. I'm sorry. I didn't know you would be here. I was trying to get it done quickly before you made it home."

"I didn't agree for you to clean my room, and I prefer you didn't unless I'm here. I don't want you going through my stuff." He opens a drawer and takes out some boxers, the ding of the brass handle sounding against the hard wood when he slides the drawer closed.

I'm about to leave the room when he suddenly drops the towel, and my eyes widen when they land on his cock. Oh my God, he's huge. Everywhere. I'm stunned, not believing he would do something like that, but I'm more shocked at his sheer size.

I spin around. "What the hell, Kalum."

"Like I said, I didn't agree for you to clean my room. You're in my room, and I'm getting dressed."

"I could leave and come back," I quip.

"What's wrong, Aura? Are you nervous?"

"No. I'm just not interested in seeing you get dressed," I snap.

I *am* nervous. The guy looks like an Adonis with straight dark-brown hair, a perfect nose, a chiseled jaw that can cut my panties in half with a hard body and a cock that is freakishly big. His body makes me feel hot and wet. I have never seen a man naked except when I was curious and Googled what a man would look like without their clothes on, but I have to say, Kalum looks better. I have no one to compare his cock to because I've never been intimate with a man before. The most Marcus and I have done is kiss, and he felt me up on my breast my junior year when he drove me home. We were kissing, and he began to lower his hand and touch my breasts, but it didn't feel right, so I made an excuse for him to stop. Marcus was understanding and patient. He respected my wishes, and that made me like him even more.

He scoffs. "Yeah, right. Every girl does."

"Well, I'm not every girl, and I have a boyfriend."

He chuckles. "Yeah, I'm sure he takes great care of you. That's why you're here cleaning my room. Please. I'm almost positive he hasn't called you since you got here and is most likely balls deep in pussy."

I flinch because he's right. Marcus hasn't called me to see if I arrived. Gina texted me that she was busy with school and would text me later, but she never did.

"You're such a pig."

"No, I'm honest. If he hasn't called, it's because you're easy to forget. Don't get all high and mighty with me like you're too good for me or some shit. You don't have to worry about me because I don't fuck ugly chicks."

I look him straight in the eyes, trying not to look at his chest. "At least we can agree we both find each other unattractive."

His eyes flicker with something I can't describe. Like it bothers him that I find him unattractive.

"Good. I'm glad we understand each other. Now clean my room and get out."

My eyes sting. Kalum has been such an ass since I got here, and I have done nothing for him to act like that toward me.

Grabbing the sheets I piled on the floor, I head to the laundry room, blinking back the tears threatening to spill. I refuse to cry in front of him.

I place the soiled sheets and pour the soap inside the washer, and when I close the washing machine door, a sob I was trying to keep at bay escapes. The tears spill, and I sniff, missing my mother and my father desperately. How could this have happened?

How could my life be turned upside down? One minute,

I'm happy with my parents, my boyfriend, my best friend at school, and in a split second, I've lost my parents and every-thing I have ever known, leaving me with practically no money, no home, and a job as a housekeeper to a privileged family with a rich snob for a son who apparently hates the fact that I'm here.

Chapter 5

Kalum

She practically ran out of my room with my sheets, and I could have sworn I saw tears in her eyes. Dropping the towel and appearing naked before her was a bold move. My first thought was to make her uncomfortable, but maybe I'd been seeking her reaction.

When I saw her swaying her hips, oblivious that I stood in the doorway of my bathroom, I was mesmerized by her body in tight black leggings and a T-shirt tied in a knot at her waist. I was right. Aura has an amazing hourglass shape with ass and tits for days. When she turned around, sensing me watching her standing there, my eyes dipped to her large breasts.

She looked like she belonged in my room with her messy bun, like she has been cleaning my room for years, not as a housekeeper, but as my girl because she wanted to.

When she told me she found me unattractive and had a boyfriend, I saw red. I smirked because I was jealous, and all I wanted her to do was forget he existed. He doesn't deserve her. What guy would let their girlfriend accept this arrangement? Why did her parents let her go? What type of parents let another stranger adopt them to be a housekeeper once they turn eighteen in a few months? It's none of my business, but now I'm curious.

Getting close to my bedroom door, I move slowly in case she walks back into my room. When I'm sure she isn't heading this way, I peer my head out and look toward the laundry room.

When the machine pauses, switching cycles, I can hear faint sniffing. Is she crying? She turns sideways, not realizing I'm watching her like a creep, and something breaks inside me. Fresh, hot tears stream down her face, and she sobs.

The instinct inside me has me approaching her. I never intended to make her cry. Something about the way she cries tears me apart. I wonder which part of the messed-up things I said caused her to cry.

When I take long strides down the hallway, her eyes widen, glistening. She quickly wipes her tears and looks away.

Between a sob and a sniff, she asks, "Is there something you need?"

"I need you to look at me," I demand.

She turns her face, and the look of sorrow laced with pain guts me. I'm not a softy by any means, and a girl crying doesn't do it for me, but somehow, Aura crying is like a knife twisting painfully inside my soul.

Another tear escapes down her beautiful face. Aura is breathtakingly gorgeous. Telling her she was ugly was me being an ass because she wasn't giving me the reaction I'm used to receiving from other girls.

My thumb softly wipes away her tears. She stands still, and I'm relieved she lets me. The soft touch of her skin shoots an electric current up my hand directly to my cock.

Leaning in so my lips are close to her ear, I whisper, "I'm sorry to have made you cry. I'm an ass sometimes."

I lean closer to her cheek and place my lips there, feeling

the salty wetness. My eyes close as I smell the soft, flowery scent coming off her skin. The way she looks is perfect. She's perfect. "If something I said crossed the line, I'm sorry."

Her eyes find mine again, and up close, her light brown eyes are striking. I could get lost in them, and it scares the shit out of me. The feelings Aura evokes inside me have me all types of fucked up. When she walks in the room, my eyes follow her like lasers finding a target.

We stand there looking into each other's eyes until she breaks the spell. "It wasn't my choice to be here. I'm sorry for barging into your life. I can tell you don't like the fact that I'm here, but neither do I."

Her words are like a blast of cold air when you're trying to keep warm. Standing back, I give her space. She wipes her face and takes a deep breath, trying to compose herself.

"I'll stay out of your way as much as possible. You won't even know I'm here. I-I appreciate your apology."

Not the words I expected to hear. Hearing them should make me feel better, but I feel none of those things. But telling her it's okay will make her think I want her around and that I have changed my mind about her staying here. If she was not attending my school or having her so close and cleaning my room, maybe I wouldn't care.

In the morning, I seek my mother out before I leave for school. I find her seated, reading to catch up on the latest gossip. She hears me approach and lowers the magazine. Her eyes find mine, and she smiles.

"Good morning, Kalum. How was the first day of school? I hope you helped Aura feel welcome and showed her around."

I lean on the edge of the sofa. "Good morning, Mom. Actually, that is what I wanted to talk to you about."

Her eyes blink fast, a telltale sign she's nervous. "Is everything okay with Aura? You have to make sure she's okay, Kalum. I know I've sprung this on you, but—"

I'm annoyed with her for not telling me her plans to bring a girl my age to live in my house, enroll her in my school, and let her invade my life. I interrupt her.

"Where did she come from? And why is she attending my school?"

My mother sits up straight. "Watch how you talk to me, young man. You may be turning eighteen in two weeks, but you'll respect me and not question my decisions in my own home."

"You know I don't intervene with your projects or whatever you plan, but I do have a problem when it involves my life. This is my senior year; you and Dad want me to take up college and eventually take over the business, and I'm fine with that. I have never told you no, but accepting a strange girl in our home and invading my space is taking things too far. I don't want her cleaning my room or attending my school. Out of all the people you could have hired, why her?"

My mother raises her hands and drops them in her lap. "Because she has nowhere else to go, Kalum."

"What is this? A charity case? I know you like to help in the community, but that is her parents' job to worry about. Not yours."

"They're dead," she says quietly.

My thoughts instantly go to the girl I have treated like shit since I first laid eyes on her and then the way the guys have treated her. The way Sarah threatened her. If provoked, Sarah and her little crew of friends could cause a lot of trouble for Aura.

Then the memory of Aura's words come back. She said if she had a choice, she wouldn't be here. It means there aren't many options or none at all.

"I'm sorry to have thrown this on you at the last minute, but Aura has no other family. Her parents were all she had. Camila has known Aura since she was a child and knew her parents very well. She'll be eighteen in three months. After the bank sold off her home and their car, leaving her with nothing, the judge granted me temporary custody for ninety days until she is an adult. She can work only four hours a day until she graduates in three months. Then after she would be offered the position on our household staff. That was the agreement. She has nowhere to go, and I couldn't say no. You know how that would make us look."

I nod, feeling like a piece of shit. Here I am with both my parents, living the best life, with all the luxuries a person could want, when other people mourn the loss of not only one parent but two. I know my mother isn't all that bad and means well. She is hiring Aura to clean. What is more irritating is that she is more worried about how people see us as a family for turning down a poor girl in need. In my mother's mind, word would get around, and she would be ridiculed for being a snob. It's not Aura she really cares about. It's her image.

Taking a deep breath, I ask, "How did they die?"

My mother's eyes soften. "A car accident. They died instantly. Aura was waiting for them to come home after making them dinner. According to Camila, she would always make them dinner when they worked late."

I nod, feeling like a bigger dick than last night when I basically told her that her boyfriend didn't care about her and is fucking some other chick because she was forgettable. She wasn't crying because of what I said. She was crying because she misses her parents and hates it here. Which means she must hate me for how I treated her, and I can't blame her. I would hate me too.

"I understand."

She stands to walk me out the front door so I can head out to school. She looks around outside and frowns.

"Where's Aura?" my mother asks.

Shit. I forgot that I told her to walk to school because I don't give rides to the hired help. Cason's words about her walking haunt me. Looking guilty, I gaze at my mother over the roof of my black Lamborghini, seeing her murderous expression. She knows something is up when I don't answer.

"Kalum St. Claire, tell me where Aura is right now," she demands.

Even if I'm six foot three and built like a house, my mother can still make me feel like a mouse with her hard tone.

Wincing, I tell her. "I-I kind of told her that I don't give rides to the hired help and that she could walk to school."

"Are you fucking crazy?"

My mother never curses. But what gets me is that she isn't mad about her walking to school.

My eyes narrow. "It was only to school. I told Henry to pick her up after school after I realized how messed up it sounded."

Crossing her arms over her chest, I know she's upset. "If something happens to that girl because of you, you will be held responsible. You will explain to a judge why you were careless and let her get hurt. It will fall on you; now get in that thing you call a car and go find her. And make sure she makes it safe to and from school."

"Yes, ma'am."

She notices I'm annoyed. She thinks it's because she is reprimanding me because of my actions. I'm not annoyed that I messed up. I'm more pissed off that she is worried about what will happen to her because of the judge and not to Aura.

Chapter 6

Kalum

Driving down the road to school, I don't see Aura anywhere. Checking the time on my car, I see that school doesn't start for another hour. *Fuck.* My stomach sinks, thinking the worst. Slamming my hand on my steering wheel, I drive through the gates and park in my designated spot in the school parking lot, noticing the cars parked in the same row. The guys are already here.

Getting out, I quickly make it inside to the lockers, scanning the hallway, but I don't see any sign of Aura. She must be here already. I need to find her, even if I have to hunt every inch of this school until I do. Quickly getting my shit from my locker on the opposite side of the hall, Brian saunters up next to me.

"Hey, brother?"

"What's up?"

"Nothing, just leaving Cason in the library."

My brows furrow. Cason in the library? "What the fuck is he doing there?"

Cason never sets foot in the library. The library is for

people with no social life or money. We have our own library at our own homes and the latest computers. There is no reason to set foot inside the school library.

Then it dawns on me, but I ask anyway, "What is he doing in there?"

I need confirmation. Only one person who attends Spencer Academy is without the same privilege.

"More like who is he talking to or, rather, who is he trying to get to agree to go out with him. The guy has it bad for the new chick."

I don't wait for Brian to keep going. My ass moves like it's on fire. There is no way I will allow Aura to go out on a date with Cason. He isn't right for her.

It's not that Cason is a bad guy. He has a great heart and a promising future as the quarterback for Spencer Academy. He already has colleges lined up, so he only has to choose. His parents have money and plenty of real estate.

This is the first time I've seen Cason smitten with a girl. It's usually the other way around. Girls know he is the type you take home to your parents.

"Where are you going?" Brian calls out, but I ignore him.

Aura is mourning the loss of her parents. All it takes is the right touch and the right words from a guy for her to give in.

Pushing the double doors, I enter the library with more force than necessary. The librarian looks up, and her eyes widen when she notices it's me. Yeah, I don't come to the library often. None of the guys on the football team do, and if we do, it's to fuck a chick in the back.

That thought has my head spinning. If he so much as puts a finger on her, I'm going to... what? I shouldn't give a fuck. Her ass is in school, safe and sound for my mother's peace of mind. That's all that should matter.

My eyes quickly scan the tables until I find her head

looking down at a book and Cason speaking softly. It doesn't look like she's paying attention, but I know she's listening to whatever he's planning and trying to convince her to agree to. Aura's shoulders are tense. She doesn't trust Cason, and if I were her, I wouldn't trust anyone either. Including me.

"Aura," I call out.

Her head lifts when she hears me call her name. I can't lie and say her name on my lips doesn't do things. Her name is beautiful, like the girl. The girl is innocence wrapped in a body made to seduce men. Her light brown hair with a soft touch of red and the light tan of her skin. Today, she wears makeup in soft, neutral tones, but it's not overdone like Sarah or the other girls. Aura doesn't even need makeup.

Her legs are crossed one over the other. I approach them, sitting on the wood table, and see that her skirt rides up, showing the smooth skin on her sexy thigh. My cock twitches in my pants, and I mentally snap out of it, trying not to embarrass myself in front of her. Cason looks at me with a slight scowl on his face, and I give him a hard stare that says *what the fuck are you doing?*

"Yes, Kalum," she answers in a soft voice.

Jesus, the way she says my name is not making this feeling in my cock any better. Even her voice is intoxicating. The softness with which my name rolls off her lips makes my heart beat faster.

"Where were you? I was looking for you."

She chews her bottom lip nervously, then looks at Cason. Watching her chew her lip has me wanting to kiss the damage she's inflicting on the soft flesh of her lower lip. It makes me want to groan.

I need to get laid. Thinking about this poor girl like that is ten types of fucked up.

Her eyes dart between Cason and me and finally land on me.

"I-I got here early and left before you were ready to leave. I-I was trying to stay out of your way like you wanted."

Cason closes his eyes and shakes his head in disappointment. She rubs her arms, and you can tell she's cold. I don't feel how chilled it is inside the library because instead of our school blazers, the football team wears their letterman jackets like the one Cason and I are sporting.

"How did you get here, and more importantly, where is your sweater?"

"I got here like I did the first day, and I don't have a school sweater."

"I can take you to school. You don't have to walk, Aura," Cason says.

My fists clench to my sides.

"She doesn't need a ride from some asshole trying to get under her skirt."

"Nah, it's better for some creep to snatch her from the side of the road because the dickhead that is supposed to give her a ride has a stick up his ass and doesn't want to be seen with her in his car. And for the record, Kalum, you know me better than that. I don't need to give a girl a car ride to get under her skirt. That's Jimmy's MO."

He gets up, clearly pissed at me. He looks at Aura and begins to take off his jacket. My lip snarls. "Give her that, and I swear, Cason, you're pushing it," I warn.

Aura begins to look nervously between Cason and me. She pushes her seat back to stand.

"Please, stop it."

We both look at her with my fist clenched and Cason fixing his jacket over his shoulders.

"You guys are friends, and you don't need to get mad at

each other." She looks at Cason. "I can't go out with you because I have a boyfriend. I appreciate you being kind to me and trying to help me out, but even if I didn't have Marcus, it wouldn't be right. I work for his parents, and I only attend here because of that fact. It feels awkward, and it probably makes Kalum feel uncomfortable that you're taking one of his house-keepers out on a date. You're a good-looking guy and you seem very nice, but like you said, you can have any girl. Don't waste your time with someone like me."

Cason frowns, and his eyes soften. I'm shocked by her reasons for not accepting any of his advances. She turned him down gently, but the fact that she mentioned her stupid boyfriend annoys me. Then her last words that she's my house-keeper and couldn't go out with anyone here makes me feel happy, but the fact that she said he is good-looking when she told me she found me unattractive is a huge blow to my ego.

Cason smiles. "You think I'm good-looking?"

That is all he heard when she turned him down. What a dork.

She gives him a smile, and holy fuck, her smile is mesmerizing. Cason swallows because she has the same effect on him as she has on me. She has a sweetness, and the way she softens her tone when trying to reason with someone has the opposite effect. All you hear is the sweetness of her voice, and you forget that she's trying to let you down gently.

"Don't get all excited, but yeah, I do."

My chest squeezes in defeat. What the hell? Cason is a good-looking guy, but not to sound like a conceited douche, I am way more handsome than him. I'm taller, have more muscle, and I have a better-looking face. Let's not forget, I can treat her better than he can.

Cason turns. "Fire her," he says jokingly.

Giving them both a sneer, I say, "If it were up to me, I

would. Unfortunately, my mother is the one who agreed to bring her on board. So here we are."

She flinches. I know it's because that would mean she would have nowhere else to go, but now I don't care. My pride has taken a secret blow, and I won't let her know that me knowing she would have said yes, if circumstances would have been different, is messing with me. It shouldn't but it does, and the asshole in me wants to see if she finds me as unattractive as she claims. She is either good at hiding her feelings or a very good liar.

I look at my phone and see there is still time to get breakfast. It will take only fifteen minutes to pick up a sweater from the uniform shop that opens early for students who need alterations or dry cleaning and get a quick coffee.

"Aura, get your stuff. Let's go."

Her head tilts as she picks up her stuff. "Where?"

"Where are you taking her?" Cason asks, confused.

"None of your fucking business, Cason. She is my responsibility, not yours," I snap, and he backs off.

"I'm not—"

My nostrils flare. "Aura. Let's go," I say in a hard tone. I'm trying not to be a dick to her, but I'm ticked off.

She says her goodbyes to my best friend. The one I want to punch in his smug face right now. She follows me out of the library, and some students who get here early look over at me with Aura trailing me, giving us curious stares. Everyone knows she works in my house as a housekeeper after school for four hours by yours truly.

It probably makes me an ass to out her like that, but I was pissed at my parents and at her for intruding in my life. The worst part is I want her. I want her to want me like I want her.

She follows me to my matte-black Lamborghini Aventador, and she looks confused, not knowing what to do.

"Get in," I demand.

She stands there, biting the lower lip I find so sexy. I walk over to open the door, and as it lifts, I realize... shit, I forgot I told her I didn't want her riding in my car.

Once I have her buckled in, my eyes trail over her smooth thighs as her skirt rides up in the low sports car. As I'm leaning inside the car, my head tilts, and I'm lost. If I don't cover Aura, I will not make it with her alone in my car. Proving my theory that she does find me attractive will be harder than I thought.

Walking around to the driver's side, I slide my letterman jacket off before slipping inside the car. When I start the massive engine, I drape my jacket over her thighs.

Her eyes find mine, and she looks relieved. "Thank you," she says softly.

"Of course."

We arrive at the shopping center where the uniform store and breakfast café are located, and I hop out of the car, opening the door for her.

Once inside the store, I walk up to where the school sweaters are located for girls. I pick one and hand it to her for her to try on. She walks over and gets thigh-high socks and enters the dressing room. Fuck me, not the thigh-high socks.

After five minutes, the lady at the counter eyes me warily. She knows who I am, and the fact I'm here with a girl probably has her asking silent questions because I'm not exclusive with any girl, including Sarah.

We just hook up for a quick lay with no attachments or emotions. At least not for me. I would make it official with her because we hang out with our friends. The only issue with Sarah is her jealous rants, but I usually turn a blind eye and ignore them. I have never fallen for a girl. Sarah is just convenient, and every guy wants her. She is pretty with a nice figure, but she is a snob with a trust fund. Her attitude isn't any better.

I can appreciate a gorgeous girl, but I wouldn't lose my head over one. That's why this thing I have with Aura needs to be checked. Maybe scaring her would do the trick. She says she has a boyfriend. She may have had one, but there is no way they're serious. Not now with what happened to her parents causing her to move away and into my house.

Entering the dressing room, I quickly click the latch shut once inside. The sight of Aura bending down in her school skirt with her thigh-high socks on has me frozen. I can see the crease of her ass where it meets the back of her thigh, and fuck me, she is wearing those sexy boy shorts.

My cock gets hard like a rod of steel in my uniform trousers, proving what I assumed all along since laying my eyes on her the first time. Aura has a delicious ass, more than my big hands can grasp. She instantly straightens and turns toward me with her hand over her chest when she notices me inside the fitting room, silently watching her.

She crosses her arms over her chest defensively. "What are you doing in here?"

I walk up to her until her back is up against the wall. Her head tilts, and her flowery scent hits me, and I get lost in her. My hand caresses her face slowly. Her breaths come out in soft pants, and I can tell she's nervous.

"I lied."

Her brows pinch in confusion. "About what?"

My chest rises and falls faster with each breath. This girl affects me like no other, and I can't explain it. All I can do is act on what I'm feeling, and what I'm feeling is crazy.

I want to be balls deep inside her while I make her come, watching her scream my name as I make her mine. I want her to acknowledge she finds me attractive and that this attraction is not one-sided. It is the only thing I want from her right now.

My lips hover over hers, and I'm relieved she doesn't pull away or protest. "I think you're breathtakingly gorgeous."

She raises a brow. "But you said you found me ugly and unattractive."

My head dips near her ear, and I whisper, "Does it feel like I find you unattractive?" My lips are inches from the skin I'm dying to kiss. I want to know what she feels like on my lips. "You feel it, too. Don't you, Aura?"

She pulls back to take a breath. "Yes, Kalum. I feel it," she admits.

She feels the pull, like two magnets that want to snap toward each other when they are near. My eyes close, and the backs of two fingers slide down to her neck so I can feel her pulse beat, and it is beating rapidly. Aura does something to me. She is permanently inside my head.

"You're so beautiful. It hurts," I tell her. Her head slowly lifts, and her brown gaze finds mine. Her soft, velvety lips part. I want to kiss her, but I know I can't. Aura is fragile right now, and I would be no better than any other guy trying to take advantage of her vulnerability. "Does this mean you find me attractive?"

Her pink tongue peeks out from her parted lips, and a blush appears on her cheeks. I give her a grin, raising my brow and waiting for her answer.

"Yes," she finally says.

"I need you to do something for me," I say softly, our bodies inches apart with my fingers still resting on her neck. She is so much shorter than me. She can't be any more than a little over five feet tall.

"Okay."

"Don't ever take another man's jacket. If you need one, I'll make sure you have one."

She nods.

"From now on, I'll take you to school. You don't walk alone. Is that understood, Aura?"

She nods again.

"Words, sweetheart. I need words."

"Yes, Kalum."

"We are attracted to each other, but it doesn't mean anything."

The light in her eyes dims, and she moves so I have no choice but to drop my hand from her neck. I know what I said is not what she expected to hear, but I was proving a point, and I made it. Mission accomplished.

Nothing can happen between us. We are too different, and we come from separate worlds. It wouldn't be fair to her. Something passes over her features, and it has me worried because she freezes and her chin lifts. Her lips form a thin line, and her eyes flash in anger.

"Fine, but don't touch me like that ever again. Are we clear? I may be attracted to you physically, but emotionally, I'm not. The fact that a guy wants to keep his attraction to a girl a secret can only mean one thing."

"Yeah, and what is that?" I quip, annoyed.

"You're ashamed of it. You don't want anyone to know because you care too much about what people think. I get why you came in here. You just wanted to prove your point. You won. Happy now?"

I'm not happy. I've made things worse by hurting her. She's right, but I wasn't prepared to feel this attraction to her, and I don't even know her.

She's our housekeeper. This is not some girl I can bang and toss aside. She sleeps in the room next to mine. I would have to look at her after I'm done with her.

"You know what?" I step back with my hand on the latch to the dressing room door. "You're right. I'm sorry. I acted like a jerk, and I took advantage of you. It was a mistake, and it shouldn't have happened. You work in my house, and once you graduate, you will be someone my parents hire to clean."

She stiffens, and the look of hurt across her face almost has me taking the words back.

Almost.

She smooths out her uniform, and I have to admire her pride. I can sense she wants to tell me to go screw myself, but it will not help her cause or her situation.

When I turn around to leave, sliding the latch, her words stop me.

"Don't worry, Kalum St. Claire. I've learned from my mistakes in allowing you this close to me. We can forget this conversation ever happened, but don't you ever tell me whose jacket I can wear because it certainly will not be yours."

I never expected her words to hit me like a spear in my back, and I instantly regret what I said.

She continues. "I may be the hired maid, but you don't own me, and I sure as hell don't belong to you. If you come at me again, I will kick you so far in your balls that you will have to artificially inseminate the day you want to have kids. Understood?"

I nod, knowing I have ruined whatever chance I had with her. I fucked up, but it's better this way. I should feel elated, but all I feel is empty. A loss I can't explain. Words I know I can't take back because the damage is done.

Chapter 7

Aura

Could my life get any worse? After having the most gorgeous guy admit he finds me beautiful, he steps back and says that I'm the hired help and he was just trying to prove a point to see if I feel the same way.

It stung.

I get that we are from different social classes and that I don't fit in, but having someone say it to your face hurts.

What an asshole.

The attraction is there, that much is obvious, but he's not for me. Guys like Kalum St. Claire are never to be trusted with your heart, and the worst part is, I know deep down he would take mine and never give it back.

The cafeteria buzzes with students talking about what they will do over the weekend. It's Friday, and every day, Kalum waits for me to get in his car. I have even figured out how the door works.

Sarah and her two friends give me death glares each morning, and when I wait for him after practice, she always makes a show to touch him or make out with him in front of me. If he only knew how much it turns me off even more for allowing her to do it.

The same girl I met on my first day sits at my table and smiles. "Hi, I'm Exie. Remember me from the hallway on the first day of school?"

Placing my hand over my mouth while I swallow a piece of homemade pasta salad Camila left for me in the refrigerator last night, I answer her. "How could I forget?"

She seems nice, but you can tell she loves school gossip. I guess in a place like this, where money is no object, it's the only thing left to feel relevant.

"Aura Rayne."

"Exie Turner." She leans close and lowers her voice. "So how did you do it?"

"I'm sorry. Do what?" I ask, confused.

Whatever it is, other people must notice. I'm worried, but then I feel a sense of relief when she smiles, her eyes lighting with excitement.

"Get the finest guy in Spencer Academy to drool all over you every time you're in the same room."

I snicker. "I'm sorry. What?"

"Kalum, silly." She waves her hand. "I know you're living in his house. Which must be crazy, by the way." Her eyes glitter as she talks animatedly. "He is always staring at you. He has never looked at a girl like that. Ever. Period."

"You're making things up. Trust me, he doesn't like me. He's just watching me because he wants to make sure I don't embarrass him or do something his parents won't approve of."

She shakes her head. "He's not the only one watching you. Cason has a thing for you too, and Jimmy..." She turns her head to look at him. He gives her a wink, and she sticks her finger up, giving him the bird.

I instantly like her. She's funny in a sarcastic way but always seems happy. It seems like nothing can bother this girl.

She turns, and her gaze lands back on mine. "Stay away from Jimmy. He fucks anything that walks, basically. He's harmless, but in his mind, if he thinks he has a chance, he'll try."

"Sounds like you know from experience."

She sighs. "Yup. Turned him down flat. Not interested. He came on to me because he knew I had a thing for Brian."

Now, I'm curious. "Who's Brian?"

"The one with dirty-blond hair sitting next to Wendy. They're a thing, if that's what you want to call it. Rumor has it that Sarah is secretly screwing Jimmy even though she's practically Kalum's girl. In Sarah's mind, they're together because Kalum is always with her and never denies anything she says about their relationship. He brushes it off because she spreads her legs or is on her knees whenever he wants. Diana and Cason used to be together freshman year, but Cason ended it with her because she wanted more, and he wasn't into her like that. If you ever get invited to a party, you will see them banging in one of the empty rooms after his third drink, but you didn't hear that from me."

"How interesting. But I'm not interested." I tell her that, but a pang of jealousy creeps inside me at the mention of Kalum and Sarah.

I have the image of Kalum naked imprinted in my mind and imagining her touching him and pleasuring him stirs something inside me that makes me want to go over to their table, pull her hair, and tell her he's mine. Then I remember how much of an asshole he is.

"So what is your story?" she asks.

I hesitate, but remember that Kalum most likely knows all

the details and will eventually open his mouth and tell people my business.

I swallow, and the sting creeps, but I let out a slow breath. "My parents passed away last month in a car accident. I have no other family. A neighbor knew the St. Claires needed to hire someone to help their head housekeeper. Rather than be sent to foster care when I will be turning eighteen in about three months, Kalum's parents offered me the spot with room and board, a two-hundred-dollar allowance, and a full year of paid tuition to attend here."

Her eyes soften. "That sucks. I mean, I'm glad you're here, but not under those circumstances. What school did you attend before?"

"Spencer Public High."

"Ooh. That's our rival school when it comes to football. This year, the guys are determined to dominate again." Her eyes light up, and she asks, "Do you have a boyfriend?"

I sigh because Marcus still hasn't called me. Gina either. I guess Kalum was right. They both forgot about me or that I existed.

"Had a boyfriend. He says we are still together, but I doubt it."

"Who is this so-called boyfriend?" She puts her fingers in silent quotation marks.

"Marcus. Starting quarterback for Spencer Public High."

Her eyes almost bug out. "You're shitting me?" I shake my head. "This is going to be fun."

"Why is that?"

She snickers. "Let's just say Kalum and your ex have history on the field. Kalum sacks him every game, and they always get in each other's faces. You need to be at that game. It's next weekend. It will give you a chance to see him. I can pick you up, and we could go together? It would be so much fun."

There's that word again—*fun*.

We exchange phone numbers, and Exie gets me up to speed with the rest of the school gossip. She tells me not to feel bad about my situation living with the St. Claire family and to look at the bright side—I sleep next door to one of the hottest guys in all of Spencer Academy.

She isn't wrong. The expanse of his hard-muscled chest and biceps makes my mouth water. My panties almost melted right off when he told me he found me beautiful until his next words crushed the feeling like a beautiful flower that sprouted, and a boot stomped on it. It questioned my relationship with Marcus and made it seem like an attraction straight out of fourth grade.

Chapter 8

Aura

The rumble of a car engine can be heard as Kalum pulls inside the garage. He places the car in park, and he grabs my wrist before I can get out. Goose bumps break out all over my skin, and his fingers wrap around my arm. My heart begins to race. Every time Kalum touches me, my body responds like it has been awakened from a deep sleep. I thought it would have gone away by now, but based on my body's reaction, it's only gotten worse.

"Are you going to clean my room? I noticed it's been cleaned since the first time you were in there, but I haven't seen you."

Removing my wrist from his grasp, I move the strand of hair that has fallen and sigh. "I thought your mother told you."

He pinches his brows, and I notice a crease forms when he does, but he's still good-looking. How can a guy make frowning look good? Nothing is wrong with Kalum's face or body. But where there is beauty, there is a dangerous dose of alphahole.

"Told me what?" he asks.

"Since you wanted space and were annoyed that I had to

clean your room, I switched with Camila. Instead of her getting the groceries with Henry, I'll go, and Camila will clean your room while you're at school. She'll leave your laundry for me to take care of when I get back from grocery shopping, and I'll leave it clean and folded in your room. I'll also take up her other duties around the house."

His mouth forms a grim line, and his voice has a strange edge. "No problem. Sounds like you have it all thought out."

Without allowing me to respond, he jumps out of the car, and I follow, closing the passenger door gently. I turn slightly and notice Henry already waiting for me.

Whatever. Kalum complains about me being around, and then when I give him what he wants, he's still upset.

Kalum notices I'm not following him when I wave to get Henry's attention. Henry gives me a respectable nod, and it's his way of greeting me.

Camila introduced me to Henry when Kalum's mother gave me the grand tour of the house on my second day here. He's quiet, dependable, and doesn't say a word.

Kalum stands in front of the doorway leading inside the house, and I can feel his heated stare on my back. I convinced his mother to switch my tasks with Camila because Kalum felt uncomfortable with me in his personal space. She was reluctant and expressed that she would talk to Kalum, but I assured her it wasn't necessary. It's a way to escape on my own and go to the grocery store. Something I loved to do with my mom so I could make them dinner before they made it home after a hard day at work.

When I was in middle school, I wanted to help my parents as much as I could, so making them dinner was one way I could give my mother a break, and my father was happy he could spend the rest of the evening with my mother as a couple.

"I'll be right out, Henry," I call out.

He gives me his usual nod again and slides into the driver's side of the sleek black car to wait. I swear, at first, I thought the man couldn't hear. He hardly says two words.

Kalum leans against the open doorway with his shoulder against the molding.

"Where is Henry taking you?"

I give him a look. "The grocery store," I answer, walking toward the open doorway. He straightens like a tall statue and tilts his head down, watching me walk into the house. His manly scent mixed with his cologne is like a breeze as I whisk by him.

I'm making my way up the impressive staircase with my hand on the black iron railing, taking one step and then the next. Kalum follows me, taking his time up the steps trailing me.

I'm excited to get out of the house and begin to quicken my pace. I make it to the top and enter the hallway leading to my bedroom to drop my backpack and retrieve my little wallet in case I need to buy myself something. I have money saved from my bracelet sales, and Mrs. St. Claire has given me the two hundred as promised every week. I'm saving every cent to get out of here unless there is something I have no choice but to buy, like feminine products.

I quickly make my way down the stairs, trying to shake the grief I'll always feel inside my heart. I slow my pace because Kalum walks briskly down the stairs.

He pauses and takes the next two steps down to be at my level. I lower my gaze to hide my excitement to get out of the house and go somewhere no one judges me, and I can be myself.

Marcus once told me he cared about me deeply. We were together for three years and always spent time together. He respected me, and I was attracted to him. But he never gave me butterflies in my stomach and never looked at me the way Kalum does.

When Kalum watches me, he thinks I don't see him from the corner of my eye in class or when he drives me to school, but I feel it. It's like he's trying to peel me back a layer at a time to see what I look like underneath, trying to figure me out. It's like time stops and everything fades away.

He turns his head slightly before he takes the next step up the stairs.

"Be careful," he mutters.

Gripping my small wallet anxiously with my bank card and the card Camila gave me to purchase the groceries for the St. Claire household, I answer softly, "I will."

After leaving the house, Henry makes the ten-minute drive to a shopping strip with an upscale grocery store, a consignment store, and boutique shops. My eyes scan the rest of the area and notice that adjacent to the parking lot is a shop that fixes street race cars and offers modifications to other types of vehicles. What captures my attention is a beautiful black Jeep Wrangler with a For Sale sign.

My eyes light up, and I glance at Henry from the back seat. "Henry, would it be too much trouble if I went over there before heading inside the grocery store?" I point behind me toward the automotive shop.

He looks over at where I'm pointing and checks the time. We headed out early enough. It would give me enough time to inquire about the Jeep.

He gives me a nod, and I grin, wondering how much they

would want for the beautiful, shiny Jeep. My mother loved Jeeps. She told me she had to sell hers back in college because she was pregnant with me and needed the money. She would show me pictures of how fun it was when you unzipped the soft cover and could feel the breeze in your hair while driving.

Tears burn the backs of my eyes when thinking about my mom and all her amazing stories. She was beautiful and kind and always had a way with words.

My father always said I reminded him of her when they first met. He said I looked

like her and wasn't surprised that Marcus immediately asked me out on a date freshman year.

When my parents died, so did everything else. It snuffed the light in my life. Everyone and everything I knew died with them, only leaving precious memories. As for Marcus, it's disappointing when you realize you weren't as important to someone as you thought you were. His avoidance and his silence are proof of that.

I get out of the car, not giving Henry enough time to open my door in my haste, and head over to the shop. Looking at the closed garage door, I notice a sign that reads, *We're open. AC inside.*

Turning the knob to the office door, I enter and notice a small office and five street racing cars suspended on different lifts. The place looks like a modern version of a race car shop you see on TV.

The garage floor gleams like a mirror, and everything looks organized. Red toolboxes and shelves align the walls, and I notice this is not just your typical mechanic shop. This is a street performance group that specializes in building cars to race.

Walking farther into the garage that smells like faint gas and oil, I call out, "Hello?"

"Give me a minute." I hear a man's voice, but when I look around, I don't see anyone. There is a sudden noise of something hitting metal. When I look under one of the sports cars on my left, I see a man dressed in overalls lying on an automotive creeper under the car.

"Oh, okay. I was just inquiring about the Jeep you have for sale out front," I say in a soft voice.

He grunts, and something slips and falls with a thud. "I said, give me a minute." He raises his voice in an aggressive tone that makes me flinch. His deep, manly voice doesn't sound like he's old.

Checking the time on my phone, I realize I'm taking too long and need to head back before I'm late. I have no choice but to leave and come back another day.

Taking a deep sigh, I turn to leave. "I'm sorry to have caught you at a bad time. Have a nice day," I say as I walk away.

What is wrong with people in this part of Spencer? They're so rude and entitled. They think they can treat people like crap.

The sound of wheels sliding over concrete echo in the garage, but I ignore it because I need to get back. The last thing I need is for Mrs. St. Claire to regret her decision in allowing me to switch tasks with Camila. Kalum has been moody since I showed up and crashed his senior year. Avoiding him is the best thing I can offer and the best therapy for his hate. Having her regret her decision is not an option for me.

My hand reaches the handle of the door to exit the garage, and the sound of footsteps reaches me. The door swings open, and I'm about to step outside when the man's voice has me stopping almost in midstride.

"I apologize for being rude back there," he says. This time, his voice is a deep rumble. "You said you wanted to inquire about the Jeep?"

When I turn around slowly, my eyes meet a dark brown

gaze. His eyes caress my face for a second longer than necessary and then he clears his throat and looks down at his hands smudged with oil and grease.

He looks around and finds a rag lying across a metal tray with wheels and retrieves it quickly. He's surprisingly young. His dark hair is straight, and he has nicely shaped eyes with dark lashes. He reminds me of a young Josh Hartnett when he played in the movie *Here on Earth*, except his arms are more muscular and defined. He's wearing a tank top under his work overalls, and his forearms are well corded with muscle from a man who works day in and day out as I watch him wipe his hands, attempting to clean them.

The door is still open, and my body turns back in the direction to leave because I have wasted too much time and answer him as I continue to walk out the door.

"Yes, I'm sorry to have bothered you, but I don't have much time and have to get going."

I squint against the sun setting in the sky from being inside the garage, so I give my eyes a minute to adjust before making my way down the parking lot.

"Shit." I hear him swear softly as he quickly catches up with me. He walks ahead of me and turns to face me, causing me to stop. "Are you really interested in the Jeep?"

"Yes, I was, but I have to get going, or I'm going to be late."

"If you don't mind me asking, late for what?"

My chin tilts up because the last thing I need is more judgment about my situation. I don't know why, but I tell him. "For work. I'm late for work."

"Where do you work?"

"Does it matter?"

He crosses his arms over his chest, and I notice he has tattoos of different cars and gears with letters written across his forearms that read *If it's fast, I built it.*

His gaze looks over my uniform, and he quirks a brow. "I've never met anyone who attends Spencer Academy and has a job."

That makes sense. I don't think anyone at Spencer Academy knows the meaning of a job.

"Now you do."

He doesn't need to know why I have a job because it's none of his business, but that doesn't stop me from asking, "How would you know?"

He smirks. "Because I graduated last year, and I'm the only one who has ever worked that attended there. I don't remember seeing you there."

"A lot of kids attend there," I challenge.

He angles his head. "I would have remembered you."

Is he flirting with me? I can't tell. His expression is hard to read, and you could tell he doesn't talk much.

I avert my gaze. "I transferred to Spencer Academy to complete my senior year." My eyes find his again. "Do you ask everyone this many questions when they ask about the Jeep?"

He uncrosses his arms and slides his hands inside the pockets of his overalls. "I'm sorry. I was curious. No one at Spencer Academy would want to buy a Jeep."

He has a point. The cars I see the kids drive are high-end cars you see at exclusive dealerships.

I look past him and realize I'm late. "Look, I really have to get going."

"You want to stop by after work?" he asks.

"I can't. I don't have a way to get here. Kinda why I'm inquiring about the Jeep."

"I could bring the Jeep to you so you could look at it."

I turn my head and look at the Jeep, admiring the rugged tires and shiny black paint. I look up, and he's waiting for me to decide. "That's not possible, and I don't even know you."

He stretches his hand out. "I'm Lane Turner, and I own Turner Racing."

My hand twitches to shake his hand, but I notice his hands are still dirty with oil. It would take me a long time to get that off my skin. I can't touch groceries with dirty hands.

"My name is Aura Rayne. I don't mean to be rude. I would shake your hand, but it's dirty."

He lowers his hand. "Right. Sorry," he says, looking at his dirty hands and sliding them inside his pockets. He looks embarrassed, and I feel bad for pointing it out.

"No, it's just... I'm supposed to be getting groceries for my boss. They have been kind enough to let me stay there. It would be very rude for me to tell you to come over and show me a Jeep when I'm supposed to be doing their shopping."

A look of surprise crosses his handsome face. I silently signal Henry with one finger, telling him I'll be over in a minute. Lane twists his body to see who I'm signaling and sees Henry give me his signature nod.

Lane turns back around and says, "Who do you work for, if you don't mind me asking?"

"The St. Claires."

His brows rise. "You mean Kalum St. Claire's family?"

I nod, and he shakes his head slowly in disbelief.

"Is there a problem?" I ask defensively.

He's probably judging me. I don't need any trouble and quickly realize it was a mistake coming here.

"No."

"I'm sorry for wasting your time, but I need to go."

I go to sidestep him, and he asks, "What about the Jeep?"

Wanting to get away, knowing I have said too much already, I keep walking but answer him without stopping. "If it's still here the next time, I'll stop by. Have a great rest of your day, Lane."

"I'll see you later, Aura."

Walking toward the grocery store, I replay my encounter with Lane. A normal person would just tell me about the Jeep, give me a price, and not ask so many questions. Some people are just nosy.

If he went to Spencer, then he must be a year or two older than I am. He must have talent to modify race cars. He isn't in some office building running his family company. Looking down at my uniform, he has a point. No one attending Spencer would inquire about a used Jeep for sale and say they work after school.

Chapter 9

Aura

"Are you ready for tonight's game?" Exie asks.

Closing my locker, I hold my algebra 2 book against my chest and look at Exie. Her eyes are full of excitement. She's asked me to go repeatedly this whole week, and I've given her vague answers. It would be a good idea to go see Marcus play and maybe Gina like old times, but I still haven't reached out. Maybe I wouldn't be welcome?

"Are you sure you can give me a ride to and from the game? It wouldn't be too much trouble?"

"Are you kidding me? I would love to hang out with you. I don't have plans with anyone. The rest of the girls in the senior class are too busy chasing guys, hoping to get their attention at the game or at the party. Everyone is going to Brian's after the game. We can go for a bit if you want."

I stop in front of my class and have three minutes before the one-minute warning bell. "How about you? Why do you want to go?"

Her thumbs hook under the straps draped over her shoulders from her bag nervously. Her hair is short, straight, and jet black, and when she's nervous, she looks down, and her hair slides forward, covering her face.

"I used to like Brian, but he doesn't know I exist. Well, he probably does, but not in the way it counts."

Brian would be no good for her with the way he ignores her and acts around Wendy at lunch. Cason would be a better match for Exie. He doesn't seem to be a bad guy. He's good-looking but not my type.

"How about Cason?" I say, lowering my voice when other students walk into the class.

"No way," she whisper-yells. "That is like wanting Kalum to ask me out. It would never happen. Guys like Cason and Kalum have standards, and I don't meet any of them."

My brows furrow. "Why not? You're pretty, funny, and have been the only one nice to me here."

Her head angles. "Really? Kalum isn't nice to you? I know he told everyone your situation, but he must be at least nice."

"Not really. That is what I meant when you said he was attracted to me, and I told you it wasn't possible. He hates the fact that I'm in his house and enrolled in his school."

"Did he say that?"

The bell rings, echoing through the hall. People hurry to get inside their classes. "Yeah, he did." I nudge my chin toward her class next door. "You better go."

She walks backward toward her class. "I'm sorry I got it wrong, Aura. Don't worry about him. Anyway, I heard he made it official with Sarah. She'll keep him company and his attention off you."

I nod and walk to my algebra class with my stomach in knots. He made it official with Sarah? It would make sense. They both come from rich families. Kalum's parents would approve of Sarah, even if she is a snobby bitch.

How he finds her attractive with that bitchy over-the-top

attitude is beyond me. I never pinned Kalum to want a girl-friend. Then my thoughts go back to the fitting room in the uniform store, and I'm glad he said it was a mistake.

It was mean and childish to do that to someone, but I warned myself about guys like Kalum. They only care about themselves and what other people think. It's better that he has a girlfriend. It's too bad she sucks as a person and is a jealous bitch. That is the type of girl Kalum wants.

Chapter 10

Kalum

"You made it official with Sarah, huh?" Brian asks.

We're changing in the locker room before tonight's game at Spencer Public High School. I place my jersey over my gear, and I'm still on the fence about making it official with Sarah.

It feels like a mistake, and I don't know why. We've been hooking up off and on since freshman year, and I didn't want any drama during my last year in high school for sleeping with different girls. How long will my relationship last with Sarah? I have no idea.

She's pretty and attractive, but I'm not in love with her. Her attitude keeps getting worse, and I'm not sure what will happen when I go to college. I haven't thought that far yet.

"Yeah. Are you and Wendy official yet?"

He nods. "Yeah, I figured it was the right move since we are always hooking up." He shrugs his shoulders. "It just made sense. Now we can go out and double date. No drama or worries except football and what college we decide to attend."

"I agree, brother. Ready to kick ass tonight?" I grab my helmet. "I can't wait to sack Johnson's ass."

"Hell yeah!" he shouts, giving me a grin.

We head onto the field with the band playing and people cheering excitedly for tonight's game. Spencer Public High is our rival school. They think they could kick our asses because we have money and can't play ball. But every time we have played them since freshman year, we've kicked their asses and won. Not by much because Johnson is a good quarterback—I have to give the guy respect as an athlete—but we have a better O-line, and Spencer Academy has me on the field.

The guys run ahead of me, and I'm walking by the bleachers when I see Johnson kissing a cheerleader. He freezes, looking behind her and pulling away. My eyes follow his line of sight, and my hand grips my helmet so hard my knuckles turn white.

Aura is frozen in place, staring at Marcus Johnson, hurt crossing her features. Exie Turner quickly grips her hand in what appears to be a form of comfort. Exie is always chatting animatedly at lunch with Aura, and they seem to have become fast friends since she obviously brought Aura to the game. I had no idea she would be here. I never pegged her to be a football fan, but the way she's looking at Johnson has me curious.

"Aura," Johnson calls out. The girl he was making out with quickly turns around with a knowing smirk on her face aimed at Aura's retreating back as she walks away with Exie in tow.

"Aura. I'm sorry," he pleads, running after her. "Let me explain."

"There is nothing to explain. I get it. Just... leave me alone," Aura says loud enough in a shaky voice as she disappears to sit in the bleachers.

I watch as his other teammates walk up to him when he

stops in the walkway. "Damn, Marcus. I thought she moved far away, and you told her about you and Melissa," Mitchell says.

"Yeah, dude. That was messed up. She just lost her parents, and you did her like that?"

"I didn't..." Marcus looks torn.

"Guess I'll give her a call and be the shoulder she needs to cry on," Tatum says, making me see red.

Marcus whirls around and grips his jersey into a fist. "Go near her, and I'll kill you," he says through clenched teeth with a murderous rage taking over his features. "She isn't like that. Stay away from her."

The dickhead raises his hands. "Alright, chill, Marcus."

So Marcus Johnson was Aura's so-called boyfriend, but he quickly ghosted her after her parents died and she moved into my house. The irony.

Now I have a better reason to kick his ass on the field. He obviously has some feelings for her, but not enough to prevent him from being a two-timing bastard. Here I thought I was an asshole. I shouldn't care because it's not my problem, but something about Aura brings out the protector in me.

Walking by them before my coach goes haywire, wondering why I'm not out there with my team, I shout, "Yo, Johnson!"

He glares at me once he sees that I'm calling him out with a sarcastic grin on my face.

"What the fuck do you want, St. Claire? You ready to get your ass handed to you?"

I chuckle, shaking my head. "I'll have you running away on the field like a little bitch. Don't worry, you'll taste defeat soon enough. You could never see what is right in front of you until it's too late."

"Yeah, we'll see."

"I think you just proved it," I counter, walking by him.

He raises a brow with a smirk, and his teammates look at me curiously, watching the exchange.

"Oh yeah, how is that?" he asks sarcastically.

He's either dumb and not smart, or he just didn't realize I watched and heard the whole thing go down with that cheerleader and him hurting Aura. I know I haven't been nice to her since she set foot in my house, but someone needs to put this idiot in his place.

I stop and turn my head with a sardonic smirk and say, "You know how the saying goes, fuck over a good girl, and it's the bitch you're left with."

He storms toward the field, and I grin, satisfied I got under his skin. If he only knew where his now ex-girlfriend sleeps at night. When I sit on the bench next to Cason, he watches me lost in thought.

"What's up, St. Claire? I saw you talking smack to Johnson. I didn't hear what exactly, but watching him storm off, it must have gone well," he says with a chortle.

"Called him out on his shit and the fact that he fucked up."

He pinches his brows slightly. "How's that?"

I don't want to tell him that Aura doesn't have a boyfriend. Because that would mean she's free to date whoever she wants.

"If you want to know who Aura's now ex-boyfriend was, now you do."

"Who? Johnson?"

"The one and only. She just caught him with his tongue down a cheerleader's throat."

He shakes his head. "That fucking prick."

"I said the same thing to myself when I found out. Now we have a reason to really kick their asses tonight. Get the team up to speed. We are going balls to the wall tonight. No exceptions."

"Hell yeah."

Chapter 11

Aura

"Did you see that?!" Exie says in excitement. We are sitting in the corner of the bleachers as far away as we can from the students from both schools.

I stand with my hands covering my mouth. "Oh my God."

Kalum sacked Marcus on the field like a rag doll. Marcus takes a minute to get up.

At first, I was worried that Kalum hurt him. I don't want to see him hurt, even if he hurt me, but it sucked to see the truth.

He moved on with Melissa, and when I saw Gina, she wouldn't look at me. She miraculously is now on the cheer team with Melissa. The betrayal stings at how little I meant to them. Melissa never liked me and would always try to flirt with Marcus.

It's weird that I don't feel jealous, but I do feel hurt. He was not only my boyfriend but also one of my best friends, and he would always tell me he would wait until I was ready. There were numerous times I told him he didn't have to be with me if he felt he needed to date other people. I'm not naive to think he didn't have needs, but he assured me he was cool with it.

It makes sense now why she was always trying to flirt with him. He was probably sleeping with her behind my back, and who knows how many other girls he's been with.

Gina once told me I should sleep with him before he found someone else, but I couldn't act on it. It didn't feel right with Marcus, and I'm glad I trusted my instincts. Mom always told me when the right person comes along, I would feel it. I would know. If you mistakenly lose your V-card to someone who wasn't worth it, then the next time you decide to sleep with someone, make sure they're worth it. She would tell me stories of her other friends back in high school and college, but most importantly, to practice safe sex and not fall pregnant. If the guy is the one and you know deep down he's perfect and treats you right, you would know.

My father wasn't her first, but she said she wished she would have waited. She also told me not to feel pressured to sleep with someone just because people or your friends were hooking up with guys. I took her advice and trusted my feelings.

Sitting back down on the bleachers, Exie leans next to me. "Did you see it, Aura? They have already taken out four guys on the field. There is no way Spencer Public High will win this game. St. Claire has been a beast on the field. The man can play."

"He's good," I admit, and I mean it. Kalum is very good on the field. The best I have seen in a long time.

When Marcus shakes it off to finish the last minute of the game, Kalum looks up and scans the stands until his eyes find mine. Marcus tilts his head in the same direction and looks over at Kalum. He shoulder checks him, and Kalum loses it, tackling Marcus to the ground. Kalum lifts Marcus like he weighs nothing and slams him down on the ground, causing his helmet to come off.

"Oh shit," Exie blurts.

Whistles sound like an alarm going off as the referees charge the field to stop the brawl as more players join in, taking their helmets off.

Standing quickly on my feet, not believing they're fighting like animals, I ask, "Is it always like this?"

"Um, no. This isn't about the game."

"What could they be fighting about?"

She rubs her lips together and places the strands of her short black hair behind her ears. "Looks like he's defending you. Why else would he look this way? It could only mean one thing, it's about you."

Why would he care? They finally break up all the players, and they go to their respective sides to finish the last minute of the game. Looking at the score, there is no way Marcus's team can win. They're losing 54–17.

When the game finally ends and the fans from Spencer Academy rush the field to celebrate, I walk behind Exie toward the parking lot. My gaze locks on Kalum hugging Sarah and giving her a kiss on the mouth.

My stomach cramps up when she wraps her legs around his waist. You could tell it's all for show, and a thought pops in my head, wondering how he would taste.

"Ready to head to the party?"

I turn to Exie. "Yeah, but just for a little while. I don't want to stay out too late."

Heading to the party is a great idea. If I ask Exie to take me home, I'll just cry my eyes out at how messed up my life is.

Coming to this game was a mistake, but the only good thing that came of it is that I know the truth.

The backs of my eyes sting with tears, wishing I had someone to talk to. Someone who would listen. I miss my mom. She would know what to do.

"You okay, Aura?"

I'm walking slowly, looking down at the black pavement and watching my black and white Vans contrast to the black road with each step I take toward Exie's Lexus.

My head lifts, and I give her a wry smile. "I'm fine, Exie. I just miss my parents is all."

"It's not because of your ex and your friend Gina?"

I shrug. "You can't change who people are. It sucks, but at least I know the truth."

Melissa, Gina, and a few other girls walk to the parking lot a few feet away. Gina looks away when Melissa snickers. "How does it feel to know Marcus chose me after all? You know we have been fucking for almost two years."

I flinch. It's one thing to assume something to be true and another for someone to point it out. The weird part is that I'm not even mad about them screwing behind my back. I never had sex with Marcus. I'm more upset about the need to lie.

Gina murmurs, "Melissa, don't."

Exie speaks up in my defense. "So that makes you the side chick. Congrats, you just admitted you're a skank who sleeps with another girl's man."

She's a real grade A bitch. She should be BFFs with Sarah and the bitch crew. Gina would also get along since she's a two-faced bitch.

I wave my hand. "Exie, let it go. She isn't worth it."

"Obviously, I am. He just felt sorry for you, but now you know."

"Melissa, leave her alone," Marcus says in a hard tone.

He comes sauntering over, freshly showered with his hair wet, wearing a fitted polo and jeans. You can see under his eye is swelling slightly from a blow he must have received from Kalum.

Getting a good look at him, I wonder how I didn't see it.

The lies and the way he would tell me I was beautiful. Every word that came spilling out of his mouth has been tainted. The times he would tell me practice ran late or when I waited for my parents to come home after making them dinner and would invite him over. He would always decline, telling me he couldn't. Now I know why. He's just... a liar.

My only regret is not spending more time with my parents and wasting it on him. The times he would take me out, he was probably hoping it was the day he would convince me to sleep with him.

Anger begins to course through me as my eyes narrow. Looking at him, I hate myself for being so naive and stupid for allowing him to use me.

His eyes soften. "Aura, I'm sorry. I never meant to hurt you."

"Of course, you didn't." I cross my arms over my chest. "You could have told me. You didn't have to lie or make up things you never felt. The only person you lied to is yourself."

My gaze turns to Melissa. "You won. You got exactly what you always wanted. A two-timing QB that just got his ass kicked on the field. You did me a favor and made me realize how much of a liar he really is, and that goes for you too, Gina. You're all a bunch of shitty liars." I step back toward Exie's car. "You guys all deserve each other."

"You're just mad that he dumped you for me."

"Whatever you want to say to make yourself feel better." I wave my hand with my palm facing up. "Go right ahead, Melissa. He's all yours. But he never dumped me."

"Aura. Please don't leave like this. Where are you staying? We can talk," Marcus pleads.

"Why would you need to talk to her? You told me it was over," Melissa chimes in perplexed.

Exie places her hands on the top of her driver's side door

with a fat grin plastered on her face. "Oh, you don't know?" she asks Marcus.

"Know what?" Marcus asks.

Exie smirks. "Who she lives with? Whose parents are her guardians."

A loud rumble of an engine as the black sports car I ride to school in each morning pulls up. Everyone's attention is on the blacked-out window that lowers, revealing a dangerously hot Kalum.

Kalum glances at me. "Are you okay?"

I nod, not knowing how to respond. He's here making sure I'm okay. He doesn't have to worry about me, but the fact he took the time to make sure I'm okay means a lot right now.

"Make sure she gets home safe, Exie."

Exie nods, and Kalum glances at Marcus.

"Don't worry about Aura. She's well taken care of."

"You motherfucker," Marcus says, his voice laced with steel.

Kalum rolls the window up, ignoring him, and drives away, the loud engine of the car coming out of the exhaust as he pulls out into the street.

"You have got to be kidding me," Marcus grumbles. "You live with the St. Claires?"

"Yep, she sleeps in the room next to his, and he takes her to school every morning," Exie says with a knowing smile. "Let's go, Aura. We have somewhere to be."

"Aura, wait," Marcus pleads.

I'm confused as to why he wants to talk. There is nothing left to say. There is nothing left for me here.

I slide inside the passenger side of Exie's silver Lexus. He walks up to the car before I can close the door.

"Whoa. Back off, cowboy." Exie points at Melissa. "Your girl is over there. You clearly made your choice."

I look up at Marcus as he tries to lean into the car. "We went from being together almost every day to never being with each other. It's okay to forget me, Marcus. Nothing is left to say except goodbye, and I wish you the best with Melissa. Now you two can be together. I'm not in the way anymore." His face falls. "It's okay if you're happy," I say softly, closing the door like the page of the last chapter in a book.

He flinches like I slapped him. Watching him from the window, I see his expression is laced with regret. Melissa tries to wrap her arms around him, but he shrugs her off while Exie pulls out of the parking spot.

"You handled that with grace, Aura. If it was me, I would have torn her eyes out and then turned on him."

"Doesn't change what he did. He lied to me for two years, and nothing will make me forget that. He could have said he wanted to be friends with me from the beginning or when he felt I wasn't what he wanted. He could have told me, and I would have understood. Sometimes people take advantage, but it's their loss because, in the end, they don't get you. Sooner or later, their true self appears, and they will hate what they see. A liar."

"I love that about you, Aura. You have this fresh outlook about life even when you have endured loss and pain."

If she only knew that sometimes, just... sometimes I wished I had been in the car with them. It's something I have never said to anyone. The judge appointed a psychiatrist, but the doctor said I'm grieving but not in a way that I would try to hurt myself. You can never stop grieving the loss of the most important people in your life. That is the part they don't tell you. It never stops hurting.

We arrive at Brian's, and it's not too far from Kalum's house. Parked cars line the street. It's dark outside, and people mill about in their respective groups, talking and shooting the shit.

We enter the lavish home through the double doors. The house has cream-colored walls, traditional furnishings, and paintings that must cost a fortune by the way they're framed.

The cream marble flooring has matching gold accents in the center of each tile. People are trying to talk over the music. Exie and I are both dressed in jeans and a simple graphic T-shirt, while everyone else is dressed to kill.

Guys wear designer shirts, and the girls are dressed in skirts and dresses two sizes too small with designer pumps. A far cry from the few parties I was invited to with Marcus. Now I know why he wouldn't take me to most of them.

Exie grabs my arm and pulls me toward the marble island to grab two wine coolers. She opens the top on both and hands me one.

"One. That is all we are having," I tell her.

I place the tip of the fruity wine cooler on my lips. Tilting it back, I wince as I take a sip, not used to the hint of alcohol burning my throat. After a few more sips, I get used to the taste and sip the rest slowly.

"Good, huh?" Exie asks.

"Not bad, I guess."

Some guys I recognize from school glance at me, but I pay them no mind. We hang out, people-watch, and talk about what Netflix movies will release soon, setting a date so we can hang out at her house to binge-watch some shows I haven't started.

When the bottle is empty, I toss it in the big trash bin, and so does Exie. "I need to pee," I tell her.

She looks up at the balcony of the second floor and sees people going up and down the stairs. "The bathroom must be upstairs. Let's pee, and then I'll take you home. This party sucks."

I grin. "I agree."

We make it up the stairs to the second floor, but all the doors are closed.

We see two doors next to each other and usually one is the bathroom.

"You open that one, and I'll open this one and see which one is the bathroom," I tell her.

"Sounds like a plan."

We both turn the door handle at the same time and freeze. When the door swings open, I can see Sarah riding Kalum on the bed. His arms are behind his head while he watches her grind on him, moaning.

"Kalum, it feels so good," she says breathlessly.

I close my eyes, and my stomach churns, trying to erase the image from my mind but come up empty. My chest squeezes painfully at the sight of Kalum having sex with someone else. Maybe the attraction I have for him is stronger than I thought.

"What the fuck?" I hear Brian's voice from the other room Exie must have opened.

My head whips to her, and I hear her stammer. "I-I'm so sorry. I was looking for the bathroom."

My eyes open. Sarah stops moving on top of Kalum, and Kalum's head tilts to the side, watching me as I release the grip of the door handle nervously and back out of the room.

"I'm sorry," I say softly, turning my head from the look of horror on Sarah's face as she tries to cover her perfect breasts and long legs.

"What the fuck?" Sarah squeaks. "Kalum, you need to check your maid. Get rid of her."

I keep walking back, mortified, until my back hits the wall on the other side of the hallway, avoiding eye contact with

Kalum. Another door opens, and Cason steps out, trying to put his clothes on.

"What happened?" he asks.

"These two don't know what the fuck a closed door means," Brian says, his voice laced with steel.

I find my voice. "We were looking for the bathroom."

His gaze travels over me like I'm a pest. "How about you get the fuck out of my house! No one invited you two."

Glancing at Exie, I see the hurt cross her face.

Screw him and his wack-ass party. Wendy peeks her head out at the same time Sarah and Kalum walk out of the room, trying to put their clothes on.

"He's right. No one invited you two outcasts. Get out," Wendy says.

Most of the senior class appears at the top of the stairs to see what is going on so they can gossip about it later.

"Kalum?" Sarah whines.

He keeps his gaze on me but answers her. "I'm sorry. I didn't know."

His expression turns cold while everyone waits for him to say something. "Leave. And don't let me catch you at one of our parties again. You're not welcome."

A lump forms in my throat, but I swallow it. Kalum is so hot and cold. He's nice one minute and then cold the next.

They don't want us here, fine. Fuck them, and fuck this school. I hate it here, but one thing I have left is my pride. Sarah smirks at me like the cat that got the cream, and from the corner of my eye, Cason looks away.

"I'm sorry. We thought we were invited. We will never set foot at one of your parties or any place you guys hang out ever again."

"Where are you going?" Kalum asks.

"None of your business." I sneer at him. "You wanted me to

hate you? Well, you got it. Don't talk to me, don't take me to school. Don't even look at me. I don't exist to you. This party is wack anyway."

"She's right, this party is wack," Exie chimes in.

I spot Dean, one of the guys from my history class, smoking a joint and nodding along with us. I walk up to him and grab the joint, taking a hit.

My mother smoked medical marijuana for years, and it used to help me with my period cramps. It was hush-hush, but my mother was understanding, and it was harmless. The pain stopped my junior year, but with everything that has gone down today, I need it.

"What are you doing, Aura?"

"You smoke?" Dean asks.

I blow the smoke up in the air. "Yeah." I hold up the white boy between two fingers. "This is good."

"Cali weed," he says.

"I gotta run, but thanks for the hit."

His eyes are glassy, but he smiles. "Anytime. You can come to any of my parties," he says loud enough for everyone to hear. "Both of you."

"Thanks, but we're good. Not our type of crowd," Exie says and gives me a wink as we head downstairs so she can take me home.

Chapter 12

Kalum

It has been a week since the party, and Aura is closed off. She doesn't even glance in my direction. She locks herself in her room when I'm around, and true to her word, she no longer waits for me to take her to and from school.

I should be glad, but I'm not. She caught me screwing Sarah, or rather Sarah screwing me, and the way Aura apologized was gut-wrenching. If she only knew where my mind had been at that exact moment, wishing it were her and not my girlfriend.

My eyes had been closed, and I didn't hear the door open because I was so focused on imagining it was her. It has always been her, ever since that day in my kitchen. I should feel guilty thinking about Aura while being with Sarah, but the way Sarah is as a person, I don't.

No one will go near Aura because I warned everyone not to talk to or even look at my housekeeper. It's wrong of me, but I'm protective of her. My protective instincts take over, and the last thing she needs is someone else hurting her, including me.

That night of the party, after Brian was a total dick to her and Exie, I had no choice but to go along with it. If I didn't, Sarah and her friends would make it their mission to destroy them both.

At lunch, she and Exie sit far away and always in front of other students, so they block the view of any of us seated at the table. Sarah slides into the seat next to me with her overpriced coffee and crackers. She's always worried about her weight, and she shouldn't be. If anything, she should eat more. She hardly has an ass to even sit on at the table.

As much as she thinks every guy wants to nail her, she isn't Aura. Aura is the exact opposite, and you can't even compare. Aura is pretty and kind and doesn't deserve the hand life has thrown at her. Sarah is stuck up, annoying, and a total bitch.

The girl I want sits across the cafeteria, hating me. The girl seated next to me, I made the mistake of officially making her my girlfriend.

"Kalum?" Sarah asks.

I place a french fry inside my mouth. "Hmm?"

She slouches in her seat. "Have you listened to anything I just said?"

I chew the french fry slowly, savoring the taste. No, I haven't, and I honestly don't give two shits about what she has to say.

You're annoying, and I can't even stand the smell of your hair.

What I really want to do is get up and walk over to the girl playing havoc with my emotions, take her to the nearest empty room, and explore every inch of her body, committing it to memory and show her how I feel about her.

"Not really," I say dryly.

Her face contorts, making her appear like a witch in a horror movie. My lip curls slightly, kicking myself for ever sleeping with her. At first, it was a quick lay. Now, she's planning our future together, and I have zero interest.

"You're such an ass."

"You've expressed this before. If you don't like my attitude, you know what to do. I'm not keeping you chained to me like a dog."

Her eyes widen, and Cason chokes on his soda.

"What is your problem?" she asks.

I grab the napkin and wipe my mouth before tossing it on my tray and standing. "I want to be left alone."

"Why? Because I question the way you're treating me?"

"Exactly. You don't even let me take a piss. It's always about what you want to do or where you want to go and how you want to do it. Notice I said the word '*you*' a lot."

"Baby, sit," she purrs.

"I'm not your baby, and I don't want to sit. I want to be left alone," I snap.

The table grows quiet except for Jimmy. "Dude, relax. She was just talking about all of us going to the county fair and what she wanted to do first."

I know I'm being a dick, but I don't know how much more I can take. She's exhausting. I'm not cut out for the boyfriend-girlfriend thing.

"It'll be fun," Wendy chimes in, lightening the mood.

I stand to throw away my trash, getting a small glimpse of Aura, just to see her face, hoping to witness her smile and maybe catch a laugh. She doesn't notice me because she's showing Exie one of her newest creations.

I recognize it because when she isn't looking, I watch how she braids the string with expert fingers, a soft crinkle forming on her forehead when she concentrates on adding a design. I can't lie and say they're not creative because they are. I would wear one, especially if she made it for me, but I don't dare ask her.

She must feel my stare because she turns her head, and her gaze lands on mine. I'm hoping she looks at me a minute longer so I can admire her pretty face, but like a dark cloud blocking the sun, her features harden like ice, and she averts her eyes. Exie looks over and rolls her eyes.

Brian and Cason walk up next to me to throw away their trash, and I notice Brian glance at Exie.

A sweet laughter blankets my ears, and I look at Aura again. Exie smiles, and they both giggle, and like a stupid idiot, I grin. If a laugh could be called music, it's hers.

Cason clears his throat. "Even her laughter is pretty," he mumbles.

He isn't wrong.

That night, I toss and turn in my bed, and I check my phone. 1:00 a.m. I place it back on the charger, and then I hear a whimper and a small noise. I quickly sit up in my bed and try to listen to see if I hear the faint, muffled sound again.

When I'm about to lie back down, I hear it again. Sliding out of my bed, I quietly open my bedroom door and peer my head out to look down the dark hallway. Then I hear it clearly—someone sobbing and sniffling.

The same feeling in the pit of my stomach comes in full force. It aches inside my soul when I hear her cry, and I can't take it. I walk toward the closed bedroom door, and I listen to her muffled sobs.

Placing my hand on the handle, I turn it, and the door slowly opens. It doesn't make a sound, and when my eyes adjust, I see her on the bed. She has her back turned, and she's curled in a little ball, sobbing her heart out.

Closing the door, I turn the lock so no one can walk in. I'm not sure if she's crying in her sleep or if she's awake, but it doesn't matter. I came in here to comfort her and to finally hold her.

"Aura," I whisper.

I don't want to startle her or, worse, scare her. She doesn't respond, so I pull back the covers cautiously. Her bed is a full size compared to the king-size bed in my room. It would be better to hold her there, but I don't want to move her out of her safe space.

What am I thinking?

As I slide my large frame quietly onto the bed, another sob escapes her. The smell of her shampoo pulls me in. She doesn't move when I get close and comfortable. My hand finds the curve of her waist above her short sleep shorts, and I try to avoid losing my mind.

Relax, Kalum. You're here to comfort her, not be a creep.

As I finally curl up next to her, her body stiffens. She turns over, and her eyes flutter open, then they widen. Her cheeks are wet with tears, and I place my finger over her soft lips.

"Shh...it's me."

Her hand rubs her face, and she sniffs. My body twists toward her nightstand, and I grab a tissue so she can wipe her face.

"You can't be in here. You need to leave," she demands, her voice above a whisper.

"I'm here, and I'm not leaving." My finger places her hair behind her ear.

When my finger touches her skin, electricity zips across my hand. Goose bumps appear on her neck and shoulder, bare from her oversized T-shirt falling off one side.

Her chest sputters from the aftermath of her sobbing. "I'm fine. You need to le—"

My mouth crashes against hers, interrupting her rant. The velvety skin of her lips parts slightly. I pull her toward my chest, and my tongue slides inside her mouth. It feels like I'm dreaming.

Her tongue twirls and dances with mine. I deepen the kiss, exploring every inch of her mouth and breathe in the scent of her skin and her hair, loving the taste of her mouth. The magic of a first kiss—what kisses are made of. The one where you fall in love. The kiss that you will always remember. The first one that carves its memory inside your heart and soul, hoping it's not the last. This is love, and she is in my arms.

The palms of her small hands lie flat against my hard chest like an imprint. An imprint that tells me we were fated to be here at this moment, that this was meant to be. I feel torn because if it weren't for the death of her parents, I would never have known that a girl so perfect existed. I wouldn't be in her life, and there is no place I'd rather be.

I fought my attraction to her with hate, and the things I said hurt her. Now, I'm on a mission. A mission to erase the hurt, the hate she feels for me, and start over. It's a secret promise I'm making to myself.

This is where we begin.

This is where I vow to make her mine.

And never let her go.

She pulls away to catch her breath. "Kalum," she breathes.

Our lips are inches apart, and my heart beats rapidly. My

teeth catch my bottom lip in an effort to keep the emotions coursing through me in check.

One taste of Aura is powerful. Something I wasn't ready for. An electric current like the ocean that quickly pulls you in and takes over.

My eyes land on her small hands on my chest like hot embers. She tries to pull them away, but my hand reacts quicker, halting their descent.

"Leave them. I love your touch on my skin," I whisper. My index finger finds the edge of her shorts and slowly traces upward. "The same way I know you love mine on yours." Her eyes lift. "We don't hate each other. You don't really hate me, and I don't hate you. We are just..."

She squirms. "Kalum, you have a girlfriend. It's not right."

My eyes close instantly, regretting having Sarah as my girlfriend. "I don't want Sarah," I say softly. My eyes open, and her eyes glitter from the moonlight streaming from her bedroom window. "I don't love her. The truth is, I thought I could stop my attraction to you by being with someone else. But I can't, Aura. Nothing works. There's this fire in you that calls to me."

She sniffs and snuggles her cheek against the pillow. My fingers trail higher on the skin of her thigh, getting closer to her core. She grips my hand and slowly raises it to my chest. "That is not going to happen," she says.

"Do you mean right now or never?" I ask.

"When the right person comes along."

"Marcus Johnson was the right person?"

I want to know how that is even possible with the way he treated her. Aura didn't deserve that. It was cruel and downright messed up.

"That's just the thing. Deep down, I kind of knew he wasn't." She shrugs her shoulder. "It's probably why I'm not hurt or jealous about him sleeping with her. It was the fact that he lied and told me things that weren't true. That is what hurt me the most and then my friend Gina. She knew, and she didn't tell me."

It can't be. That's impossible.

"Aura?"

"Yes," she answers, licking her lips.

"Have you ever...?"

"No. I've never slept with a guy before."

I nod because I feel like I swallowed my tongue. *Holy shit.* Aura is a virgin.

"That is not possible."

"When you have had the same boyfriend since freshman year and turned him down many times, yes, it's possible. Like I said, it didn't feel right. Now I know why."

"He didn't deserve you."

Neither do I. I don't deserve someone like her. It makes sense why Marcus was so defensive about her. She never allowed him to sleep with her, and then she found out about his lies. It felt good to punch him in his face for hurting her. I did it all for her, not caring if I had a girlfriend, and I would do it all over again.

"I guess," she mutters.

"Are you crying because you miss your parents?"

She gives me a slight nod.

"I'm not an expert on death or anything. I can't tell you I know how it feels because I don't, but I do know one thing." I point toward the middle of her chest. "They live inside you. You have the precious gift of their memories. No one has them but you, and they will live through you. You need to celebrate their lives and be happy you had their love. Show the people you care about how much you know how to love because some people live their whole lives and never experience it."

"Have you?"

"Have I what, sweetheart?"

Her tongue peeks out, and she wets her lips. "Felt love? Been in love with someone?"

My thumb traces her jaw down to her chin. I'm relieved she doesn't pull away from my touch.

"No. Never."

She changes the subject before I get to ask her the same question. Has she ever loved someone? Do I want to know?

"I stopped crying. You can go."

My hand slides to her small waist. "I'm not going anywhere. Roll over."

She does as I ask and gives me her back. I adjust my erection before moving into a spoon position, draping the covers over our bodies. Her body is so small compared to my large frame. She feels small and delicate. I bury my nose in her hair and fall asleep to her scent.

Chapter 13

Aura

The sun streams like a white light against my closed eyelids, filtering into the room. The feeling of warmth and a faint smell of cologne fills my senses. It feels like I'm floating in a dream. My head snuggles against something hard and warm, not soft like the pillow I'm used to. My eyes flutter open, and I squint until my vision adjusts to the sunlight.

My head tilts up, and my gaze meets Kalum's grin and morning hair.

"Good morning, gorgeous," he says, looking like a male model with his left arm behind his head.

I bite my lip nervously, looking down at my body sprawled over Kalum's shirtless chest. My stomach leaps. His muscled thigh is between my legs. I push myself up and almost decide against it because I can feel his erection by my hip.

"If you keep moving like that, we won't make it out of this bed, princess."

He keeps calling me beautiful endearments that any girl

would love to hear from a guy like Kalum. He's gorgeous any time of the day, and last night, he had been so sweet.

"I'm sorry, but I have never slept in a bed with a guy before. I am not used to... you know."

His grin widens, and he raises his brow. "I'm glad I'm your first," he says in a husky tone.

My cheeks flame, and my heart beats wildly. Heat rushes through my body, with the awareness that his erection is hard like steel under me. My nipples strain and need pools between my thighs. I want nothing more than to feel him against me the way I want, but this is Kalum.

Mean Kalum I can deal with.

Nice Kalum is dangerous.

He can melt my panties in a puddle at my feet with one word and a single caress.

Sliding out of bed without touching his manhood, I notice my breasts can be seen through my shirt, and my shorts are too short for comfort as I stand at the edge of the bed. He makes no move to get out. His legs almost hang over the end of the mattress at the foot of the bed, making him look funny.

"It's Saturday," he says.

I check my phone and see a missed text from Exie telling me she'll be here around five to pick me up and head to the fair. "Yeah, I have plans."

He shrugs his shoulders. "I do, too. What are you up to today?"

My eyes are trained on my phone, reading the rest of the text saying her brother will also be there and a couple of his friends.

Sending her a message thanking her for the invite and telling her it's cool, I look up. "I'm going to the county fair with Exie. She invited me."

He stiffens, and when I raise my head, he looks away. "Yeah, that is where I'm headed with the guys and—"

"Your girlfriend, Sarah," I finish for him.

Hearing it out loud is like acid burning my tongue. What he sees in her is beyond me except she reminds me of Melissa, a girl who can give a guy what he needs between the sheets.

It's the only thing I can come up with. When Kalum kissed me last night, it was like nothing else mattered. If he kisses Sarah like that, it's no wonder she's a possessive bitch. How she could sleep with Jimmy behind Kalum's back, even after Kalum made it official, is beyond me. I take a deep breath.

"I promise to stay away. You won't even know I'm there."

"Aura."

I raise a hand. "It's cool. I understand." I sigh. "It was why I said it wasn't right for you to be inside my room. I appreciate you staying with me last night. You were great and were there for me when I needed someone."

"But," he blurts out.

My eyes soften, and my heart constricts. What I want to say is how I crave this side of him so much more. How he's perfect.

But he isn't mine. He belongs to someone else, and I refuse to be the housekeeper cliché, sneaking around with the owner's son. He's right. We have a strong attraction to each other, but it would never work. I don't fit in, and he would be ashamed of being seen with someone like me. His parents would most likely kick me out if they found out.

"You have a girlfriend, and she doesn't deserve his house-keeper allowing her boyfriend in her room late at night. It's wrong, and I don't want any trouble. I'm not in the best position, and this isn't my home."

"This is your home."

I shake my head. "I work here—cleaning and doing the

laundry and grocery shopping." I walk over and pull open the sliding door to the wall-to-wall closet, revealing one suitcase, a box with pictures and memories of my parents, and five Spencer Academy uniforms with three pairs of shoes. "This is what I am and all I have to my name." I wave my hand, showcasing the few items I have inside. "We're too different."

I had condensed my belongings to one suitcase after throwing away most of my clothes that were old with age and looked threadbare.

"There is only one world, Aura."

"Tell that to everyone you know and see what they say. I'm not trying to argue with you. I'm tired of hating you, Kalum, and I want to be civil with you, but this is my reality. Staying away from you and your friends is the smartest choice."

"What if I don't want you to stay away from me? What if I want to spend time with you and get to know you?"

My arms cross over my chest. "Where would Sarah fit in? Last time I checked, your car only has room for two."

"That can be taken care of."

I can't allow him to dump her because he wants to spend time with me in secret. Like the ugly girl a guy calls to secretly hang out because she's nice and a wonderful person on the inside.

My nostrils flare, and I lick my lips. "Don't you dare break it off with her because you want to hang out with me all of a sudden."

"That is not your choice," he says, standing to his full height.

His ab muscles flex with each breath he takes, his shorts hanging low on his hips. I can feel my mouth water at the sight of him standing there, battling with himself.

My hands itch to run over every dip and groove on his skin to see how they feel. The memory of being in his arms replays in my mind, and it was the first time since my parents' death that I felt wanted. That someone cared enough to comfort me at a time when I felt dark, alone, and scared. The worst part of it all is that I want to be in his arms again, even if it's wrong, even if he could never be mine.

"You're right. It wasn't my choice. It was yours, and you chose her. I saw it with my own two eyes that night at the party after you and your friends threw us out. I sure as hell am not going to be your second." My tone vibrates with the sudden rage I feel, remembering that night when he turned from savior to villain in a split second.

"I did it to protect you."

"Oh yeah, how?"

He walks closer, but I don't back down from his gaze as it locks on mine, lowering in a caress down my body and slowly traveling back up and stopping on my teeth chewing on the corner of my lip.

His thumb stops me from breaking the skin, sliding slowly to where my teeth dig in. "You're hurting those pretty lips, and to answer your question, I don't want anyone to mistreat you. Only I can mistreat you."

"Why is that?"

He grins playfully. "Because I'm the only one who can make you feel better."

My expression turns to ice. He thinks playing with me is fun. I've already played into his games, and he flipped the switch on me. "You need to go. You wouldn't want to be late for your date tonight."

I would be no better than Melissa and Marcus if I allowed lines to be crossed.

Our kiss was amazing, but it should have never happened. He says he doesn't love her, but he must feel something toward her, or he wouldn't have slept with her all this time. The first day of school, he made a point of displaying PDA.

He backs away toward the door with a forlorn expression. When the door shuts, I close my eyes, relieved that he left because I wasn't sure how long I could keep myself in check with him. Kalum has the power to make me go soft with a touch, and with the right words, he can erase the hurt like a balm that heals a gaping wound.

Exie picks me up from the house shortly after Kalum left. He probably had time to think about last night and how it was a mistake to kiss me because he has a girlfriend and the fact that I'm practically the maid. I didn't tell Exie what happened because there is no point in telling a story that has no future.

She said we would meet her brother by the front entrance to purchase our tickets.

"I'm so excited you get to meet my brother and give him the bracelet you made for him. He loved the one you made for me. He also said he wanted to give you the money himself."

Exie loved the bracelets I made, so I made her a couple, and apparently, her brother had also wanted one.

"Okay. I hope he likes it. Thank you for helping me sell them."

She pulls her Lexus into the spot the fair staff guides her to and says, "Anytime. I love to help my best friend out."

My heart soars at her words. After everything that happened with Marcus and Gina, I thought it would be a long time before I could call anyone my best friend.

We walk up to the entrance to purchase our tickets and the wristbands that give us access to unlimited rides when I see a face I thought I would never see again. Lane Turner.

Exie waves at him and grabs my hand to pull me forward. When I'm standing in front of him, he gives me a knowing grin. "Hi," he says.

I'm speechless. I never figured that Lane and Exie were related. Now thinking about it, they have the same last name, but I hadn't put two and two together.

I can see the resemblance—they both have dark hair and dark brown eyes, and when they smile, they both have the same faint dimple in their left cheek.

Lane wears a long-sleeved fitted shirt with the sleeves scrunched up, showing off the tattoos on his forearms, jeans that hang low, and a baseball hat.

"This is my best friend Aura, the girl I've told you so much about. She's the one who makes the cool bracelets." She points at the other two guys. "This is Blaze and Dex. They work with my brother at his shop."

"Hey," they both say with a wave.

"Hello," I say softly. My gaze lands on Lane. "Hello, Lane."

Exie's head whips back and forth, and she waves her finger between us. "Wait, how do you know each other?"

"She came by the shop and was interested in the Jeep," he answers.

She quirks a brow. "Oh. So you knew it was her I was talking about the whole time?"

Lane glances at his sister, a look of guilt crossing his features. "I did. I'm sorry, Exie."

Why would he keep that from her? Was he afraid I would stop being her friend or something stupid like that?

Lane looks back at me. "How come you never stopped by again? You're not interested in the Jeep anymore?" he asks.

I love the Jeep, but a quick Google search let me know there was no way I could afford it. The Jeep he's selling is way newer than the ones I saw listed, and it would take me years to come up with the money working for the St. Claires.

"I-I'm not sure it's a smart move for me right now. I'm sorry if I led you on about my interest in buying it from you."

I lift my wrist, showing him the bracelet I made, and turn the small wooden charm with my signature for all my hand-made pieces. "Here is the bracelet you ordered." I unclasp it and hold it out.

He takes it from my fingers, and his eyes light up when he looks at it. He lifts his head and smiles. "I like it. I like it a lot."

I let out my breath, relieved. I would hate to make something someone will pay for that I spent my time on and have them hate it. I return his smile, and he stares at me for a second too long, not saying a word. Dex gives him a nudge.

He blinks and swallows. "Oh, my bad." He slides his hand inside the front pocket of his jeans, retrieves the money, and hands it to me.

"Thank you. I hope you really like it," I say.

Then there is silence.

Exie claps her hands together. "Okay, let's get to it," she says, breaking up the awkwardness.

She walks with me behind her brother and his friends. "I think my brother likes you," she whispers.

I turn toward her, frowning. "I don't think—we don't know each other. That is not possible."

She snorts softly. "I have never seen him stare at a girl the way he was staring at you just now."

We head to the ticket booth, and his friends go first and pay for their tickets and bands. Lane steps up to the booth ahead of Exie and me.

I slide my hand in the pocket of my worn, ripped jeans to retrieve the money for my ticket and the band. Lane turns around with two extra bands and two extra tickets, one for me and his sister.

"How much do I owe you?" I ask him.

He shakes his head. "It's on me," he says with a smile.

"That's really sweet, but I can't. It wouldn't be fair. You paid for the bracelet, and I would feel really bad if you paid for my ticket too."

"It's okay, Aura," Exie chimes in with a laugh. "My brother's loaded."

I swallow nervously and hold out the money in my hand to him. "I can't. Please take it."

He places the band on my wrist and looks at the money like it's diseased. "I'm not going to take it, so it's best you put it away. It's my treat."

With a deep sigh, I reluctantly place the money in my pocket. "Thank you."

He nods and turns to his friends waiting for us by the gate. "Let's go. What ride would you girls like to go on first?"

I look around to take everything in.

"I think we should hit the fast rides first before we eat so we don't get sick," Exie says.

That makes perfect sense. The last thing I need is to throw up in front of everyone. I've been to one fair, and it was when I was younger. My parents always encouraged me to go, but I felt guilty about spending the money.

"Okay."

We walk ahead of Lane, Blake, and Dex. "Told you," Exie says softly with laughter in her eyes.

Lane is attractive, but I have enough on my plate with Kalum and my personal issues right now. My thoughts go to Kalum, wondering if we'll run into him. I hope not. I know if I see him with Sarah, it would be the same as walking over a broken glass.

We walk toward the midway rides as the sun sets in the sky, the lights from the coasters becoming brighter. The smell of cotton candy mixed with corn on the cob billows in the air from the tents as we pass by.

The laughter from people riding rides and the generators making a humming noise surrounds us as we pass each concession, ride, and carnival game.

We wait in line, and Lane stands behind me with his hand in his pocket. His friends talk about their latest build in the shop, and Exie scrolls through her phone. When it's our turn, the ride operator stops me from getting on the ride with Exie.

"I'm sorry, girls, you'll have to ride separately or with someone bigger. The ride is really fast, and it's for your safety." He points at the sign that shows smaller individuals need to go with someone taller.

I'm petite and short for my age, and Exie is about my height. Lane steps forward and places his hand on my lower back. "Exie, ride with Dex. I'll ride with Aura."

We get on the ride, and Lane makes sure I'm buckled in. The ride goes up and swings in the air in a clockwise motion. He double-checks the straps, making sure we are both secure. He places his arm behind me and gets a thumbs-up from Dex, signaling Exie is strapped in.

I'm nervous and afraid the gravity will throw me against Lane. I don't know him well enough to feel comfortable around him.

If it was Kalum, you wouldn't think like that. I don't know why I'm comparing. Kalum is at this same fair on a date with his girlfriend. Lane takes off his baseball hat before the ride begins and places it behind his back. His straight black hair is flat and falls over his brow.

"Has anyone ever told you that you look like a Josh Hartnett when he was younger?" I blurt, instantly regretting my thoughts leaving my mouth.

He chuckles. "Sometimes. Is that a good thing or bad thing?" he asks, licking his lips.

My palms sweat. He's so close I can smell his cologne. Not too light but not offensive.

I shrug and smile. "Good, I guess."

He leans forward and whispers, "I was trying to get you to admit that you find me good-looking."

My hand grips the bar. I won't admit it. Look what happened last time.

The ride makes a rumbling noise and begins to swing in the air. My stomach drops at how fast the ride spins. A scream escapes me when it swings rapidly in the air, and I instinctively grab onto Lane. He holds me close, and we both laugh as the ride spins. I laugh so hard every time the ride swings and changes directions, tickling my stomach.

He holds me close until the ride stops, and I'm smiling. It feels like the pressure has been lifted off my chest, and I have a reason to smile and laugh again.

Even if it's only for a moment.

"That was awesome," Exie says excitedly as she walks down the steps. "Come on, Aura." She grabs my hand and tugs me forward until we get to the next one and the next.

I don't have to ride with Lane again, but he stands right behind me and always makes sure we are secured in every ride.

When we can't take it anymore, we head to finally get food, but Exie stops in front of a carnival game where the prizes are oversized bears that would hardly fit inside your car.

"Those are huge," I tell her.

Exie's eyes light up. "I know. I want one. You should try to get one too, Aura."

"I don't know. It looks kinda hard."

You have to throw the loop into the center bottle like a frisbee to get the main prize. I see numerous people in line and watch the ones trying to throw the loop but missing every time.

I would love to win one, though. I have never had a bear that big before, but I'd love the feeling of winning more than the actual bear.

Lane and Blaze leave us waiting in line to go get some food. Dex is looking at everyone trying to throw the ring, when I hear someone giggling in the line on the other side.

When I look up, Sarah whispers to Wendy, covering her lips. Wendy looks over at Exie and me.

"Damn," I mutter.

Exie looks up, and she sees what has me muttering to myself. My heart beats like a rapid knocking on a door when Kalum, Brian, and Cason come into view. Sarah is still whispering to Wendy, and they begin to openly laugh.

"I think we should go. We could come back," I say softly to Exie.

The light in Exie's eyes dims when she spots Brian with his hand wrapped around Wendy's waist. Sarah turns around and winds her arms around Kalum.

"You're so good at this, Kalum. You know how I love to reward you after you get me stuff," she purrs.

He nods but says nothing. I know she's doing it on purpose. She loves to show people she's with Kalum. Kalum looks like every girl's fantasy of a high school boyfriend in a simple blue hoodie and jeans. Sarah leans her blond head against his chest.

Kalum, Brian, and Cason haven't noticed us, but as the lines get shorter, and we get closer, I grip Exie's wrist. "Come on. Let's just go," I say softly.

But it's too late. Sarah sneers at us when we are about to leave. "Oh, look. It's the maid and her sidekick. I'm surprised Kalum's parents give you time off from cleaning toilets."

Kalum's head snaps up, and he steps back from Sarah. He's surprised to see me and realizes I've been standing in line the whole time. Brian and Cason glance at Exie and me, lowering their gaze.

"Let it go, Sarah," Brian warns.

Exie's fist clenches, and she curls her lip. "I guess Saturdays are Kalum's." Exie makes a motion like she's looking behind them. "Gee, Sarah. Where's Jimmy?" Exie places her hand over her mouth. "Whoops, did I say that out loud?"

Sarah's eyes almost bug out of her head. "You stupid bitch."

Kalum, Brian, and Cason raise their brows. Sarah's expression looks murderous.

"Don't call her that," I seethe. "Shut the hell up."

I'm surprised I'm being mean, but she's mean to everyone. I can't blame Exie for putting her business out like that—a person can only take so much. Kalum tries to hide his grin and scratches his cheek with his index finger.

"You're just a jealous, broke bitch who has a future in cleaning other people's piss from their toilet. I dirty my man's underwear. You just clean them when I'm finished," she spits.

"Sarah," Kalum warns, his voice laced with steel.

She glares at me in a fit of rage. "What? It's the truth. No one wants her around. You said so yourself when she first showed up. Not even her parents want her. Probably why she ended up as one of your mother's pet projects."

Everyone standing in line glances at me with looks of pity. Tears burn in the back of my eyes, and my heart sinks that he told everyone that he didn't want me. But what hurts the most is the reminder of my parents.

Dex places a hand on my shoulder, and I look at anything to distract me from looking at Kalum. "Don't pay that bitch any mind. She hates her life and gets off on putting others down," Dex says.

To my relief, Lane and Blaze approach with sodas and cotton candy. He frowns and then glances at where Kalum and his group stand. Dex speaks softly to Lane, and his head snaps up to look past me. His lip curls, but then his eyes soften when they land on mine.

The only moment today I had that I felt free was on a carnival ride with Lane. The reminder that I can't go to my real home right now has me feeling like I'll break down.

"Could you take me on another ride, please?" I ask in a shaky voice.

I need to get out of this line and do something other than stand here, listening to how messed up my life is right now.

He walks up to me and nods. "Yeah, I'll take you on every ride if you want." He places my hair behind my ear. "Look at me." He raises my head with his finger under my chin.

Tears threaten to fall, and I'm trying to blink them back the best I can. Lane brushes his thumb on my cheek when one tear escapes. He then slides his hand inside the cotton candy bag and places a piece on my lips, and when I open, it melts on my tongue, tasting sweet.

"Does it taste good?"

I nod, and Exie comes into view, concern marring her expression. "You okay, Aura?"

"Yeah," I say after swallowing.

"Forget about the stupid bear. Let's go have fun. Don't listen to her." Exie turns her head at a glaring Sarah and Wendy. "They all deserve each other," she says loud enough for them to hear.

The line moves along, but we step out of it, and right before we leave, we hear Sarah raise her voice. "Are you kidding me, Kalum?"

Kalum's face is hard and murderous. "We're over. Find a ride home."

"You're making a mistake. Any guy would kill to be with me."

Kalum sneers, and he waves his hand toward the crowd of people rubbernecking. "Well, hurry up because they're all waiting, including Jimmy." Her face is red like a bomb waiting to explode. She crosses her arms in a huff, embarrassed.

"You're going to regret it," she says in a shaky voice.

Kalum laughs sarcastically. "I regret entertaining the thought of you, and for the record, you're a horrible lay." He clenches his teeth. "I'm done. And stay away from Aura."

Chapter 14

Kalum

The look of hurt on Aura's face when Sarah mentioned her parents had me seeing red. Sarah went too far this time, and I care too much about Aura to allow a selfish bitch like Sarah hurt her.

Then I had to watch Lane Turner striding to her like her savior, touching her. The way she whispered something softly to him and then he fed her the cotton candy was so intimate.

I wanted to punch his fucking lights out. I figured she would meet Lane since she's good friends with Exie, but what gutted me the most was when he swiped her cheek, and I saw the bracelets on his wrist. She made one for him.

Lane and I go way back. We've been friends since high school. He would talk about cars and race on the backroads to see which car we could push faster. The guy is a genius in the race car world. He can build any car. I respect and admire him. He's self-made and a good guy.

Since he's a year older and graduated before me, I expected him to follow in his parents' footsteps like all rich kids do and take over their company or attend college first. Lane did neither. He attended a mechanic school and is now a certified mechanic and works on many makes and models.

It's his passion, and he's living his dream on his terms and has made a lot of money on his own. Lane didn't need a trust fund or his daddy's help. He made money on the street fixing cars and opened his own shop.

I stomp around the fair alone in a fit of rage. I should have taken Aura to the fair and broken it off with Sarah earlier. Sarah and her friends hate girls like Aura and Exie because they don't need to be fake or obvious.

I stop in front of a similar game with those ridiculous over-sized bears hanging from a fence, and I wave at the attendant.

"I'll play the game, but how much do you want for all of them?"

"Excuse me?" he asks, not sure if he heard me correctly.

I swipe a hand over my face. "You heard right. How much?"

He knows I want the bears, so I'm sure he'll inflate the price, but I don't care. I'll do anything to put a smile on Aura's face and redeem myself.

"You have to play ten games, and then I'll give you a price for all of them." He places twenty buckets of about fifty rings on the edge of the wooden area. "Is it for your girlfriend?" he asks, wiping his beard with a knowing grin.

I pull back the sleeves of my hoodie. "I'm hoping she'll be... if I didn't already ruin my chance with her."

The old man chuckles, combing his long gray beard with his fingers. "When the right girl smiles, she becomes a question to the man interested in her. That man could spend his whole life trying to find the answer."

The rings cling against the bottlenecks as I throw one after the other, missing most of them. *Tell me about it, old man.* After the third bucket, my wrist aches, and I have only made about four.

After two hours, my phone dings, letting me know Aura is home. I had Camila send me a text when she made it home safely.

She said her friend Exie dropped her off and not Lane. Even if Lane and I go way back, I stay out of his way, and he stays out of mine.

Except when we race once a month at the track in the fall when the temperatures cool, letting his latest build and my Lamborghini run at optimal speed. Since he made his own money and refused to take over his father's conglomerate, it forced his parents to leave most of it to Exie.

The worst part about him being around Aura is that she sees him as her hero, and I'm the villain. Brian walks up to me while I settle with the old man and the ten bears he has left.

"Need help?" Brian asks.

I nod. "Yeah."

"Is this for who I think it is?"

I grab three of the bears and lift them. "Is it that obvious?"

He chuckles. "You're really into her, aren't you?"

"I should ask you the same thing. The looks you give Exie are enough for even me to figure out. Pushing her away is only going to make her run into the arms of someone else."

Brian's nostrils flare, and his jaw ticks. "Oh yeah? Like who? We warned everyone away from them and banned them from my parties. Who in their right mind would defy us at Spencer?"

I shake my head, handing him three of the bears. "The guy who stood close to her in the line checking out her ass while her brother was buying food. That's who."

Brian's fist clenched on the bear.

"Easy. Don't fuck up the bear before I surprise her. She was waiting in the line, hoping to win one."

Brian snorts. "Yeah, before the queen bitch spit her vitriol at them. Aura was right. She's annoying. So is Wendy. I wish they came with an off switch so they could shut the fuck up."

We make it with the bears and three giant trash bags with the rest of the furry stuffed animals to the parking lot. Thank God Brian brought his truck so they all fit. Fitting ten oversized bears inside a sports car is not going to happen.

He closes the back passenger door of his truck. "How is it going to work if she agrees to give your sorry pigheaded ass a chance after you have treated her like dirt?"

I open the door to my Lambo, and the door swings up. "How is what going to work?"

"Her cleaning the toilets and dating you," he volleys back.

I slide inside the red leather seat and roll the window down when he does the same with his front passenger window. "That's easy, she doesn't. With me or not, I'll make sure to take care of her."

I just hope she chooses me.

Chapter 15

Aura

The sun streams through the window, but when I take a deep breath, a faint smell of a man's cologne is in the air. When my eyes flutter open, I gasp and spring up from the bed. Gigantic bears crowd my room. There are ten in total, ranging from pink, blue, and even yellow. I grab the one on the foot of the bed and notice they're the same ones Exie and I wanted at the fair. The ones that were nearly impossible to get. Who could've—

Quickly getting dressed in leggings and a T-shirt, I brush my teeth and knock on Kalum's bedroom door. I knock again before trying the handle. When no one answers, I turn the knob, and the door swings open. Kalum stands in the middle of his room, scowling at me.

He's shirtless, wearing sweats and barefoot. He must have just gotten out of the shower because his dark brown hair is wet.

"Why didn't you answer when I knocked on the door?"

He walks toward me and reaches out above my head and shuts the door. "Are you with him?"

"What?"

"Are you with Lane Turner?"

I shake my head and pinch my brows together. "No. We're just friends."

"It looked like more than that from what I saw."

"He was being a friend and a good person when he saw me hurting."

"The way he touched you, Aura..." he says, raising his tone.

"Who the hell do you th—"

He lifts me, laying me on his bed. He walks back to the door and turns the lock, the click echoing in the bedroom. Moving back to me, he kneels on the bed between my thighs and hovers over me.

"What are you doing, Kalum?"

He lowers his body so his face is inches away. His lips hover over mine a breath away from kissing me. "What I should have done the first time."

He slides his tongue over the seam of my lips. The mint taste of his breath and his tongue coast over the sensitive skin at the corner of my mouth. I whimper when the hot need pools between my thighs. He rubs his erection over the seam of my leggings between my legs.

"Kalum," I plead against his lips.

"You're mine, Aura. All mine," he whispers softly.

He slides his hand between us to the part where the tip of his erection rubs on my sensitive clit.

"Have you touched yourself here, baby?"

His tongue slides inside my mouth and swirls, sucking my bottom lip like it's the most delicious topping of a cake.

"Yes," I say.

His fingers find my clit, and he rubs circles over it, making me ache. "Have you done it here in your room?"

I nod.

He flicks my clit and slides his finger up and down my slit over my leggings in a rhythm that has me panting.

"Were you thinking of me?" he asks.

I can't think, I can't speak, and all I want is for him to give me my release. He looks down between my legs and cups me.

"Yes," I hiss.

His eyes caress my skin, dark with lust, his fingers continuing to rub in circles, and my breaths come out short and fast.

"You're so wet, Aura. I can feel you soaking my fingers."

"Kalum," I whisper, rubbing myself on his fingers. "What about Sarah?"

"I'm not with Sarah. I ended it with her because all I can think about is you. All I want is you."

He removes his hand from between my legs. "Kalum," I beg, grinding my hips.

He curls his fingers over the band of my leggings and swiftly slides them down my legs along with my panties. He raises himself to slide my shirt off over my head.

He trails kisses up to my breast and rasps against my skin, "Can I taste you, Aura?"

I love the way he looks at me. The way his words drip from his lips and the way he asks if he can have a part of me. I don't have the willpower to deny him because I want him.

"You can taste me, Kalum."

He closes his eyes. "Fuck," he breathes.

My eyes close when his tongue takes one nipple in his mouth. My hands slide between the strands of his hair, and he groans. His mouth makes a popping sound when he pulls my nipple out of his mouth.

"You taste so good, gorgeous." He sighs when he takes the other one.

"Please, Kalum. Don't stop."

He groans, and he releases my nipple. "Never."

He trails kisses down my stomach to the apex of my thighs, lighting my body on fire. I'm so wet, and I don't know what to do without touching myself, but he does. When I tilt my head to look at his head between my thighs, I blush because he's openly staring at what no other man has seen, touched, or tasted.

When his tongue flicks my sensitive flesh, my head tilts back.

"Oh God. Kalum, please."

His tongue slides inside me while he sucks, and he groans. I moan and grip the side of his head, not wanting him to move it away and stop him from pleasuring me. He twirls and sucks in a rhythm. My back arches, and I release his hair and grip the bedsheets.

"Yes."

He answers with a groan, and the sucking sounds of his mouth on my clit play like a melody. My nipples are hard, wet, and hot, and I'm grinding on his face.

"Kalum, I'm coming," I whisper-yell, and a hard wave comes crashing, making me feel like I'm suspended in the air outside my body. An electric current rips through me so powerful it causes my thighs to shake. He doesn't stop and drinks from me like a man starved. He pulls his swollen lips away from mine below with a kissing sound.

I bite my lip when I see him look up, and my arousal is all over his lips and chin, glistening as he swipes his tongue, trying to catch every drop. "I could do that to you all day and night, and it still wouldn't be enough."

He kisses between my legs, and a bubble of laughter escapes my lips as the stubble of his jaw tickles the soft skin on the inside of my thighs.

He smiles and stands to walk into his bathroom. He returns with a washcloth and cleans the mess we made. He dresses me slowly, pulling my leggings over my legs, then holds the arms of my T-shirt so I can slide my arms through.

"Ready?"

Grinning, I look around. "Ready for what?" I ask.

He leans close and pecks me on the lips. "Breakfast. I've already had mine, but you must be hungry," he says playfully, giving me a wink.

Why? Why me? He could have anyone.

"Kalum?"

"Yeah?"

"What does this all mean? Us? This? The bears?"

He lifts my chin with two fingers while I'm kneeling on his bed. "This is the beginning."

"Of what?" I ask, confused.

His eyes bore into mine like he's trying to see the window into my soul when he gazes at me. "Of us," he says.

Chapter 16

Aura

"Where are we going?" I ask.

"You'll see."

Kalum says he's taking me on a surprise joyride and to bring my swimsuit and a change of clothes. I'm wary but excited. His parents are out of town, and he showed up and knocked on my door this morning and asked if I would go with him.

"I want to take you to a place I thought you might like. It will keep your mind off other things."

He means it will help me get my mind off mourning my parents. Thinking about them makes my chest squeeze tight and my throat close.

For the past month, Kalum has changed. He has acted more like a good friend than an enemy. He takes me to school, and I wait for him in the library after school until he finishes practice.

He doesn't taunt me anymore, and on the nights when I cry, missing my parents, he holds me. He's careful when entering my room and always locks the door. I cry on his shoulder, and he soothes me, and it's the greatest feeling in the world.

To be held.

To feel safe.

I wrap my body around his, knowing he doesn't expect more, but my favorite part is when his lips touch my forehead in a kiss.

At night, it's like we're in a bubble he has created. A shield against the outside world that can't be penetrated. Some nights, I dream of him and hope that he dreams of me too like a sharing of souls.

Once he sees I packed a light bag, he walks down the hallway, and I follow. When we step outside, my eyes light up.

"Is that yours?" I point at the white Jeep.

"I rented it."

Why would he rent a Jeep? He opens the door, and he already has the top down. It has a soft top that can be opened electronically, a newer model than the one I was interested in purchasing from Lane.

My thoughts briefly think of Lane and the night at the fair but quickly disappear when Kalum slides in the driver's side after placing a book bag in the back. My eyes trail over his football T-shirt with his school logo and his number sixty-eight on the lower left part near the hem. His light gray shorts show his muscular legs. My eyes trail over his large hands and muscled forearms. Kalum is gorgeous.

Girls give him doe eyes in the hallways, but when he looks at me and smiles every morning, it feels like rain falling violently from the sky. The force rippled inside me.

I try to play it off, but then I remember what he did to me with his tongue between my thighs. He gave me the most intense orgasm I have ever had. It was beautiful, and it was mine. It was our secret.

He places the car in gear, and we head toward the open road. The wind begins to pick up as the car increases in speed, and the memory of what my mom said about her time in college with her favorite Jeep brings a smile to my face. To experience something similar to what my mom did forges the memory together, bringing me closer to her in reenacting a memory she shared with me.

"Do you like it?" Kalum asks, raising his voice over the wind.

My head turns, and the huge grin on my face has him smiling.

"I love it!"

On the way to wherever he's taking me, I tell him about my mom and the Jeep she had in college she had to sell when she fell pregnant with me. I also tell him about the Jeep Lane Turner had for sale at his shop that I couldn't afford.

"So I got it right?"

"With what?" I answer.

"Renting the Jeep and taking you on an adventure."

"Yes. This is the most fun I've had since forever."

He knows I mean the accident involving the death of my parents. Why I feel like telling him this, I have no idea. I guess it's because he stays quiet when crying at night and the fact that he's always there holding me until I fall asleep and I wake up in his arms. He hasn't tried to touch me since that morning he ate me out on his bed.

He has respected the fact that I'm not like the girls he's used to having casual sex with. He knows that I see sex as something special that needs to be with the right person. Like the first time you see the sun set. Because you'll never see another one like it.

This change in him is refreshing, and it means a lot that he has been there for me at night when I'm at my lowest. He could have stayed acting like he did when we first met.

We arrive at a state park. There is a lake where you can swim with white sand like at the beach. There are picnic tables to the right with grills. On the far side is a dock for fishing.

"This is beautiful, Kalum," I breathe.

The sun is out, and the Jeep rolls over the gravel with ease. There are few people since it's still early September, but the summer heat is still in the air, heating up the day.

"Ready for a swim?" he asks.

I smooth my windblown hair, and I feel refreshed and exhilarated that I get to go for a swim at the beautiful lake, looking like a crystal as the sun gleams off the surface.

In the distance, you can see small boats, one pulling a wakeboard. I hop out of the Jeep, glad there are restrooms, and head inside to change into a modest bikini.

When I emerge, Kalum is already ready for a swim, his massive body with tattoos covering his smooth tan skin.

To know that just this morning, I was wrapped in his arms, feeling warm and safe. Not even Marcus looked like that, and he plays football.

When I walk up, his eyes trail slowly over my bikini. His eyes darken for a second, but then his mouth turns up in a smile.

He holds out his hand. "Come on. I've already tested the water. It's still warm."

He guides me to the shallow part and then farther until the water is up to my neck. Under the water, I can feel the brush of his knees every now and then.

"Did you ever swim back home?" he asks.

I slide my wet hair over one shoulder before I answer.

He studies me and gets closer, but I don't step back. I've gotten used to the feel of him near my body. He isn't handsy, which I can appreciate, and he makes sure not to make me feel uncomfortable around him.

"My neighbor had an aboveground pool. When I was seven, my mother took me to get free swimming lessons at the community center. There was a group of volunteers from a foundation to teach kids how to swim to prevent accidental drownings. As you can tell, I didn't come from money." I shrug. "I had fun with friends from my neighborhood. They would come and go until high school when I met Marcus and Gina."

The mention of Marcus has Kalum's expression hardening.

"How long were you with Marcus?"

"Since the first week of my freshman year until I moved here with you."

"Why Marcus?"

I look down to see if I could see my feet below, thinking how to answer the question. He probably is wondering how I didn't see the betrayal. How I didn't notice, and why out of all the guys attending Spencer Public High, I chose to be with Marcus.

"He was nice and didn't pressure me to have sex. I would tell him to stop, and he would. He was safe, and my parents liked him for the most part."

Kalum gets close, and my legs wrap around his waist, my arms winding around his neck. The smell of his cologne drifts off his skin.

"Why me? Why do you let me touch you and not him?" he asks, his voice husky.

His lips are inches from mine. His thumbs slide under the strings tied around my back. My skin tingles under the water in the wake of his touch. My nipples are so hard under the bikini top, they ache for...

His lips.

Anything if it's Kalum doing it.

How did I fall under his magic spell? I don't know. But it happened.

"I like the way you touch me. It feels right."

The way he's patient and listens to me. The way his touch burns a fire across my body, searing it in my mind, committing it to my memory. I don't think I could ever forget him.

"Like this." His lips brush over mine, and I slide my tongue inside his mouth. He sucks my tongue, and I suck his. My breasts rub against his muscled pecs, and we kiss like star-crossed lovers. A forbidden embrace. A forbidden touch and a forbidden kiss.

We both know what's at stake. My existence and well-being in his house. The disapproval from his parents and his friends for sneaking around with the poor future housekeeper.

Right now, we don't care because it's just us, and nothing can ruin this moment. We are in each other's arms, our breaths mingling and our skin touching. It's perfect. It's us.

Chapter 17

Kalum

When I saw the way her face lit up when she saw the Jeep, I knew I made the right decision. I had to pull some strings to rent it since I'm not eighteen yet, but I made it work. Aura is a simple girl who finds joy in the most trivial things. She isn't about designer labels or overpriced dinners. She enjoys the good in people and always looks for it in everyone she meets. She's like a breath of fresh air in a stuffy room. Her gorgeous smile makes my heart skip a beat, and I can't help how I feel when I wake up with her in my arms. I'm always careful, so everyone at home is none the wiser. But I have never wished my parents to travel away from home the way I do now.

When she cries at night, I want to take away her pain and wipe away her tears. She's the most precious gift, and I can't help myself. I've fallen for her. Like stars that collide and slowly become one, admiring how perfectly we fit.

I place soft kisses all over her mouth and move down her neck, holding her against me. My fingers slide up her soft skin to the side of her breasts. My head tilts, and I see we are the only ones in the water. Her nipples are hard under the triangle scraps of fabric that make her bikini top, and I would give anything to slide the fabric to the side and take each one inside my mouth.

My lips find her neck and nibble where her pulse beats rapidly. "You're beautiful, Aura." My fingers find the band of her bikini bottoms. "Is this okay?"

She gives me a nod, and it's all I need to slide it to the side and swipe my finger on her clit. Her intake of breath tells me she feels the same way I do right now.

I leave her exposed underwater, and I lower my swim trunks, brushing the tip of my cock against her clit in a discreet rhythm. Her lips part, and I plunge my tongue inside.

A moan escapes her throat, and I groan at how hot I feel. I rub the tip over her clit, careful not to go any farther. I want us both to get off without taking her completely.

Aura's so responsive even though her touch is innocent. I could tell that idiot Marcus didn't touch her or, rather, she didn't allow him to touch her, and my ego is stroked by her giving me permission. To be the first one to touch her so intimately. She says the person she chooses must feel right. I want to be the one who does.

I break the kiss while I subtly rub against her so anyone who looks this way can only see two young people locked in a passionate kiss instead of getting each other off while swimming in the lake. Her eyes are full of want when I glance at her. Her lips are swollen from my kiss, and her skin is flushed.

"Do I feel right, Aura? I want to know if this feels right." I rub her clit with the head of my cock, stroking her tight bud underwater.

"Yes, Kalum. When you touch me, it feels right."

Her eyes close, and a soft moan escapes her lips. That is all

I need to hear to turn us around so my back is to the shore and no one sees her. My fingers brush her nipples. Her breathing picks up, and I grip my shaft with my other hand.

"Hold on to me, princess. I'm not going to go further than this. You deserve better for your first time."

"I want it to be you."

Jesus. This girl will be the death of me. I have died and gone to heaven. Her heaven.

I rub the head of my cock faster on her clit, and she leans back, her nipples slightly exposed. My left hand holds her, and her hips tilt in a rhythm. We watch each other, and it's the sexiest thing to see her beautiful upper body floating in the water while I rub her pussy. Her clit throbs, and I know she's close. So am I. The tingle from my balls gives me a signal that I'm going to come, jerking my cock and rubbing my sensitive tip over her.

"I'm about to come, baby."

Fuck, this is better than any meaningless sex I've ever had. Aura is inside me, and I have accepted she always will be.

She rubs frantically over me, and my nostrils flare. "I'm coming," she whispers.

I bring her close, and I kiss her mouth to drown out her moan as she comes all over me. It's the sweetest thing I have ever heard. I come, but I'm careful it's outside of her. We are both breathless and lost in each other. It feels like we're flying high in the sky.

After making our way back to the beach, we lie out on our towels. Her body gleams with drops of water as the sun dries our skin. Her body is perfect. Her breasts fit in the palms of my hand. The sweetness between her thighs is like honey on my tongue, and the smell of her hair is like those flowery candles you want to keep burning just so the smell can linger in the air.

"Do you come here often?" she asks.

I grin because I'm sure she's wondering if I bring girls here.

"Not since I was five with my dad. He took me fishing one time, and it was at this park." I point toward the boats on the far side of the lake. "It was a day just like this, and it was so peaceful. It was one of the best days I ever had with my father."

She turns so that her body faces mine, and I stare at her, mesmerized. She's so pretty and petite. She's so much shorter than me, and I love it. She weighs nothing when I lift her and take her in my arms.

When I'm with her, the whole world fades away. It's just us inside a cocoon of our own making. My parents would never approve of me being with her, but I don't care. I want her and only her.

"You never came back or went fishing again?"

I shake my head. "No. He never had time after that. Work and the family name always came first. They have groomed me to take over the family business after I graduate from college." I sigh. "As much as I love football, I would disappoint my parents if I chose to play instead of working at the family business. In their eyes, it's just a sport to pass the time."

"And what do you want, Kalum? What would you like to do?"

Lying down, I place my hands behind my head and look up at the sky. What do I want? She's the first person to ask me that. No one has taken the time to ask me what I want. There is only one thing I *know* I want.

Her.

I want her.

I don't tell her that.

I'm falling in love with her, but now is not the time to tell her. She just lost her parents and needs to figure out what she wants to do. I want whatever that is to involve me.

"I don't know, but I'm going to figure that out before I graduate."

That is the only answer I can give her right now. When the time is right, I'll tell her. Soon.

Chapter 18

Aura

Kalum told me last week that Thursday was his birthday. After school, I went to the grocery store with Henry and picked up some stuff, but I paid for it with my own money. I purchased balloons and everything I needed to make a surprise homemade birthday cake.

The Jeep is not there, so I assumed Lane sold it already. It was really a nice Jeep, but there was no way I could afford to buy it. I never mentioned it to Exie or asked who purchased it from her brother. The subject of her brother hasn't come up, and the way I feel about Kalum, I'm honestly not interested in Lane, not in that way. Kalum has stolen my kisses and my heart.

I'm walking out to the parking lot, and my phone vibrates.

My heart sinks that I'm not invited, but I understand. People have already noticed we are closer than before. Kalum doesn't allow the bitch crew or any of his teammates to call me names. No one approaches me at school except Exie. I have to say I'm grateful. My thoughts roam, wondering if Sarah and the other girls got invited to celebrate his birthday. A wave of jealousy hits my stomach, but I block it out when the black Rolls-Royce pulls up, and Henry opens the back door.

I didn't know what to buy Kalum for his birthday, so I made a special bracelet with his name engraved on it. The guy has everything, and my budget is limited. The bracelet is thicker than anything I have ever made, so it took me more time to complete. It has been a challenge to hide it from him. Kalum watches me while I make them in class, and I didn't want him to see what I was making, so hiding my next creation has been a challenge.

He makes sure the coast is clear at night and slips inside my bed. We sleep together almost every night. No sex, just sleep, and we talk about everything in hushed whispers. Our favorite foods, what we are into, what movies we haven't watched with promises to go to the movies one day.

I sigh, disappointed I didn't get to finish the bracelet yet, but I wanted it to be perfect. I bought the best material to make it. It's a bracelet meant to last forever.

I text him back.

> Aura: I can't wait to see you. I miss you already. Have fun and stay safe.

Three bubbles pop up, and then they disappear.

"Is everything okay, Miss Aura?" Henry asks, his gray eyes looking through the rearview mirror. Is my disappointment that obvious?

I give him a fake smile. "Everything is great, Henry. I can't wait until I get home to make Kalum his cake."

Henry nods, but his expression tells me he's not so convinced. He drives through the gates of the St. Claire mansion. Sometimes, I feel like it's an institution, a prison, and I'm completing a sentence. In a way, I am.

The only thing good is Henry, Camila, and Kalum. Mr. and Mrs. St. Claire see me as the hired help. Not fit to be anything more than a poor girl who, under bad circumstances, needs a job. They overlook that I'm third in class. I have excellent grades, and I'm only trailing first by two points. Kalum is ahead of me academically by one point. He was surprised when he found out.

I batted my eyelashes and said I came from smart parents who attended college, even if my father had no choice but to drop out. Kalum said he admired them for not giving up on each other. My heart soared when he talked so well about them, not judging their decisions. My mother could have aborted me and moved on with their lives and could have been successful. My father wanted to major in accounting and attended Penn State with my mother.

"Hi, Aura," Camila greets me when I make it into the kitchen. "Everything is ready."

I smile. "Thank you."

I get to work, and once the cake is in the oven, she eyes me warily and lowers her voice to a whisper, "You like him, don't you?"

I place the balloons around the small table in the kitchen so that when he arrives, we can sing "Happy Birthday" and cut the cake. My mother taught me to make the triple-layer chocolate mousse cake that melts in your mouth.

"I do. Very much. I think I'm falling for him," I whisper back.

She nods and then sees my expression.

"What's wrong?"

"I'm just scared. I know I shouldn't feel this way."

She shakes her head. "Why not?"

I sit in the chair and watch the time to make sure the cake is cooked just right. "We would never work, Camila." I lower my voice. "If they found out, they would get rid of me. You know that, and you know why."

Camila comes from the real world; she knows that his parents would never approve of us, and no one on this side of town, including his friends, would accept me with him, even if I didn't care what anyone thought. Kalum comes from a world where what other people think matters the most.

Her expression turns grim, and she nods in understanding. Then she smiles when the timer dings, signaling that the cake is ready. I prepare the cake and set it on the table. I check my phone, and it has been three hours already. Camila suggests placing the beautifully decorated cake inside the refrigerator to avoid it getting spoiled.

Thanking her, I make my way and finish some house chores, take a shower, and work on Kalum's bracelet. After two more hours, I look at the time, and it's way past the time I'm usually up, and Kalum hasn't texted me to tell me he's on his way.

I feel bummed, but I understand it's his birthday, and he wanted to spend it with his friends like he must have always done before I came into the picture. These people have been in his life way longer than I have.

Checking my phone, I see it's almost eleven at night.

I hear a knock on the door. My head lifts, and it's Camila. My door opens, and she stands in the doorway. My eyes are glassy, but I make sure not to show any emotion. She must sense it, but she doesn't call me out on it. Camila has known me and my parents since I can remember.

She holds her hands together and gives me a small smile. "Mrs. St. Claire informed me they had a celebratory dinner for Kalum with all his friends at an exclusive restaurant in town after football practice. She said they wouldn't be back until late. It's his eighteenth birthday. It's a big thing for them, I guess."

"I understand," I croak. My paltry homemade cake wouldn't hold a candle to what his parents and friends have planned for him.

She frowns when she sees me get up. "Where are you going?"

I give her a smile. "To clean up. My momma taught me better than to leave my mess downstairs. I left the balloons and plates out."

She shakes her head. "I wouldn't dream of it. You spent hours making and decorating that cake." She wags her finger at me playfully. "I know you spent your own money on it. The balloons and the cake and all the decorations weren't on the receipt when you came home with the weekly grocery run for the St. Claires."

Busted. I have a feeling Camila knows about Kalum and me sneaking around, but that's okay. This just shows I'm chasing a pipe dream with Kalum. I was right. This would never work, and whatever I offer is nothing compared to what he's used to and that includes me. Whatever I'm feeling needs to stop.

I raise my chin. "I did. I paid for it with my bracelet sales, but that's okay. I'm sure he had a better cake with his family and friends."

"I doubt that, sweetheart."

"Would you please make sure everyone who works here gets a slice, including Henry? I would hate for such a good cake to go to waste. I'm sure they would love cake. Oh, the balloons, I'm sure whoever has children or grandkids would love them," I say with a smile.

I don't want her to see the sadness I feel right now. It would cause her to worry.

"Are you sure, Aura?"

"I'm sure, Camila. It's okay, really. I'm fine. It's just a cake and some balloons. Thank you for helping me. I made sure all the cleaning in Kalum's room and the laundry were done when I came upstairs. I didn't want to fall behind or, worse, Mrs. St. Claire to think we weren't keeping up with the house."

"Thank you, sweetheart. I would have done it, but being the angel you are, I'm not surprised."

Chapter 19

Kalum

I wanted to send Aura a text on the night of my birthday. For the past three days, she has avoided me. She locks her door at night. I think I hurt her. It wasn't my intention, but my parents and my friends had a surprise party for me after school.

I couldn't tell my parents I wanted to head home because of Aura. They were suspicious because I turned my friends down for a house party. The only person I wanted to spend time with on my birthday was her, and I made myself out to be a liar.

On the car ride to school the next day, I explained what happened. She smiled and said it was all right, that she understood.

I'm heading out to my car, placing my football bag and change of clothes inside. Henry walks up after parking the black sedan in my parents' driveway.

"Kalum, I haven't had the chance to thank Aura. I was wondering if you could thank her for me when you see her."

What does he want to thank her for? Henry isn't allowed

inside the house unless one of us gives him access, and Aura rides with me from school or hangs out with Exie.

Camila went to get groceries with Henry this week. Aura has midterms coming up and a project for school due.

My mother has excused her for the next three weeks, and she has been up in her room. My feeling is that she's dreading turning eighteen tomorrow and she'll be officially a hired member of the staff. If my plan works out, all of that will change.

"What would I be thanking her for, Henry?" I ask as I stand a few feet away.

"Oh, the delicious chocolate triple layer cake she made the night your parents gave you a surprise birthday with all your friends. You were out late, and Camila gave everyone a slice of the cake and some balloons to some of the staff's kids." He wrinkles his forehead, and my heart sinks. "I thought the balloons were odd, but the cake was beautifully decorated. It had these little sparkling candles, but I didn't mind. The cake was superb. Honestly, the best cake I have ever tasted. It must have taken her quite some time. I heard she spent hours making it."

"It was that good, huh?"

My heart drops, and shame claws my skin. What should I say? Throw up the cake? It doesn't take a genius to know it was my surprise cake. She never said anything. She said she understood.

The next words out of his mouth make me feel like the biggest piece of shit on earth, solidifying the reason for her behavior. I royally screwed up.

"I was wondering the other day why she wanted to stop and buy balloons and cake supplies. Aura is the sweetest thing on earth. She paid for all those items out of her own pocket to make us all that splendid cake."

Aura must think I don't love or care about her.

No one has ever made me a surprise birthday cake with balloons. My parents hire catering companies and chefs for any event they host. My mother would chop her fingers off before making me a cake. I would be surprised if she even knew how to make one.

Fuuuck.

"I will. I'll tell her when I see her."

If she'll talk to me. I ruined her surprise, and I won't ever get it back.

The restaurant was posh and over the top like my parents and my friends' parents. They even invited Sarah, her parents, her friends, and their parents.

Cason was the only one at the table who could sense how upset I was. He was the only one who knew I didn't want to be there. Lane texted me well wishes and told me to tell Aura he said hi.

Like I said, Lane and I are boys. Even if we aren't up each other's ass, we still keep in touch on birthdays and certain holidays. Guilt ate at me when I saw it was close to midnight, and my birthday was practically over.

I read my text to Aura and felt like shit. I told her I wanted to spend it with her, and it was the opposite of what I did. Sarah tried to get me to fuck her in the bathroom or give me a BJ in my car.

She was pissed when I told her I would never touch her again and to forget about us getting back together. She asked me if it was because of Aura, and I was honest and told her yes. She laughed. I told her to fuck off.

She said Aura and I would never happen. I told her she was desperate. She left in a huff, telling me I would call her. If she only knew that was never going to happen.

Henry smiles. "Thank you, Kalum."

After the game, I need to fix the mess I made and hope Aura will forgive me. If I would have known, I would have made it back home. I was worried about my parents finding out how I felt about her. I also didn't know how to tell her that my parents invited Sarah, her friends, and her parents. I knew it would hurt her on top of me not showing up. I didn't want her to think I was using her.

Parents with money are more powerful than people think. They can disown you or make the other person suffer, and I would die if that happened. No matter what, I'll make sure Aura doesn't suffer. I'll protect her. She thinks she has no one, but she has me, and that will never change.

Chapter 20

Aura

It's seven thirty, and I'm in the dining room. Mr. and Mrs. St. Claire wants to have a word with me, and I'm nervous. They probably got wind of Kalum and me, and they want to send me away.

My birthday is tomorrow, and I'll officially be an adult. No one knows it's my birthday at school, just Exie, Kalum, his parents, and the staff know. Camila is making a cake to celebrate. For me, it feels like a death sentence. Where would I go? How will I support myself?

Kalum's mother and father sit at the dining table, and my stomach turns in a knot. I sit on my hands to stop fidgeting.

"Tomorrow is your birthday, and that means you're officially an adult. I have the papers that officially end our guardianship agreement." She slides a manila folder to me. "I want you to enjoy your day. Henry will take you anywhere you wish to go. Kalum has plans to go on a trip with some friends."

He knows it's my birthday, and he's leaving? My throat squeezes because I thought he cared. A part of me thought he did. I avoided him because I needed space to lick my wounds in peace. To dissect my feelings for Kalum.

Kalum's father smiles at me warmly. He looks like Kalum but with graying hair. He has the same authoritative air. His mother is poised, and you can tell she has wit and an airy disposition.

"We also wanted to let you know that we don't need you to be employed as our housekeeper. Camila found someone," Mr. St. Claire says.

It feels like all the air has escaped my lungs. Kalum's mother gives me a wan smile and pulls out a white envelope.

"I understand," I croak.

"We heard about the rumors Kalum started, and he apologizes for divulging information around school. That was in poor taste. As a family, we are incredibly sorry."

In other words, you look bad in front of the charity events you frequent with the other rich families. She finally slides the envelope. I place it on top of the folder.

"That is a check for a hundred thousand. It should give you a fresh start, money for school, and enough to cover your expenses. You can still have a great life, Aura. I'm sorry we can't stay to celebrate your birthday, but we have an emergency with one of our projects in New York."

Basically, it means get out. A huge knot forms in the back of my throat. I have nowhere to go. I wished they would have waited until I graduated or given me more time.

I raise my chin and look at both the St. Claires. "Thank you for everything, and I appreciate your generosity. You have been kind and have done more than I could have asked for. I wish you all the best."

Taking the folder in my hand, I walk as fast as I can to my room. Once I close the door, I slide down the door and let the tears I've been holding back slide down my cheeks.

I watch the clock on my phone until it strikes midnight. I pack all my clothes in one suitcase. I have five thousand dollars to my name. There is no way I could take their money. Rich people have a way of throwing money at problems when they make mistakes, thinking it's the right thing to do.

Kalum won't be back. His parents said he had plans with his friends. It was a mistake to let him get too close. Not because I regret his kiss or his touch because I don't. I shut him out after his birthday, but I had my reasons.

When my father met my mother, he would never do the things Kalum has done. My father knew how special my mother was and wouldn't risk losing her for a second.

Men like my father simply don't exist anymore. A love like theirs is the kind written in poems. The kind you learn from. The kind you wish for. A rare connection. I thought I found it, but I was wrong.

Maybe their death clouded my reasoning. I wanted to feel loved so badly that I didn't realize I was the only one with stars in my eyes. I thought he felt the same way, but maybe all I saw was what I wanted to see, a reflection of how I felt. I thought I felt safe in his arms, but I was just his secret.

The dirty looks and smirks Sarah gave me in the hallway gave away what I assumed. What I heard in the bathroom after lunch the following day.

Sarah was with him on his birthday when he said he wanted to spend it with me. Her friends and his friends were all there with his parents. They were talking about college and their plans after graduation and how Kalum and Sarah looked good together. How his parents loved the idea of them together. I felt like I was being ripped piece by piece.

The Uber drops me off at the shopping center, and I'm glad it stopped drizzling. I remember Henry passing a hotel on the way to the grocery store but couldn't get the app to calculate a ride. The closest destination was the shopping center. The sound of an engine roars in the empty parking lot, causing me to cover my ears.

I look up, and it's coming from Lane's shop. There is a sports car with the tail end sticking out one of the bays with flames shooting out of the exhaust. I pull my suitcase down the sidewalk toward the hotel two miles down the road. I can see the sign in the distance.

A car drives past me. The headlights are blueish white, blinding me as it drives on the empty wet road. The taillights brighten when the car brakes hard, coming to a complete stop. The car waits as I walk down the sidewalk with my rolling suitcase containing everything I own. I'm nervous, and tears spill down my cheeks.

When I pass the car, the passenger window rolls down. "Aura?"

I sniff. "Lane?"

He pulls the brake and gets out.

I point at the hotel. "Could you take me to that hotel over there, please?" I ask.

He opens the passenger door of the car. He takes my suitcase and places it in the back seat. He slides in the driver seat, reaches over, and buckles me in.

"Thank you," I say just above a sob.

I'm seated at the all-night diner with a cup of coffee. Lane is seated across from me, and I tell him what happened, leaving out what happened between me and Kalum.

"So they just tried to buy you off?" I nod. "Does Kalum know?"

I shrug. "I'm not sure. He was playing an away game, and they said he had plans after. I didn't want to stay longer than I should."

His eyes soften. "Are you hungry?"

"No. I don't have much of an appetite right now."

He pays the bill before I get the chance to place the money over the check on the table.

"Please, put that away," he says.

"Are you taking me to the hotel now?" I ask, sliding the money back into my wallet.

He stands and looks down at me. "No. I'm taking you to my house."

My eyes widen, and I shake my head. "I can't impose on you like that."

"I'm hardly there. I'm too busy on my latest build at the shop. It's no trouble. I'll take you to school in the morning. No exceptions."

I nod. "Okay. I'll figure something out as soon as I can."

"Take as long as you need, Aura. Friends look out for each other. My sister will be breathing down my neck when she finds out tomorrow. There is no way I could leave you at a hotel."

His house is big. It's a one story not far from his shop. Not overly flashy but expensive. There are hardwood floors throughout with white couches and cream-colored walls. It's simple and modern. He has numerous awards for building cars and racing along a single wall. Pictures with different cars on the track.

"This is all you?" I point.

He stands with his hands in his pockets. "Yeah. It's all I ever wanted to do. There is nothing more important to me than my next build. My next creation. It's a passion that lives inside me. It feeds me and keeps me feeling alive. Nothing else matters... I feel... free."

"How about having a family of your own?" I ask.

He shrugs. "Never thought that far. How about you? What do you have a passion for?"

"I love creating bracelets. I wanted to have my own store one day."

"They're beautiful and different. They look authentic and well made."

He pulls his sleeve up. He's wearing the one he bought from me. I need to tell him I don't want to attend school tomorrow. I'd rather not run into Kalum and the rest of the snobs.

"I'm glad you like it." I clear my throat. "I want to skip school tomorrow."

"I can't let you do that. School is important."

"It's my birthday," I counter, not wanting to tell him the real reason.

"Oh." He pauses. "Like right now?"

I sigh and give him a smile. "Yeah, like right now."

"O-okay, that means it's a long weekend for you. Got it."

He walks past me to the hallway that leads to his bedroom. He turns his head and says, "Follow me."

He opens the door to a massive main bedroom. I follow him inside and grin because his bed is unmade, and he has a pile of dirty clothes in the corner. His room is not dirty but messy. A person who wakes up, gets dressed, and runs out in the morning.

He runs a hand behind his neck. "I know it's a mess, but I have a lady who comes once a week to help me clean. Like I said, I'm never home. I would tell you to use the spare room, but all the other rooms are empty," he rushes out. "No one comes here, and when I visit my parents and my sister, I stay over at their house in my old room."

I place my hand over his arm. "Lane."

"Yeah?"

"I don't care about the mess, and I want you to know I'm grateful for you giving me a place to stay, even if it's for the night." I pause. "I'll take the couch."

He faces me. "I can't have you sleep on the couch. I'll take the couch. You take the bed."

When I look up, his dark brown eyes framed with dark lashes soften, and something passes between us. A weird feeling, but it's more like friendship than anything. At least for me. For him, I'm not so sure. Lane is hard to read like a closed book. Exie says he's an introvert. He keeps to himself and only has a close group of friends. She says he doesn't get along with their parents and does his own thing. He doesn't agree with their way of life or decisions.

"Stay with me. You don't have to go, and if you want to leave, all you have to do is tell me, and I'll understand."

My forehead rests against his chest over his gray long-sleeve T-shirt. He smells like fresh-ocean cologne mixed with gasoline and burnt rubber. I'm torn and feel like my heart has been stabbed into a million pieces. I have nothing and nowhere to go.

What choice do I have? If I asked my only friend, who is his sister, she would tell me to stay here with him. Whatever happened with Kalum is over. I don't think he meant to hurt me, but in the end, his family would never accept me. He would choose them. The way he chose not to tell me he was with Sarah that day.

I left him a letter before I left, wishing him well. I'm grateful his family offered me an opportunity at Spencer and a place to stay. My situation could have been worse.

I meet Lane's gaze. "I'll stay, and if you go, I'll go with you."

Chapter 21

Kalum

When I make it home, it feels empty. It's late, and I don't want to bother Aura in her sleep. I have a big day tomorrow planned for Aura's birthday. I want it to be her day and all about her.

Camila is baking her a cake and a big breakfast when she wakes up so everyone can celebrate before I take her to a cabin I rented in the mountains. Just the two of us. It's the first time I have ever done something like this for a girl, but Aura is different.

I awake at first light and smile to myself, excited. After taking a shower, I knock on Aura's door, but I don't hear her moving around. I knock again, and after a minute, I turn the doorknob, and it opens. My eyes scan the room, and my stomach fills with dread. All the bears I gifted her are neatly placed on the edge of the bed, facing each other. I frown when I see a piece of paper and an envelope.

Looking around the room, I notice all her things are missing. I yank open the closet door to find that her bag and all of her things are gone. I panic.

I grab the envelope and paper folded on the bed so force-
fully that I almost crush it in my hand. I take a calming breath,
open it, and read it.

Kalum,

I'm sorry for leaving without saying goodbye.
Your parents informed me they wouldn't need me
after I turned eighteen. I'm not sure if you
knew when that day was, but if you're reading
this, then that day is the date on this letter.
Your parents have been generous and kind to
offer me a place to stay when I had no place to
go. They offered me a generous amount of money
to start my life, but I couldn't take it. It
didn't feel right. They heard the rumors of me
being your housekeeper from school, so they
thought it best for me to start my life on my
own terms.

In my heart, I always knew this was where
I was meant to be. I can count on one hand the
times I smiled while staying here, and they were
all with you. I'll never forget the small moments
we had and the small words of wisdom you
shared with me that night when I was in my
darkest moment, so I thought I would share mine
with you. My father once told me when you meet
that special someone, don't let them go even for a
moment, because you never know if you'll ever get

another chance. I hope you find that someone,
Kalum. When you meet her, don't ever let her go. I
wish you the best, and I hope you find love
one day.
Love,
Aura Rayne

I drop the letter on the floor as a blinding rage clouds my vision. I blame myself and my parents. I open the envelope and see the check for one hundred thousand she didn't take. Under the papers, there is a thick black, white, and gray bracelet she made, and it has my name woven with red letters with a little charm that reads *Made by Aura*. My fingers run over the letters wishing her name was with mine.

Emptiness washes over me, an emptiness that will always be there if she's not with me. I lost her.

A knock comes from the bedroom door. When I look up, Camila stands in the doorway with a tray.

"What's wrong?"

Her hands shake when she looks around. She notices that all of Aura's things are gone. Her eyes catch the bracelet and letter in my hand. She places the tray on the nightstand and kneels in front of me, where tears begin to fall, forming a puddle on the floor. She takes my hands in hers. Her eyes lift, and fresh tears slide down her cheeks. I blink back my tears.

"Oh, Kalum. What have they done?"

She means my parents and their meddling. They knew I fell in love with her, and what I had planned for her today proved it. When I first laid eyes on her, I didn't recognize it. I tried to fight it. Then I tried to hide it. My mother must have never thought I would consider a girl like Aura, but they were wrong. They never thought I could fall in love with her.

They lied to her. They made it seem it was because of a rumor and that they took advantage of her situation. But it's all lies.

My parents didn't want their son to be seen with a girl who came from no privilege or a wealthy family. It's all about the St. Claire name and how they stand in the community. Deep down, I knew if I gave in to my feelings for her that she would be attacked somehow, but I never thought my parents would be the ones to do it.

The invitation to Sarah on my birthday and her parents. I was surprised when they showed up, and they made sure I stayed. They made sure I didn't make it home.

I can't believe they would stoop so low. I'm so angry, I can't think. But I can't tell them to go fuck themselves and leave because they would make our lives hell. Aura doesn't deserve that. She deserves love and stability. I underestimated my parents, and I have never felt more ashamed to have been born into a family the way I do now. A cold, heartless family that only cares about themselves.

I sniff. "I'm going to make them pay for what they've done. I need you to help me, Camila, because I don't know how to go on from here." I pause and blink back more tears threatening to fall. "You knew her parents?"

She wipes her face. "Yes, I was very close to them."

"Good. I need you to tell me everything about them and about Aura. I want to know everything they shared, how they loved. Everything. I need you to remind me, Camila, because I won't be the same after this. They want the ruthless CEO? Then that's what they will get."

Chapter 22

Aura

Two Months Later

"**A**re you ready?" Lane says.

"Yeah," I answer.

I'm excited to be on the track with Lane in his supercar. I'm seated between his legs in the driver's seat. Lane makes me feel free. He says I'll love the adrenaline rush. He wasn't kidding when he said his passion was building engines and making cars faster.

He sets the launch control on the car, and my stomach has butterflies swarming like bees in anticipation. I've seen him drive it from the sidelines, and this car is lightning-fast.

Manufacturers across the world wonder what his secret is, but he keeps it under lock and key in a special journal. Lane took me to eat the morning of my birthday, and we celebrated with Exie. It was the first time I celebrated my birthday without my parents, and it was emotional, but Lane and Exie were there to get me through it.

I was able to finish high school a couple of months early by taking online classes. I never returned to Spencer. Lane decided to move to Charlotte, North Carolina, and open another shop.

Lane left Dex and Blaze to manage the one in Pennsylvania, and I was secretly relieved he wanted to move. Since that night, Lane has never left my side, and I've never left his unless he's building another car— another one of his projects. He always includes me when revealing it for the first time. He wants me to see it first before he shows it to anyone.

When he's busy, I spend my time making my next creation for the next customer, and it keeps my mind busy. Thanks to Lane, I've gotten many orders for bracelets in the past month. He shows everyone my pieces and how special they are because there are never two that are the same.

He places his hands on my waist, and I settle deeper between his legs.

He clears his throat. "Aura, baby. If you keep squirming like that, I'm afraid we are going to crash into that wall over there."

"Huh?" My head turns to catch his gaze. Then something hard pokes me on my butt, and I take a deep swallow. "Oh."

I bite my lip, not knowing what I should do, and let out a shaky breath. Lane has never touched me inappropriately or pressured me to have sex. I have never felt more comfortable being with a man besides Kalum.

Exie told me Kalum would leave for college once he graduated and that he gave up playing college football. Her parents heard that his parents wanted him to take over the St. Claire dynasty as CEO.

He has never been seen at parties or with another girl since I left. At times, I wanted to reach out but thought it best to let him go.

Lane revs the car, causing my heart to beat fast. His erection still poking me from behind.

I squirm once more, and he buries his face in my hair.

"Aura, I need to get the lap time, baby." His voice is husky as he speaks into my hair.

"I'm sorry," I say, disappointed.

He told me he dated on and off, but his shop and his time were always his priority. When he took me to the shop, he only had time for his next build. It was his focus, and nothing beyond that mattered. I understand his passion and his love for what he does. I see in his eyes when he shows me something new he built the way his expression changes when he looks at a car.

He doesn't hang out with a bunch of friends or go to parties. It's not who he is, and none of that makes him happy. *This* makes him happy. This moment on that track. Even if it's illegal with me on his lap. He wants me to learn how to drive his car and race on the track. I have no idea why, but he said he wanted me to understand him. Understand why he does what he does. I tried to take the driver's seat, but my hands shook, and I was afraid I would crash or hurt someone on the street. So here we are. He places his hand on the steering wheel, presses the button, and slams his foot on the gas.

The car lurches forward, pinning me against him. My heart beats wildly inside my chest as the adrenaline takes over. It feels like the fair ride we went on. My stomach drops. The markers on the pavement blur past us like tunnel vision. Lane expertly switches gears, and the engine's roar is like an explosion when the valve releases.

He presses the brake until the timer clocks the car at zero to sixty in one point nine seconds.

Lane shouts, "Hell, yes!"

His team runs out toward the car with the widest grins on their faces.

"You did it! You son of a bitch, you did it!" one of them shouts.

I'm not sure what he did, but whatever it is, it must be great from the reaction he's getting on the track. My ears ring from the loud exhaust of his car. I never asked what car this was, but he always takes me in it, and people just stare at it when we drive by on the street. There must be something special about the car I'm not privy to. I have never seen one built like this one, and it looks like something you see in the TV show *Car and Driver*.

Lane opens the door so I can get out. I smile and step aside, his team rambling on about lap times and mechanical parts of the car. Lane lifts the hood while one guy checks the tires. The weather is cool as we enter fall and, according to Lane, perfect to test out his build.

Crossing my arms over my chest, I watch how excited everyone is for Lane. The wind picks up and blows my hair in my face. When I get a handle on my hair, I look up, and Lane stands in front of me.

His expression softens. "I couldn't have done it without you," he says, giving me a hug.

I breathe in his familiar scent of cologne, gas, and burnt rubber. He's safe. He's home.

The house Lane purchased in Charlotte, North Carolina, is a two-story home with four bedrooms and a three-car garage. It has one of those hanging gas lanterns when you walk up to the front door that I love so much.

When he was house hunting, he asked me to come along. The real estate agent showed us different properties in the area. After she showed us the last one, we went for coffee, and he asked what I thought. He said he couldn't decide. He laid out four pieces of paper on the table. They each had pictures of the houses, but I kept staring at the one with the pretty wood double door with the gas lantern. I told him it was up to him and what he thought was best.

He got up and excused himself to the restroom. When he came back, he was quiet. He picked up the papers and told me he had made his decision. I was relieved from being put on the spot. How could I choose a place when he was paying for it? It was bad enough I felt I was taking advantage of him.

After a week of waiting until the paperwork went through, I smiled when he pulled up to this house. He knew.

I place my hand on the soft fabric of a dress I was able to get on sale at a boutique shop in downtown Charlotte. It has light pink spaghetti straps, almost the color of powder, and hits almost mid-thigh. I paired it with a cardigan and let my hair down. I applied makeup in nude shades, hoping it doesn't look overdone.

Sitting on the edge of the bed, I slide my feet into nude pointed-toe ankle boots. Exie had sent them over as a birthday gift from Neiman Marcus. They're extravagant and from a designer I can't even pronounce.

Lane knocks on my door, and I call out, "Just a minute." I check once more in the mirror to make sure I look okay.

When I open the door, Lane looks at me from head to toe. When his gaze lands back on mine, he has an unreadable expression, and I'm not sure if I'm overdressed. I chew the side of my lip nervously and look down at my outfit.

"Do I look okay?" I ask. "I could change."

His eyes widen in panic. "No, please," he begs. "You look... beautiful. I'm just...nervous." He smiles and grabs my hand gently and pulls me toward him.

I visibly swallow. He looks handsome with his fitted, long-sleeved black crewneck sweater and stone-washed jeans. His hair is straight and long with one strand curled across his forehead. He has a faint stubble that looks sexy with his dark eyes framed by dark lashes.

He cups my face in his hands, and the smell of citrus from his cologne envelops me. He angles his head slowly and captures my lips. The kiss is gentle and soft.

My hands grip his strong shoulders, and I love the way he's patient. How he doesn't want to overstep and ruin the moment. He pulls back, breaking the kiss, but I move forward and capture his lips once more, sliding my tongue inside his mouth. His hand slides down to my lower back and pulls me against him. I feel how much he wants me. There's no question that Lane Turner wants me.

He takes me to a nice restaurant in Charlotte called the Bentley, and we're seated at a corner table for two. We receive curious glances, and a man wearing a black suit with a blue tie nods at Lane.

I lean forward and whisper, "Do you know him?"

Lane shakes his head. "Never seen him before."

The server approaches, and we place our order. After a few seconds, Lane furrows his brow and continues to scan the menu.

"Will that be all?" the server asks.

I ordered the least expensive plate on the menu. There is no way I could order anything that would cost Lane more than necessary.

"Yes," I reply, glancing at Lane. "Unless... Lane?"

Lane hands the server his menu. "I'm good," Lane says while I hand the server mine. When the server walks away, I can see the concern in his expression. The same one he gives me when I refuse to take the money he leaves me in the box on the kitchen island for groceries. Or the fancy car he has parked in the driveway for me to use, and I take an Uber instead. There is no way I can take more from him. I don't pay rent or utilities. He pays my cell phone every month ahead of time. He also has a cleaning lady who comes three times a week and refuses to let me clean the house.

"Aura…"

A man no later than his twenties walks up to our table. He glances at me and smiles, making my skin crawl with the way his gaze lingers on my breasts. I lift my chin, clearly offended.

"I'm sorry for interrupting, but you're Lane Turner, right?"

"Who's asking?" Lane says with an edge to his tone.

The man holds out his hand to Lane. Lane looks at his outstretched hand like it's a snake slithering around him and he wants to chop its head off.

"My name is Patrick, and I work with NASCAR." Patrick angles his head slightly in my direction. "Who might this lovely lady be?"

Lane looks up, his nostrils flare. "I'm trying to have dinner with my girl, and you're rudely interrupting my time with her. I would appreciate you keeping your eyes planted elsewhere, and if you so much as look her way again, I'll beat you within an inch of your life, and when I'm done with you, I'll run over your corpse with my car to make a point."

Patrick drops his hand. "I-I'm very sorry to have disrespected you or her in any way," Patrick stammers. "Please accept my apology."

"Fuck off," Lane snaps.

Patrick quickly steps away, but he never glances in my direction again, heeding Lane's warning.

I lower my gaze. My palms sweat. I never thought Lane would be capable of violence, but the way he threatened Patrick was laced with promise.

Aura?" I look up, and his eyes soften. "I'm sorry to have

frightened you. I would die before I hurt you, but I'll never allow anyone to disrespect you or make you feel uncomfortable." He grins. "Let's get out of here."

"Okay," I say with a smile.

As we wait for the valet driver to bring Lane's car outside the restaurant, Lane places a soft kiss on my temple. "How about a burger?"

My stomach growls at the prospect. "That would be perfect," I answer with a grin.

Chapter 23

Aura

We make it back home, and a charge is in the air. Like a short-circuit, sparks fly when he stops in front of my bedroom door.

He slides a piece of hair behind my ear, and my insides flutter when he leans close and slowly captures my lips. I wrap my hands around his neck. He groans when I deepen the kiss. Our mouths read each other like poetry, one line at a time.

He pulls back, out of breath. My hands glide up his chest, feeling the ripples of his hard, lean muscles under my fingers. I stop over his heart, and it beats wildly.

He angles his head and takes in a sharp breath when my hands slide down to the waistband of his jeans.

I hesitate. My eyes lift, and I whisper, "Take me to your room, Lane."

He places his hand over mine. "You don't have to, Aura. If you're not ready…"

My fingers interlace with his rough ones. "I want you, Lane."

"I know, but "—- he adjusts the thin strap of my dress over my shoulder—"are you sure you want it to be me?"

There is something beautiful about the way the heart beats with the flutters in your stomach the moment you fall in love with someone new. The way mine is right now. I try not to compare his touch to Kalum...the way he kisses me. The way his eyes hold me. I try not to, but I do. Then I think of Kalum doing the same thing to someone else. The way he did with Sarah. How simple it was for him to forget me when she was around. How much more he gave her when he had me.

Then my thoughts go back to this moment with Lane. How different it feels after he kisses me. The tingles on my skin after he touches me in the places Kalum never did. And I want more.

I want Lane.

"I wouldn't want it to be anyone else but you."

The pad of his thumb rubs over my bottom lip. He takes my hand and tugs me into his bedroom. He pushes the door open. The light from the hallway filters into the room. My eyes fall on the king-size bed with white sheets in the center of the room. He walks to the gray nightstand, reaches under the lamp, and flicks the switch, basking the room in a golden light, like the sun when it rises.

He turns around and studies me for a few seconds. He steps close, my eyes level with his chest. He slowly removes his sweater, and I watch the ripples of his muscles contract over smooth skin to the deep *V* disappearing in the waistband of his jeans. His body is ripped, built like the engines he builds.

He pulls the sweater over his head and drops it on the floor. His eyes scroll over my body. "I want you, Aura."

He removes his jeans until he's clad in only his boxer briefs. His erection is huge, the tip of his cock straining against the band. My teeth trap my lower lip, wondering how he would taste. He slowly slides the straps of my dress over my shoulders. I turn around, pulling my hair to the side. He pulls the zipper, his finger on my skin leaving a trail of heat.

I can feel the heat from his mouth when he places a kiss on my back. His fingers when he slides my dress down my arms, and it puddles at my feet. My bra goes next. My nipples harden, and my body shivers. I turn, and he lifts my chin to meet dark brown eyes full of promise.

"Lane..."

"You're perfect."

"Thank you," I manage to say because his words have me melting, and I can't help falling in love with him.

I never thought I would ever fall for someone else after Kalum. When I would cry at night, Kalum held me. His kiss seared my soul, hoping for the day he would make me his.

I honestly thought for a moment I was, but reality caught up with me. The reality that I'm homeless, and I don't belong in Kalum's world. I thought for a second that he loved me.

But Lane looks at me like I'm his world. The only person who has cared for me when I had no one. He treats me like I'm a fragile piece of glass, but he looks at me like I'm his rock. Like I'm the most important person in his life. If only he knew that right now, at this moment, he's the most important person in mine.

I'm on the bed, and he kisses my nose, my eyes, my jaw, and my neck. I arch my back, seeking his lips over my skin. His tongue trails down the valley between my breasts. His tongue flicks my nipple, then the other. My panties are soaked between my legs. I'm panting and writhing under him.

"Lane," I say breathlessly.

"I want to be inside you, Aura."

He lowers his boxers, and his erection stands proud, with a tiny bead of precum sliding down his shaft. He strokes himself, and I watch his muscles contract. The way his hair falls over his forehead. His full lips when his tongue glides over them.

His hands glide up my thighs, his fingers slide under the thin straps on my hips, and he slips my panties down my legs, tossing them over his shoulder.

He rubs the tip of his cock over my slit. He angles his head and stares between my legs. His thumb presses on my clit. I let out a whimper, and a surge of energy slides up my thighs and pierces my clit. I'm wet, and I grind my hips, seeking more.

He settles his face between my thighs. His eyes flick up and hold my gaze. "I need you to be ready for me, Aura. I don't want to hurt you."

I nod, holding myself up by my elbows and loving that he's so gentle and caring with me. His tongue is soft when he swipes my clit, and my head tilts back. I look at the ceiling when his tongue dips inside, stroking me in a rhythm. My climax builds. His mouth swallows me whole. He licks and sucks while he breathes through his nose. My fingers slide through the long strands of his dark hair.

"Oh God, Lane." I buck against his mouth. "Mmm...yes," I cry out. I fist his hair and tug. He doesn't protest and flicks his tongue faster and faster. "I'm coming," I say breathlessly. He groans. My heart beats wildly as my clit pulses in his mouth.

He lifts his chin, glistening with my arousal, and licks his lips, wishing there was more. He kneels on the bed with his hard cock.

"Everything about you is... perfect."

"You sure know how to make a girl fall for you, Lane Turner."

The man can make a girl feel like she's the only thing in his orbit.

Tonight, he said I was his girl, and it was the sweetest thing coming from his lips. His claim that I was his had my heart doing a little flip. The way he notices everything about me. He knew the whole time I had never been with a man in the true sense. The way he knew that Patrick made me feel uncomfortable the instant he laid eyes on me.

He brushes the tip of his cock and pushes in slowly. My body trembles at how full he makes me feel. He groans and holds himself over me. "You're so tight, Aura." His teeth snag on his bottom lip. "Please tell me if I hurt you, Aura. Please tell me and don't be afraid. I'll stop," he breathes. "I promise."

"Don't stop, Lane."

He takes my lips and pushes deeper past my barrier. I stiffen, and he freezes. I take a breath, and he moves slowly. I let out a moan when the pain turns to hot pleasure, and he slowly begins to move inside me.

My thighs open wide when he finds a rhythm while he kisses me. It feels like the earth is shaking, and I'm quaking inside. A feeling so powerful that I'm speechless. He moves inside me like the tide in the ocean, peppering kisses all over my face and neck.

His lips ghost my ear. "I love you, Aura."

A tear slides down my face. "I love you, too," I breathe.

He continues to move inside me with measured strokes until we both crash. Colliding like a hurricane in an earth-shattering release, we're left sweaty and breathless in the aftermath. Our eyes meet, and it's beautiful. Our love... is beautiful.

Chapter 24

Aura

Three Months Later

"**A**re you going to tell him?"

Exie visits me while Lane goes to the track to test his car. He has been working nonstop on it. Night after night, he has been at his shop working on his latest build like a scientist in a lab finding a cure.

I flush the toilet after throwing up my lunch and open the bathroom door. "Tell him what?"

She grins at me knowingly. "That I'm going to be an aunt."

"Shit, is it that obvious?"

"Sweetheart, you have thrown up three times since I showed up. You're... definitely... pregnant."

I look down at my still flat stomach under Lane's Turner Automotive T-shirt.

"You think so? I thought maybe it was something I ate. I started feeling like this early this week," I tell her.

I had a hunch, but I didn't want to cause Lane any more pressure. He has been working at the shop tirelessly. There is only one way to be sure.

When I return with Exie from the pharmacy, she's hot on

my heels like a mother bear. "Come on. Pee on the stick. I want to know," she demands.

I enter the bathroom and follow the instructions, pee, and wait. After the required time, I pick it up and slide down the freestanding tub in the main bathroom, feeling like my stomach hit the floor. I'm pregnant with Lane's baby.

The bathroom door opens with Exie holding a clothes hanger. "Really? This isn't funny," I snap.

She tilts her head from side to side. "So yay or nay?"

I hand her the stick. She takes it and lets out a loud squeal. "Yes, I knew it!" she shouts.

"Knew what?" Lane asks, leaning on the doorway.

I didn't hear him walk in or his car rumbling down the driveway. Exie quickly hides the stick behind her back. "Nothing," she mutters.

He glances at me sitting on the bathroom floor and sits next to me. "Is your stomach still bothering you, Aura? Do you need to see a doctor, baby?" he asks, his voice laced with concern.

The back of his fingers slides down my face, and I turn my cheek into his palm. "Yeah, but it's not what you think."

He pinches his brows, and his head snaps up to look at Exie. I nod when her eyes find mine, and she hands him the pregnancy test.

"I'm pregnant," I say softly.

He holds it in his hand and stares at it. He doesn't look happy or sad. He doesn't say anything.

I should have waited to tell him, but I couldn't keep this from him. I love him, and he says he loves me, but this is a huge step. I had a feeling he wasn't ready to take the leap into having a family. After a while, my heart sinks because he won't look at me.

"Lane?"

Nothing.

Exie's mouth forms a grim line. I stand and silently exit the bathroom.

"Do you want me to kick his ass?" Exie asks. "Maybe it will get him to talk."

"He isn't ready, and it's a big responsibility. I should have been more careful," I say softly.

"I'm going to head out with some friends. I'll call you. It will give him time to think. Lane's a thinker and a planner. It will give you guys time to talk it out." She gives me a hug. "He loves you." She pulls back. "You know that, right?" I nod. "He would never let you go, Aura. He'll take care of you and the baby. No matter what happens."

"Thank you, Exie. Call me later."

I walk to the bedroom and sit on the bed to finish the bracelet I was working on. I hear footsteps, the front door slams, and then the sound of his car.

He's left.

He didn't call or come home. I called him four times, but it went straight to voicemail. My chest squeezes. It hurt that he wouldn't tell me what he thought or how he felt. My heart told me to give him time and not to pressure him. He would eventually come back. But he never came home.

A week has come and gone with no sign of Lane. I went to the urgent care clinic, and they confirmed I was three months pregnant. I saw the little embryo on the ultrasound, and I'd never felt more alone than at that moment. I wanted to share it with Lane. For him to see something bigger than both of us. A tiny little being we created.

When I came home, I cried for hours. I was alone, wishing he was holding me.

The following week, I gave up thinking he would come back. I tried calling him, but it went to voicemail. Exie called me, but I ignored her calls. I wanted to talk to her, but I couldn't. I felt like telling her that her brother was an asshole. And that he left me. None of that would give me him. None of that would get Lane to come back.

In need of some fresh air, I order an Uber. I'm craving a burger and found a local spot, refusing to take one of his cars.

When I make it inside, I sit at a table outside and people-watch. I think about the baby growing inside me and how I'm going to raise a child on my own. I run the math in my head to see if I could keep selling jewelry to support myself and a baby, but I quickly realize that it would be impossible. My fingers wouldn't be able to keep up.

That leaves me getting a job and finding an apartment. I didn't plan to fall pregnant. He probably thought I did it to trap him. I'm broke, I'm homeless, and I don't have any family left. It's probably why he wouldn't talk to me. Why he left me. Why he won't answer my calls.

I'm lost in my thoughts, and I see a digital billboard with a huge picture of Kalum that reads, "Youngest CEO takes over company." My eyes take in his features, remembering the nice things he said that first night and how he held me. His parents and how they easily wanted to get rid of me. Kalum called me a total of twenty-six times, but I never answered. He left messages pleading for me to call him back, but I blocked his number and never called him back. It was over.

What would be the point? To say he was sorry? The result would be the same, and even if he offered me money like his parents did, I wouldn't take it. The young housekeeper with no future.

Lane has been there for me and was my safety blanket. My solace. The quiet man who loved building his cars more than life itself. He won me over by simply being there as a friend, then as a lover. Until he walked out on me pregnant with his baby without a single word.

Lane is a man of few words, and I thought patience was the way to handle his silence, but this is different. This is about a life we made together, growing inside me by the minute. Does Lane want me to leave? Is that why he never came back? Is that the message he's trying to send me without voicing it out loud because he feels guilty? The same way Kalum's parents asked me to leave. He doesn't want me because of who I am. His parents wouldn't accept me or my baby. He's ashamed of me.

After three hours, the light from the diner shuts off, and I stand, having made my decision.

Chapter 25

Aura

"Is that all I can get you?" I ask the couple seated in booth three. They nod and smile, letting me know they're good when I set down their plates.

I asked the manager at the diner if they were hiring. I was relieved when she told me she needed one more person for the night shift, which gave me some time to make bracelets. They also helped me find a small one-bedroom one block over. It's not the best, but it prevents me from having to purchase a car or Uber.

"How are you feeling today, Aura?" Nick asks, pouring sugar into his coffee.

Nick is a regular at the diner and works at the bank across the street. After two months of working at the diner, I'm showing, and my apron doesn't hide my small baby bump.

"I'm fine, and thank you for asking. That's really sweet."

He smiles. "If you need someone to walk you over, I have time tonight. I don't have any plans."

"That's nice of you, but I think I'll be okay."

It's a nice offer, and Nick has never given me a reason to

think he was creepy. My creep meter hasn't sounded off in my head. His offer seems sincere, but I have gotten used to being on my own.

"I'm not taking no for an answer. I'll follow you, and when I see you safely cross, I'll go on my way. I worry about you, Aura. Walking alone at night...it's not safe."

Nick has been coming to the diner a few nights a week. On slow nights, conversations about my family come up. It's something I've gotten used to being pregnant. My answer to everyone is the same. My boyfriend and I broke up, and I'm going to be a single mom.

I shrug. "I'm kinda used to it."

"If you ever need any help or anything, you know where to find me across the street. I would give you my number, but I don't want to seem disrespectful."

Like I said, Nick is nice. He seems like a standup guy, but so did Lane. Kalum was—Kalum. Lane never showed up when I left, a huge sign that he didn't care. He never called to see if I was okay or needed anything. He was gone. His message was plain and simple. He was done with me.

The following week, when my shift was over, I took Nick up on his offer for a walk home.

"Ready? You got your coat? It's a little cold out," Nick says.

I nod, but when I pull out my coat, he frowns.

"You need to get something thicker than that," he says, pointing at my coat.

It's either a thicker coat or paying the light bill and not freeze to death inside the apartment.

He works at a bank but is not the brightest. He obviously hasn't put two and two together and figured out I'm broke with a baby on the way.

I walk with my hands crossed over my waist to keep myself warm as Nick walks beside me. There is a loud roar of an engine followed by a loud pop. It gets louder as the car drives down the road.

Lane pulls up in his car. Nick stands back as the driver's side door opens.

Lane points at Nick. "Who is this asshole?"

"Hey, man, I don't want any trouble," Nick says with raised hands.

My teeth clench so hard I might saw them off. "What is your problem, Lane? Are you out of your mind?"

Lane flinches like I slapped him. He's wearing a red racing jacket with different patches of brands from sponsors all over it with a black T-shirt and jeans, making my stomach flutter. It's like the baby senses him, but then I remember he left me. He left us.

"Who is he?" Lane questions.

"Someone making sure the six-month pregnant girl gets home safe. You know, because the guy who knocked her up gives two shits about her now that she's an inconvenience," I retort. "Go back to your garage and leave me alone. I have nothing to say to you. I don't want to see you. If you want a picture of your son, you let me know where to send it?"

He calms down and walks up to me. "We're having a son?" His eyes land on my stomach.

"Yes."

My heart clenches watching him blink back tears, but I shake it off. I found out we were having a boy this past Monday, but I hadn't shared it with anyone. I glance at Nick, and he's staring at Lane like he's a celebrity.

"You're Lane Turner. The man rumored to have helped build the fastest car in the world. You're like the Michael Jordan of the car world," Nick says in bewilderment.

Lane rolls his eyes. "Do you mind? I'm trying to fix things with my girl, and you're kind of ruining it."

I have never told anyone at the diner or Nick who my boyfriend was. Lane has made a name for himself working on super cars with major car manufacturers. People come from all over the world so he can modify their cars to make them faster.

"Where were you?" I ask Lane.

"Taking care of things." He wipes his hand down his handsome face. "A lot of things."

"You couldn't tell me where you were or answer your phone when I called?" I shake my head, and tears slide down my cheeks. "You couldn't call or say, 'hey, I know we're pregnant, but give me some time' or 'hey I want you to leave, Aura, get out.'"

"I know. I'm sorry. I never wanted you to leave me, but I need you to get in the car so I can explain."

"No. You don't get to do that. You had your chance," I say in a hard tone and walk away.

"Aura... don't."

"Why don't you go build another car, Lane? You don't need a baby to get in your way, and from what I can tell, you don't need me."

"I'm not leaving you, and you're not leaving me. Wherever I go, you go. Remember?" he shouts.

I whirl around. "Where you went, I wasn't invited. So there's that. You left me."

Lane catches up to me, pinching his nose. "I didn't leave you. I would never leave you. I already told you I had to take care of something," he says.

Is he insane? I think he has inhaled too much carbon monoxide. He thinks that is all he needs to say, and I'll run back to him.

"Is everything okay, Aura?" Nick chimes in.

I forgot he was still standing here when I walked away.

"Leave!" Lane roars as he marches over to him with his fist clenched.

Nick's eyes widen at the look of rage across Lane's expression. "O-okay. I'll go," Nick stammers, and he takes off in the opposite direction.

"You didn't have to do that," I scold Lane.

"No man comes near you. Do you understand? No other man."

"It's a little too late for that. I'm sorry, but... it's over, Lane."

I walk briskly across the street to my apartment building. The car roars when he gets behind the wheel and pulls up next to me.

"Get in, Aura."

"Go home, Lane."

He parks in an available spot and follows me up to the apartment. I place the key in the lock and open the door to the practically empty studio with only a single bed.

"This is where you're staying? In this?"

Rage boils in my veins. How dare he judge me? After he left, I was all alone. I turn around and surprise him when I drive my hand back. *WHACK!* I slap him hard across his left cheek—enough that my hand stings.

His head whips back like a spring, and his eyes widen when he places his hand on his cheek.

"Get out!" I yell.

He steps forward, and I step back.

"How dare you judge me? Where were you when I was alone? Where were you when I was at the doctor? You haven't heard your own son's heartbeat." I push him hard toward the door. "You come here and judge me for trying to take care of myself and your son. Get out. Leave me alone."

"I'm sorry, Aura. Please. It's not what you think."

"It's not what I think? It's what I know, and one thing I do know is that you don't abandon someone you love." Tears flow down my cheeks, my body trying to hold back the sobs at how easily he walked out on me without a single word. The memories of how lonely I felt inside that house, wondering what I did that was so awful. Why he would abandon me because I was pregnant with his child. "You don't love me, Lane. It's okay. I'll be fine in my small bed in my small apartment with my waitressing job. You can go now."

"I'll never leave you."

"Are you listening to yourself? You did leave me. That's why I'm here. You weren't even there when I packed my stuff. You didn't even know, and it's obvious that I don't matter to you. That you're ashamed of me." My chest is heaving, and he has a look of defeat, but I don't care. He isn't who I thought he was. "I have a shift tomorrow so I can pay for my shitty apartment with my shitty bed."

He finally walks out, hanging his head. "I'll see you tomorrow," he says.

"Don't bother," I say, slamming the door in his face.

Chapter 26

Aura

It's been two weeks since Lane showed up. He comes in the diner every day and sits at the booth in the back and waits until I'm done with my shift. When I clock out, he follows me to my apartment in his car to make sure I make it home safe every night.

I walk into the diner for my shift. Lane is sitting in one of the booths. His head snaps up when he hears the chime of the bell from the door. Tammy at the register gives me a smile.

"Good afternoon, Aura. He has been waiting for you for about an hour," she says, motioning to Lane.

"Thank you, Tammy."

After the third day, my boss and Tammy found it odd that Lane was always at the diner exactly when my shift started and would leave when my shift ended. I had no choice but to tell them he was my baby's father and my ex-boyfriend.

Tammy found it sweet, but when I told her what he did and how he left me all alone, she told me to make him sweat. Since they're not in the racing world, they haven't noticed that

Lane Turner is in their diner waiting on his baby momma until her shift is over.

Customers walk in, and I get to work. I hand out the menus and head over to Lane's booth. I take out a pad and pen, ignoring the scowl on his face. "What can I get you?" I ask.

"You back in our house."

"That's not gonna happen. Are you going to order something or are you going to sit here and watch me?"

"Why?"

"You know why, and I hate repeating myself. I don't like that house. It reminds me how I got here, and I want to move on, and so should you."

"Is it the house? You don't like it?"

I take a deep sigh. My feet have started to bother me more and become more constrictive in my shoes. I shift my weight to give my other foot a break.

He notices, and he frowns. "What's wrong?"

My feet are swelling like pumpkins each day, but I don't tell him that or that my clothes hardly fit and I don't make enough to buy bigger ones. It's not his problem, but mine.

"Nothing. Now order, or I'll take the next customer."

"Fine, I would like"—he scans the menu—"a burger with fries and a Coke."

"We have Cherry Coke. It's your fave."

He grins. "I'll take it."

I go put his order in and work for the next three hours until my break.

After a month, I notice he's getting antsy. After placing his order, Lane picks at his food and sits at the booth the whole time until he sees me head to the back toward the restroom. I'm about to close the door when he barges in and closes it behind him and flicks the lock.

"What are you doing?"

"Turn around," he says in a hard tone, but I don't move. "I'm not going to ask again. I said, turn around."

"Lane—"

He spins me around and bends me slightly, and I grip the sink. He slides his hand under the skirt of my uniform and rips my panties. I gasp and clench my thighs.

I'm sensitive. Everywhere. I'm wet, and my thighs are sticky from my arousal. I read in the book I got at the clinic that offers health care for single expecting moms that hormones from pregnancy make you want to have sex. I guess what I read was true. I'm extremely sensitive and like what he's doing.

A few times in my tiny depressing shower inside my apartment, I pleasured myself. Most of the time, I thought of Lane, and then one time, I guiltily thought of Kalum. I immediately stopped, shut off the water, and cried myself to sleep. I was ashamed of myself. I blamed it on my hormones, but deep down, I wasn't so sure. I didn't get off.

Lane looks at me through the mirror. I can hear the zipper of his pants, and I close my eyes. I want him to touch me. I need him to touch me. My skin prickles with anticipation. Goose bumps form all over my skin, and my stomach flutters. Not because of the baby but because of what Lane is about to do to me.

"Lane," I whisper.

In one swift movement, he slides into me so fast my feet almost lift from the ground.

"Hold on, Aura. I need you. I can't be without you. I'm sorry for hurting you. Please, Aura. I'm so sorry."

I don't protest. He moves inside me, and I clench around

him like a tight vise that makes him groan. The slapping of our skin echoes in the small bathroom.

He slides his hand over my stomach, and with every thrust, he says each word in a caress. "You're so beautiful. I'm so lucky to have you carrying my baby. You have given me so much, Aura. There is nothing I could give you that amounts to what you have given me. I love you, my angel. I'll always love you. Please, forgive me. I can't lose you. I'm not the same without you." I moan when he plays with my clit and arch my back. "Come for me, Aura. There is only you."

He thrusts into me while frantically playing with my clit. I come, his name escaping my lips. "Lane." He places the palm of his hand flat over my stomach so it doesn't hit the sink, protecting me, protecting our son.

When my shift is over, he opens the door for me to get inside his car.

"Lane?"

"Yes, Aura," he says, buckling his seat belt.

"What kind of car is this?" I ask.

I meant to ask him before but never got around to it. I don't know much about cars except what he has shown me—what the mods do and what purpose they serve.

He smiles and revs the engine. "An r35 GT-R."

"Oh. I know what you build is a big deal, but is this an expensive car? Like a Porsche?"

He chuckles and pulls out onto the road. "The makers of Porsche can't beat it. It's worth more than a Porsche and a Lamborghini because I built it."

I tilt my head, Nick's words the other night replay in my head. That Lane was like Michael Jordan in the race world for building the fastest car in the world.

"I'm sorry I'm asking all these questions. I just don't really know much about cars and their worth because my parents only had one car, and it was used."

"I love when you ask. It shows you care what I'm into and what I do."

He doesn't drive past the speed limit, which I can appreciate. Some young guys with modified cars line up and try to provoke him to race, but he ignores them. Lane continues to drive carefully and doesn't go too fast. It's quiet and doesn't play music. For Lane, the sound of an engine is music. It's his Beethoven.

I never liked driving his cars because I know how much they mean to him. As a form of respect, I don't like touch any of them. There are times he's disappointed I don't. It wouldn't bother him if I did. He taught me to drive a stick shift and how to listen to the engine while shifting gears. He said I should learn, just in case of an emergency, so I agreed.

"Lane."

"Yes."

"Where are we going?"

"Home."

"This doesn't look like the way to the house."

"It is, Aura. This is the way to our home."

This was not the way home. The houses are spread out and have huge gates in each driveway.

He turns onto a street with a single driveway leading to a tall gate. It's so tall that there is no way you could jump over. There are cameras that shift when we pull up on each of the giant pillars.

"Where are we?"

The gate slowly swings open. When he revs the engine, the rumble vibrates the snug seat and calms my nerves. There is a big flutter and a poke from inside my stomach. I look down where my apron is still tied around my protruding waist.

"Lane?"

"Yes."

"Do that again."

He glances at me. "Do what again?"

"Rev the engine."

The car rolls forward, and he places it in neutral and revs it, sending the same humming vibration through the seat. I feel it. The baby feels it, and it's soothing. The baby pokes me again once it stops.

I smile and rub my stomach. "The baby likes it. He likes it, Lane."

He smiles, places his hand on my stomach, and does it again. There is a slight poke in my stomach, and Lane's eyes widen. He brakes. "Did you feel that!"

I giggle. "Yes, Lane. I felt it."

"That's amazing," he says. "He likes it."

"Like his daddy," I tell him.

He helps me out of the car, and I look over to see a one-story house that looks like a celebrity mansion.

"Whose house is this?"

"It's our house. I bought it because you didn't like the other one except for the gas lighting. This house has cameras and security. It's a fortress. No one can come in, and the baby will be safe here. I also made sure that there were no stairs. So you would be more comfortable. I also hired a driver, so you don't have to drive yourself. He'll take you anywhere you wish to go."

My brows rise. "You thought of everything, huh? How can you pay for all this, Lane?"

He snorts, and the door opens and an older lady named Kate greets me. "Welcome, Mrs. Turner."

My head whips to Lane, but he entwines his fingers through mine. "To everyone, you're Mrs. Turner."

"But I'm—"

"You are, and you will be... Mrs. Turner."

He gives me a tour of the house. There is a huge area rug in the living area. There is also another one in the bedroom so the baby can crawl and not hurt himself. He already has the house baby-proofed. He thought of everything. The room has a massage chair and nonslip tiles on the bathroom floor. It's the most extravagant house I have ever set foot in besides the St. Claire home. The St. Claire home is luxurious but cold. This home is decorated with warm touches.

No sharp objects or edges could harm a small child anywhere in this house. The white granite is rounded everywhere it's placed, and the kitchen is stocked. There is nothing to do except relax.

He shows me to the main bedroom and opens the closet to reveal a large section of maternity wear and rows of designer shoes, including dress shoes, sandals, and sneakers. There is a large overcoat. I rub my hand over the rich texture of the brown coat. There is a black one next to it.

"That was Exie," he says, pointing at the closet. "She loves designer stuff and wanted you to dress in style."

Exie and I kept in touch after I moved out of the other home. She said she would kill Lane, but I always made excuses for not calling her like I should. I was upset at Lane, and she was starting college and a new life. Lane refused to take over his parents' company, leaving it up to Exie.

My shifts at the diner were in the evening, and I could not be on the phone. During the day, I slept in the early morning, and in the afternoon, I would continue fulfilling as many orders as possible. I needed the money. Our schedules didn't align. She offered to help me out. She offered me money, but I refused. She sighed and let it go because it was what I wanted.

I glance at Lane and feel the need to apologize for slapping him. It wasn't right, and I'm not prone to violence, but I was hurt. My hormones were raging. I was stressed and felt cornered.

"I'm sorry I slapped you the other night. I was upset with you."

"You had every right to feel that way." He pulls me toward him. "I was wrong for leaving you like that. I'm sorry. Please stay and be my wife. I promise to always take care of you, but you have to promise to leave the diner. My pregnant wife cannot work in a diner as hard as I work." He shakes his head. "I can't allow it."

I laugh as happy tears stream down my face and fan myself. "Yes," I say. "A thousand times, yes!" He lowers his gaze and places the palm of his hand on my belly. "What are we going to name him?"

"Lane Jr.," I say.

Lane's eyes lift with pride in his expression. "I like it. I want to call him LJ Turner for short." I smile. "But my favorite is calling you Aura Turner." His throat moves when he swallows. "I'll always love you, Aura. You're the air I breathe."

Chapter 27

Aura

Five Years Later

Staring out the floor-to-ceiling window in New York City overlooking the skyline, I focus on the blue sky, feeling motionless, speechless, heartbroken, and lost. The pain in my soul breaks me in half repeatedly.

"Mommy? We are high up, aren't we? I can see the cars from up here."

"Yes, baby," I croak, trying to swallow the lump in my throat. I can hardly speak, but I can't cry in front of LJ.

The door opens, and a man in a tailored gray suit walks in with armed security and a police officer. The armed security guard holds a large box with an electronic lock and places it in front of me on the lacquered wood desk.

"My sincere condolences, Mrs. Turner. Your husband was a great man." I look up, and tears blur my vision when I give the man a slight nod.

Lane died a month ago on the track. A rear tire that was too hot had a blowout, causing him to lose control. He crashed into a wall at one hundred eighty miles an hour. He was pronounced dead at the scene. He told me he would be home later that day but never made it.

LJ makes engine noises as he races his cars on the floor. He reminds me so much of his father. I miss Lane so much it hurts.

The man motions for everyone to turn around when I enter Lane's code. It was the day I met him for the first time. The beeping noise makes a sound with a loud click, and the top opens. Inside is Lane's journal, a flash drive with all his builds, and a large sealed yellow envelope, only to be opened upon his death.

I leave the journal and the flash drive inside because they're valuable. He secured it with armed security to make sure it didn't get in the wrong hands. I close the box, letting it secure the lock in place. Lane always warned me to be careful that the information he had inside was worth a lot of money to certain people. They could harm LJ or me to get to it.

I take a deep breath and open the envelope. I pull out a handwritten letter from Lane.

To my wife,

I love addressing you as my wife. I feel honored to call you that. You have given me more than I could have ever asked for. You have given me love, a beautiful son, and my legacy. You have made me the happiest man on earth. To have a gorgeous wife to call my own. Every day I work and build the next car and the next. All for our future. I told you once that my greatest love was building the next car and making it the fastest. I lied. My greatest love is you. It was always you.

I fell in love with you the first time I laid eyes on you. I couldn't get you out of my head. When you walked past my shop that night, I knew it was fate. I knew something bigger than all of us brought me you, and I promised myself to never let you go. Now, for the hard part.

If you're reading this, it means I'm no longer with you or with Lane Jr., and for that, I'm sorry, Aura. The day I disappeared was the same day you told me you were pregnant with Lane, and it was the same day I almost died on the track. It scared me. If I had died that day, you would have struggled with our son, and I couldn't let that happen. I couldn't risk leaving you like that. So I left, and I planned. To leave you my legacy. My dream is to live on through you and our son. All my hard work couldn't be for nothing. It couldn't end like that. All the nights away from you and LJ were to build a future for us. If I didn't make it, at least you and Lane would be taken care of. I'm sorry for leaving you so soon, but I knew it was a possibility.

I left you everything, Aura. All the money, my cars, my legacy is in your hands to pass down to our son. He'll continue what I have built. People will offer you the world for it. Don't. It's worth more than you can imagine. I did it. I help build the fastest car in the world, and you own it. What does that mean? It means you have the blueprint inside the box. The foundation. The other cars I left you and built are one of a kind, and there is nothing like them.

I love you, my angel. I love you so much. I couldn't have done it without you. You're the lightning to my tidal wave. The spark I needed to make it work. You're the key to everything I have ever dreamed of. It was you, and it will always be you. By the time you're almost finished reading this letter. There will be a knock on the door, and armed men will come inside the room to take you. Do not be afraid. I sent them. They will protect you, and there is only one person I trust to protect you and our son. This was all arranged the day I left, and you thought I didn't love you. I couldn't tell you this because I hoped to God it would never happen.

I know I wasn't your first love, but I was glad to be your second. You gave me my dream, Aura, and now, it's my turn to make sure you have your happiness. Goodbye, my love. I'll always love you.

Till death do us part,
Lane Turner

Tears run down my cheeks as sobs wreak havoc through my body. As promised, a knock sounds on the door, and six men walk into the room with guns and bulletproof vests. They're quiet when they move inside the room.

LJ is too busy playing with his cars on the carpet to notice.

Another man enters. I'm crying, and my makeup is running. He waves his hand to the men standing against the wall to step back.

"There is someone who will escort you along with these men to an undisclosed destination. There are a lot of paparazzi, and it's for your safety as well as your son's," the police officer says.

I sniff, trying to stop crying, but I can't. My lip quivers, and I'm scared. A tall shadow of a man towering over the lawyer and the police officer enters the room like a Goliath, and my heart drops.

Kalum.

His eyes scan my face. Tears fall like fat raindrops down my neck. When I glance at LJ on the carpet, he concentrates on getting a closer look at his cars, oblivious to the scene unfolding. Kalum's eyes follow the path of my vision. His face is hard and unreadable. While his attention is focused on LJ, I wipe my face and notice how much he has changed. He no longer has the face of a teenager but of a man with a dangerous air of authority. He's tall, with his tailored suit perfected over his massive build. When he glances back at me, his dark hair is coiffed with a clean-shaven, sharp-angular jaw, the same straight nose, and lips so perfect they could have been used as concrete like a work of art.

His demeanor is also different from when I last saw him. A man I no longer recognize. My instinct is to protect my son. Kalum tries to make eye contact with me, but I refuse, and the only thing that feels right is to hold LJ.

. . .

"LJ," I call out. LJ looks over his shoulder at the sound of my voice. His forehead pinches into a frown when he notices the men standing like soldiers in the room.

I open my arms. "Come to Mommy. Bring your cars, sweetheart."

He looks down and scoops the cars in his arms as fast as he can and hurriedly runs into my arms, shielding his face in my embrace. My hands soothe him by making lazy circles on his back. He's incredibly shy and doesn't like talking to strangers. His head lifts, his handsome face, the spitting image of his father. I smile, assuring him that everything is okay.

"We need to get going," Kalum says sternly.

I try not to look at him. He isn't my friend but was sent here by my husband for whatever reason. Whatever feelings I held in my heart for Kalum died the night his parents wanted me gone.

When I was forced into his life, Kalum found me to be an inconvenience, and even though he tried to be nice because we did have an attraction to one another, he was also heartless. I hope he found someone who could love him the way he deserved.

I have to be strong for LJ. Lane warned me that I was a target for information only I have access to if something were ever to happen to him and that includes our son. His family wants to destroy what he built, and with him being by my side. I always thought it was impossible. But I never thought something like this could happen. But accidents happen, and it's something we have no control over. Lane is gone.

The armed guards escort LJ and me, with Kalum trailing us like we're celebrities walking out of the building in the middle of New York City. Flashes from cameras blind us, and people shout.

"Mrs. Turner, who will run Turner Automotive?"

"Are you going to sell?"

LJ grips my black fitted dress, hiding his face on my side, holding his toy cars. A driver opens the rear passenger door of a sleek black Maybach.

I hesitate. "It's all right. It's safe," Kalum says behind me.

I guide LJ inside the car first, and I follow. He sits in the middle, and I sit on the far side. To my surprise, the right passenger door opens, and Kalum slides inside. The smell of his cologne permeates the air in the confined car mixed with expensive leather.

Kalum sits, looking straight ahead, and says, "We need to talk."

"I have nothing to say to you. If you could, please drop me off at my hotel."

"I'm afraid that's not possible. The media knows you're here, and they want answers that you're not ready to give them. His parents are not happy with his decision regarding his will. You and LJ will stay with me at my penthouse."

My gaze lands on his profile. "I prefer my hotel, where I can get my things and take the next flight out of here."

He shakes his head like I'm a child, making my insides boil. "As I said, you'll stay with me at my penthouse. It's not safe for you or LJ. They want to pressure to sell. They want the information you have access too. You know that your in-laws are not happy with your husband's decision to leave everything to you. They will do anything to destroy it or make you sell his company and his patents."

"I know that. I'm fully aware," I snap.

His head turns to me, and the expression on his face is hard and unreadable. There is a tic in his jaw, but then his eyes soften. He looks at LJ sitting between us while he digs the cars into the leather like it's the pavement on a track, making imprints with the wheels.

"You and LJ are my responsibility. Get used to the idea of me being around because there is no other person Lane trusted except me."

"Why would he trust you with me? Why would you care what happens to me or

to my son?"

He avoids answering the question, and it pisses me off. Why? Why would Lane do this? My happiness is with Lane, not this nightmare sitting in a car. A man I have no wish discussing my life with.

"I'm really sorry about Lane."

LJ's head pops up at the mention of his father. "Mommy says Daddy is in heaven. Right, Mommy?"

The back of my eyes sting with fresh tears that don't seem to stop.

I give LJ a watery smile. "Yes, baby. He's in heaven watching over you."

"He's watching over you, too," he says in his little voice. "Daddy told me to take care of you when he's gone. He said he loves you sooo much that he wanted to make sure someone looked after you."

"I do too, baby. I'll always love both of you very much," I say in a shaky breath, looking out the window and trying to compose myself.

I'm trying not to let LJ see me cry all the time. He understands that his father is no longer with us, but Lane expressed his love for us when he was home and made sure our son knew he loved us both. There are times I don't think I'm going to survive without Lane with me.

"I'm sorry, Aura," Kalum says quietly.

I can feel his gaze but still can't look at him. I can't.

He reminds me of memories I buried a long time ago. We're both different people, and I'm mourning the loss of my husband. The man who took care of me when no one was there. Took me in and showed me love and gave me a home. A family.

LJ makes noises, digging the car toy in the leather.

"LJ, honey, please don't do that to the seat with the car."

He looks up with a worried expression and then glances at Kalum. He looks at the leather, and his lips tremble.

"It's okay, Aura. He can do whatever he wants."

"He could ruin your car."

"I'll have it replaced if something happens. It's no issue. I want him to feel comfortable when he's with me. I want *you* to feel comfortable with me."

"I don't want to be with you or around you," I quip.

"I'm sorry, but there is no other choice. It's for your son's and your safety. It's done."

I know Lane informed me in the letter I have in my lap about men escorting me somewhere safe once the news is out that I'm finally meeting lawyers, but I never thought it would be Kalum, of all people. The safe is in an armed vehicle traveling behind us, and I wonder where he's taking us. He said his penthouse, but then what? The media have been in a frenzy since Lane's death, but all I can think about is how to move forward without him. How can I when I have my past sitting next to me?

Chapter 28

Aura

We arrive in front of an elegant building. The doorman waits for us to exit the car. Kalum does not let the driver open the door for us and opens the side closest to the entrance.

We are shown up to the top floor, and the elevator opens directly inside what I assume is Kalum's penthouse.

LJ and I both exit the elevator with Kalum right behind us, but being in an unfamiliar place, LJ and I both pause and survey the apartment.

Scanning the opulent space, with white marble floors, gray carpet, with chrome and glass furniture, I find it cold and soulless.

LJ must sense the same thing. He looks up, his forehead furrows like his father does when they feel uncomfortable with their surroundings. The apartment feels impersonal and nothing like we're used to.

Our home has life, a coziness to it that screams love and a family that spends countless nights together watching movies, having dinner, and spending time with one another. This place screams emptiness and lack of feeling.

Kalum drops his keys and turns around in his impeccable suit. "Is there something wrong?"

LJ clutches his cars to his chest.

"Everything," I say, scanning the living room and open kitchen. "Is it possible you can take us back to the hotel?"

Kalum walks toward us. His size is intimidating. Ruthless and cutthroat. His arm stretches every possible inch of his suit jacket. He's still attractive. Beautiful. You can tell he spends hours in the gym.

His hard expression lacks warmth. The way he moves around the room is robotic with an edge of coldness to his demeanor.

Memories of when I first met him come back. He hated me when I walked into his life. I expected he would have married a girl like Sarah or found someone to share his similar interests and social status by now.

This place looks like a bachelor pad. No pictures adorn the walls, and the furniture is meant to look good but not to sit on or watch TV with a cozy blanket and eat popcorn. The dining table is glass with a chrome base and is not meant for a five-year-old to sit and have dinner. The better option is to sit on the floor.

"What's wrong, Aura?" he asks, his voice laced with worry. His gaze lands on LJ and then back at me. "Tell me."

"I appreciate your concern for us, but this is really unnecessary." I look down at LJ and then meet his gaze. "We feel uncomfortable here. This is no place for us to stay. It's generous of you to allow us inside your home, but like I said, unnecessary and an inconvenience to you. You must have a wife or girlfriend. It would make her uncomfortable for us to be in your space."

Kalum glances around his penthouse and slides his hand inside his pocket.

LJ squeezes my dress with his fist. "Mommy, can we go now?" he whispers.

"I'm trying, baby."

Kalum looks nervous, but then his expression turns serious. Almost lifeless. Like this apartment.

"There is someone I want you to see. You two could catch up, and maybe she can help you with LJ."

The change of subject has me curious. I want to get the heck out of this cold, lifeless apartment, but I am curious about meeting someone from my past, wondering who could help me with LJ. Not that I need help with taking care of him. I've never hired even a babysitter. He goes with me everywhere I go. I trust no one that isn't his father or Exie.

Lane never allowed his parents to spend time with LJ. Lane told me his relationship with his parents was always strained because they wanted him to take over Turner Industries, and Lane's passion was street racing and engines. His family didn't agree, but he didn't care. Turner Racing Automotive was Lane's passion.

The elevator behind opens, and when I turn around, an older lady with gray hair and tan skin greets me with a smile. "Aura."

I sigh in relief. I give her a tight hug with tears streaming down my cheeks. "Oh, Camila. How I've missed you." She steps back, tears streaming down her plump cheeks. She looks down, and her eyes soften.

"Oh, Aura. He's beautiful." She leans down, and LJ's expressive eyes give her a once-over.

"Hello, it's nice to meet you. I'm LJ Turner," he says in his soft voice.

"Oh, my. You're very well-spoken. My name is Camila, and I have known your mom since she was your age."

His eyes light up. "Really?"

"Yes."

Camila straightens and gives me a sad smile. "I'm sorry for your loss, Aura."

The backs of my eyes burn like a wildfire. "Thank you. He was... everything," I tell her with a watery smile.

"I can tell," she says.

"I'll be in my office," Kalum says as he walks away.

"How did you end up here?" I ask her.

"When Kalum left for college, he rented a place off campus and took me with him. His parents protested, but he didn't speak to them unless it was about the family business since—"

She looks at Lane as he crouches down on the floor and plays with his cars, using the almost invisible grout lines on the marble tile as a track.

"Since I left," I finish for her.

"Yes. Since that night, Kalum has been...different."

I nod and figure it was because he felt guilty. He called me nonstop the next day, but I thought it best I didn't answer. Because I was never going back. I promised myself I would never set foot inside that house. I don't regret it because it brought me to Lane.

I try to feel sympathy for Kalum, but in all honesty, it was for the best. During the months I stayed with Lane, I thought I was deeply in love with Kalum, and maybe I was, but it was nothing compared to the love Lane showed me.

For months, I thought he'd left me when I told him I fell pregnant because he didn't want me or the baby. I was a mess, but he showed me how wrong I was to ever doubt his love for me. He showed me just how much he loved me ever since. He never left me alone unless he was in his shop building a car.

"He says you'll be staying with him for a while. The media are going crazy asking questions about how you'll run the company and who will be at the track. They expect you to sell and will do whatever it takes to offer you anything for Lane's builds and his car."

"I know, but I won't sell it. It will be passed down to LJ when it's time. I'll make sure of it. Lane trusted me."

"That is why you should stay with Kalum for a little while." She rubs her forehead. "I'll help you with LJ if you need me. It will be no trouble. This is New York, and there are times when it's not feasible for you to take him everywhere."

I smile and know she's being kind, but I have a life in North Carolina. We have a home. All of our things and memories are there.

"I know, but we can't stay here. This is not"—I look around once more to make sure Kalum is still in his office—"a place for us to stay. It's not a place for a child."

"Did you tell him that?"

"I tried, but then you arrived, and he sauntered off. I know Lane sent him, but I'm still trying to figure out why. It doesn't make sense."

Camila gives me a soft smile. "Why don't I watch LJ for a minute, and you go talk to Kalum and tell him how you feel?"

I trust Camila and have known her almost my whole life since my parents bought their house in Spencer. Camila was our neighbor, and she would watch me when my parents couldn't. She would not let anything happen to LJ.

I take a deep breath. "Okay. Where is his office?"

"Third door to your right."

"LJ?"

He looks up. "I'll be right back. I'm going to talk to Kalum. Don't give Camila a hard time, alright?"

"Yes, Mommy."

Chapter 29

Kalum

The way she looked when I walked into the boardroom at the office, where I was instructed to meet her by Lane's lawyer, broke me. She tried to hold back the tears in front of everyone so she could be strong for her son— their son. When I looked at him, it was unmistakable. He looks like his late father. They even have the same hair, face, and eyes. He looks at his mother like she's the center of everything. And she's.

Letting her go was the hardest thing I ever had to do in my life. To know that another man I respected and admired had everything. Because he had her.

I knew deep down the day at the fair when he approached her, and she looked at him like he was her protector because he was. Lane was there for her when my parents practically tossed her out. I cried like a pussy for months, and when I stopped crying, the hate replaced the hurt. Not for her or for Lane but the hatred for my parents. They took what I wanted most, and I lost her in the arms of another man.

I'm not sure what his purpose was for me to watch over her

and his son in the event of his death. I don't understand it. It makes sense she needs protection for a while against lawyers, family, and people in high places trying to take advantage of a woman who just lost her husband, and according to her, the love of her life. They know she's vulnerable and doesn't have other family members to help her.

The way she talks about him makes my gut clench because deep down, I'd hoped when I was eighteen it would've been me. That her son out there in my foyer would have been mine. She's still as beautiful as I can remember. She's stunning. Motherhood adds more to her appeal. She must have looked beautiful pregnant.

A knock sounds from the door, interrupting my thoughts.

"Come in."

I straighten in my chair when the door swings open, and she stands in the doorway looking beautiful with her black dress molded in all the right places. The armed guards kept glancing her way, admiring her beauty, and I almost lost it. It took me back in time for a moment when she was mine.

Even when she cries, it doesn't diminish how stunning she is. It brings out a protective instinct inside, and all I want to do is kill the bastard who caused it. My fist clenched, and I made sure I followed directly behind her. Men will be like hound dogs in heat looking for a bone, knowing she's vulnerable and wealthy.

Her husband made sure she would want for nothing, and neither will his son. The man was hard to dislike. He did everything right except staying alive. Now, she's alone and heartbroken.

"What is it?" I ask.

She stands in the doorway and makes no move to enter.

"We need to talk."

I wave my hand to the modern leather chair. "Please, have a seat."

She nods and takes a seat, but I notice she leaves the door open. I wonder if it's because her son is outside, and she wants to make sure she hears him, or she doesn't trust me.

Pulling up the security camera on my screen that gives me a direct view of LJ, I turn the screen toward her.

"Close the door," I demand.

She does as I ask and closes the door without protest and returns to sit in the chair across from my desk with her gaze locked on mine. I'm testing her, and she knows it. She knows that I want to know if she fears me. If she's afraid to be alone with me.

I remove my cuff links and roll up the sleeves of my dress shirt. I'm not doing it to intimidate her, but I want her to see that I'm comfortable around her. I don't need to be businesslike around her or her son. She has gone through a lot already with the loss of her husband, so the last thing she needs to worry about is her safety and being around someone who makes her or her son uncomfortable.

She looked around like the apartment was an institution. A prison. And I didn't know what to do or say to make them feel more welcome. I was glad I had instructed Camila to meet me here when she arrived. Aura looked relieved when she saw her get off the elevator. They both did.

"What do you want to talk about?"

She looks at the monitor and watches her son with the softest expression, full of love. I could imagine her looking at me the same way. My stomach clenches at the thought, and so does my... cock. *Get a grip, Kalum.*

I have sworn off marriage. Aura was the only woman I could ever see marrying, but I let her go when news broke that she married Lane. She didn't have a wedding or grand affair. It was released by the racing world that the great Lane Turner married the love of his life. I knew I never stood a chance. When it was announced they were waiting for the birth of their first child, I saw my chances evaporate into thin air and decided that it was best to move on. It didn't thwart my plans to get back at my parents for what they had done to her.

To me.

To us.

It was their fault for kicking her out of my life. I was eighteen, dependent on my inheritance, and thrust into my family's expectations. I would have given it all up for her, but I was still in high school, and when I graduated, Aura's best friend Exie told me that Aura was fine and in love with her brother. It was a blow I never expected. Aura never returned my calls or sent a text. I knew there was no way I could get her back or offer her the life Lane could. Even if her happiness wasn't with me, I loved her enough to let her go and be happy with him. She deserved to be loved by a man who would do anything for her after the loss of her beloved parents.

She takes a deep breath. "I know that you feel I need to stay with you, and I get it, but we can't stay with you here."

"Why?" I ask.

I know they feel uncomfortable, but I want details so I can rectify them. I want them to feel relaxed for a little while until things die down and she can return and raise her son. She's grieving. She needs time to think about what she wants out of life and what she wants to do, and I have a company to run, business deals to make, and money to be made. I have way more than I need, but my purpose is to make even more. It's selfish to want more money, but I have my reasons.

She scans my office. Her eyes meet mine, and I try not to make it obvious that I'm aware of her sexually. If the circumstances were different, I would swipe everything off this desk, lay her flat on her back, and bury my face between her thighs, reminding me of how she tasted when she came on my lips the first time. It thrilled me to know I was the first to taste her sweet pussy. No woman has ever tasted as good as Aura. Believe me, I have tried to find one, but nada.

"Your apartment is nice but not a place for LJ. He loves to play with his toys, which are basically cars with tracks. Toys would damage your pristine floors, and the furniture is not the kind to have a five-year-old sit on. I would basically have to tell him to stick to playing and eating on the floor."

"You would do no such thing. I won't allow it. He isn't a dog but a child."

She gives me a small grin. "I'm glad you agree with me and understand. I'll call an Uber, and we'll be on our way."

She moves to stand. I frown, and panic begins to take hold of me. She's leaving?

"Wait...you can't leave... I understand."

Her brows rise, and I glance at the monitor, watching her son slide the cars on the marble. As I look through their eyes, I'm sure their home is equipped for children to play with and a kitchen to make cupcakes and popcorn. I get it. She wants her son and her to feel comfortable under the circumstances.

"I have an idea."

I don't, but I will. I can't watch her leave. Lane wanted me to watch over her upon his death. His lawyer said a letter will be delivered before the year is out. Why? I have no clue, but Lane was a strategic son of a bitch.

We were friends in high school, but not best friends like Cason or Brian, with whom I still keep in touch. We respected each other, and I knew he would be good for Aura.

"What idea is that?"

"You could stay in my house. It would be better than staying here. A good place for LJ and for you. No one can bother you there, and you'll have security at all times. You won't even know that they're there." I take a deep breath. "If they know you're not at your main home, they won't go looking for you there."

She nods. "How long? He doesn't need to be frightened by all the media and cameras or his grandparents imposing and making demands. Lane never had us in the limelight, and we preferred to keep our personal lives as private as possible."

"I know."

I do know. Aura was never at public events, which sparked controversy as to why Lane Turner always hid his family and never took them to any races involving his builds. Now she's on every page and social media news outlet as the woman who inherited everything from her late husband. Car manufacturers and racing companies will hound her to sell her rights to his builds and his cars, including his patents on certain tech for imported vehicles. His cars are probably worth more than his company, and she owns them all. Lane's family has connections and will do anything to take them from her.

"Until it all dies down, and they all back off. I'll be there to guide you and protect you and LJ. Nothing will happen to you, and no one will pressure you to do anything you don't want."

"Okay. I just need to get my things in order and a car to be brought up to your house. Lane needs to be with all the things he's familiar with."

"I took the liberty of bringing your things from the hotel."

"How?" she asks.

"I own the hotel you're staying in."

She rolls her eyes. "Naturally."

"I wanted to save you the hassle," I say with a grin.

I lean back in my chair and familiarize myself with the beauty of her face. The curve of her breasts under her simple black dress. Her pretty thighs up to the indent of her waist.

The flare of her hips makes her look sexier since giving birth to her son.

She smiles. "So where is Mrs. St. Claire or a girlfriend I should meet?"

"I'm not married, and I don't have a steady girlfriend at the moment. I do date, but no one is serious enough for you to meet."

"Oh. I thought maybe you would have found someone special by now."

I shake my head. "I'm not interested in settling down, getting married, and having children. I'm focused on my company and running it."

The light in her eyes dims for a split second, and then she gives me a smile. "I understand. You were never the type to settle down, but I still have faith in you finding her. I know she'll be amazing."

I chuckle. "You were always trying to find the good in people. There is no need to bring your car or anything like that. I can arrange a car for you to use. It will be no trouble."

I have to get a house and a car, and fast. I grab my cell phone and send my personal assistant Janine a text.

Kalum: I need a house fit for a five-year-old and his mother as well as a suitable car.

Janine: Who's the lucky lady? Please tell me you're ready to settle down with someone.

Kalum: Nothing like that. I'm helping an old friend who passed away.

Janine: This friend wouldn't be Lane Turner, would it?

Kalum: Yes, it would.

Janine: His wife is gorgeous, Kalum. I would love to meet her.

Kalum: No.

Janine: Come on. Everyone is talking about her. She's so pretty. No wonder her husband kept her hidden.

Kalum: Get me the house and the car, Janine.

Janine: You suck. Fine. What house and what car? What is the budget?

I should give her a budget because she can go overboard, but I look at Aura seated in front of me and then at the monitor where her son is making motions with his mouth as he imitates engine noises. I figure, what the heck.

Kalum: No budget, and I need it fast.

"Is everything okay?" Aura asks.

I look up from my phone. "Yeah, everything is fine. I'm just letting my personal assistant know the change of plans. I'll get with my lawyer to get with yours and settle your house and all your belongings in the meantime. I just need a week or two to get everything settled. Do you think you could stay here?" She looks down at her hands on her lap. "It's short term, Aura. I can extend your stay at the hotel, but..."

"We'll stay." She looks up. "Two weeks, Kalum. I hope you don't mind toys and smudges all over your nice furniture. I'll clean..."

"No. You don't have to clean my apartment. I hire people for that, and I don't mind you and LJ in my apartment. Smudges and toys don't bother me."

"Okay."

I hate lying to her right now about me already having a house somewhere, but I can't risk her denying my help. I promised myself when I was eighteen that I would take care of her if she needed me. She doesn't see it, but she needs me.

. . .

After settling a date with my lawyer to meet with hers to settle her house and move their things when I secure a house, Janine will handle the transition until everything is settled.

"Is he okay?" I ask from the hallway.

Aura walks out of the spare bedroom and closes the door halfway. "He has his iPad and headphones. He'll be fine."

After Camila left for her apartment one floor down, LJ was antsy. He kept looking around, and it pained me to see he was uncomfortable. I called Janine and told her to find a place fast. I didn't care what it cost.

"How about you?"

She looks up. Her eyes and nose are red from crying. I can't imagine the pain she must be feeling. The pain and confusion her son is feeling at having lost his father at such a young age.

"I'm..."

"I know, Aura. I'm here if you need me."

Her lips are pink and full. I'm drawn to them, but I need to get a grip on my attraction to her. She's grieving, and the last thing she needs is a man trying to take advantage of her. She loves Lane. Enough that she forgot about me. Enough that she gave him a son.

"Thank you, Kalum," she says and walks inside the room next to mine.

She didn't answer my calls or texts. I looked for her at school. I slept in her bed until the smell of her was gone. After a while, I accepted she was never coming back. I accepted she chose Lane, and I lost her forever.

New York is the city that never sleeps. People are on the streets at all hours. Police officers patrolling. The lights in the building never shut off. Just like my mind when it comes to the woman currently sleeping in the next room.

My glass of brandy is almost empty. The ice melts like the wall I have built around my heart because of Aura. The only woman I could ever see marrying. The only woman I could ever see having a life with. Children. And she's taken. Unattainable.

I look around my apartment, and I can see it through their eyes. The marble over the electronic fireplace. The sharp edges of the glass coffee and dining table. The chrome gleams from the base of the leather chairs. The white carpet on cold marble that needs to be dusted every two days, or it will create a film, turning it gray. The white carpet that's steam cleaned every month.

My eyes focus on the six-foot canvas of a naked woman hanging near the dining table. Pink nipples and the curve of hips drawn with an expert hand. I had it commissioned by an artist in the art district. The image of Aura naked in my arms haunted me for so long that I had to get it out of my head, but I didn't include her face. It would have been obvious if I had.

It's three o'clock, and like most nights, I sit in the armchair and stare out the window with the view of the city. Every so often, I look at the painting, drinking a brandy, and think of another life. A life I could have had.

Placing the glass in the sink, I hear a whimper. I pause, wait a few seconds, and there it is again. I close my eyes, and I'm eighteen again, waking up in my bed to the sound of the girl haunting my thoughts. My dreams.

The hallway is dimly lit by the lamp I made sure to leave on in case Aura needed to wake up and tend to LJ in the spare room. He's in a strange house away from everything he knows after losing his father. I'm sure he has trouble sleeping.

I'm about to pass the spare bedroom, telling myself I shouldn't, but her sobs break me. I push the door open slowly.

Aura faces away from me on her side. She sighs, and then her body trembles as another sob wracks her small frame.

My knees touch the edge of the bed, and I tell myself not to do it, but I can't. I can't leave her like this. Crying and alone.

When I pull the comforter gently, she turns to face me. Her cheeks glisten from her tears. She's been crying for a while. There is a huge wet spot on her pillow.

"Kalum," she whispers in a trembling voice. "What...?"

Her eyes go wide when I slide next to her in the queen-size bed. I'm shirtless and in my Tom Ford pajama pants, but I couldn't care less. I'm not here to take advantage of her. I'm here to hold her. To comfort her.

"I'm here, Aura."

She sits up on the bed, and a sob escapes her throat. I wrap my arms around her and pull her to my chest. The smell of her hair hits me, and I'm back in my parents' house holding her when we were teenagers.

"I-I miss him, Kalum," she says in a trembling voice. "I miss him so much."

My nose stings because I miss him too. He was a good man. A good friend even if he had what I wanted. He didn't deserve his life to end the way it did.

"I know, Aura." I close my eyes. "I'm here for you... I'm here for you both."

She wraps her arms around my neck, and I hold her tight, hearing her grieve for the man she loves. My heart rattles inside my chest in the storm of emotions I buried years ago. Emotions that started with infatuation covered up by vexation because I didn't know if it was love. But our storm was beautiful, destructive, and one of a kind.

It was ours.

It was us.

CHAPTER 30—— KALUM

"How was last night?" Janine asks, walking in my office and placing a file on my desk. I lean my head back and look at the ceiling. "That bad, huh? You look like shit. You're not sleeping again."

"Show me what you found."

I'm irritable.

Being reminded of Aura crying last night gets me in a sour mood. I hated seeing her hurt and broken like that. There was nothing I could do about it. All I could do was hold her until sleep claimed her.

"How is she? I mean, I get she must be grieving. She lost her husband."

"Janine," I say in a warning tone, leaning forward and opening the file. "I don't want to talk about it right now. I need to find them a house."

"What's wrong with yours?" I spread the sheets of different properties available in the Hamptons and place them side by side to compare them.

"It's an icebox."

"I beg your pardon?"

I look up. "It's cold and a bachelor pad, Janine. No place for her son. He needs space and a place they will both feel comfortable."

"Is she the reason you have dark circles under your eyes and look like shit?" she asks curiously.

She's fishing for information about my feelings for Aura. I can see it in her eyes. She wants to know if we have a past. Of course we do, but she wants to know if there is more, and I'm not at liberty to talk about my past. It's buried where it belongs.

Chapter 30

Aura

Two Weeks Later

Kalum insisted we be taken by helicopter to the Southampton area. The houses down below are right on the water. Some have swimming pools and tennis courts. I'm not surprised Kalum has a house here. His family was extravagant and extra. Kalum was the same way with his flashy car and designer labels. Apparently, nothing has changed.

Lane was different even though he came from money and the same circle of friends as Kalum. He built his cars even if they're probably worth more than the average Ferrari or Lamborghini. He wasn't flashy but was a car enthusiast. Anyone into them would know what was under a hood and how much a car built by Lane Turner cost.

We land, the propeller causing the trees to blow in disarray. Lane is looking around in excitement with his headphones on. His eyes shine bright because it's his first time in a helicopter.

Kalum said he would be here when we arrived. It took him the two weeks to get everything sorted with our main home in North Carolina. My lawyer agreed with Kalum about being watched and the concern for my safety. There were different cars parked on the road leading to the house, and then the fear of being watched settled in the back of my mind.

Exie called and told me her parents were upset about Lane leaving me everything in his name. Nothing in the will belonged to his parents. Even if there was, Lane knew I would refuse to accept it.

When they found out I was pregnant with LJ and Lane and I were getting married, I was subjected to his parents' vitriol every chance they got. The arguments when Lane's father would call, and Lane defended me. They accused me of taking advantage of Lane by falling pregnant. I kept my distance from Exie so they wouldn't give her a hard time because of it. They found out that I was staying with Kalum. I'm sure Kalum's parents had nothing nice to say about me. Lane's mother never accepted me and kept LJ at arm's length.

I haven't touched a dime of Lane's money since his death. Everything I have saved through the years from making bracelets is what I have been using for my necessities. I instructed Lane's lawyer to place everything in a trust for LJ. I didn't want anyone to think I married Lane because of his money. If they only knew I never asked Lane for anything. He would tell Exie to buy me clothing because I refused to use the bank card he had left in my name unless it was for our son.

My parents taught me growing up that you spend what you earn, and if you didn't earn it, then it's not yours to spend. The only thing I earned was what I made with my hands. My bracelets. It was a miracle I sold out every time I listed a new collection online. It motivated me to keep making them.

The copilot opens the door and waits patiently for me to get LJ unbuckled. When he assures me it's safe, I step down, holding him close.

A black Rolls is parked out front, reminding me of when I

was seventeen. The driver's door opens, and my eyes almost bulge out of my head.

"Henry?"

Henry gives me a grin.

I smile and run up to him with LJ in tow. "How are you, old man?" I give him a hug, and he gives it right back.

"Aura," he says softly. He pulls back, and his gaze darts to LJ. "Is this your son?"

"Yes," I say breathlessly. "This is LJ."

LJ gives him a once-over and smiles at the old man. "Hi, my name is LJ Turner."

Henry bends his knees so that he's at eye level with LJ. "I'm Henry. It's nice meeting you, sir. You're a very lucky boy."

LJ beams at Henry. "I have the best mommy in the whole world. She loves me lots."

"I bet she does. If you want to go anywhere with your mommy, you can count on me to make sure you get there."

LJ surveys the car with a keen eye and frowns. "This car doesn't go very fast. I can tell. It doesn't rumble." LJ makes a rumble with his voice like the sound he's heard in his father's shop.

"I'm so sorry, Henry. He's used to—"

"I understand. Does Kalum?"

"Does he what?" I question.

"Understand what he likes."

I tilt my head. "I don't need to worry Kalum about LJ and his needs. I'm shocked that Lane reached out to him at all. I didn't know they knew each other that well."

"They knew each other before you came along. They would race out on the backroads. All the kids into cars like that did. Kalum and Lane were close."

"Daddy would race with Kalum?" LJ chimes in.

Henry glances at LJ. "When they were kids. They went to the same school."

"That is so cool. My daddy was the greatest. He can make a car faster and faster. I want to be just like him when I grow up." LJ looks at me with a smile. "Right, Mommy?"

I ruffle his hair. "Yes, baby. Just like Daddy."

"Well, let's get going. Kalum will be arriving shortly. He wants you and LJ settled."

After fifteen minutes, we arrive at a gated mansion.

"Wow," Lane says in awe, looking at the house.

The kind of house they feature in *Better Homes & Gardens*.

"Yeah," I say, matching LJ's enthusiasm.

The house is a single story with a charming appeal. It's built for a big family. Not a single man who works in Manhattan. Why would Kalum own this impressive home? It's enormous.

The house has a modern cottage feel. The wind whips my hair with the hint of the salty sea air as we make our way up the pathway leading to the white wooden front door. The door opens as we approach, and Camila appears with a warm smile.

"How was the helicopter ride? Did LJ like it?" she asks excitedly.

"Oh, yeah. He loved it," I tell her.

"Kalum is waiting for you in the kitchen," she says.

When we walk inside, LJ spots the white fluffy couches and smiles as he tests their softness and comfort. The home has a cozy feel and is so much better than Kalum's New York City apartment. This house has white oak wood floors and cream-colored walls.

The kitchen comes into view, and Kalum is set up with his laptop on the island on his phone, speaking in a hushed tone. His suit jacket is draped over the stool, and the sleeves of his white dress shirt are rolled, giving me a glimpse of tattoos and corded muscle. His dress shirt fits perfectly over his broad shoulders, and his dark hair is swept over to the side. I didn't think he would be here already. He made it before we got here.

The man is gorgeous. If I thought he was good-looking when he was in high school, Kalum St. Claire, the business-man, is sinfully hot. Tall and handsome with a face to die for. He always reminded me of those *GQ* models on the cover of magazines I would see in the grocery store back in Spencer.

He spots me walking toward the island, disconnects the call, and stands while he shuts the laptop. He looks over and grins when he sees LJ testing all the seating areas in the living room.

He nudges his chin toward the living area. "I guess that means he likes it here."

"Yes," I say, admiring the chef's kitchen with wood accents. "Your house is beautiful.

The light filters in through the living room windows as the sun sets, giving the house an ethereal feel.

"I'm glad you like it."

LJ walks down a hallway, but I frown because he's looking around for the light switch. "It has to be somewhere," he mutters to himself.

I walk over and spot a light switch on the opposite side of the wall. I push it on. He walks down the hallway and begins to open every single door.

"Kalum?"

He turns his head. "Yes, Aura."

"Is this really your home?"

"It is now. Why?"

I stifle a laugh. "You don't seem to know where anything is."

He takes a deep sigh and faces me. My head tilts because I'm five feet to his six-four. His eyes rake slowly down my simple white T-shirt and skinny jeans, finally landing on my face. I unconsciously swipe my long hair over one shoulder. His gaze lingers on my hair for a second longer than necessary.

"Your hair is longer," he points out.

My skin tingles when he's near, and there is a flutter low in my belly. It sounds crazy because I just lost my husband. The minute my gaze lingers on his chest a second longer than necessary, guilt slowly creeps in, and I look away.

Shame overcomes me at my reaction. I should feel absolutely nothing around him.

"Yeah."

"It looks good," he says huskily. Then he clears his throat. "I asked my assistant to purchase a house because my apartment is clearly not suitable for you and LJ."

My hand covers my face. "Please tell me you didn't buy a house just so we can stay in it for a short while."

"I did."

My hand falls. "Why? It wasn't necessary. It would have been better at a hotel."

"Not in New York and it's not suitable for LJ either. He clearly needs his space and a place to play with his cars and other toys. This house has a pool, a yard, a living area, a generous kitchen, and is on the water with private beach access."

"You didn't have to go to so much trouble. This place must have cost a fortune, Kalum." I shake my head. "You didn't have to do that."

"It's done, Aura. I want you and LJ to feel comfortable while you stay with me. My lawyer informed me that your lawyer says there is a lot of media presence at the front gates of your home. Companies will harass you and come after you to buy you out or, worse, threaten you. That is a lot to handle when you just lost a husband and LJ lost his father."

My eyes well with unshed tears.

"I know it hurts, Aura. I see the love you have for him. The way you take care of LJ. It's plain as day you both loved each other. I'm trying to wrap my head around the fact that he asked me to watch over you both. Of all the people, it should have been Exie."

"Exie took over the family business, and Lane wasn't on speaking terms with his mother or father because of his choices. Those choices also included me. They weren't very happy when we married because of the way we did it, and—"

"Because you don't come from a predominant family and have money."

"Yeah. I guess he thought it would put Exie and me in a bad spot with his family. It wouldn't be good for LJ and his future."

"I guess Lane and I both agree on one thing. We don't give a shit about what our parents think and don't let them dictate what we want for our future. It makes sense. But there is one thing I don't understand, Aura."

"What is that?"

"What do you want for your future? What do you want to do? I understand LJ's future is secure, as it should be, but what about you?"

My eyes lower because, for the first time, someone has asked what I wanted. All my time with Lane, I waited for him. He was quiet and reserved but focused on Turner Racing and his builds. He showed me his work and taught me things I never thought I would learn about cars and how fast they could go.

He made sure my needs were met, and when he was vocal, he would tell me he loved me and that everything he was doing was for us. When I had LJ, my life revolved around raising him, but Lane did not ask me what my dreams were or what I wanted to do.

"I-I don't know," I stammer. "I guess having LJ, I never had time to think about it. There weren't many options for someone like me."

His parents washed their hands of me the year I lost my parents. I had no money. I had no one. Not even him.

"Let's find the main bedroom so you can get situated. Camila chose the room right next to yours for LJ so you wouldn't have to worry if the main bedroom was too far."

"I could have taken the room next to his. The main should be your room."

"I'm not staying."

"Oh... I thought—"

"I'm staying in my apartment in the city. It's convenient. I can't—"

"Stay."

He flinches when I hit the mark. I get it. He sent me and LJ away. I should be relieved, but the fact we are being sent here to hide away like a secret annoys me. I know it's for my safety but still.

The house feels like a trap like we are in a witness protection program. Kalum wouldn't want to be seen with us anyway. He has a life, and I'm sure he entertains a slew of women. This is a favor from a friend who passed away, and maybe he feels doing this would help him relieve the guilt about what happened between us.

"I live a fast-paced life, and I'm always on the go. I have business meetings and—"

I raise my hand to stop him. "You don't have to explain anything to me. You have a life, and honestly, you don't have to do this. I appreciate it, and so does Lane, even if he's no longer with us. I already feel bad for imposing on you. I could go back, and I'll figure it out. It really is no big deal. I can handle it on my own."

"No," he says in a hard tone. "If I agree to something, I'll go through with it. I agreed, and I wasn't only Lane's friend back in high school, but I was also yours. Lane and I weren't that close, but we were friends."

I scoff. "Fine. But one thing I want to make clear about this crazy arrangement is that you're doing this for Lane. We were never friends. We were never anything. You hated the fact that your parents agreed to have me stay in your home. My presence was a nuisance and an inconvenience."

He walks up to me. He's so close I can smell the hint of his expensive cologne. My breathing picks up. His expression darkens. "Was it?"

"Was what?" I challenge.

"Was it an inconvenience when I tasted you?"

I never thought he would bring it up. I thought he forgot about it and probably wouldn't even remember what I looked like without my clothes on.

How many women has Kalum had since then? He's rich, gorgeous, and can have any woman he wants. I know I don't compare to any of the women Kalum is used to. Lane was the only man to ever make me feel pretty. He would always tell me I was pretty and that he loved me. For a girl like me, that was enough.

What is he trying to prove by bringing up the past? This is not high school. He followed the path his parents laid out for him, and they made sure I was nowhere near him.

The memory of how easily they cast me aside and threw me out plays in my head. The memory of rolling my suitcase down the sidewalk on my birthday, scared and alone.

"Don't bring up things that are not important."

He steps closer with less than an inch between us, the heat

of his body mixed with his scent permeating all around me. Every breath I take is mixed with his heat and scent.

"Look at me."

I meet his gaze, holding it for a beat. His nostrils flare, and his lips are set in a hard line. The energy crackles between us like a whip.

I'm glad LJ is with Camila. I can hear their voices behind me as Kalum and I stand toe-to-toe, staring at each other. Our pasts seeking answers to things left unsaid.

Chapter 31

Kalum

er anger makes my cock harder than steel, and all I feel like doing is taking her to the main bedroom in this enormous house and showing her how much I want her. How much I crave her. I thought being away from her all these years would change how she affects me, but I was wrong. It's worse. I want her more than the air I breathe, but I can't touch her. It's wrong in so many ways. I keep reminding myself she's mourning the death of the man she loves.

I wish that little boy was mine. I imagine he was ours, that he looked like me or maybe both of us, but then I come to my senses. I don't want a wife, and I don't want children. When the time comes, because my family's legacy depends on it, I'll take a wife. But for now, I'll have meaningless sex when I want and how I want.

Aura is not the woman I can take to bed and tell her to leave when I'm done. She's the kind of woman you marry. There was a time I wanted that with her, but it wasn't in the cards. And time is a fickle bitch. It passes, and you would think time heals all wounds. But it doesn't. When you least expect it, it consumes you like a blazing fire, burning your waking thoughts and taking the air from your lungs.

I cannot have feelings for the woman in front of me. She belonged to another man. A man who trusted me to make sure she's safe. Lane Turner's parents want to take his legacy from her and sell it to the highest bidder. They will make sure she doesn't see a dime. They want her penniless. Exie has tried to convince them to leave her alone, but her control is slipping.

People from my world are ruthless, and when they want something, they will destroy whoever and whatever to take it. They will do anything to make her sell it, or they will destroy it. Right now, it's her against the world. I'm the only one who can save her.

My eyes travel down her shirt. Her nipples are hard against the soft fabric of her bra. She feels it. The same way I do.

Her eyes follow the path of my gaze. "Some things never change, do they?"

"The fact that I want nothing more than to slide my tongue between your legs and reacquaint myself with the taste of you. I'm a man, Aura. I like to fuck. That will never change."

"I'm not the same girl you had cleaning your room when she had no other choice. I'm not the girl you can sweet-talk with your charm and good looks to get her to lose her head and fall for your lies."

I chuckle. "You had a choice to say no when I was making you come on my tongue. You sure as hell didn't say no then." I lean closer. "And I bet you wouldn't say no now."

Thwack!

Heat spreads over my cheek. She slapped me hard. My hand instinctively wraps around her wrist in a solid grip but not hard enough to hurt her. My eye twitches from the sting, but it's nothing I can't handle.

Her eyes flash. "Fuck you."

"That can be arranged. Tell me when and how you want it."

I prefer her to be mad at me. It's better than having her want me for any other reason than what I can offer her. Safety.

"Never," she spits.

I snort. "Good. I can never offer you more than a quick fuck anyway." I lower my voice. "Besides, I prefer a woman with a little more experience. You were never my type anyway." I tilt my head and scrutinize her with my gaze. "Pretty, but plain." She flinches.

I know I'm being an asshole, but it's better to put a barrier between us. She won't be getting anything more than my help from me.

No one should take away what her husband wanted her to have. His family shouldn't have a choice, but that is not the way they see it.

"I want to leave," she grits. "I don't want to stay with you or have anything to do with anything that belongs to you or your family. I hate you."

"Trust me. I would prefer not to get involved in your late husband's battle, but he asked me for this one favor upon his death, and I'll honor it, Aura. You're right. I'm not doing this for you. I'm doing it for Lane and his son."

Keep telling yourself that, asshole.

The mention of Lane has tears running like rivers down her cheeks. My chest clenches at the sight. I didn't want to make her cry. It breaks me inside, but I'm trying to make the best of this nightmare. I need to calm down and convince her to stay, but I can't stay here. Being near her stirs up old memories better kept where they belong. In the past.

Chapter 32

Aura

Six Months Later

It has been months that Lane and I have been staying at Kalum's house in Southampton. Sometimes I feel we should go back to North Carolina. Kalum tells me I'm not out of the woods regarding Lane's parents' lawsuits contesting his will. They want to take everything away from me and LJ, stating I'm not entitled to anything and that I used Lane for his money.

"I'm sorry, Aura, but it's best you remove the Turner name. It will help calm things down. It will help prove that you never intended to capitalize on the family's influence."

"Mr. Schwartz, it's unfair. I have never touched a single dime of Lane's money."

"I know, Aura. I know, but they don't know that. I did what you told me to and let their lawyer know that you placed everything in a trust for LJ and are managing it until he turns of age. That will make them back off and avoid pursuing the forgery investigation."

The lawyer Lane trusted to handle his will if something

happened to him has helped me, but Lane's family is relentless. They have tried to paint me out as a gold digger. I don't even live in my house, for Christ's sake.

Lane's mother has even threatened to take LJ away from me. I had to stop going to the doctor when I couldn't sleep because I was afraid she'll use it against me and say I was unstable. Mr. Schwartz is right; I have no choice but to sign the papers to change my name.

"Fine. I'll sign them. Change my last name to Rayne. I need to get a job anyway."

"You know you don't have to work, Aura."

"I do," I insist.

"He never wanted you to have to work because you needed money, Aura. He felt strongly about that."

I take a deep sigh. "Yeah, but he didn't realize the lengths his family would go to in order to destroy what he built. Come to think of it, this was his dream and what *he* wanted. All I wanted was to be with him, but now he's gone. I'm left with no choice."

"Don't do this, Aura," he says, "It will feel like I failed him. Where would you work?"

"Don't worry. I'll figure it out. Y-you have a nice day, Mr. Schwartz, and thank you for everything," I stammer before hanging up and letting the tears fall.

I have to talk to Camila and ask her how much she would charge me to watch LJ so I can get a job. Lane's parents still haven't figured out where I'm staying, and I have Kalum to thank.

The following week, Mr. Schwartz sent me the court document to update my driver's license with my name changed. It hurts having a name I was used to being called for so long taken away. I felt like I belonged to the man I loved when he honored me with it. But now, I'm back to square one.

My phone rings while I sit on the bed in the main bedroom in Kalum's home in Southampton. The sunlight filters through the windows of the sheer curtains. I'm looking at the screen with Dex's name flashing.

"Hey," I answer.

"Hey, how are you and the little man?"

"He's good. He's with Camila, eating lunch in the kitchen. She helps me a lot with him."

"I'm glad. Kalum is not such a bad guy after all."

"Yeah, so far," I say distractedly.

"I'm sorry, Aura. I don't think Lane knew the extent his parents would go when he left everything to you."

"He left it to his son," I correct.

"You know that is bullshit, right? He loved you so much, Aura. I have never seen Lane so happy. You meant everything to him."

My throat tightens.

"I know, Dex. But he's gone," I say and change the subject. "How's the shop going?"

"Business is great. We have so many customers coming in. I had to make a waiting list to work on cars and accept deposits. Blaze, in Spencer, says he's swamped. Every street racer wants a build from Turner's shop."

"Sounds great, Dex. Have you heard from Exie?"

Dex and Exie have been dating, but I'm not sure if there is more going on with the way Lane's family is. I try not to call her phone in case her parents are around. I wouldn't put it past them to have her phone line tapped.

"She's good. She wants to see you but has been waiting for the right time. Anyway, I called you because we need to take Lane's car on the track to get a time after I install his last modification on it."

Lane was supposed to install a mod to his car but never got

the chance to do it. It was supposed to be a game changer for the GT-R. He never made it home, but Dex knows how to install it.

I shrug my shoulders, even if he can't see me. "Okay. Do it. Get it done."

"It's done, boss lady. I need you to drive it on the track, Mrs. Turner."

I swallow. Why me?

"Why can't you do it?"

"Only you and LJ are allowed to drive that car, and I think LJ is too young at the moment. Ten years is too long to have it sitting there by the time LJ can at least get behind a wheel."

"No way, Dex."

"It has to be you, Mrs. Turner," he teases.

Lane taught me how to drive, but it was for fun. The first couple of times I did it, I was on his lap. After a while, he liked me there for other reasons. I have to do this for Lane, but Dex needs to stop calling me Mrs. Turner.

"Fine, I'll do it," I tell him.

"Yes," he says with excitement.

"But Dex?"

"Yeah?"

"You can't call me Mrs. Turner."

"What? Why?" he asks, confused.

"His family threatened to sue me. They said I'm using their name as a brand to capitalize on it outside of being Lane's widow."

"You have got to be shitting me! Those motherfuckers."

"Tell me about it. I can't fight them. They have strong influences with good lawyers. I'm okay with being Aura Rayne."

"Fuck, Aura. That is so messed up. I'm sorry."

"Me too, Dex. Let me know when you need me, and I'll make plans to head over there."

"Okay, let me get the details and set a date. I'll call you to let you know. Bye, Aura," he says, sounding defeated before hanging up.

Chapter 33

Kalum

"So how's Aura?" Cason asks, sitting in front of my desk at my New York office.

"She's okay, I guess. The security you have on detail has reported no issues. I called Camilla. She is doing good."

Cason pinches his brows together and raises a finger. "Wait...are you telling me you don't see her? When was the last time you physically saw her?"

"The day I showed her the house she's staying in," I say sternly.

He wipes his hand over his face. "You're telling me her husband basically gave you the green light, and you haven't spent a day with her? The girl you let go because one of our friends fell in love with her. The girl you were going to throw everything away for, and you left her in a house you bought for her and her son... by the way, for twenty million. You're telling me you haven't tried to tell her how you feel about her?"

"Felt about her as in I don't anymore."

Cason scoffs. "You're such a liar."

The door opens, and Janine walks in. "Who is such a liar?"

"Your boss."

"About what?" Janine asks.

"Aura," Cason says.

Janine shakes her head and hands me a folder with the status of a new building I'm constructing in New York.

"He has her hidden in a twenty-million-dollar house and refuses to visit her. If you could see the way his expression changes when you mention her," Janine says. "It's priceless. Photo worthy."

Cason laughs. "Janine, you should see the way he looks at her. It will give you hope that he could love someone."

"Stop putting things in Janine's head. I'm not in love with her. The poor woman lost her husband and has a son to raise, with said husband's family trying to destroy her because he shunned them until the day he died. Any feelings I had for Aura, which were more of the teenage sexual variety, are in the past where they belong."

"Then you wouldn't mind if I see her?" Cason taunts.

My knuckles turn white when I grip the desk. Cason has always liked Aura since high school, and imagining him with her makes me want to reach over my modern glass desk and rip his throat out.

"Leave her alone, Cason," I warn, looking at the file.

"Well, at least it will be nice for her to know who has provided all her security. She'll feel... safer."

Cason started his own protective service company, branching out from his family's worldwide protection services for the super rich. He's made a name for himself in the States working with powerful leaders who travel worldwide and need the best of the best, sparing no expense. Cason's company, Zenith, is the world's most sought-after private security company. Like me, he's also single and doesn't like being in a relationship. We usually hang out and shoot the shit when we're not working or fucking our flavor of the week.

"No," I say. "Is the security detail ready for tonight?"

He leans forward. "You're seriously contemplating taking out Meredith when you have a gorgeous young woman all alone that I would chop off my right arm to spend one night with?"

"What's wrong with Meredith?"

"She's not Aura. That's what's wrong with her."

"You're right. She isn't," I explain. "She doesn't expect anything but a good time, and that's what tonight is all about. A good time."

Cason rolls his eyes. "Whatever, brother. I sure hope you know what you're doing because—"

"Because what?" I interrupt him, getting annoyed.

"Nothing. You're right. She just lost her husband," he says.

<hr>

"Yes, right there. Don't stop," Meredith screams as I thrust into her from behind. After our night out with some business associates, we went dancing, then headed to her apartment in Manhattan. I never take women to my apartment because they get clingy or read more into it.

The headboard on her iron bed bangs against the wall, and I slow down, knowing I'm making a dent in the wall, but when I look closely, I'm not the first. I look down and pull out slowly to make sure the condom is secured.

Yep. All good.

I need to make this quick because I'm bored. This is the last time I'll see Meredith. She's starting to annoy me, and her time has run out. One month is long enough. I never last more than a month with anyone I date. I lose interest, and the appeal fizzles out.

"Yes, Kalum. Faster," she says before a moan.

I pump into her, my hips crazed, but I can't come. I've tried, but her scent just doesn't do it for me. What Cason said about Aura messed with my head. I was fine, dammit. The more I'm away from her, the better it is for my sanity.

I close my eyes and imagine it's her, and my cock comes back to life. I pump four more times, and finally, the sensation at the base of my spine has my balls drawing up, and I come, spilling inside the condom.

"Yes, Kalum. Oh my God. I'm... coming."

Thank God, I tell myself. I block out her moans and pull out quickly, dispose of the condom, and get dressed.

"You don't want to stay the night?" she asks coyly, walking around seductively.

Meredith has a voluptuous body. Her father owns a lucrative import/export business, which makes her an heiress. She's nice arm candy but isn't smart and loves Daddy's money. That's all she talks about. My father this, and my father that. Good luck trying to fill those shoes. I'm glad I'll never be one of them.

Sliding my arms through the sleeves of my white dress shirt, I answer, "No."

She walks up to me and drags the tip of her red-manicured nail up my chest. I watch her finger trace the indent of my chest muscles with disinterest.

"Is there any way I can change your mind?" she whines in a little-girl tone.

"I'm sorry, but I have to go."

I don't mean to be a dick, but I can't take it anymore. I want to head to my apartment and take a hot shower and scrub myself with strong body wash, taking her scent off my skin, and never set foot inside her apartment again.

"When do you want to do this again?"

I quickly finish getting dressed, then grab my wallet and keys off the dresser. "I'll call you," I tell her without looking back and exit her apartment.

Damn Cason and his stupid mouth.

Chapter 34

Aura

"**A**re you sure, Camila?" I ask.

"Of course, I can watch LJ," she says and then asks, genuinely confused, "Why do you need to get a job, Aura? I don't understand."

I'm in the kitchen making LJ pancakes while he watches TV.

"I need the money."

"That can't be right, Aura. Lane left everything to you."

"It's not my money, Camila. It was money intended for our son. I've had enough of his family claiming I married him solely for his money."

Camila frowns and looks at me while I mix the batter. "But you're a Turner."

"Was," I counter.

"What do you mean was?"

I look up and meet her gaze. "They threatened to sue me if I didn't change my last name. I'm no longer Aura Turner. Apparently, they can sue me if I use it when I sell my bracelets online, so there's that. Even if I only make a few thousand bucks, they can sue me for way more than that."

"That is stupid and preposterous, Aura."

"I know, but they have more money than God, and I can't risk pissing them off. They already think I can't take care of LJ on my own."

"Are they crazy? You're the best mother I have ever seen. Just like your parents were to you. LJ loves you."

I give her a warm smile. "Thank you, Camila. It means a lot coming from you."

"Has Mr. St. Claire called you?"

"No, and I don't expect him to either."

She frowns. "Do you really have to work?"

"Yes, I do. I have used up my savings in the past six months. Have you found out how much the utility bill is here in the winter?"

"Yes, I'll leave it on your nightstand, but I don't think Kalum will be happy about you paying for utilities. I'm surprised he hasn't noticed."

"I haven't paid rent since we started staying here. Paying the utilities is the least I can do. I also haven't touched the debit card he left to buy groceries. I found a job at a local diner not far from here. In a way, having my name back to Aura Rayne wasn't such a bad idea. They won't know who I am, and all I have said is that my son and I are staying with friends for a while until I can find a place."

"You're not serious, are you?" she asks.

"About?"

"Moving."

"Camila, I can't stay here forever. I can't go back to my house either. The more I stay out of the limelight, the better."

After I made pancakes and made sure LJ was fed, I head out in an Uber to the diner. I know I could have used the Merc parked in the garage, but I refuse to drive it. The last thing I need is for anyone to say I'm taking advantage of Kalum.

After months of crying and feeling sorry for myself, I learned one thing. I need to move forward. It means getting a job and making a living to support LJ and myself. My son's future is secure, and all I need is to save enough money to move to a house I can afford. LJ is being homeschooled with Camila's help until we can find a permanent place to live.

Mr. Schwartz will handle the sale of our home in North Carolina and place the funds in a trust for LJ. Dex and Blaze have all the cars secured and all our belongings placed in storage until I can find a new home.

I enter the diner, and the bell chimes. A woman who looks to be in her early sixties looks up from behind the counter. "How can I help you?"

"My name is Aura Rayne. I'm the one who called about the server position."

She points outside to the two men in black suits. "Are they with you?"

Shit. I forgot about the security Kalum hired for me.

I raise my finger. "O-one second," I stammer and exit the diner.

"Excuse me?" I motion to get the attention of one of the guys.

The blond one stands tall and puffs his chest out. "Yes, Mrs. Turner. Is everything alright?"

I roll my eyes. "Yes. Everything is fine, but do you have to follow me everywhere?"

"Yes, Mrs. Turner."

"I'm not Mrs. Turner." He frowns.

"Not anymore. I had to change it... listen, I'm trying to get a job, and it's weird to have two guys in black suits following me. Is it possible for you to find something else to do while I'm at work? Take a break. Go for a walk."

"I'm afraid I can't—"

"Please," I plead. "I need this job. I know it seems weird, and you don't understand, but I really need this."

His eyes soften, and he looks at the other guy in the suit with brown hair and brown eyes. "You really need this job?"

I glance at the entrance of the diner. The lady is talking with someone and watching this way. I look back at the bodyguard. "Yes. I really need this job. I know it seems... stupid. Why would Lane Turner's widow need money, but you don't understand. I don't come from money, and my late husband's family wants to take whatever he left me if they think I can benefit from it. I have no family except for my son, but until he's of age, I have nothing to offer him. They will not stop until they destroy what his father was trying to leave him. My husband wanted nothing to do with them, and I know why, but this is the best I can do for us right now."

Both men look at each other and then back at me in disbelief. "Are you fucking shitting me right now?"

I shake my head. "No. Trust me. They're powerful people, and they have money and connections in places you'd never think it was possible to have. They will find a loophole, and all they need is a reason. They don't want their name associated with me."

The blond one nods. "My name is John, and this is Milo. We'll keep watch but far enough away so they don't question you here."

I sigh. "Thank you," I say with a smile.

John smiles nervously. Milo elbows him. "You're welcome, Mrs.—"

"Aura. Aura Rayne."
"Okay, Aura."

Chapter 35

Aura

I'm glad I was given the morning shift five days a week, and it's not far from Kalum's house. It has been three months, and still, Kalum hasn't called me. Instead, he leaves messages with Camila. She gives him an update but doesn't tell him about my job at the diner and neither do the bodyguards. They drive me to work every day instead of me paying for an Uber since they need to follow me anyway.

Most people living in Southhampton have money, so the tips I have received are generous. I haven't decided where to move yet, but I'll know soon. Things have died down a bit with the media. I can't believe how much time has gone by. It seems like it was yesterday, and the ache in my chest is still there when Dex called me while I watched the TV in horror as the flames were being extinguished. Lane's body was burned to ashes. A lump lodges in my throat, and I'm unable to swallow every time I think of that moment.

"Hey, are you okay?"

I snap out of my thoughts.

"Oh... I'm so sorry. What can I get you?" I ask.

The young guy seated in the diner's booth stares at me.

"I would like the special, and if it's possible, your number."

My gaze lands on his face after the last part of writing down his order. "The special. Coming right up."

I hand the ticket to the kitchen and take a deep breath.

"That's Bradley. His father is a whale," Nancy says as she saunters up to me.

"A what?" I ask, confused.

"A whale. Rich. Bradley is a nice guy, not stuck-up like the usual trust fund kids around here. He's twenty-six and single." She glances at him and continues, "He keeps staring at you." She lowers her voice. "All the guys who come in here stare at you, but you don't notice. Do you?"

"No. I don't. I have a son to think about."

"I know your husband passed, but sometimes we need someone to talk to. Friends. You're far too young to alienate yourself because of your husband's passing. It's not as if you're disrespecting his memory, but you can't be alone all the time, sweetie. Judy wants to hang out on Saturday. If I babysit, maybe you girls can hang out." She bumps me playfully. "Maybe go dancing," she says, giving me a wink.

The bell rings, signaling the food is ready. Nancy smiles at me and pulls the ticket and hands me the plate.

Judy asked if I wanted to go for a girls' night out, but I declined. Camila offered to watch LJ so I could go out, but I declined, not wanting to leave LJ more than I had to. She also refused the money I offered to watch him while I work.

A guy enters the diner with light-brown hair and eyes the color of green emeralds and takes a seat across from Bradley.

"Is there anything else you need?" I ask as I place the plate in front of Bradley.

He looks at the plate of hot food, then looks up with a smirk. "You forgot to give me your number."

"I'm sorry, but I'm not interested."

He raises his eyebrows. His friend chuckles. I'm sure Bradley is not used to girls turning them down. Bradley has dirty-blond hair and blue eyes with a Ralph Lauren polo knit sweater fitted over his broad frame.

I glance at his friend, who is now openly laughing at him. Bradley looks embarrassed, but I'm honestly not interested.

I feel bad for Bradley.

"I have a son, and he's all I'm interested in right now."

His friend stops laughing. They both stare at me with surprised expressions. I'm sure they didn't expect me to be a single mom. It should scare Bradley off. I turn to leave the table to take the next customer's order.

"Is that the only reason?"

I turn back around. "Excuse me?"

"Is that the only reason you won't give me your number? Because you have a son? I know you don't have a husband or boyfriend. No guy in their right mind will ever let a girl as pretty as you work at a diner." I look down at my retro pink uniform. "I wouldn't."

I look up and catch Judy's smile in the next booth serving other customers. Kalum's last words come flooding back. "*I prefer experienced girls. You're pretty but plain.*"

Lane said I was *pretty* all the time. Even in bed, he said my pussy was pretty. I thought I loved when he said it, but now, I hate being called pretty. It makes me feel like I'm this delicate flower that could easily break. Weak. Fragile. Plain. It's like calling a guy cute all the time. Lane didn't like me working in a diner, but here I am, and I'm tired of being called pretty. And maybe I am plain and not good enough to be called beautiful, but I'm not weak.

I raise my chin. "You're right, my husband wouldn't want

me working in a diner. Not much he can do about it since he's dead."

Bradley looks down like I kicked his pet turtle. It's not how I wanted this conversation to go, but it hit home. At least Bradley will have some sense and back off.

"Mommy!" LJ runs toward me as I enter the house.

"Hi, sweetie. How was your day?"

"Super-duper fun. Camila and I made cupcakes."

"That is awesome," I tell him, ruffling his straight black hair.

Camila sits on the living room couch. The TV is on the *Entertainment and Gossip Show*. The flash of paparazzi is on the screen, and cameras are flashing in front of a fancy club in New York. A black Rolls pulls up, the back passenger door opens, and Kalum exits with a tall, statuesque woman on his arm.

My stomach clenches, but I push it down. The woman is wearing a cream-colored gown with a daring *V* in the front that looks gorgeous against her deep-red hair.

The headline reads *St. Claire is still a month strong with the heiress*. They look great together. He's tall and handsome in his tailored designer suit, and she's voluptuous and beautiful. Her red hair is rich, matching her lipstick.

Camila looks at me warily and then back at the TV.

"They look great together," I tell her.

Camila frowns. "She's awful."

"Really? Then why would he still be with her?" He places his hand on her lower back possessively when they step forward. She stops and looks left and right, posing for the cameras with Kalum at her side.

His words about his taste in women repeat in my head like a mantra. *"You're not my type. Pretty but plain."* The woman he's with is none of those things. I can see why he would be with her. The same way he was with a girl like Sarah. I never stood a chance. We both moved on, and I'm happy for him.

"I have no idea," she explains. "She's rude and annoying. I don't like her, and I think he should dump her."

"She's beautiful."

"No, she's not. You're beautiful." She points at the screen. "She has makeup and a good surgeon."

I snort. "I've been told I'm pretty and plain. Nice even. But certainly not beautiful." I point at the screen when the camera lands on her face again. "That woman is beautiful, and she looks great on his arm. I could never pull that dress off. I'm too short."

"If you ever wear something like that."

"I have no place to go that would require me to wear anything like that." I wave down at my diner's uniform. "This is what I need to wear. I serve coffee, milkshakes, and greasy burgers. Besides, I prefer a hot dog from a hot dog stand down on a street corner than to sit in a stuffy restaurant and eat an overpriced meal that tastes like crap."

Camila giggles. "You have a point."

"I'd rather sit here eating a cupcake with you and LJ than be caught eating at some uptight place where everyone judges you."

"Are you ever going to go out on a Saturday? It's tomorrow, you know."

"I have no one to go with, and I have no idea where to go."

"A movie with a friend sounds nice. I can watch LJ for a few hours."

I watch LJ stuff his mouth with a cupcake full of chocolate, playing with his cars. "I'll think about it."

Chapter 36

Kalum

"Quick question." Janine strides into my office.

"What is it?"

"I know I'm being nosy, but I was looking over your credit card statements."

Janine is my personal secretary and also my personal assistant. She handles all my personal bills, which makes my life a lot smoother.

"And? What's wrong?"

"Who's paying for the utilities and groceries in the Southampton house?"

I frown. "What do you mean? I am."

Janine shakes her head. "No, you're not. The bills are being paid, but nothing has been charged to your card."

I straighten in my chair. "Since when?"

"Since you bought the place. Nothing has been charged. No food, light, gas, or water."

I snatch my cell phone and call Mr. Schwartz, Aura's lawyer, and place it on speaker.

"Hello?"

"Mr. Schwartz, this is Kalum St. Claire."

"What can I do for you, sir? If this is about Aura and her staying with you," he rushes out. "I spoke to my wife, and we will gladly have her and LJ stay with us. It's no trouble. You have done enough, Mr. St. Claire."

"What? No," I say, confused. "What are you talking about? That's not why I'm calling. Why would you suggest that?"

He sighs. "Then what can I do for you?"

"I'm calling to ask why the utilities and food are being paid. I made it clear that I would cover Aura and LJ's expenses."

"I didn't," he says.

"Then who is?"

"She is."

"How?"

"It's called working, Mr. St. Claire. She hasn't touched a dime of Lane's money since he died. She sold everything except the cars and two shops and placed it in a trust for LJ when he's of age."

"Why?" I ask, raising my tone. "Why didn't you tell me?"

Janine backs up. She knows I'm pissed and have a temper. I'm not mad at her but at myself. Of course, she wouldn't take a dime from me. The things I said to her the last time I saw her.

"She asked me not to say anything, and she's my client after all." He pauses but doesn't hang up.

"There's more. Tell me."

"Yes, Lane Turner's parents threatened to sue her for using the Turner name in any way since it's a global brand. I'm sure you were already aware of their intention. They wanted her to remove it legally, or they would sue her for damages. She wants to keep her son's future the way his father wanted him to have it. He left her money, Mr. St. Claire, but you know how Aura is. With all the threats she received from his family, knowing they have people in very high places, she agreed and signed the papers, removing Turner from her last name. She's using her maiden name. Aura Rayne."

Fuck.

"Where is she working?"

"I don't know. I'm assuming it's somewhere local. I'm sure she has kept it a secret from everyone. She's a very independent girl. I love the fire in her spirit. It's a shame that Lane died, and she was left to deal with this. I don't think he realized what lengths his family would go to destroy what he built. He loved Aura, but she didn't deserve this. Like I said, if it's too much trouble, my wife and I, we'll look after them. It's no trouble at all."

"No. She has me."

I hang up and look at Janine.

"I have never wanted to dig up someone from the dead before and strangle them," she says in a hard tone.

"Why do you say that?"

"Because if you know you have powerful parents who are assholes from the get-go, what makes you think leaving a fortune you built that your parents did not agree on would stop them from destroying it? Give the girl a break. Threatening to sue the poor girl like she's a thief," Janine says, shaking her head in disbelief.

"Send some of my stuff from my apartment to Southampton."

"What are you going to do?"

"Stay with them," I quip.

Janine gives me a smirk. "Domestication. I like it."

"Don't get your hopes up."

"Don't worry, boss, I have them all the way up." She wiggles her eyebrows. "I get to meet her."

"Don't get any ideas. She's off-limits."

"Ha! I knew it," she says, smiling. "You're interested in her.

The way you protect her is so barbaric. I love it! That is exactly what she needs."

"What is that?"

"A ruthless motherfucker like you. That woman means more to you than anyone, doesn't she?"

I stay silent, not answering her because I'm not sure what I feel for Aura right now. I know that I have to protect her. I have to be there for her. I haven't because I'm afraid. I'm afraid of falling for her all over again.

Chapter 37

Aura

"Chocolate milk, please."

I'm in the kitchen getting LJ a snack before he washes up and heads to bed.

"One chocolate milk coming right up."

"Yesss," he says excitedly. "Chocolate milk is the best."

I smile because I loved chocolate milk when I was a kid. At least he got that from me.

I'm trying to reach over and grab the chocolate powder from the cabinet when I hear the door open and the beep from the alarm being disarmed.

I look down and realize I'm wearing boy shorts and a tank top. Shit. Not the clothes I should wear in case I have company. Camila is fast asleep in her room.

The only person who would have the code is the security guys Kalum has on detail or Kalum himself.

We hear the door close, the lock turn, then footsteps before Kalum's massive body comes into view.

"Kalum?"

"Jeez, the guy is huge," LJ whispers, his eyes going wide.

I grin. He is huge.

My eyes wander appreciatively over his tall frame. His bulging biceps strain his soft cotton T-shirt. He's wearing sweats slung low on his hips with sneakers, reminding me of when we were back in high school.

"Hi," he greets us, but his gaze focuses on LJ.

Like he needs his approval, and it's kind of cute.

"Hi, Mr. St. Claire," LJ says in his little voice.

"Please... call me Kalum."

"Okay, Kalum." LJ's gaze travels up to Kalum's face. "How did you get to be so tall?"

"I don't know. I just grew," he says with a smile.

"I want to be tall, but I'm not sure if I will because Mommy is really short, and Daddy was not tall like you."

"He was tall enough," Kalum says.

"Yeah, but not like you. I want to be really tall, so I can help Mommy grab the chocolate powder from the cabinet."

I blush because I am short. I need a stool or small ladder to reach for things.

"She's having trouble, huh?"

"Yep."

"I can fix that."

Kalum watches me from across the island and looks behind me with the cabinet door open and the chocolate powder on the top shelf. I look over at the couch for the blanket I leave there when we watch movies.

When I spot it neatly folded in the corner, I quickly move over to the other side and grab it, wrapping it around my body for modesty.

I can feel his gaze tracking my movements. Flutters erupt in my lower belly, and my spine tingles. Goose bumps rise on the back of my thighs where I feel exposed at how short my boy shorts are. My ass cheeks are practically hanging out.

"I'm sorry. I didn't know you would be stopping by," I tell him, pulling the blanket to cover my backside.

He clears his throat. "I'm staying."

I quirk a brow in surprise. "Staying? Don't you have work? A girlfriend?"

"I'm staying," he repeats. "I do have work, I own a helicopter, and no, I do not have a girlfriend. I was seeing someone, but I ended it."

"Oh... I'm sorry. Um...I saw you on TV. I thought she made the one-month mark, but I guess not."

"She couldn't hold my attention for long."

"Not enough experience?"

He grins. "She had enough. She was just too clingy."

"What does clingy mean?" LJ asks.

I laugh. "When someone wants to be around you all the time."

"Then I'm clingy with you, Mommy. I love to be around you all the time."

"Me too, handsome. How about that chocolate milk?"

I walk over to the kitchen when Kalum reaches for the powder and sets it on the granite countertop, and I open the lid to prepare it for both of us.

I look over at Kalum. "Would you like some?" I ask softly.

"Yes," he says, sweeping his gaze over me.

I make three cups of chocolate milk, and we sit in silence as we drink. Once LJ is done, he jumps off to brush his teeth and head for bed.

"Do you need me to tuck you in?"

"Nope, I got my headphones," he says and runs off.

Kalum raises a brow. "Headphones?"

I smile. "When I was pregnant with LJ," I explain, "Lane drove me to the house he bought for us after I got off work."

"You worked while you were pregnant with LJ?"

"Long story," I say, waving my hand. "Anyway, he picked me up in his car. The exhaust and engine were loud but would vibrate with a deep hum inside the cabin. He was opening the gate, and when the car moved forward in first gear, the engine caused the seat to vibrate like a massage chair. It was the first time I felt LJ move in my belly. It was the craziest feeling to feel him like that for the first time. It was the sound of the engine that did it. Now, every time he has trouble sleeping or winding down, he needs to hear it."

"Hear it?"

"The engine. The sound of the exhaust. It makes him go to sleep. It calms him. Like it did for his father. I don't have the car, so I recorded Lane's car, and he listens to it on his iPad through his headphones almost every night."

"Wow. That is crazy, but I get it."

I wash the cups in the sink, and he's silent, watching me.

"I can sleep in the other room, and you can have the main bedroom," I offer.

It's his house, and he has been generous. It's the least I can do.

"That is unnecessary. But I need to talk to you."

I stiffen. "About?"

Does he want us to leave? Shit, I didn't think about that. I have to check how much I have saved already. I need to start looking. I know it was only a matter of time before we would need to go.

"I can start looking and move out. It's no trouble, Kalum," I rush out.

He gives me a look like I have offended him. "I didn't come here to tell you to move," he says. "I want you to stay. You and LJ don't have to move anywhere. This is your home."

"I appreciate your help with my situation, but this isn't my home. It's your home or your family's home."

"I bought it for you, Aura. For you and LJ."

I pause, looking around the house like I'm seeing it for the first time. My eyes take in the grandeur of the home. A home I feel comfortable in.

"Why?" I ask.

"Because you and LJ didn't like my apartment. You were right. My apartment sucks if you think about it." His gaze travels over the kitchen, and he grins. "Not a place to make good-tasting chocolate milk at night."

I grab my hair and twist it up in a messy bun. "Why? You didn't have to do that. You have no obligation to us whatsoever."

"I wanted to. It's my money, and if I want to spend it buying you a house so you and LJ can feel comfortable, then that's what I'll do. I don't want to fight with you. I want to help you."

"Okay."

" I heard that you're working, and why haven't you used the card I left you?"

I lower my gaze and shrug. "I felt bad that you were paying for everything. It was the least I could do."

"You don't have to work. You have enough—"

"It's not my money," I interject. "All he wanted was for his son to keep his legacy alive. His vision. The name he built for himself."

I hate that people keep telling me that. The money Lane left me was for his son, and it's not mine. I hate having to repeat myself. No one fucking gets it. Nothing he left is mine. If I were to touch it, I would be sacrificing LJ's future. I'm the keeper he trusted to carry out his dying wish.

"You know that's not true. He loved you, Aura."

"He loved his dream more. He can write me a letter telling me otherwise, but I know the truth. I was just there to help him carry it out. I'm a fucking target for his family now. They want to prove a point, and I know they want to make it through me."

He sits on the couch and leans forward, his elbows resting on his thighs. I glance at his wrist, and that's when I see the bracelet I made him all those years ago. He's wearing it. You almost can't see it with the tattoos inked all over his skin, but it's there.

I take a seat next to him but keep a respectable distance. With the pad of my finger, I run it over the braided thread. A surge of energy shoots up my arm. His head tilts, and he turns his wrist, letting me touch it. He laces his fingers through mine.

Our eyes meet. "I won't let them take anything away from you, Aura. It's not theirs to take. If you don't want to touch the money he left, then let me help you."

"How is it any different if I take money from you? You can't save me, Kalum. I have no problem working and paying bills like a normal single parent."

He shakes his head. "Let me help you, Aura. Please... I can help you. I can make them go away, and they will never bother you again."

"How?"

How is he going to do that? They will come at me with everything they have. His parents and Lane's are friends. They're worse than the Turners. They will do whatever it takes to make sure I disappear.

"You let me worry about that."

"Your parents aren't any better, Kalum. I'll not just have his family but yours against me too."

His jaw clenches. He levels me with a hard stare. "My parents are the least of your worries. I'll take care of the rest, but you need to trust me, Aura. You think you can do that?"

What choice do I have? Exie is my best friend, but she can

only do so much. She's a Turner. She's tied up taking over the family business.

"Okay."

"Good," he says, relieved. "Now, let's try to get some sleep."

We get little sleep. We stayed up all night catching up on all the things he did since I left. How he played football in college but refused to go pro. How he was able to get tattoos when he was seventeen when he vacationed in Hawaii with his parents. Cason's decision to branch out and build his empire in the private security world.

It was like seeing Kalum in a new light. A friendly light. No animosity. No judgment. It was like we were best friends catching up on old times. In reality, we were getting to know each other. It makes it hard not to like him more than a friend. It makes it harder not to remember how he made me feel in his arms.

Chapter 38

Kalum

"How was your night in your new home?" Janine asks when I walk out of the boardroom.

I had a meeting with the developers, and they want to have dinner.

"Good. I need you to get Aura on the phone in my office."

I need to ask her to go out with me tonight. It has me on edge. I hope she'll agree. I don't want to take anyone else but her.

"This doesn't have to do with you needing a date for tonight's dinner, does it?" she asks curiously.

"It does," I tell her as I walk in my office. "Get her on the phone."

"Are you going to ask her out on a date?"

"It's not a date. I just need someone to go with. You annoy me enough at work, so I can't deal with you at dinner, too. It will raise questions, and then people will think there is more between us."

"In that case, I'm on your side and will do whatever is necessary to get her to agree."

She sets the phone on speaker and dials Aura's number. It begins to ring, and I look at Janine with raised brows.

"What?" she asks.

"You can go now," I say, waving her off.

"Alright. Alright, I'll leave, but tell me if she says yes."

"Hello." Aura's voice fills the room, and my cock strains in my pants.

Fuck. Everything about this woman does it for me. Even her voice turns me on.

"Hi," I greet her.

"Hi."

I'm nervous as fuck. For the first time in my life, I'm worried that a woman will turn me down when I ask her on a date.

I clear my throat. "Um... how is LJ doing?"

"He just finished having lunch. How is your day going so far?"

"Good." I pause. "Listen, I wanted to ask if you have plans tonight."

She pauses. My hands begin to sweat. "No, just finishing a couple of bracelets. I have some orders I have to fulfill."

I slide the mouse on my computer and open the window to Aura's website. I've bought all her bracelets since high school. All of them. I know it makes me a creep, a stalker, or even a weirdo, but they sell out fast. I started buying them all when I could. I have cases of them. They're all made by hand. Her hand.

"Oh... um... I was hoping you would go to dinner with me tonight. It's a business dinner... with clients."

Silence.

More silence.

I check the screen to see if she hung up. "Aura?"

"Yes, I'm here. Um... I would love to, Kalum, but the truth is... I don't have anything to wear."

"That's not a problem. I can have someone pick you up and take you shopping. Of course it will be on me."

"I can't let you spend money on buying me clothes."

"Aura?"

"Yes, Kalum."

"Please do this for me. I know it's last minute, but I don't trust anyone else to go with me."

I tap my fingers on the desk. I'm sweating and almost to the point of begging. The anticipation of getting her to agree is killing me.

"Okay, I'll go."

I fist-pump the air like a five-year-old who got what he wanted for Christmas.

"I'll have my assistant pick you up within the hour. Oh... and don't worry about LJ. I'll have Camila watch him and send over new toys he can play with. We'll be back late."

"Okay."

Chapter 39

Aura

He wants to take me out to a business dinner. I'm nervous. I call Exie because I have no one else I can talk to about this. I feel excited and guilty, all at the same time.

"Yes, sis?"

"I have a problem."

"What is it?" she says in a serious tone. "Who do I need to get rid of?"

I laugh. "Nothing like that. I have enough trouble with your parents."

"I'm sorry, Aura. My brother didn't think things through. I don't agree with them, and if you need anything, I'll send you whatever you need."

"I know you're stuck in a bad place. I appreciate the offer to help me, but we're good."

"How is the Kalum situation going? Is he still hiding you away in the Hamptons?"

"Yes. I got a job."

"Fuck. Why?" she whines.

"Independence."

"My brother would kill me if he knew I allowed this shit. Come on, Aura." She moans. "You know he would be upset about you getting a job while taking care of LJ."

"I like it, Exie. But that's not why I'm calling. Kalum asked me to go with him to a business dinner with his associates. I agreed, but I have no idea what to wear. He's sending someone to pick me up and take me shopping.

She snorts. "It took him long enough."

"What do you mean?"

"Come on, Aura. You know how Kalum felt about you since you left."

I frown. "That was a long time ago, Exie. He's doing this for Lane for whatever reason."

"Yeah, right. Keep telling yourself that, but be careful, Aura. I don't want you getting hurt. Sometimes I think my brother is crazy for asking Kalum for his help, but I get it."

"Get what?"

I don't know what she means. I'm confused about the whole dynamic between Kalum and Lane.

"It was his way of making sure you were taken care of by a man who would do anything to make that happen. It was no secret Kalum was heartbroken when you left. He was closed off, and if anyone mentioned your name, he would lose his shit."

"Why? He hated the fact that his parents brought me to his home."

She blows out a puff of air through her mouth, making me pull the phone slightly away from my ear. "Do you remember when you were a little girl in school, and you saw a little kid in class pick on the same girl all the time? You know... pulled her hair, tripped her, or stuck gum in her hair so everyone would laugh at her? What would our mothers tell us when we would ask why?"

"He secretly liked the girl he was tormenting."

"Exactly. Kalum liked you since the first day he laid eyes on you. I think he fell for you."

"He would have said something, Exie. He always told me he didn't want a relationship and that he was a no-strings type of guy. He says I wasn't his type."

"Look, I know it has been about a year since Lane died, but I want you to have an open mind here. You deserve to be happy. You need to find out what you want instead of feeling stuck behind someone else's dreams. You stood by my brother and supported him with everything. You forgave him when you thought he left you pregnant and alone. He was there for you when you had no one."

My eyes fill with tears because it's hard to let go of someone who was there when no one cared. I gave him my heart. "I love him, Exie. I love Lane," I choke out through my tears.

"I know. And trust me, it's hard for me to tell you this. As his sister, I want to tell you hell no, but as your best friend, I need to tell you yes. You'll always love Lane, and you gave him the best part of you already, but he's gone, Aura. He isn't here to help you pick up the pieces. Kalum will be the barrier against my family and their righteous shit. He's willing, and I think my brother was right."

"Right about what?" I sniff.

"He knew, Aura." She takes a deep sigh. "Lane knew Kalum was in love with you before you fell in love with him. I guess he thought if something happened to him, he would trust Kalum to do the right thing. They were friends before, Aura. Before you. Do you remember when you told me about the lake?

"Yes," I say, my voice trembling with emotion.

"Kalum was in love with you, Aura. Everyone knew it. The way that boy looked at you... anyone could see it. I did, but I was on my brother's side because my brother fell in love with you too."

My heart beats wildly inside my chest. How could I have missed it? Why didn't he say anything? The phone calls. The bears he left in my room. The ones I wanted at the fair. The memory of his kiss. The way he touched me and then his parents forcing me to leave.

"I understand."

"His parents did everything possible to get rid of you because they knew, Aura. They knew that Kalum would choose you, and he would always choose you."

"Unless I chose differently. I chose Lane."

"Yes," she admits. "You chose Lane, but now things are different. I don't know what will happen or how Kalum feels now after all this time, but what you need to focus on is you and what you want. What is best for LJ, and I know you'll do what feels right. I can't make my parents back off, but I can tell my best friend and mother to my nephew to be happy and fuck what everyone else thinks."

She's telling me to take Kalum's offer for help and not feel guilty. The most he can offer me is friendship after everything. There is no way he feels the same way he felt back then. I got married, fell in love, and had a child. I chose to be with Lane, and I have no regrets. Lane gave me a family and a home. His dying wish was for me to be happy.

I tell Exie we should meet in New York later in the week so she can see LJ.

The doorbell rings, followed by a knock on the door. It must be the person Kalum sent to pick me up because security let them through.

I open the door and see a tall brunette with the most expressive green eyes staring back at me. Her mouth curves in a grin as she sweeps me from head to toe.

"You must be Aura. I'm Janine, Mr. St. Claire's personal assistant and secretary."

I give her a smile. "Yes. Kalum said I should be expecting you to help me pick out a dress for tonight."

"Not just any dress. *The* dress," she says enthusiastically.

"I hope it's not too expensive."

She walks in and smiles. "Honey, that man wants to buy you whatever you want. He has never given me a limit when it comes to you, and I can blow money like the wind."

Camila comes inside from the patio area with LJ in tow and beams when she spots Janine. "Hello, dear. Have you come to whisk Aura away to make her beautiful for her date tonight with Kalum?"

I shake my head, alarmed. "Oh... it's not a date. I'm just doing Kalum a favor."

Janine acts like she doesn't hear me. "It's a date," she says to Camila, ignoring what I just said.

Camila smiles like me going on a date with Kalum is normal. "We'll be fine while you're gone. I have a whole night planned with LJ. Kalum told me you guys would be out until late. He'll be just fine with you gone. Right, sweetie?"

"Yep, we have a whole day planned, and Mommy can go out and have some fun. She's always working."

I caress his handsome little face. "Oh honey, I'm just trying to save money."

Janine raises her brows. "You don't have to. Kalum doesn't want you to worry about a thing."

Crossing my arms over my simple black T-shirt, I sigh. "I know, but I don't like to take advantage of his hospitality."

She snorts and waves her hand toward the front door. "Come on before my mouth gets the best of me in front of LJ."

Henry drives us out to the city in the Rolls, with security trailing us in a black Maybach.

"So is there a particular designer you like?" Janine asks, scrolling through her phone.

I shake my head, not being able to remember the ones on the clothes Exie sent me. "I'm not familiar with too many, except the ones my best friend would get me. I hate overspending. My husband was never frugal with me or LJ. I guess I felt guilty having been brought up with parents who clipped coupons. I didn't see the point of spending five thousand dollars for a handbag when you could get one in a department store for twenty-four ninety-nine."

"You're entirely too good for Kalum. I can see why he cares for you so much." She looks up from her phone. "You're so genuine."

Cares for me?

This is a small favor I agreed to do for Kalum. There's no way Kalum still has feelings for me anymore.

I did fall in love with him. That night I spent crying in the diner when Lane picked me up off the street, I poured my heart out to him. How it hurt to be kicked out of Kalum's parents' house. My parents' death. I didn't tell Lane how I felt about Kalum. I couldn't. Kalum made me forget about everything when I was with him. You can't put a feeling like that into words and expect someone to understand. There was nothing to deny or regret. Kalum was my first love.

I was heartbroken on my birthday. I get he called me after, but there was nothing to say. There was no way I could ask him to give up his future for me and go against his parents.

Lane understood me. In Lane's eyes, I was not the leech Lane's mother painted me out to be. She said I was a parasite. I'll never forget his father's words when he got on the phone. *"She's not worthy of the Turner name, Lane. All she did was trap you by getting pregnant."*

His father's words sliced into me like a knife, but I acted like I didn't hear them on the phone. I remember Lane was quick to end the call, but the damage was done.

I knew to be discreet and try to make my own money from knitting my bracelets. I never asked for anything or went shopping. I felt ashamed. I couldn't provide for LJ and me on my own. My fear was for him to think I trapped him. That one day he would change his mind and believe them.

When he asked me if I wanted something, I said no. Maybe he sensed it, or maybe he didn't, but I would never know because he never pushed. He left every morning and returned later in the evening. Every. Single. Day.

I never complained or told him he was spending too much time at the shop. When I asked for him to go to the park or zoo with Lane, he always said he was busy. I understood. He was working and providing for us, and what I made selling my paltry bracelets would never amount to what Lane made money-wise.

I stare out the car's window as it makes its way into the city.

"Are you okay?" Janine asks.

I turn to Janine and give her a smile. "I'm sorry. I was just wondering if we really have to buy a designer dress? It can't be from a secondhand store or maybe a department store? They really have nice things if you look."

Janine looks at me like I grew a second head. "Um... I don't think—" She pauses. "Look, there is nothing wrong with buying something from those places, but it's a little more upscale where Kalum goes to take his high-profile clients. I'm thinking Balmain would look great on you since you're so petite."

The car stops in front of Saks Fifth Avenue in Manhattan. Security opens the door, and we are escorted inside. Janine walks ahead. My eyes widen at all the handbags from each designer with security tags. We reach the elevators; security holds the elevator doors, and we go up to the women's clothing floor.

"Janine." An older woman walks up and kisses each of her cheeks. "It's good to see you."

"Hey, doll. I have come at Mr. St. Claire's request for his lady," she announces.

"Oh, I'm no—"

The older lady studies me and smiles.

"So you're Kalum's lady." Her gaze sweeps me from head to toe. "Yes... I can see it. You're breathtaking, my dear."

"I was thinking Balmain for tonight. Baroque jacquard dress, short, tight, high neck with a double strap sandal, black and gold."

The woman's eyes light up. "Oh... yes, I have the new collection, and it will look perfect on her. Chic, classy, but very sexy. Her legs will look like they go on forever." She walks to the Balmain section on the floor. "I have to be careful with you, Janine. You might take my job," she teases.

"And give up my good job with Mr. Sensitive and Conde-scending? Never," Janine says playfully.

"He's that bad, huh?" I chime in.

"Yes, but he's nice and reasonable when it comes to you for some reason. It's like he can't say no."

"We're just old friends."

"I think he wants to be more than friends, but I don't want to pry into your personal relationship." She stops at a rack of dresses. "Oh, wait. Maybe I do. I love a good love story. Even if I prefer women myself. Either way, love is love."

I like Janine and her craziness. She's a great assistant to Kalum. She has a way of making sense while keeping you on your toes.

Chapter 40

Kalum

I wait for her to be dropped off at the front of the restaurant. My clients are already inside, seated at the table, but I'm dying to see her first. To walk in with her by my side and take her to dinner. My hands shake. The Rolls pulls up with Cason's men trailing.

I wave them off when I step out. I want to see her first.

Janine texted me a few minutes ago with two words. *You're welcome.* Whatever that means.

When the car stops in front of the exclusive restaurant, cameras flash in rapid succession when I open the door. One long slender leg with golden skin slides out. My breath catches in my throat when Aura, with her silky straight brown hair with a hint of red, slides her slender hand into mine, and I help her out. Her makeup is perfectly applied in nude shades, and I swear, I stopped breathing for a second.

I ignore the camera flashes behind me as my eyes rake over her. She looks sexy from the designer knitted dress to the delicate nail polish on her pretty toes. She looks like a model from the cover of *Vogue*.

When I pull her to my chest, I close my eyes briefly so I can smell the flowery scent of her perfume. I'm almost tempted to ditch the dinner and place her back in the car. I fight the urge to take her back to my apartment and peel that dress off while I taste every inch of her skin. I want her all to myself.

"Do I look okay?" she asks in a soft voice.

"You look perfect. You look gorgeous, Aura. Thank you for coming with me."

She gives me a white-toothed smile. Her straight white teeth against her lips make my pulse beat uncontrollably. I give her my arm, and we walk inside the restaurant.

We make it to the table where both men are seated. They stand when they see me approach with Aura.

"Hello, gentlemen. Aura, these are my business associates." I point at the man to my left. "This is Mike Ryder." And then I point at the man seated next to him. "And this is Frank Ipstein. I have an upcoming project in a partnership. They're building a tall skyscraper here in New York that I am funding."

"Hello," she says with a nervous smile.

I don't like the way Mike looks at her. A little too hard for my taste, but I let it slide. This time. I give him a hard stare when I catch his gaze. He wipes his brow nervously. Frank smiles at us both but looks away and takes his seat after Mike.

I hold out Aura's chair beside me.

When Mike takes his seat, he glances at Aura once again when she scans the menu. I talk about our business to avoid reaching over and strangling him. I don't know why, but when I see anyone who looks at her like they're fucking her with their eyes, I want to commit murder.

After we agree on the date when construction will commence, Mike clears his throat. "So Aura. How is it that you know Kalum?"

She lowers the menu. "Oh, we're old friends."

I don't miss the gleam in Mike's eyes at her answer. He licks his lips like she's a steak on the menu. I clench my teeth so hard they're about to snap off. We are old friends, but I don't like the way that sounds.

Because it means she's available. She isn't your girl. Her husband is dead, and she can talk to or date whoever she wants. Eventually.

She picks up the menu and looks at it for a while longer and then sets it down. She gives me a small grin. Then she innocently bites her lip. Mike's eyes follow the movement, then dip lower, leering at her chest. When he finally looks up, her lips form a grim line.

Fucking hell.

How much do I care about this deal? I wipe my mouth with my hand like I have something on my face, watching Mike.

Frank looks nervous. Mike glances at me. He must read my expression because he motions for the server.

The server quickly approaches. "Yes...what would you like to order?"

"I'll have the Chilean sea bass," Mike says.

"I'll have the filet with scallops," Frank says next.

The server looks at Aura. "I'll have..." She stalls and then continues, faltering momentarily. "A house salad with water... please."

I frown and notice it's the cheapest item on the menu. She drops the menu and places her hand on her lap and looks around the room.

Mike leans close. "You know... you can order whatever you like. I'll be more than happy to pay the bill. Maybe we could go somewhere after dinner," he says, giving her a wink.

Fuck it.

I dismiss the server and look Mike dead in the eyes. He

leans back in his chair and seems panicked by my expression. He knows why.

"Look at her one more time," I say through clenched teeth. "And I swear, I'll take this fork and stab your eyes out. If you so much as talk to her, I'll end you." I reach over the table like a madman in a movie, grip him by the throat, and squeeze his pathetic excuse of a neck.

The utensils and empty glasses rattle on the table. People seated at the other tables gasp with wide eyes, but I don't care. He makes a funny noise, trying to get air inside his lungs. His eyes bulge out his pathetic excuse of a face.

"Please, Kalum. Let him go," Frank pleads.

I let him go. Mike's hands grip his neck in a coughing fit.

"Are you insane?" he chokes out, gasping for breath like a fish out of water.

"When it comes to her... I am." I lean close. "And for the record, she's mine. Whatever deal we had is off." I point the fork in his face. "Go ahead, look at her again," I taunt. "I'll fork your fucking eyes out," I say with a raised voice. "Do you understand me?"

"Yes." He nods. "I-I'm sorry."

"Fuck you," I say, and then to Frank, "The deal is off." I make sure he's aware that I'll never do business with him.

"Please, Kalum. He's sorry," Frank says apologetically.

"No," I snap.

I look at Aura, and she's wringing her hands. I toss her dinner napkin on the table and pick up her small Balmain designer bag.

"Let's go, sweetheart. I don't want you in front of this asshole."

I'm sure I'll be on the news, but I don't care. I would never let anyone disrespect her like that. Ever.

"I'm sorry," she says once we're in the car. "I shouldn't have come."

"I wanted you to come."

"But your business deal?"

"There will be other ones. I have other deals lined up, and you're more important to me than any business deal, Aura. That man was wrong and disrespectful. He made you feel uncomfortable, and I won't allow it. Fuck him." Her legs are crossed, showing smooth skin. Her dress is so short I can see a hint of her black lace thong between her legs, making my mouth water. "Are you hungry?"

"Yes."

"What would you like to eat?"

She tilts her head to the side and smiles. "I would like a hot dog."

I chuckle, shifting in my seat. "A hot dog?"

"Yes...with mustard and ketchup."

The thought of a hot dog shaped like a penis going inside her mouth has me wanting to bust out of my pants. I motion for Henry to stop at a hot dog stand on the corner.

I get out of the car and buy us both one. Her eyes light up, and it makes me want to get her all the hot dogs she wants.

I slide in the car with our hot dogs and Cokes. "You're the best," she says.

I smile at her praise and hand her the food. I nod at Henry, already instructing him to head toward my apartment.

"I hope you don't mind finishing the rest of our evening at my place."

She shrugs, eating her hot dog. Her tongue licks her lips, and I squirm in my seat. I'm trying to adjust my raging hard-on without freaking her out and ruining the moment. I find a comfortable spot for my cock in my pants while Henry drives us to my apartment, hoping she doesn't notice.

Chapter 41

Aura

The elevator doors open to Kalum's apartment. I'm still a little nervous about what happened at the restaurant with Mike and Frank. It isn't the first time a man has looked at me like I'm cattle, but the way Kalum grabbed him scared me. I know Kalum would never hurt me, but the way he looked at Mike, it looked like he would kill him. I felt horrible for putting Kalum in that position. His business deal was ruined because of me.

"I'm sorry about tonight," I say.

He waves his hand. "It's nothing."

"It's something. You lost money because of me."

He turns around. "Nothing is worth more than someone disrespecting you. Not to me."

My heart beats frantically with every passing second he looks at me that way. I should feel ashamed of the heat between my legs. For wanting him. It's wrong, but my body is saying it's right. My head is muddled, and I can't think.

"Aura?"

"Yes, Kalum."

"Can I kiss you?" My head lifts, and the confusion melts away when I see the desire in his eyes. His black dress shirt is open at the throat, the swirl of colors of his tattoos peeking out, taunting me. "I want to kiss you. I need to kiss you, Aura. Just a kiss."

I close my eyes, relieved that I threw away the hot dog wrapper and can of Coke before entering the elevator.

He moves forward in a rush, lifting me. Everything is happening so fast. My legs wrap around his waist and my arms around his neck. He walks me to the huge window overlooking the city and pushes me against the smooth glass. My ass feels the cold surface underneath. The short dress bunches at my waist. I feel his hard length between my legs.

His lips caress mine, brushing gently at first. Then his tongue licks the seam, parting them slowly, and I remember. Our first kiss. The way my heart beat to the rhythm of his lost in his embrace. *Oh God. Please forgive me.* I whimper when he slides his tongue inside my mouth. His hands spread wide on my outer thighs, holding me to him.

He slides them higher. The thin lace of my panties is the only barrier between the hard ridge of his cock and the lips of my pussy.

My fingers slide into his hair, and he deepens the kiss, his tongue reacquainting itself with the taste of my mouth releasing and fusing together. A jolt of electricity flows through my body down to my core. I'm wet, rubbing shamelessly over the head of his cock. He pushes into me, letting me feel what my pussy craves.

He breaks the kiss, sliding his tongue down my neck and then back up over my chin to my lips.

"Kalum?" I say breathlessly.

"Yes, baby," he says before catching my bottom lip with his teeth.

I pull back, licking the spot where his teeth were, arching my neck, grinding my hips. "Don't stop."

"Fuck... Aura," he groans.

"Promise me."

He carries me to his bedroom and lays me on his bed. I want him. I want to know what being with him would have been like. He was almost my first everything. I loved Kalum. If he had uttered one word that told me he wanted me, I would have given my heart and soul to him on a platter.

My legs are wrapped around his waist. He looks down at my black lace panties and leans back, then slides his fingers into the sides by my hips and pulls them down my thighs over my heels. He slides his hand under me and slides the zipper down of the minidress, releasing the fabric from my chest down my arms.

When he peels it down my legs, I'm left in only my heels. He raises himself on his elbows and lowers his gaze down my body, lingering between my open thighs, making a wet spot on his white sheets.

"You're beautiful," he whispers.

My heart soars at his praise. He lowers his head between my thighs, slides his tongue from the bottom of my slit over my clit, trailing up my torso, and sucks each nipple.

"Oh God," I breathe.

"Do you know how beautiful you are, Aura?" he whispers against my skin.

He kisses up my neck until he reaches my mouth in a scorching kiss. I love that he's fully clothed, and I'm only in my heels, but I want to feel his skin on mine.

His arms strain against the fabric of his dress shirt. My hands land on his muscled chest and rip his shirt open. The buttons scatter like tiny beads, hitting the pristine marble on the floor. Anyone from the building across can see us from the large window in his bedroom. I turn my head, the city lights casting shadows across the walls. He follows the path of my gaze and reaches to grab the remote on the side of his bed. He presses a button on the screen, the glass darkens, and then "Dusk Till Dawn" by ZAYN begins to play softly.

"They can't see," he says softly as the back of his fingers slide down my cheek.

My heart beats like a drum. A mantra before a ritual. He removes his shirt. My hands slide over every inch of his hot skin down to the rippling of his ab muscles, tracing the ink from his tattoos under my fingers. I lean forward, placing small kisses on his chest and up his neck, breathing in the scent of his skin.

He removes his pants and boxers in one swift movement. He cups my cheek with one hand and fists his cock in the other. His beautiful body hovers over mine. His brows pinch in concentration like he's holding himself back. His arms bulge. Tremors rake through his body.

"Fuck," he mutters under his breath and then looks up. "You're like a fantasy come true."

His breaths come out faster with each stroke of his cock over my entrance. I grind my hips, seeking more, but he holds my gaze. His brown eyes hold mine like a part in a movie he doesn't want to miss.

"Kalum, please," I beg.

He laughs through his nose, and his gaze dips. "Patience. I have wanted you like this for a very, very long time."

After the last word leaves his lips, he pushes inside me. My back arches. A hiss escapes his lips. He stretches me inch by inch until he's deep.

"Fuck... you feel so good, baby."

I feel so full.

His large muscles flex as he begins to thrust in deep, measured strokes. His gaze holds mine as he moves.

"I love the way your pussy grips my cock, Aura."

He leans close, and I swear my heart is about to pop out of my chest. He pulls out and slides me effortlessly to the edge of the bed, flipping me over. He turns his head to the side, where an enormous mirror is on the left wall. I steady myself since I still have my heels. He grabs my waist firmly. I can see the reflection of us in the mirror and then feel the tip of his cock from behind my entrance. "Look at how beautiful you look when I take your wet pussy from behind," he says with his cock at my entrance. "I'm going to come so deep inside you... so deep."

He slides in deep, and I gasp when he starts fucking me. He grabs my breast with one hand and teases my nipples until they're red and hard.

"Kalum," I moan.

His hands cup my ass, spreading me wide and watching me through the mirror. I whimper when he angles his body slightly to the side, hitting me deep. My climax builds hard and fast.

"Do you know what you do to me, Aura?"

"More, Kalum. I want more."

"I want you, Aura. I want you so fucking much."

His thrusts are deep and fast, his hips wild as he takes me hard in long strokes.

My nails dig into the mattress.

My back arches.

I scream. "I'm coming! Oh God... I'm coming!"

His hands grip my hips like in a vise, and I know I'll wear his marks on my skin. He pumps into me while I'm riding the wave of my orgasm. His skin slaps against mine.

"Fuck," he growls. "This is mine... all mine."

I feel my walls grip his thick cock, and the heat of his cum spills deep inside me.

We stay like that for a minute. Neither of us moves. His cock remains seated deep inside me, twitching.

He pulls out slowly. My legs shake, and I place my hands on the mattress to keep me from collapsing.

He pulls the blanket, turns me around, and slowly removes my heels. When he's done, he lifts me and places my head on his pillow. I gasp when he holds my hands above my head with one hand and opens my thighs with his other hand, spreading me wide.

"Kalum," I call out.

He slides into me again, and we both groan at how good it feels. I'm wet, cum dripping between my thighs, our bodies fused together, moving as one until we reach another release as powerful as the first.

"I'm making a mess," I say as the trickle of cum drips under me.

"We're both making a mess. Don't worry, I'll tell the cleaning lady it was you. If not, she'll think I'm a dirty little boy who jerks off." He gives me a kiss. "It will be our little secret, being that you're the only woman I've ever had in my bed in this apartment."

I bite my lip to keep from smiling. "Keep doing that, Miss Rayne, and I'll have to bite the other side of that sexy lip of yours." His lips dip to my neck, biting gently. "I'm going to have to mark you here." He smiles against my skin, kissing every spot he nibbles. "And here."

I giggle and squirm under him. "I bite my lip a lot. It's a quirk I've had since I was little."

He kisses the tops of my breasts. "Let's see what other quirks you have," he says huskily.

I'm so screwed.

He feels amazing when he slides deep inside me, making me come for the third time and fourth time. He makes love to me for hours until we are both spent. I don't think I've ever come so many times in my entire life. He kisses and caresses every inch of me. I don't think there is a spot left on my body he hasn't explored. A spot he hasn't touched. I'm drowning in the ocean of him.

Chapter 42

Kalum

"Like this?" I ask LJ.

"Yep. The pancakes bubble, and you flip it when it gets crispy on the edges."

I flip the pancake, and then voilà. It flops without breaking. His little voice is adorable. He's been giving me step-by-step instructions on how his mom makes him pancakes in the morning.

"Got it."

"You see?" His eyes light up. "You did it. You have to make sure it isn't mushy, or it will break and taste horrible," he says with a grimace on the last part, making a funny face.

"How did you get so smart?" I ask him.

LJ is smart for his age. He explains things. He analyzes them in a way that makes a grown-up understand them better.

"That's easy. I pay attention to Mommy. She's smart and pretty." He angles his head. "Do you think my mommy is smart and pretty?"

"I do."

"My grandma and grandpa don't like my mom very much.

They said mean things about her. When my daddy wasn't paying attention, she would cry. They're not very nice, but my Auntie Exie is the best."

I lean on the counter after I place the pancake on the plate and slide it over to him after shutting off the burner on the stove.

"Don't worry. I'll make sure your mommy never cries again unless it's because she's happy."

LJ takes a piece of pancake inside his mouth with gusto. He chews and scrunches his forehead in thought.

"Promise?" he says between bites.

"You have my word."

He nods once. "Okay, Kalum." He forks another piece and swallows. "I trust you."

I laugh, and then I hear the doorbell ring. My phone goes off. It's a text from security.

> Security: You have a visitor. A Miss Turner. She says she's related to Miss Rayne.

> Kalum: It's fine. Let her in.

I walk over to open the front door, but Exie barges inside the house.

"Well, hello to you too," I say sarcastically.

Exie is rambunctious and always gave me a hard time when it came to Aura. I figured out the reason when I visited Lane the day after I saw him with Aura and his friends at the fair, and Lane admitted he was interested in Aura.

"Where is she?"

"Aunt Exie!" Lane shouts, jumping off the chair and running into her arms.

"There's my little man! Where's your momma?"

"Sleeping, but Kalum made me breakfast."

"He did?" she singsongs.

"Yep. It's good, too. He's a good listener."

"It was my first time making pancakes."

Exie rolls her eyes. "Oh please, it's not that hard."

"Actually, I couldn't have done it without LJ's help. Right, buddy?"

"Right," he beams.

"Where's my best friend?"

"In the main bedroom, last door on the right," I tell her, but her eyes meet mine before she saunters off toward the bedroom.

She knows.

Chapter 43

Aura

My eyes flutter, but I squint against the bright light of the sun from the windows. I hear the bedroom door open and then close. Then Exie's voice.

"Don't you look well-rested?"

I sit up on the bed and grip the cream-colored sheet over my naked breasts. I rub my eyes, look around, and then look at my best friend. The memory of last night floods back and guilt slowly creeps up my neck from the throbbing soreness between my legs.

"What time is it?" I say in a sleepy voice.

"Noon."

I push my hair away from my face. "Shit."

"Relax," she says and sits on the bed. "You rode the magic train, didn't you?"

I fall back on the bed. "Is it obvious?" I moan.

She snickers. "The man is shirtless, dressed in sweats in all his tatted goodness, making pancakes for my nephew, when he let me inside. Looks like he liked the magic train just as much as you did."

I look at the ceiling. "Go ahead, say it. I'm a ho. A heartless tramp."

"Was he as good as they say he is?"

"Oh my God, Exie," I whine. "How can you ask me that?"

"I'm just curious." She pats my thigh over the comforter. "Remember what I told you. It was bound to happen. It should have happened a long time ago, but it didn't. Now it did. Stop feeling bad about it."

"How can I not feel bad about it? My husband was his friend. A friend I have a child with."

"My brother is dead and left you with a big mess to clean up, I might add, and you have mourned and cried. It's time you stop crying and feeling bad for everyone else because of what they think, and yes, they were friends, but as much as I hate to say it, and he does get on my nerves"—she points toward the closed bedroom door—"that man out there has suffered in giving you up. He loved you first, Aura. This is his second chance, and I have a gut feeling he wants you to give him that chance."

I place my hands over my eyes to stop the sting. I feel guilty because of Lane. This is wrong, but my heart tells me deep down it isn't. It was sex. That's all it was. Kalum doesn't want marriage or children. I'm fine. I'm good.

I close my eyes, and the feeling inside my chest that squeezes and flutters tells me one thing I'm afraid to admit, even to myself. I'm in love with him all over again. I'm in love with Kalum St. Claire—even though there is no way he'll ever love me back the same way.

I tilt my head and look at Exie. "You're aware that his parents hate me just as much as your parents do. His parents kicked me out of their house and tried to pay me off so I'd leave quietly."

She snorts. "Yeah, I know, but he obviously gives zero fucks about what they think. To prove a point, he bought a house in the Hamptons for twenty million for you and my nephew so no one fucks with you. He also has a driver, security, and someone you trust to help you out with LJ. I'm sorry, but if that isn't a sign that he cares for you or has some deep feelings swirling in that black heart of his, then I don't know what is, but what I do know is he's been on your side through it all."

I change into simple leggings and a knitted cropped sweater and head to the kitchen with Exie trailing me. I stop short when I see Kalum on the couch watching cartoons with LJ. All the air escapes my lungs at the sight of them sprawled on the couch with LJ lying on Kalum's side like they have been doing this every day.

"Jesus, I hate to say it, but he's every single mother's dream," Exie whispers. "And you know how I feel about the way he goes through women, but he was always different with you. The way he's with LJ right now, I can't hate him even if I wanted to."

"I know. That is what makes it so hard," I whisper back.

Old feelings I thought were long buried in heartbreak are surfacing. Feelings that should have never resurfaced because I moved on with Lane.

"Hey," I say with a smile.

Kalum and LJ turn their heads at the same time and both gift me a smile. My heart squeezes in my chest. One is my first love, and the other is the spitting image of his father.

"Hi, Mommy. Did you sleep well?"

"Hey, gorgeous," Kalum greets me in a husky voice.

"Yes, baby. Mommy slept well. Have you been a good boy and been nice to Kalum for watching over you this morning?"

His eyes light up. "Yep, I even showed Kalum how you

make pancakes, and he did a great job. Now when you sleep in, he can make them for me."

Exie clears her throat. "Come on, kiddo. Let's get you cleaned up."

He gets up, fist-bumps Kalum, and follows Exie after giving me a morning hug.

"Thank you for watching him and making him breakfast. You didn't have to do that."

Kalum sits up, and my eyes trail over his ripped chest and torso. I squeeze my thighs, reminding me why I'm sore. Every ridge and curve of his muscles under taut, smooth skin brings back to life the memory of him moving inside me.

"It was my pleasure. I wanted to spend some time with him so he can feel safe and comfortable around me if you aren't around or... if you're tired."

The way he says his last words causes heat to creep up my neck. The delicious soreness between my legs is a reminder of why I'm so tired this morning.

"Thank you."

I make my way into the kitchen to make coffee and clean up any mess they have made. He gets up and stands right behind me while I prepare the Keurig. I can feel the heat of his body when he places a soft kiss on my neck. Goose bumps skate over my skin, igniting a fire between my legs. My nipples harden under the soft cotton of my bra. His fingers graze my waist, and he pulls me to his chest. I can feel his hard erection on my lower back.

"I want to be inside you every chance I get. Making you mine over... and... over," he says. "Despite the thoughts battling inside your beautiful head, just remember, you were mine first."

My heart skipped a beat, or it stopped beating, or I think he took it out of my chest. Before I can voice my inner thoughts, the front door opens and closes with the chime of the alarm. Then heels click against the wood floor. The loss of heat when Kalum steps back. The pulse drumming in my veins.

"Well, well. It all makes sense now. And I can't blame you. You could have done it without an audience, but hey, looking at you together, I get it," Janine's voice drawls.

"What the fuck are you talking about, and what brings you here, Janine?" Kalum says in an irritated tone.

My head turns, and she gives me a wink. She's obviously used to Kalum's sarcasm and condescending attitude.

"Did you really have to grab him by the neck and threaten to scoop his eyes out with a fork? I mean, you could have kicked his ass in an alley somewhere where no one was watching and made your point. The guy is threatening to sue you for assault. The only reason I believe you terminated the deal and threatened to basically kill the guy was because of her. I think...you know, the scooping of the eyes out part gave it away."

"He disrespected her and was a total creep. He kept fucking her with his eyes, and I wasn't going to sit there and take it."

"Well. He's threatening to sue you unless you move forward with funding the project."

"Fuck. No. I'll never do business with him again. He can go fuck himself, and if he wants to sue me, fine. He'll have to build his fucking building in Alaska because when I'm done with the bastard, the only thing he'll build will be made from Legos because no one is going to fund him for shit. He sat there, staring at her chest, licking his lips like a dog, and offered to pay for dinner and asked her to leave with him to fuck her."

My eyes go wide. I didn't realize how upset Kalum was about that creep trying to make a pass at me in front of him at the restaurant.

Janine holds up her hands. "Fine. I'll handle it with your lawyer."

"What happened?" Exie waltzes in with LJ.

LJ has his toy cars and runs off to the living room to play with his new track set that Kalum must have sent over yesterday.

Janine gives Exie the details about what happened last night.

Exie gives me a smirk over Janine's head.

"Stop looking at me like that," I tell her, pressing the button of the coffee machine.

"You're Exie Turner," Janine says.

Exie smiles at Janine. "In the flesh. I wonder..." She points at Kalum with her thumb. "How do you put up with him? I would have stabbed him by now."

"Trust me, you get used to him after a while. And since I'm not into men, it works out."

"Why are you two talking about me like I'm not here?" Kalum asks, looking through his phone.

"Because we can," Exie says sarcastically. "I don't work for you. I don't answer to you. I'm here because you're helping out my best friend, but I appreciate what you did at the restaurant."

Kalum rolls his eyes and shakes his head. "I did what anyone would have done in that situation. You would have done the same thing for a friend. It was wrong, and he deserved it."

A friend? That's how he sees me? I grip the handle of the fridge and close it with more force than necessary.

Hurt washes over me followed by regret. Regret for giving in to Kalum so easily. I slept with him after a night out. It wasn't even a date. He asked for a kiss, and I begged him to fuck me. The back of my eyes sting. How could I have been so stupid to think I meant anything more to Kalum than any other woman he's been with. He's a man, and like he said, he likes to fuck. I'm holding on to feelings of the past, interpreting them as something more in the heat of the moment. Last night didn't mean anything to him.

Chapter 44

Kalum

It's been two weeks since that night with Aura. I have avoided her because I don't know what to say. She has been distant ever since that day Janine scolded me about what happened at the restaurant. Mike has backed off, but I'm more nervous about what I'm about to do. A step I'm about to take with my parents. Something monumental that needs to happen for my sanity, or everything I have sacrificed will have been for nothing.

The door to my office opens, and Janine strolls in. "Your parents are in the conference room with the..." She clears her throat. "Colorful bears and the TV is on with the rest of the board members on a Zoom call. I wanted to ask..."

I lean back in my office chair, watching her fidget.

"What, Janine?"

"Why would you have ten bears, one seated in every chair, and two envelopes?"

"You'll understand at the meeting when I share the news."

"What news?"

I get up from my chair and straighten my Tom Ford suit

jacket. "You'll see. Everything has a purpose, and they will all understand mine."

We enter the boardroom, and my father is the first one to speak. "Kalum. What is the meaning of this meeting? And why do you still have these bears? If I have to look at these bears a second longe..."

I raise my hand to stop him from rambling. "Please," I say calmly and wave to the other two vacant seats. "Have a seat, Father." And turn to my mother. "Mother."

Once they're seated, I unmute the screen.

"Ladies and gentlemen, I'm ready to begin this meeting so we can make our announcement before the press release."

"Yes," they all say in unison.

I look at my parents while I hold both envelopes made out in their names.

"I have called this meeting because of an important decision that has been made by all board members regarding your futures with the company," I announce. "You have been active members and founders of this organization, but as silent holders, we have come to the conclusion that you're no longer needed as active members."

"What is the meaning of this, Kalum? Have you lost your mind?" my mother says, her face red with rage.

"Actually, I haven't lost my mind," I say carefully. "You see, I have sacrificed my life for this company, and the other board members agree. As the current CEO, I have quadrupled what both of you have generated in profits, and apparently, I have the majority share. Based on the votes of the other board members, we outvote you. We have come to the decision that you'll no longer be on the board of this company, and I am prepared to give you your remaining share, plus a bonus. You have more than enough put away for the rest of your lives, so this will not affect you financially."

"What is the point of this, Kalum? You cannot take the company away from us. We built it!" my father roars, slamming his fist on the table.

"Like I said, I'm freeing you of any obligation from the St. Claire conglomerate. Both of you are no longer needed."

I slide the white envelopes across the table. They open them, and my mother is the first to look like she'll faint. She places her hand on her chest. "One hundred thousand dollars!" she cries. "Are you out of your mind?"

I chuckle sarcastically. "You see these bears?" I point, and everyone looks at them. The board members on the screen, my parents, and Janine. "I'm going to share a story with you all about the meaning of these bears and why they're important to me. My senior year of high school, there was this girl I met in my own house, of all places. She had nowhere to go after her parents were killed in a car accident when she was seventeen. My parents took her in, wanted me to be nice and make sure she fit in because she would make a great housekeeper once she turned eighteen in three months. You know how rich people are; they take advantage of the less fortunate, but one thing that never crossed their minds was that their beloved son and heir to their company and fortune would fall in love with her. She was beautiful and had a heart made of gold. She was kind, and all she wanted was love and a normal opportunity, but the only option she was given was to be a housekeeper to a rich family and had no choice but to agree. She was top five in her class but had no money to go to college. Alone with no family.

"Once my parents found out how I really felt about her and what I planned on the day of her birthday, they decided to take matters into their own hands. Their son could not possibly be with the girl destined to be their housekeeper. In their eyes, that was not allowed. In their mind, she was good enough to clean toilets but not for their son. I tried to hide my feelings for her the best I could so no one would notice because I had the gut feeling my parents would make her suffer. She met a friend at school, and then she met her friend's brother. He was a good friend of mine. Graduated before I did but fell for her the same way I did. You would think the girl had a special spell with her smile, but that wasn't the case. She was just genuine and beautiful. Wholesome. Fun to be around. I couldn't help myself. She didn't care what my last name was or if I had money…"

The room falls silent, listening, waiting for what I say next. I look at the bears, and the memory of that night comes back. The night that I lost the girl I was madly in love with, and she didn't even know it. "I left for a football game the night before she turned eighteen. I had a surprise, you see. I had rented a cabin for the whole weekend. The night of the fair, I spent hours winning her these bears you see seated in every chair in this boardroom. It wasn't the bear she was happy to see when she woke that morning. It was the fact that *I* had won her the bears. I was the happiest guy alive that morning when I saw the delight in her eyes. I was able to impress the girl I loved by getting her these stuffed bears. But when I came home the night of the football game, I didn't want to wake her. I had no idea what my parents had done. I didn't think anything of it.

"The next morning, I found a note with the bears on her bed. My parents offered her one hundred thousand dollars to leave and never come back. They lied to her and told her that rumors in the community caused them to make the decision." My tone lowers, and I hear Janine's intake of breath. "They told her I made plans with my friends for the weekend. They said it was a good offer. What they didn't want to say was that they didn't want the community to know that their son was in love with the housekeeper. She left that night with only a suitcase to her name walking on the sidewalk. Homeless and alone. She left the money and a note wishing me well. Saying that she was thankful for my parents' hospitality and that all she wished was for me to be happy and find someone to love. Her best friend's brother found her walking on the sidewalk near the strip mall where she would go to buy groceries for my parents every week. He took her in and gave her a place to stay. She finished her school online, and I never saw her again. She must have thought the worst of me. I tried calling her to explain. To tell her that my parents didn't understand, but she never answered my calls."

"What happened?" Janine asks from behind me.

I don't tell them about the time I spoke with Lane about Aura and what my plan was. I have never told a soul about my conversation with him. Man to man, friend to friend, about a girl we both loved.

I tell them the part that wrecked me. Forcing me to let her go because I was too late. I never stood a chance with what they did. I had nothing to offer her. I was barely graduating from high school, but Lane was older than me and was already well-off. He could do for her what I couldn't.

"She fell in love with him and ended up getting married and having a child." I point at my parents with their checks in hand and both of their mouths agape. "You took her from me. Now, I'm going to take something from you. I want you to feel what it's like for someone to take something you love the most."

"You can't be serious, Kalum," my father says in disbelief. "We're your parents."

"And she was the love of my life. You wanted me to be the CEO... I'm the CEO, but on my terms, not yours."

"You have to get over it, son. She married Lane Turner."

"Because of you!" I roar. I wipe my face. "Now you know why I can't stand to look at either of you. You kicked her out like she was nothing because she didn't have the right last name. You're no different than her late husband's parents, but there is something none of you counted on, and that was how much I cared for her. Now... you all understand."

I look up at the screen. "Thank you all for attending."

"Yes, sir," they all say in unison.

"For the record, sir," Timothy says, leaning forward on his camera. "You have all of our support."

Chapter 45

Aura

The sun finishes setting on the horizon as I look at the ocean behind the house. It's getting cooler, but I need to make peace. When Lane died, his request was for his ashes to be spread out at sea. He said it was a way I could talk to him from anywhere I was. He didn't want to be buried in a cemetery. He said he wanted to be free.

I feel guilty about my feelings for Kalum and my love for Lane. The waves pound against the shoreline like a calling. Like he's listening. He said I was the lightning to his tidal wave, but all I hear is the storm of the sea.

"I have to let you go," I whisper. "I'll always love you, Lane. I'll never forget you and promise to take care of our son with everything that I am, but I love him. I think you knew I always did and always will. It doesn't mean I have to choose. I just... wanted you to know."

I talk to the wind, to the sea, and hope wherever he is, that he listens. That he understands my bleeding heart. I walk to the edge of the shore and touch the cool water from the sea. When

I turn around, Camila stands a few feet away with a blanket in her arms.

"He'll understand, my love," Camila says softly.

"I hope so."

She knows me well enough. She knows what I'm doing out here.

"You're in love with him all over again, aren't you?"

"Yes, but he doesn't love me. He's never said it, and I don't expect him to. I'm not good enough, just like I was never good enough for Lane."

"Oh, honey," she says, walking up to me. "That's not true. The problem is... you're too good for any of them. You must believe that."

Tears spring from my eyes. "I try to do the right thing, but it comes at a price. I can't keep paying that price because I'm losing myself, Camila. I can't stay here."

She wraps the blanket around my shoulders. "If that is how you feel, then go, but I'm coming with you. It's what your mother would have wanted. I promised that if anything happened to her, I would look after you. I'm not leaving you and LJ. I'll help you with him. You're not alone, Aura. I have faith in Kalum, but I understand. You cannot force someone to love you."

<hr>

"Are you ready?" Dex says as I grab my helmet and look at Lane's GT-R.

"I hope so. Are you sure I can do this, Dex?"

"He showed you how to drive the thing. He wanted you to be the only one to drive it besides LJ. I can't go against what he wanted. They want you to speak on behalf of Turner Automotive before you take it to the track to clock how fast zero to sixty and the quarter mile."

NASCAR tried to recruit Lane, but he wasn't interested. He loved Japanese imports and modifying them. Major manufacturers took notice and offered Lane millions for his built engines and how he tuned the vehicles. Anyone can make a car go fast, but can the car withstand the test of time without having issues? That's what Lane did. He built flawless engines, and every street racer enthusiast wanted their car built by Lane Turner.

"You got my music, Dex?"

"It's up on the speaker on the track, Aura. The media are televising this on the air."

I take a deep breath. *I'm doing this for Lane,* I tell myself.

I walk up to the podium, squinting at the camera flashes. I'm nervous that Lane's parents are here. They're unhappy with how much attention I'm getting for driving Lane's car on the track.

A major reporter from ESPN starts rambling off questions.

"Mrs. Turner? Please tell us what is expected of your husband's latest build. Everyone is dying to see how fast it is. We all know his record has been beaten in different circuits, but nothing is quite like a car built by Lane Turner. He builds truly impressive machines. Is it true he can modify Lamborghinis and not just Japanese imports?"

I plaster a fake smile for the camera and begin. "Thank you all for being here. My name is Aura Rayne, not Mrs. Turner. I know that sounds confusing, but according to my husband's parents and specifics with his inheritance from the Turner legacy, apart from my late husband's company in the automotive industry, I was told that I could not use the name Turner." Voices begin to rise as people look at his parents in shock and dismay. "Please. Please, I am not saying this to attack them in any way, but legally, I must not be addressed as Mrs. Turner. My name is Aura Rayne. That doesn't mean much to some because my parents were not wealthy or famous. They passed away three months before I was eighteen. I have no family except for my son and my best friend Exie and a handful of friends who really know me. The only thing I'm known for is the bracelets I sell online." I shrug my shoulders. "I'm no one special, but my late husband always made me feel like I was. He taught me to drive his cars and how to answer most of your questions. He left his legacy to his only son, LJ. Dex and Blaze"—I point in their direction—"are the backbone of Tuner Automotive and, with my help and the instructions Lane left, will carry out what he wanted."

Dex has LJ on his shoulders, cheering. Blaze smiles, and Exie gives me a thumbs-up.

I smile and wave to LJ, whose face is lit up with a smile.

"I'll take Lane's car to the track and give you his latest time, and I know deep in my heart it will be the best and fastest because it was built by him with his heart and soul. Thank you."

I leave the podium. Reporters are shouting, and cameras flash.

"Aura, where can we buy your bracelets?"

"Aura, is it true the Turners disowned you?"

"Aura, do you think his son will be just as great as his father?"

I close my eyes and head to the track where the imposing car awaits me in all its glory.

Dex wears a smile, holding the driver's door open. "Just like he taught you, Aura. You're quite the famous widow. Social media is going apeshit with you right now."

"Yeah, I guess. This is for Lane."

He hands me my helmet. "He couldn't have married a

better woman. He loved you, and you were everything to him. I know I keep saying it, but he wanted me to always remind you."

"Thanks, Dex."

I place the helmet over my head and secure it. Then I slip my fingers in the leather gloves before sliding in the cockpit of the car.

I rev the car like Lane taught me and prepare the launch mode. The engine roars with the sound of the exhaust. My heart beats uncontrollably. There are over three thousand horsepower under the hood. The screen on the car mapping is on to record the lap time. It will be quick and scary, but the cooler temperatures have the car running at its best.

I grip the steering wheel and let out a breath. *I can do this. I can do this.* I repeat in my head. "Unstoppable" by Sia blares from the speakers on the track. The roar of the car spikes my adrenaline.

The flag goes down, I press the gas, and the car shoots forward, almost jumping from the line. Adrenaline courses through my veins. Tunnel vision takes over my eyesight.

Chapter 46

Kalum

The GT-R is on the jumbotron in Times Square. A crowd in the streets stares in awe as the most gorgeous woman sits behind the wheel of the impressive car as it takes the track by storm. Fire shoots from the tail end of the exhaust. People are cheering.

"If that isn't woman empowerment, I don't know what is," Janine says from behind me.

I smile. "It is, isn't it?"

"I think I'm in love." She sighs.

I snort. "Good luck with that."

"I'm kidding. I know how you feel about her. What I want to know is, what are you going to do about it?"

I scratch my brow. "I'll give her time," I say absentmindedly. "I think she needs some time."

"I know it's none of my business, but... why?"

I turn to face her. "Because I wouldn't survive ... if she still chose him. Even if he's no longer with us. I don't know how I would handle that."

"You won't know if you don't tell her or show her how you

feel, Kalum. It's time you show her what she's always meant to you."

I walk in my office and see an envelope with my name scrawled across it on my desk. The last time I saw one just like it was when Lane passed.

I turn it over and open it, wondering what my good friend wanted to tell me when he thought the time was right.

Kalum,

If you have received this letter, it has been almost a year since I've been gone. Knowing Aura, she would have waited this long before venturing out on her own, not caring if my wish was for you to look after her. Knowing her, she would have placed every dime in a trust fund like I figured she would for our son and not touch a dime. She was always like that. She must have thought I didn't notice how she would avoid buying anything for herself, but I did. I noticed. I should have tried harder, but I was so wrapped up in my selfish ways with my cars that I neglected her in a way. The purpose of this letter is hoping you can look out for her either way. If you haven't found someone... or maybe you have, but if you haven't and you still love her the way I know deep down you always will, then do what I should have done and put her first. Love her like I should have loved her, and if anyone deserves Aura, it's you...

Like you said that night you bought the Jeep for her, if you love someone enough, you let them go, even if they don't come back to you. If that's not love, brother, then I don't know what is. That Jeep brought her to me, and hopefully, it will bring her back to you. I may have had her past, but you have her present, and now, you have her future. I trust you with my son, and I trust you with the girl we both fell in love with and promised to take care of. As you trusted me to care for her, I trust you to do the same if I am gone. We both knew it would happen. A guy can only escape death on the track by pushing the limit so many times. My time is up, and now it's your time. Make the most of it, Kalum. Never doubt the love she had for you. I saw it that night in the diner when she poured her heart out to me. It was her love for you that was in her heart. I wanted you to know that.

P.S. Don't let her pick the least expensive item on the menu.

Your friend always,
Lane Turner

I place the letter on my desk, not believing what I just read. The fucker was always a strategist. It's creepy how he knew that he would die earlier than expected. He was a loner and an introvert, but we fell in love with the same girl.

The door from my office opens, and Janine enters. She's the

only one who enters without knocking since she knows my work habits and my schedule.

"Are you going to try to win your girl back? Woo her?"

"Woo her?" I volley back. "Who the hell says that word anymore?"

"Well, you need to do something and not let her go this time. She'll be back after some dinner Camila told me about."

I frown. "Dinner? What dinner?"

She waves her hand as she picks up the file with my next project and prospectus. "Some family dinner they want Aura and LJ to attend at some country club in Spencer. She's staying with Exie, and they'll drive up there."

Why? So they can make her feel like an outsider and remind her how she doesn't fit in their world of snobby, rich people? Not on my fucking watch.

"Get my plane ready to go to Spencer."

She looks up with raised brows. "You're just going to show up there?"

I shoot her a glance. "Get the plane ready, Janine."

I need to be there for her. For them. It's not just for Aura; it's for LJ, too. They're a package deal. The Turners are like vultures circling, waiting for their next meal. They saw the reaction the media and everyone had today on the track. They want to put her down and feel empowered. They're just upset they couldn't control Lane the same way my parents tried to control me.

It was what Lane and I had in common. We knew who our family was and what they were capable of. He had his way, and I have mine of how to deal with our families.

Chapter 47

Aura

"Are you sure this looks okay?" I ask Exie.

I'm looking at myself in the floor-length mirror, wearing a white pantsuit with nude high heels. Exie recommended I wear them.

"You look hot, and that outfit gives you an air of confidence. That is the look we're going with to deal with my parents and their country club dinner. They want LJ to be part of family functions."

"Funny how Christmas and birthdays don't count. Like I'm desperate for an invite, but you know what I mean."

"I know what you mean. I can't even show up with Dex. They would have a fit. They want me to marry some wealthy prick from the right family. This is how Lane felt and why he left as soon as he graduated and didn't take a dime of their money." She sighs. "They hate the fact that he did the opposite of what they wanted."

I swipe the brush over my hair one last time before we leave. "That includes marrying me and me having LJ. I'm not who they wanted for your brother."

"They'll get over it, and it's why you need to just show up, say hi, and then bye. End of story. They can't say you didn't show up and tried to keep LJ from them."

It's easy for her to say because she's their only living daughter and the only one to inherit and run the family company. But I don't tell her that.

It's like I'm going to meet the executioner.

Camila is going with Dex. It was the only way we could get Dex to go without causing a fuss with the Turners. They will lose their minds if they discover that Exie and Dex are together.

I can't wait to head back to the Hamptons. Kalum's home has been a hidden sanctuary. Our own hideaway where no one can attack us or show up and demand anything.

We arrive at the over-the-top country club in Spencer. I'm a hot mess. My palms are sweaty. My shoes are too high, but I blame that on being nervous.

"Are you okay, Mommy? Your hand is sweaty and is shaking a bit," he whispers.

I let out a breath as I walk behind Exie and Camila. "I'm okay. Just a little nervous, sweetie."

"It's okay, Mommy. I won't let them get to us. I'll protect you. If they say or do anything, I'll tell our friend Kalum. He'll help us."

My chest tightens. They have gotten close since that day he made him breakfast.

"I know, baby, but we got this. You and me. We're a family."

The country club is like those you see on TV, with beige marble floors, traditional wall paneling, and jazz music playing softly in the background.

Exie lets the hostess know that we are with the Turners and that they're waiting for our arrival. We are escorted to a long table with white chairs inside a restaurant that caters to the super rich. Servers pass us by in black-and-white uniforms, ensuring the wine and water are topped off for each guest.

"There they are," Lane's mother says in a fake voice. Like she's missed us. All fake and all lies. I notice other people are seated at the table, but I don't recognize who they are.

"Hello, Mrs. Turner." I give her my best smile. I glance at Lane's father. "Mr. Turner."

He gives me a smile, but it doesn't reach his eyes. "Hello, Aura."

His cold eyes land on LJ. His expression softens a fraction but then hardens like he wants to accept his grandson, but something inside holds him back. It's sad not to want to embrace your own grandson when he's the spitting image of your dead son. A son you had a strained relationship with.

I sit in the far corner with LJ, Camila, and Dex. Exie greets her parents with a curt hello while their eyes follow Camila and Dex.

"I'm glad you all could make it. We haven't spent much time with LJ," Lane's mother says.

My face heats, but I maintain my composure. They could have attended his birthday. We had a small cake and gifts at the house in North Carolina. It was the first birthday he had without his father present, and it was hard on all of us a month after Lane passed. Christmas wasn't any better, and you would think his parents would have a soft spot for their only grandson, but instead, they sent an email from their personal assistant. What type of monsters do that?

"We have been spending time in New York. You're all more than welcome to visit," I say.

"Oh, yes. I heard Exie mentioning something like that," Lane's mother says. "Where are you staying exactly? The Bronx? East Harlem? It must be hard since you're working, but at least you did the right thing and placed LJ's inheritance in a trust his father left him."

My teeth grind together. She always thinks I'm poor, and she already knows I put everything in the trust and would not touch a dime from her lawyer. She always makes a point that I wasn't entitled to a dime Lane left me.

"Actually..." I look up, and my stomach flips. Kalum is walking to my side of the table. "If you would excuse me and pardon my interruption. Aura and LJ, along with Camila, are staying in an exquisite estate in the Hamptons right on the water." Kalum adds, "Truly a gorgeous home. You should stop by and spend some time there with LJ." Kalum's voice drips with a lethal dose of *watch what the fuck you say next*, bitch.

He looks handsome in a tailored blue suit that takes my breath away. His hair is swept back, and his dress shirt is open at the base of his throat, giving me a glimpse of his tattoos and hard muscles. His suit jacket stretches across his broad shoulders, making my panties soak right where I'm sitting.

His gaze finds mine, and a look of molten lust swirls in the dark depths as they caress my face.

LJ grins and whispers, "Told ya, Mommy. He's here to save us from the evil witch."

Mr. and Mrs. Turner have their mouths slightly open. Camila coughs. Dex grins.

Kalum gives LJ a wink and says, "Hey, kiddo."

"Hi, Kalum," LJ says with a beaming smile.

My heart lurches in my chest at how cute he is and how much he trusts Kalum. Kalum grabs a chair, lifts it like it weighs nothing, and places it between LJ and me.

"And how can she afford such extravagance, Mr. St. Claire? Please do tell since you have invited yourself to our family dinner," Lane's mother says flatly.

"Mother. Stop it and leave her alone," Exie chides.

What a bitch. I want to claw her eyes out, but that's what she wants. She wants me to make a scene.

Kalum chuckles. "Why are you so worried about Aura's finances and where she's living instead of how she's doing? She's caring for your grandchild after your son's death? It has been almost a year, and you haven't visited her or made an attempt. I know this because I was the one who gifted her the estate."

My mind is going a hundred miles an hour, like one of Lane's cars. What is he doing? I can see his side profile. He's calm and collected, but I know this side of Kalum. The lethal side I have witnessed living with him at his family's home when he strikes.

Everyone's eyebrows rise at his admission of the gift. Who gifts an estate to a woman unless they're... together. Friends. No, not friends. Lovers.

"Are you trying to say what I think you're saying, young man?" Lane's father asks.

Exie looks at me with a grin. Dex looks at Exie. Camila smiles at Kalum like he hung the moon.

"I'm taking responsibility for Aura and LJ.," Kalum admits and gets up from the table.

"What would your mother say?" Lane's mother says accusingly.

"What can she say? She was voted out of the company, along with my father. Early retirement," he adds. "I own it all."

Silence blankets the room.

"If you'll excuse me. LJ and Aura have a flight to catch. This has been fun, but under the circumstances, you understand that New York is getting cooler, and Aura and LJ need to stay warm, and my plane is waiting."

Relieved, I stand, and we say our farewells.

Exie gives me a hug and whispers, "Get the hell out of here. I'm sorry my parents are such assholes, but I need you to give that man a chance."

My eyes lower because I'm not sure I can.

Chapter 48

Aura

I wake up in bed with little feet running on the hardwood floors to the main bedroom. Kalum is staying in one of the guest rooms at his own request. I'm relieved because I don't want to confuse LJ. I look out the bedroom window, and it's still dark outside.

My bedroom door is pushed open. "Mommy. It died," LJ says as he jumps on the bed.

Tears stream down his face, making a wet spot on his car pajamas.

"What died?" I ask worriedly. My heart pounds with dread.

"My iPad with the sound of the engine. I forgot to charge it on the plane, and I can't sleep. I need to hear it." He makes a motion to his ears.

His body shakes with a sob, and my heart breaks.

"Let's charge it."

"No, it takes too long, and the battery will not hold for me to hear it, Mommy. I'm sorry for crying and waking you up. I'm so sorry."

My eyes sting as a single tear slides down my cheek. I don't have one of Lane's cars here in New York. They're locked up in the garage in Lane's shop.

"What's wrong?" Kalum's voice filters from the open doorway.

"Um... his iPad died, and he can't hear the recording. I think the dinner with his grandparents stirred up feelings, and he just needed to calm down and get to sleep. It happens. The track and the car. The dinner and everything that was said. I think it was too much for him."

Kalum walks farther into the room with his sweatpants slung low on his hips and his hard chest.

I'm hugging LJ to my chest with his face buried in my neck. Kalum gently slides his hand in soothing strokes over his back.

"Hey, kiddo," Kalum says softly.

"Hey," LJ chokes out.

"I have an idea. If you promise to keep this a secret? What if I said I could let you hear the real thing?"

LJ's head snaps up. "How?" he asks, his voice breaking.

My gaze lands on Kalum's and my heart melts. He's so good with him. How LJ is drawn to him when Kalum has a solution for everything. He would make a great father someday.

Kalum sits down on the bed. His biceps bulge with the movement. He gives me a wink, and I swear my heart skips a beat.

"Remember when I told you that your daddy and I were very good friends?"

He sniffs and wipes his face with a tissue I hand him from the nightstand.

"Yeah," LJ says.

"He built something for me a while back, and I would like to show you. No one knows he modified the engine for me, so it's a secret. You want to see it?"

LJ looks up at me with bright eyes. "Can we, Momma?"

"Yeah, baby."

We dress warm and follow Kalum to the detached garage on the side of the house. I haven't opened any of the four garages since staying here.

Kalum presses the button on a fob, and the garage door opens, revealing a Lamborghini SVJ. LJ looks at me with a bewildered look on his face. His forehead creases like his father's when he's unsure about something.

LJ points at the car. "My father built the inside motor of that car?"

"Yep. I like Lamborghinis, and even though he doesn't, he said he could make it go faster, and I believed him." Kalum walks to the back and shows him Lane's signature tag mark on the back of the engine. *"Built by Turner."*

LJ smiles, his eyes lighting up like the Fourth of July. "He did! Mom, look, Daddy worked on this one."

"Told you," Kalum says, giving him a grin.

"Lane modified this?" I ask as I rub my hands together over my gloves. The smoke of my breath swirls in the air.

"He did. I asked him one night, and he said he would work on it for me and only me. You know he preferred Japanese imports, but this one"—he points—"he modified it for me. It's one of a kind."

He unlocks it and opens the door upward. "I can't go above a certain speed since you have to hold Lane in front, but I can figure out a safe way so he can fall asleep by listening to it. There is a road right out here that is quiet. I won't go past second gear and will rev it slowly so he can feel the engine and hear the sound."

"Is it loud?" LJ asks with excitement.

"Very."

Kalum buckles us in tight and makes sure we are secure, then slides in the driver's side.

"Ready, kiddo?"

LJ nods, and he snuggles closer, strapped snugly in the red leather seat. Kalum starts the massive car, and the engine purrs to life. The exhaust rumbles, and my head angles slightly. A sense of déjà vu washes over me when I'd done this with Lane. My eyes close, and I feel the engine's vibration behind us.

Kalum plays "Faded" by ZHU as he rolls the car slowly without giving it too much speed but roars the engine so LJ can feel it. After fifteen minutes, LJ slowly drifts to sleep. Kalum drives down the road for a while. When LJ is completely asleep, he drives slowly through the metal gate down the driveway.

He places the car in park and slides the back of his fingers over the side of my face. "I just wanted you to know that I'll do anything for you both. I'm here, Aura, and I'll never leave you two alone."

"Thank you."

He studies me, and I'm not sure how long we sit there staring at each other with LJ sound asleep in my arms in the driveway, but there is no place I'd rather be.

Chapter 49

Aura

The sun streams through the massive window of the main bedroom. It's Saturday, and I shift in the bed but feel something big beside me. The memories from last night come flooding back, but I don't remember coming to bed. I remember LJ was upset about his iPad, and then Kalum came to the rescue and shared his car with us.

My eyes flutter open, and my breath catches in my throat. The bedroom door opens slightly, and my eyes widen when I notice Camila standing at the door. My eyes wander back to LJ curled up against Kalum's side, both sound asleep.

"Rough night?" Camila asks softly.

"Yeah."

I tell her about LJ and his iPad issue and how Kalum came to the rescue.

"There is only one word I have for you, sweetheart. Fall."

The way they're sleeping together takes my breath away. He treats LJ as if he was his own son.

"It's okay, Aura. Just let it happen," she whispers.

I smile. "I have."

"Good. Give him a chance."

Easier said than done. I have enough on my plate with Lane's parents, and Kalum's parents would never approve. It's like going through the same drama all over again, and that wouldn't be fair to Kalum. If he wants to be here for us, I'll let him.

***

"Will that be all for you today?" I ask the lady seated in the booth before I set the bill down on the table.

"Yes, dear. Thank you." I give her a smile and move to the next booth, but my steps slow when I notice it's Bradley.

"Hello. Let me know when you're ready. In the meantime, what can I get you to drink?"

He looks up, and his eyes soften. "Hey there, gorgeous. A Coke would be good."

I write it down. "I'll be right back."

When I get back to the booth, Bradley clears his throat. "I saw you on TV," he points out.

It seems pointless to work at the diner to some when they find out I was married to Lane Turner and live in a big house. They must think I have all this money.

"Yeah."

"I know it's none of my business, but why are you working here?"

And here it goes. The annoying million-dollar question.

I make little circles on my notepad with the pen. Judy walks up next to me and replaces the ketchup bottles. Bradley waits for me to answer him, but I'm at a loss for words.

"You come from a rich family, don't you, Bradley?" Judy says, grabbing the empty ketchup bottles.

"Yes," he says proudly.

She nods, but everyone knows that.

Working at the diner with Judy has been fun. We talk about the customers and the regulars. Where they live. Who's a snob. Who isn't. I would have never thought she would come to my rescue.

Judy juts her hip out. "Well, some rich families don't agree or like it when their sons marry poor people with no money. They think because they're poor, they're taking advantage of them. They don't believe in something as simple as maybe their son fell in love and vice versa. They look at relationships like a transaction or a partnership. They see a girl who doesn't come from a predominant family as a threat. I'm sure you're a smart guy and can figure out her in-laws weren't sold on the idea and want to take away what her husband left for his family."

Bradley swallows nervously but says, "I'm sorry, but not all families are like that."

Judy snickers, then lowers her voice and says, "Yeah, right."

He leans back and watches her walk away with a scowl. When his gaze lands on me, I give him a dry smile. "So what can I getcha?"

Poor Bradley doesn't realize how people from his side of the tracks think about people who work regular jobs and don't have chauffeurs. They're good enough to work for their sons or daughters but not be—with their sons or daughters.

"Is that what they did to you?" he asks, looking at the menu.

"Did what?" I say, playing dumb.

"Threaten you with their lawyers. I never stood a chance with you, did I?"

"No, and it's not because of any of that. It's because I'm in love with someone."

"He's a lucky man. I hope he realizes that, but if you need a friend or someone to talk to." He points toward his chest. "I'm your guy."

"I know you think it's dumb that I'm working here, but it gives me purpose, and I don't mind."

"He doesn't know, does he?"

"It doesn't matter. Now what can I get you, handsome?"

Bradley's eyes light up. "Keep talking to me like that, and I might make it my mission to whisk you away."

He knows I'm not flirting with him. Bradley is a good-looking guy and doesn't seem creepy or anything, but I think Judy is more his type.

"Why don't you ask Judy out?" I blurt.

He nudges his chin toward Judy, wiping the table. "Judy doesn't like me very much."

"Why?"

"Because a good friend of mine broke her heart. He left her for a girl he knew from way back. The girl moved back from where she went, their parents set them up, and he broke it off with Judy for no reason. She's had a chip on her shoulder ever since. She doesn't go out like she used to and apparently hates my guts, too."

I never realized that Judy was nursing a broken heart. That must suck to fall for someone and then they just ditch you like you meant nothing to them. Now I feel bad for turning her down when she asked me to hang out with her.

I saunter up to her while she picks up an order from the kitchen.

"Hey, I'm free tomorrow night. How about that movie? It's Tuesday, so there won't be many people."

She smiles. "Really?"

I shrug. "Sure, why not? I really haven't made any friends since I moved here."

Her eyes dim, and she says, "I'm really sorry about your husband, Aura. That must have been really hard."

"I'm no stranger to loss and heartbreak. I lost my parents before the start of my senior year in high school."

"And I thought I had it bad."

I make it home, and Camila is thrilled to hear I have a night out with Judy to the movies.

"I won't take long. It's just a movie, and I really think she needs a friend. Exie's been busy with work, and she lives far away. I can't expect too much of her right now. It would be a good thing to talk and socialize with someone."

"I think it's a great idea."

My phone vibrates, and an incoming text comes through.

> Janine: The boss wants you to come to the office for a meeting. Can you come now?

I look at the time, and it's four. I pinch my brows, wondering why Kalum wouldn't ask me himself.

> Aura: Is everything ok?

> Janine: Everything is peachy. He's in a meeting and couldn't get out in time and asked me to call you before it got too late.

> Aura: Ok. I'll head out and meet you at the office.

> Janine: Awesome. :)

After showering, I get ready, dressing in a wool form-fitted dress and long coat. It has gotten notably cooler in the evening, and I don't want to freeze to death. Henry waits out front, and Camila makes dinner for LJ. I kiss them both and head out toward Kalum's office building in the city.

Chapter 50

Kalum

"**I**s she coming?" I ask Janine when I walk out of the board meeting. I've been busy with the store I want to open in Manhattan for Aura and her designs.

"Yep. Henry is on his way with her now."

I smile because I'm dying to see her.

Every night, I sleep in the room beside hers. It's hard not to walk into her room and bury myself inside her, but I don't because of LJ. I don't want to confuse him or make him feel uncomfortable. We haven't been affectionate in front of him either. *Baby steps.*

I walk into my office and freeze. Meredith leans on my desk in a seductive pose with a long coat. I'm assuming she wears nothing underneath except for some lacy lingerie. Before, I would have welcomed the intrusion, but now my stomach bottoms out, and dread snakes up my spine.

"What are you doing here, Meredith?" I say, irritated.

"I've missed you, Kalum. I haven't heard from you in a while," she says in a naughty voice. "It's never bothered you before."

"I need you to leave right now."

I hate to be an asshole, but I didn't invite her, and I figured she would've gotten the hint when I didn't call her or answer her calls since that night I left her apartment. The last thing I need right now is for Aura to walk in and think the worst.

She walks slowly, opening her coat, revealing exactly what I assumed. She's wearing a lacy number that does nothing for me. I'm not even hard. She places her hands on my chest, and I grip her wrists to push her off. But luck isn't on my side. The door to my office opens, and Janine stops, her eyes widening with Aura right behind her.

My gaze lands on the most important person in the room, and the look on her face breaks me. Her smile dies a quick death, and her eyes lower to the ground. Her eyes glass over, and Meredith's words make it ten times worse. I have never laid my hands on a woman, but I want to strangle her.

"Excuse me. We'll just be a second. Right, baby?" she coos. "It's been a while."

Janine backs up after shielding Aura from the scene in front of her. "Sorry to have interrupted. I thought we were having a meeting. I guess I misread the message earlier," Janine says in a tight voice.

Fuck.

I shove Meredith away. "Get out," I say in a voice dripping with venom. "If you come to my building unannounced again, I'll have you thrown out. We are done. I didn't call or plan to call you."

"It's because of her," she seethes, closing her coat and raising her chin.

I know she saw Aura. You could tell from her expression and the way Janine shielded her from watching Meredith's hands pawing all over my dress shirt.

"It will always be because of her. Now get out and don't ever come back."

She lowers her head in defeat. She knows her stunt has backfired. Had I known she could show up like she did, throwing herself at me, I would have made my point sooner.

I open the door and turn to the secretary seated at the desk by the elevator.

"Call security and make sure she's shown out and is not allowed back in. Where are Janine and Aura?"

The girl scrambles to pick up the phone. "Yes, sir. I think Janine and Miss Aura are in the boardroom."

"Let's see how long she lasts," Meredith says as she enters the elevator.

"Get the fuck out," I growl, raising my voice.

My patience is wearing thin, and this bitch is pushing me to my limit. I look down the hallway at the brown wooden door. There is only one way I can fix this. I need to show her.

I hurriedly walk down the hallway and open the door. Aura stares out the window, looking at nothing.

Janine quirks a brow. "Finished?"

I moved to close the electric shades on the windows by the double doors.

"Leave us, Janine. Make sure no one knocks on the door and lock it on your way out."

"Sure thing," she says and walks out.

My chest aches because she must think I'm a piece of shit.

"It's not what you think."

"It's fine." She gets up, and panic surges through my veins. "Doesn't matter what I think. You don't have to explain yourself, Kalum. I understand."

"What do you understand?"

"That we are just friends, and whatever we shared or had... meant nothing. Like it always did and always will. I would like to leave now."

I swallow, and the tightness in my chest increases with every breath. "I don't want you to leave."

"This was a mistake. I'm not sure why you brought me here, but right now, I really have no interest in anything you have to say or anything to do with you. Whatever happened... shouldn't have happened."

"What we shared was never a mistake."

"You have proven to me that it was. Thank you for all you have done for me, but please, if you can find it in your heart, please leave me alone."

She goes to move, but I can't let her leave. I refuse to lose her again. I cup her face in my hands. "Look at me, Aura."

She looks up, and our eyes meet. "I don't want her. She showed up, and I was trying to get her to leave. What you saw was not what it looked like." My head lowers, and my lips brush hers. "I haven't been with anyone since you. I don't want to be with anyone but you." I push her coat off her shoulders, and it slides to the carpeted floor. Her form-fitting dress molds to her soft curves. Her hips flare from having LJ, and my cock stiffens, remembering how those hips felt when I gripped them from behind.

"Do you know how badly I have wanted to sneak into your bedroom at night— wanting to be inside you? I have held back because of LJ. I don't want him to ever think I'm replacing his father, and it scares me to think that he would hate me if he saw me kiss you."

"He likes you, Kalum. You're so good with him. He would never think that of you," she says softly against my lips.

"Get on the table, Aura," I say against her lips.

She walks over and unzips her dress and lets it fall down

her shoulders to the floor. She sits with her legs slightly parted on the wooden boardroom table in nothing but her lace bra, panties, and heels.

The sun is setting in the New York skyline, giving the room a glow through the tiny space of the window blinds. I undo my pants and pull my raging hard-on out of my boxers and fist my cock.

Her eyes dip to my hand. "What are you doing?"

"I'm having a meeting. Tell me you want me between your thighs, Aura. Tell me you want me to fuck you right here."

Her nipples harden under the lace cups of her bra. My eyes trail down her taut stomach to the glistening wetness between her thighs.

We stare at each other for a beat until she says, "I want you between my thighs, Kalum."

The way she says my name is my undoing. I grip her thighs. She removes my dress shirt and slides her fingers down my chest and over my stomach. My cock bobs between us. She opens her legs wider. My fingers find the sides of her lace panties, and I rip them off her.

"You don't need these when you're with me. I want you to come into my office and sit on my desk while I feast on your pussy for lunch."

She whimpers when I brush the head of my cock over the lips of her pussy. "Do you want me to eat that sweet pussy, Aura? Huh, baby?"

"Yes," she says breathlessly. "But I want you inside me, Kalum."

I nudge her lips open, and she takes me like a ripe flower. The head of my cock slides inside, gripping my head in a tight vise. I push in deeper. She arches her hips forward and leans back on her hands, pushing her breasts in my face. I push my cock in, spreading her open like a gift.

I close my eyes and grunt as I fuck her cunt in deep, hard thrusts.

"Kalum..."

I fuck her like a madman. Our bodies begin to slap inside the room, and I swear if I could have her like this after every board meeting, I would never miss a day of work in my life.

"I want this pussy wrapped around my dick." *Thrust.* "I'm going to come inside you so deep, baby." *Thrust.* "Every chance I get, I'm going to come inside you. Don't you ever doubt me, Aura. I want you. I need you."

Her legs grip my hips, and she lies on her back. The straps of her bra slide down her shoulders. The cups of her bra barely cover her hard pink nipples.

"You're so beautiful, Aura. Tell me you're mine."

"I'm yours," she says. Her pussy clenches, and I know she's close.

I slide her down slightly so I can go deeper and pound into her, my muscles clenching as I grip her thighs. I fuck her hard. I fuck any doubt she had that I didn't want her.

"I'm going... to... come," she says in a breathless pant. She's panting and writhing on the table. "Please, Kalum. Don't... stop."

My balls tighten, and we both groan as we come at the same time. Her pretty pink nipples bounce as I thrust into her, emptying inside her. Weeks of holding back while she sleeps in the next room have me coming in full force.

Chapter 51

Aura

He pulls out of me slowly, and I wince. Kalum has a huge cock, and when he pounds into me, it leaves his mark. I look down at my swollen pussy. Cum leaks between my thighs onto the table. When I look up, he's staring at the mess he made.

He places his fingers on my soft, swollen flesh, and my face heats. "You have a beautiful pussy. It's even more beautiful when I have tended to it like I just did." My nipples react like two traitors. "Don't ever doubt how much I want you. Ever," he says.

I nod, but I'm at a loss for words. What do I say? My love for him is in every kiss and every breath.

He moves over to where napkins are stacked on a credenza by the coffee machine. He returns with a bottle of water, pours a small amount over the napkin, and wipes me gently.

"I'm sorry I was a little rough. I can see you're swollen. Are you okay to stand?"

Is it that noticeable? He was gentle, even more so than the

first time we had sex in his bed. I look around for my ripped underwear.

"I'm not a delicate flower, Kalum. I can handle it," I admit, but my mind still wonders why he wanted me here. I'm glad he cleared up the redhead situation in his office.

My heart dropped, breaking into a million pieces when I saw how she touched him.

At first, I thought he was backpedaling, but it wouldn't make sense. Why would he bring me here if he wanted to fuck the redhead? I recognized her from the gossip news on TV.

I watch him get dressed. His smooth skin slides into his dress shirt. He turns and catches me ogling him. He gives me the sexiest wink.

"I'm all yours, beautiful. I can dress slower if you want," he teases.

I look away with a smile. I want to crawl under the table and hide from embarrassment. He knows I find him attractive, and his air of confidence makes it hard not to melt under his gaze.

He slides his boxers up his thighs, and I quickly fall to my knees. His eyes widen when I grip the length of his semi-hard cock sticky with cum.

I look up and lick the tip. He sucks in a breath and rolls his eyes.

"Mm..."

"Holy. Fuck," he whispers.

I take him in my mouth and softly suck on his sensitive tip. I may have only gone all the way with one man in my life, but I made sure I pleased him. What I didn't know, I read about and learned from watching porn in secret.

I suck his cock and take him deep in my mouth until he hits the back of my throat. His girth fills my mouth. It's amazing how my body reacts to him like it has been deprived for so long. The touch of his skin. The taste of his cum on my tongue.

"We taste so good together, Kalum," I say against his cock.

I can't get enough. I grip his hips and relax my throat and let him fuck my mouth.

"Jesus, you're fucking perfect. So perfect taking my cock in that sexy mouth made just for me."

He pulls out, and I suck his balls gently, splitting them in half with the flat part of my tongue. I wrap my hands around his length and jerk his cock at the same time as sucking his balls. A moan escapes my throat, and he groans.

His fingers slide into my hair. My eyes flick up. My hand dips between my legs, and my fingers play with my clit.

"Play with that swollen pussy, Aura. Fuck... I want to come down that pretty throat."

He fucks my mouth, his balls hitting my chin, and he comes. Spurts of hot cum slide down my throat, and I swallow.

He lifts me from the floor and places me on the table. His head is between my thighs, and he begins to suck my clit until I cry out when I come. When I'm done, he licks me clean.

He slides my dress down my thighs, licking his lips, and says, "See, panties are pointless."

"Why did you want me to come?"

"You gave me more than I deserved, but I initially asked you to come because I have a business proposition for you."

That gets my attention. He finishes dressing and makes sure we are presentable. I pick up my coat and drape it over the chair. I move to clean the table, my cheeks turning bright red.

"Leave it. That is where I sit. Now I have something to remember when I walk into this room."

He opens the door and undoes the blinds. After ten minutes, he sends a message on his phone, and it must have been Janine because she opens the door with a file in her hands.

She narrows her eyes at Kalum and gives me a knowing smirk. "I'm not going to give you shit because that woman was escorted out of the building and asked not to return. The breathy moans that could be heard by the elevator had Melissa biting her lower lip."

Kalum gives her a grin. "We were talking, and I was making sure Aura was aware that she's the woman I'm seeing."

He moves the chair back to the spot where I was spread-eagled and gives me a wink. Butterflies swarm my stomach. Is he making us official? Are we dating?

Janine slides the folder to him and takes a seat on the far right. He opens it and takes out a bunch of documents.

"This is a proposition I have for you. I know you're over-whelmed with making your jewelry by hand, but since you have so much demand, it would be good to try out a pop-up store for you to sell them here in New York. I have found the best spot, and Janine will help market it."

I look at the address, and it's an exclusive part with boutique shops, but I don't have the money or enough supply to sell them. There is no way I could pull it off.

"I love the idea, Kalum, but I don't have the money or supp—"

"Money is no problem. I'll give you all the money you need. I want you to have this. You have been doing it for years, and there is so much demand."

"I don't have the supply for a store."

"I do," he quips.

"What?" I say, confused. "How?"

He scratches his brow and looks at Janine. Then his gaze lands back on me. "I bought most of them."

I shake my head, not quite getting what he's saying. Did he just say he bought most of them? How? When?

"How?"

"Since high school. Every time you put them up on that craft website. It was me. I have boxes of them all made by you."

I frown. All this time, it was him. All the money I made. It was him.

"Why?"

"Because I needed to feel close to you in some way, and it was the only way I could. In a way, I thought one of them could have been for me. I only had one, and it was the only piece I wore that mattered."

"Oh," I whisper softly.

Janine fans herself with the manila folder. "I'm about to cry. This is some *The Notebook*-type shit right there. Who would have thought you were such a romantic? Jesus, you're making me want to go straight."

"But wait...Um... you want to sell them?" I ask curiously.

"Only certain ones. They will be exclusive, and we will market '*Made by Aura*' as a brand. Your brand and your identity. This is who *you* are."

He moves closer and points at the paper like the CEO he is. The power coming off him is why he's so successful in business. It takes my breath away at how smart he is.

"How would I pay you back?"

"Trust me. The speech you made at the track has made you quite the girl next door who was taken advantage of, and the demand for your bracelets under your name is quite the trend right now."

"Look at the comments on social media."

Janine opens the comment section after my speech and the videos on IG of me speaking. Everyone wonders where they can buy my bracelets and other jewelry to support me. Requests have been pouring into my website, requests I can't quite fill with working at the diner. I never thought I could make a living making jewelry by hand.

"Fine. I'll do it as long as you get your money back. All of it."

"Done. Ms. Rayne. I'll get it all in writing. Everything is done in your name only. I'll just be the bank in a way to make you feel better, not because I want you to pay me back."

"Yes. Mr. St. Claire," I say his name in declaration.

"Kalum. You'll always address me as Kalum. You don't work for me, Aura. We just have a business agreement, and you're the owner of your brand. Now look this over and take your time and sign them. You can look it over with Mr. Schwartz, and I'll cover his fee."

I smile. "Thank you."

"Anything for you, Aura."

"So you're like a business owner," Judy says excitedly.

I gave my notice to Nancy at the diner since Mr. Schwartz assured me that the agreement Kalum drew up was all in my favor. No interest and Kalum is basically helping me out. He said it was the most generous contract he had ever seen. An interest-free loan with no risks.

Exie was excited and happy for me. Even LJ was jumping up and down because he loves to wear the bracelets in his favorite colors with his name stitched inside them. I have added little beads with accessories and stones I found at a local supply store. I notice Kalum never takes his off. He's always wearing one. At first, I thought it was the same one, but now I notice he changes them.

"Yep. My boyfriend..." I trail off, not used to calling him that.

"It's okay, Aura. He's your boyfriend."

"I know, but he really hasn't labeled us, but I'm assuming he is."

"Thinking about how you two met in the first place, I think there is more behind it all. How do two guys not hate each other over the same girl?" She places a strand of her brown hair behind her ear and sits down on the bench, waiting for the theater to open the door. "I mean, that is crazy. He sent the guy you cried about when his parents were a bunch of assholes by kicking you out on your eighteenth birthday to watch over you in case he died. That shit's like fate."

"Fate?" I ask, tilting my head toward her and pinching my brows. "What do you mean, fate?"

She sticks popcorn inside her mouth. "Fate. Events beyond someone's control. Things that were supposed to happen when you're fated to be with someone. I believe... you were destined to be with Lane and have his child but also destined to be with Kalum. It's probably why you fell in love with both," Judy explains. You married Lane, but you were always meant to end up with Kalum. It just wasn't the right time. It was Lane's."

It makes sense in a creepy way. I believe things are meant to happen, but I also believe in free will.

"I guess."

"I know this is messed up, but what if Kalum told you he loved you before his parents did what they did? Would you have been with Lane and married him?"

Deep down, I'm scared to admit it, but I know the answer.

"No. I would have chosen Kalum. I would have never been able to fall for Lane because I would have never left Kalum's side, but if Lane was alive now and Kalum told me he loved me after all this time, I would choose Lane and my son because I wouldn't abandon my family. Deep down, I love them both, but I would do right by them."

"I don't know, but all I know is something about the whole

thing is hidden. Love is a big emotion and the center of every-thing we do. It's what we take with us in the end, Aura."

"My mom used to say that. She used to say without love, nothing matters. It's all we have in the end. Love or hate." I take a sip of soda and clear my throat. "How about you and Bradley's friend?"

"Who? Nick. He wasn't in love with me. He lied to me when he said it, and he used me. I'm a girl with no money. My parents are divorced, and my mother manages a restaurant in town. We barely make rent. The second month I started working at the diner, Nick came in with Bradley. He was a sweet talker. We went out for six months before his family found out, then his childhood sweetheart moved back. It went all downhill from there."

"What an ass. What happened?"

She laughs sarcastically and flicks a thread off her jeans. Judy is pretty with brown hair and brown eyes with two tiny dimples on her cheeks. She's twenty-four and going to college online for her hospitality degree. She wants to land a good job and help her mother out. I admire her for her hard work and passion, but a sadness lingers behind her eyes.

"He would make excuses when I asked why he hadn't called. Then I saw him with her one day. I was walking home on my way to pick up my mother from her shift at the restau-rant, and I saw them heading inside together. They were out on a date. I was heartbroken. When I confronted him, he denied it at first. I kept pushing when I asked why I couldn't meet his parents or why I wasn't invited to his birthday party. He was annoyed, but I wanted the truth. I think I needed to hear it from him, and he snapped." Her voice shakes with sadness. "He said I wasn't the type of girl he could bring home. I was just a girl he was dating, and he liked me a lot but wasn't serious about me. I was a server at a diner, and his parents would not approve. When I asked him why he told me he loved me, he said he didn't know and that it was a mistake. He said he loved Elizabeth. "

"What a complete asshole. It makes sense to think Bradley is the same way, even if he swears he isn't."

"He's friends with the guy, and they hang out, so he knew. He comes to the diner all the time, and he never gave me the heads-up. He could have at least said, 'Hey, don't take dating my friend seriously. His family has a big influence on who he dates, and he'll break your heart,'" she mocks.

I place my hand on hers. "You know what? He doesn't deserve you, and it's better to know now than battle a rich family. They can make your life hell. Trust me, I know."

"They all suck."

"Yeah," I agree. "Some people just suck. Rich and poor."

Chapter 52

Kalum

Cason walks into my office as I make my way out. "Hey, I got your text. Where did she go?"

He means Aura. I was losing my shit a while ago when I got an update from the security detail at the house that Aura was out to the movies with a friend. A friend I have not heard about. Jealousy filtered into the pit of my stomach for the first time in a while. I have never felt jealousy like this since... I found out Aura married Lane and then when she fell pregnant with his child.

I wanted to ask her who she was with, but I wanted to see for myself. They said she left for the movie theater. I called Cason to let him know that his security detail did not go with Aura, and they reported that she had requested to go alone. Apparently, they have become fond of Aura. Who knows what else they have let her get away with.

"I'm sorry, brother. You know how Aura has that effect on people. I'm sure it's just a friend."

He must see the scowl on my face because he's trying to calm me from going over there and kidnapping her. I wouldn't kidnap her, but she needs a reminder that safety is a major concern. She's by herself, and what if something happened to her? What would happen to LJ?

"The chopper is standing by," I tell Cason.

"I'm coming with you. Who knows what you'll do when you get there? I can see that look on your face."

"You know me well," I mutter.

"When it comes to Aura. There is no telling what you'll do."

The helicopter touches the helipad, and we wait until it's safe to exit. The driver waits with the driver's side door open to the blacked-out Rolls.

When we arrive, I park the car in the front. I look at the time, and the movie is about to end. Camila told me it was some chick flick. If she wanted to go to the movies, I would have taken her.

Chapter 53

Aura

Judy pushed the door so we both could exit the theater. "The movie was okay. She could have given the guy a second chance, but he was kind of a douche to her, so I guess it was a good thing she chose to stay single and hoped to find the right one someday."

"I guess, but he was kind of hot," I say with a laugh and throw the empty popcorn bucket in the trash. I open the pack of gummy bears and pop a red one in my mouth.

"Look who we found," a voice I don't recognize says from behind us.

Judy turns around, and she stiffens. I follow her gaze, and I guess this is Nick standing next to Bradley.

"Hey, gorgeous," Bradley says with a smile.

"Hey," I say, my voice fading.

Bradley glances at Nick and then at Judy. "Hey, Judy."

"Hey, yourself," she says.

"Look, we gotta get going," I say, stepping forward.

Nick steps forward, blocking me. "Aw, come on now. Why don't we hang out? Bradley has been telling me all about the sweet piece of ass who works in the diner. He can't stop talking about you. Maybe we should all hang out." He looks at Judy. "How about it, babe? I know you miss me."

My nostrils flare in annoyance. "Why don't both of you fuck off." I move to go around, and Bradley grips my wrist. "Let go," I warn.

"Look, Nick is harmless. He doesn't know how to act sometimes," Bradley says.

I try to move my hand out of his grasp, but when it won't budge, I wish I had my security with me. I didn't want to look out of place with Judy and make her feel weird and uncomfortable with two guys following us around. I thought Bradley was an okay guy, but Judy was right. They're both self-entitled pricks.

"Let me go," I say again through clenched teeth.

He looks up, his eyes widening when a shadow looms. Bradley flinches when he connects with his face. Bradley falls, hitting his side on the carpeted floor.

My eyes widen when I see Kalum charging him. Nick looks behind Judy, and Cason comes into view with a menacing look.

"Leave, or I'll make you. If you or your bitch-ass friend comes near them again, I'll make it my mission not to only kick your ass, but I'll destroy you and whatever hole you crawled out from as well," Cason says in a menacing voice.

"Y-yeah. What are you, her man or something?" Nick says.

He looks at Judy and then back at Nick. "Maybe."

Kalum has Bradley by the throat and is lifting him off the floor. My hands cover my mouth.

"Kalum," I call out.

Kalum looks at me but doesn't release his hold on Bradley. Bradley's lip is split open, and blood drips on his shirt.

"He wouldn't let you go. He better not have hurt you, Aura.

Because right now, the way I'm feeling, I'm going to break his fucking face."

"He didn't hurt me. He just wouldn't let me go. Let him go, Kalum. He isn't worth it."

Bradley looks at me and then at him. "I'm sorry. I would never hurt her. She loves you. She told me that she loved you."

Kalum releases him, and I can't believe Bradley told him I loved him before I did. Bradley and Nick quickly run out of the theater. Kalum glances at me but says nothing.

I glance at Cason, and he gives me a grin. "Hey, stranger."

With a small smile, I say, "Hey."

I look at Judy, and she looks at Kalum and then at Cason. "I'm Judy. Aura's friend. We appreciate you guys coming when you did. I'm sorry to meet you all like this," Judy says apologetically.

Kalum holds out his hand. "I'm Kalum, Aura's boyfriend."

Judy shakes his hand. "I'm Judy. I work with Aura. She gave her notice, and we have been meaning to hang out."

Judy gives me a knowing grin and then looks at Cason. I feel bad I didn't tell him about Judy, but I was planning to. So many things happened yesterday, and I was excited to hang out and talk with Judy after hearing about Nick. I wanted to be a friend that she felt she could count on.

"Thank you. Nick's been an ass since we broke up. I didn't realize how much of an ass until now. He has a girlfriend, so I don't know what his problem is."

"He won't be bothering you anymore," Cason bites out.

I don't think he liked hearing that Nick and Judy used to date. I think Cason thinks she's hot.

Henry pulls up, and Cason rides in the back with Judy to see her home safely.

Kalum opens the door for me, and I slide in the blacked-out

Rolls. The smell of leather hits my senses. He walks around and gets in on the driver's side.

"Are you sure you're okay, Aura?"

I shrug off my coat and place it in the back seat. "Yeah, I'm okay. Is your hand okay?"

I see his knuckles are red, with the light filtering through the windshield from the overhead lights in the parking lot. His strong hands grip the steering wheel, and he lifts the hand he punched Bradly with. He opens and closes it.

"Nothing I can't deal with. It doesn't hurt."

He drives down the road but in the opposite direction of the house. He parks at a hotel and marina.

"Why are we here?" I ask.

The dock lights reflect off the water and the boats as they sway. He doesn't answer and gets out of the car, walks around, and opens the door. I grab my jacket and exit the car.

I follow him inside the hotel. I send a quick text to Camila and tell her I'm with Kalum. She sends me a quick update that LJ is fast asleep and not to worry. I cooked him dinner and made sure he was in his pj's watching TV before I left for the theater with Judy.

He has been doing well with being homeschooled with Camila. I have enrolled him in online classes that help him with reading and math.

Kalum always dedicates an hour or two each night to LJ. It's so hard not to fall in love with a man who cares so much about you and how your son feels.

He murmurs something to the lady at the front desk, and she hands him a key card. The lady smiles warmly as Kalum entwines his fingers with mine and guides me farther into the hotel.

He opens the door to the room and closes it with a thud. The room has a cottage feel. A large king-size bed with French-styled shutters over the windows. He opens the French doors leading to the harbor, and the view is breathtaking.

"Kalum."

"Take off your clothes, Aura."

He gets close, and his dress shirt is stretched across his tight chest. He walks me back to the bed, and I have no choice but to sit.

I look up, and he stares at me. His dark brown eyes melt me like chocolate.

"I love you, Aura."

He said it! He loves me.

I begin to remove all my clothes, throwing my jacket, then my long-sleeve T-shirt until I'm naked.

Once he removes his clothes, he leans over me and slides his big hands up the length of my arms over my head. The cool air sends a breeze into the room, and my nipples harden, begging for his touch.

He kisses my neck, down my chest until he reaches between my legs and begins sliding his tongue inside my pussy.

I moan. "Kalum. Yes... fuck. Yes."

"You taste so fucking good. I never thought I could taste pussy this sweet," he rasps against my clit.

"Kalum," I moan, running my hands through the strands of his dark hair. "I love when you eat my pussy, and I love it when you're inside me."

He pulls away and raises his body over mine. "Me too, baby. I brought you here because what I have to say I need to tell you alone, and I can't go another night without telling you."

I'm nervous. My core throbs for him, but I know what he has to say is important because, in my heart, I know things are shifting. He's becoming the air I breathe, and slowly, he's becoming everything I need in my life. I can't picture it without him in it.

"I have never stopped loving you, Aura. I loved you since the first time I kissed you. I fell in love with you, but I was too scared to admit it. I needed to protect you because there was no way my parents would accept us, and I was right. I was broken the day you left. The letter you left me broke me. I never got the chance to tell you how much I love you."

I snuggle into his chest, and he holds me. I close my eyes and remember the way he held me when I cried because of the death of my parents. He was the only one who held me and kissed me when I mourned their death.

"Kalum..."

"I had a whole weekend planned for us, baby. I wanted to tell you how I felt the weekend of your eighteenth birthday and hoped you'd accept my love. I wanted to make you mine in every sense. My heart has always been yours, Aura. I thought I could let you go, but deep in my heart, I never did. I had to watch you fall in love with my friend, marry a man who wasn't me, and give him the most beautiful son I have ever had the pleasure to meet. I loved you so much that I made a pact with a friend to love you when I couldn't be there for you because there was nothing I could offer you. My parents threatened to disown me and make sure to ruin you."

Tears stream down my face because I thought he didn't want me. I thought I imagined the connection between us. A connection I had never felt with someone. Except Lane. He made a pact with Lane. But why? I would have waited, but then I would have never had our son.

A sob bubbles up my throat.

"It's okay, baby, don't cry. Time just wasn't ready for us. Things happen for a reason, and we both loved you. No matter who you ended up with, me or Lane, there was no wrong choice because we both were in love with you at the same time. He was ready to give you what I couldn't, and I loved you enough to let you be happy and safe from anyone who would hurt you. It was all planned, Aura. I have letters, too, the same way he did, in case I passed. I always wanted you to know that I loved you, and he was okay with that, and so was I. What mattered the most was you. Now what matters the most is you and LJ. I didn't tell you this because you were mourning your husband, and it was wrong to put this on you. But I want to be honest and tell you that I'm scared."

I wipe my cheeks with the back of my hand and look into his eyes. "Scared of what?" I whisper.

What would he be scared of? He's brave for what he did and what he admitted. He could have moved on and forgotten about me. I thought him helping me was because he was doing right by a friend, but this is different.

"That after everything, you would always choose him over me. It's wrong, and I feel ashamed to say it, but you loved him just as much, if not more, and I can't compete with that."

"Shh." I place a tender kiss on his lips. "If I had known how you felt, I would have never left. If I had never left, I wouldn't have fallen in love with Lane, but you did what you felt was right, and there is no right answer. We meet people in our lives, and it's their time with you. It was his, and I loved Lane. I don't regret a minute of it because it gave me LJ, and he's everything to me. Lane was my second love. You were my first love, Kalum, but now, you're my last. I love you." His nostrils flare, and he crushes his mouth to mine.

We make love for hours in the dark, with only the moonlight filtering through the open doors from the balcony.

We make it home before LJ wakes up. Kalum sleeps with me alone for the first time, and I smile when the sun rises. But I know he's gone to work when I feel the empty side of the bed and smell the scent of his cologne.

I make my way to the kitchen and see an envelope with my name on it.

It's addressed to me, but I recognize the envelope. It looks like the one I received when Lane died.

I take it and walk outside with the blanket over my shoulders. I sit under the cool breeze with the sun rising on the horizon.

What do you have to tell me? I ask Lane inside my head.

I open the letter and read the simple, curt message scrawled in Lane's handwriting.

> *Aura,*
>
> *If he told you, I'm going to tell you the words you need to hear. You have my blessing. It was always about you.*
>
> *We both love you,*
> *Lane Turner*

I hold the letter tight in my palm and look out at the sea. The salty sea air blows my hair. "I love you, too," I whisper in the wind. But there is a man I need to give my love to and the chance he deserves.

I walk inside the house.

"Mommy," LJ says, running into my arms.

"Hey, sweetheart."

"Where's Kalum?" he asks with hopeful eyes.

"He's at work, sweetie."

He frowns. "Bummer," he mutters.

"He'll be back from work later."

He grins. "Is he your boyfriend, Momma?"

I don't want to lie or keep anything from him.

I sit on the couch, and he sits beside me, and I take his hand. "Would you be okay if he was?"

He looks down at our hands linked together. "I would like for him to be with us. So I'm saying yes. I want him to be there for me like Daddy was," he says with a sniff.

"Oh, honey. I think Kalum would be honored. He likes to be there for you, and what you think about him matters a lot to him."

He tightens his grip on my hand. "I miss Daddy, Mommy. I know he's gone, but Kalum is here, and I don't want him to leave. Ever."

My chest aches, and I take deep breaths and try not to cry in front of him. He feels conflicted like I do. He feels what I feel in my heart. Conflicted with the love and loss of his father, and Kalum sweeping into our lives like a storm wreaking havoc with our hearts.

Chapter 54

Kalum

I walk into my office and sit at my desk, then pick up the phone. "Please send Janine in," I tell Melissa over the receiver.

"Yes, sir. Right away."

Five minutes later, Janine waltzes in with her knee-length pencil skirt, looking like Mary Poppins.

She takes a seat in the chair in front of my desk as I type away on my schedule. She has her notepad in hand with a pen, ready to take notes of what I need.

"I need flowers sent to Aura, and please inform security and everyone in this building that she has full access to the building and my office at any time." I can see Janine smirk as she takes notes. "Did you catch her size when you took her shopping the first time?"

"Yes, I did," she quips.

"Good, I need the latest collection of everything she would like sent to the house in the Hamptons, and I need another wardrobe for the penthouse in the city."

"What would you like the card to say?"

I stop typing and look at her while she's tapping her pen on her notepad. Shit. I didn't think about that part. I have never sent a woman flowers before. I've only ever taken them out to eat, fucked them at their place, then left. I lean back in my chair and loosen my tie, lost in thought.

"Write this down." I make a motion with my finger toward her notepad. "What is the worst part of your day? That is what I want you to write on that card when you have them deliver the flowers."

Janine grimaces. "Really? That is what you want to tell her? A normal man who is crazy about a woman would write 'I'm thinking of you' or 'Miss you. You tasted great last night.'"

I chuckle. "I'm going with what I told you. I want to know what the worst part of her day is so I can make it my mission to make it better. I don't want her to have a bad part of her day." I lean my forearms on the table. "I want to make her happy."

Janine's eyebrows shoot up. "I never thought about it like that. You really care about her."

"Janine, Aura is the love of my life. My first and only love. Everything in her life matters to me and her son."

"Her pop-up shop is almost ready. We just need the merchandise so I can announce the location with marketing."

Do whatever you need to do. I want her dream to come true.

Chapter 55

Aura

There is a knock on the door, and one of Cason's security guys enters the house with a beautiful bouquet of bloodred roses. Then another guy carries two more in white and pink. Flutters swarm in my stomach.

"Oh, my goodness," Camila exclaims.

"They're beautiful," I whisper.

Camila grabs one, and I grab another one to place on the dining table and one on the island in the center of the kitchen.

"He really wants to make an impression, doesn't he?" Camila says.

"Wow, Momma. Those are really nice," LJ says in awe, looking at all the roses, running over to each one and smelling them.

I sigh and grab the single card in the bouquet of red roses. "Yes, they are, sweetie."

I open the small envelope, and it reads:

What is the worst part of your day?

This is so Kalum. I fish out my cell phone from the back pocket of my jeans and tell him.

Aura: The worst part of my day is not waking up in your arms. The second is when LJ asks me with sadness in his eyes why did you leave. That is the worst part of my day. When you're not with us. The best part is when you are. Thank you for the flowers.

My phone vibrates instantly with an incoming message.

Kalum: You both are everything to me.

I smile and place my phone back inside my pocket, but it begins to ring. Camila pinches her brows when she sees the look on my face when I see who's calling me. It's Lane's mother, Mrs. Turner.

I answer the call. "Hello."

"This is Caroline, Lane's mother. I need to talk to you about LJ."

She rambles on the phone, and my stomach bottoms out when her threats spill through the phone as I look at LJ writing in his workbook. After she hangs up, a ringing sound assaults my ears. She can't. She wouldn't. Why can't I be happy? Why are they so evil?

I drop the phone on the dining table with a thud.

"What's wrong, Aura? What happened? Who was that?"

I place my hands over my face. "It was Caroline. She wants LJ. She says I can't take care of him properly as a single mother. He's a Turner, and she can provide better for him than I can."

"But that is not true. Look at where we live and you have the pop-up store and everything going. "

I close my eyes and slide my hands down my face. "Yeah, all that is great, but I haven't received a dime until the funds clear after sales, and everything is in a trust. She pushed me to do that to set me up, Camila. On paper and in front of a judge, the Turners will make it seem like he's better off living with them based on the life they could provide. They will twist things around to make it look like I'm struggling, and they could force me to sell Lane's cars, shop, builds, maybe even his company. It's their endgame. I doubt they care about Lane. When they ask for my financial statements, I look like I can't afford where I live and would need to sell assets to create liquid cash flow and, in the end, they get what they want, to destroy what Lane built under their name to make a point. They can pay people off. All sorts of things money can buy."

Camila's mouth opens like a fish when she sees how I painted it all out. How it will go through lawyers, judges, and the court. The well-being of Lane Turner Jr.

"You have to tell Kalum, Aura."

I shake my head. "All I've been is trouble for that man. Maybe his parents were right in getting rid of me. There is nothing he can do."

"Don't underestimate him, Aura. You need to tell him."

I lower my head and slide my fingers through my hair. "You know I'm not. I have to pay him back for the pop-up store, and this is not his fight but my own with my husband's family. This is not his problem. He's better off being with some heiress."

"You know that is not true. It will all work out, Aura."

I get up and walk toward the bedroom. "I'm not sure anymore, Camila."

Chapter 56

Kalum

It has been a week, and I have moved my schedule around to have Aura wake up in my arms, but she's distant. Something is wrong, but she won't tell me. The pop-up store was a success on the first day of opening. She sold out of every design, but her smiles don't reach her eyes, and I'm confused. I thought she would be happy. I have asked her if she's okay, and she says everything is fine, but her spark is gone. Something is wrong. Is she not happy? Does she miss Lane?

I'm looking out the floor-to-ceiling windows of my office.

My phone rings, and it's from Melissa out front. "Yes."

"There is a Miss Exie Turner wanting to see you, sir. Do I let her in?"

I roll my eyes. Great. What does she want? "Let her in," I reply.

The door opens, and Exie Turner enters wearing a blue pantsuit. The poster child of the female CEO. She made the cover of *Forbes* as one of the most influential businesswomen to own a billion-dollar fortune, the Turner fortune. She has almost as much money as me. Almost but not quite. I beat her profit margin by a couple of billion.

"What can I do for you, Exie?"

She crosses her arms over her coat in her hand. "We need to talk, and it's about Aura."

My head snaps to attention. "What is it?"

She sits and levels her stare on me. Her expression is hard and serious, and I have a feeling I'm not going to like whatever she's here to tell me.

"My parents are gearing up with lawyers." She blows out a breath, and her left leg is shaking.

"Tell me, Exie. What is going on?"

"That means she hasn't told you."

"Told me what?" I snap.

The fucking suspense is killing me. I want to reach over my desk and shake it out of her.

"They're threatening to take LJ away from Aura. She put everything in a trust that LJ can only access when he's of age, and he's still too young to make any decisions. My parents are expressing their concerns over her ability to provide adequately for him in the same capacity as they could. My parents are going to get a court order from a judge to have LJ stay with them because they can provide a more stable environment than Aura. They will want to see financial statements that we both know only show Lane's assets, cars, and his company."

"They want to blackmail her so she sells it. This is not about LJ and his lifestyle."

"Exactly," Exie says.

I lean back in my chair but then get up and walk over to pour a scotch. I turn my head. "Want one?"

She sighs and places her coat on the chair next to her. "Yeah."

I pour her a glass and hand it to her. "What are you willing to do?"

She looks up. "Honestly, she's my best friend, my brother's only love, and the mother to my nephew. Anything."

"How much of the company do you own?"

"Majority share, and I placed some in Aura's and LJ's names. She doesn't know."

"How is your parents' retirement? Do they have enough?"

"Of course, they wouldn't threaten her if they didn't feel a sense of financial empowerment. They have more money than they know what to do with. Since my brother's death, I'm the sole beneficiary. Why? What are you proposing?"

I level her with a hard expression, taking a sip of my scotch. The cubes inside the glass move with the amber liquid. "Retire them like I did mine and outvote them with the board. Take away their power, and in return, it will give you your freedom with Dex."

Her face softens. I can tell she's in love with him. Dex was Lane's right-hand man. He runs Turner Automotive and takes care of the shops and sends reports to Aura on a weekly basis. The guy is loyal but has the same issue Aura has with her in-laws. He doesn't come from a privileged family, so their relationship is hidden.

"That would piss them off, but if they move forward, they still have enough money to get even with Aura. Even in the sense of dismantling what Lane built. They were never happy Lane deviated from the family business and built cars to race. He moved out when he turned eighteen and never looked back. It was against their wishes, and let's not even talk about his marriage to Aura and the fact he had a child with her. My parents don't believe their children should marry for love but for convenience and money."

"We share a similar issue with our beloved parents, but I see things differently. I'm sure you do too."

She takes a long sip of the scotch that makes her eyes water. "I do," Exie croaks.

"Slow down there, slugger."

She coughs, and her eyes water. "What is this?" She holds up the glass like it's nuclear.

I chuckle. "Macallan Fine and Rare, aged scotch."

"It's smooth, but shit, it's strong," she declares.

"I opened it for the occasion."

She coughs and clears her throat. "What occasion is that?"

"It's time I propose to Aura and make her my wife. She'll be untouchable as a St. Claire."

She smiles. "You really love her, don't you?"

"With everything that I am, Exie. Her and LJ."

I tell her the pact I made with her brother, and for the first time, Exie Turner sees me for who I really am and not the monster she thought I was. How much I love her best friend.

Tears stream down her face when I tell her the story of two young guys falling in love with the same girl. What lengths they would go to protect the one girl they both loved forever.

Chapter 57

Aura

I look at the test in my hand in disbelief. I missed one pill, and now I'm pregnant. One pill.

I lie down on my bed and stare up at the ceiling. No wonder I can't stand the smell of eggs. They smell rotten, and I just feel like sleeping and puking. Camila made me eggs with toast this morning when I was so tired from working the store. All the customers walking in placed orders for more handmade designs, but my stomach wasn't having it. I figured I had eaten something that didn't agree with me, but then I remembered when I fell pregnant with LJ, and it hit me. I went to the grocery store nearby and was relieved to find they had pregnancy tests on hand.

After drinking a ton of water, I thought I would float. I took three tests, and they all yielded the same result. I'm pregnant. I'm pregnant with Kalum's baby. I look down at my still flat stomach and feel flutters in my belly. A baby is growing inside me. Our baby.

I walk out of the bathroom, and Camila stands in the

hallway watching me. I look down at my scroungy socks over my gray leggings.

"How far along are you?"

My eyes lift, and her expression softens. I tell her. Why hide it? "About two months along, give or take."

"Does he know?"

I shake my head. "I don't know how to tell him, not with everything going on with Lane's parents."

I received the documents from their lawyer with dread. I haven't sent it to Mr. Schwartz yet. The walls are closing in on me fast.

"Tell him, Aura. You need to be honest with him about everything. He'll be there for you. He loves you, and I know the news will make him happy."

I give her a hug. "You think so?" I whisper.

"I know it."

"Tell Henry to wait for me out front."

She nods. "I'll stay with LJ."

"Are you sure?"

"Yes, I think you need to tell him first, and then you can tell LJ."

I make my way inside the St. Claire building.

"How can I help you?" the security guard asks before I reach the reception desk.

I glance down at my simple long coat and sneakers and know I look out of place in the beautiful building with black marble floors.

"My name is Aura Rayne, and I'm here to see Ka—Mr. St. Claire."

His eyes widen when he hears my name. He grabs his security badge so fast he practically rips it off his suit jacket.

"Right this way, Miss Rayne." He guides me toward the elevator without question. I look over, and Cason's men nod and take a seat in the expansive lobby.

Once the elevator opens, I stride toward the young woman with designer glasses seated at her desk. She smiles at me warmly.

"Hello, I'm Melissa. I hope you remember me from... last time," she says awkwardly.

Oh God. I tighten my hold on the letter-size envelope I'm holding, slightly embarrassed from the last time I was here on this floor when Kalum and I were fucking in the boardroom.

"Yes," I answer shyly.

"You're more than welcome to go right in. He already knows you're here."

"A-are you sure he isn't busy? I don't want to interrupt," I stammer nervously.

I'm hesitant to walk in like I own the place. I didn't call first. I should have called him.

"Mr. St. Claire gave everyone strict instructions that you're not to wait when you're here to see him. You can come whenever you wish."

"Oh. I'm sorry. I wasn't aware I could just—"

She waves her hand like it's no big deal. "Please. You don't have to explain. Go right ahead."

I give her a warm smile and walk toward the imposing door to Kalum's office. I turn the knob slowly, and the door swings open. His head lifts from whatever document he's reading, and my breath catches in my throat. He's so handsome, with his gray dress shirt fitted to his frame. It's tailored, accentuating his muscled chest, bulging biceps, and trim waist. He looks like a model. His hard, angular jaw and perfect lips, and brows shaped over expressive dark eyes.

When he smiles, I feel it all the way to my toes inside my sneakers. My legs clench slightly before taking slow steps toward his desk after letting the door close behind me.

He stands, and I hold my hand out. "Please, I'm sorry to have interrupted you. I came because I needed to talk to you, and maybe it could have waited until you came home, but I'm here."

The concept of home being where we all have been living. Time goes by so fast, and I realize we've all been living together like a family for months.

He sits back down and gestures for me to take a seat. "You can visit me whenever you want, Aura. I like it." He grins. "Is everything okay? Do you need something? Are you hungry?"

"I need to talk to you about something very important, and I didn't want to discuss it over the phone."

"What is it, Aura? Tell me."

I sit in the chair in front of his desk and place the papers from Lane's parents on my lap. I even took the pregnancy tests as proof. I'm scared he'll be upset. He told me he didn't want kids or marriage, and I'm petrified of his reaction. It's not fair to keep it from him, and he should know.

"If it's about Lane's parents and their threats, I already know about it, and I'm going to take care of it."

I frown. "How did you know?"

"Exie," he quips.

"Exie?"

He nods and gives me a smirk. "She came to see me and told me. I'm not upset that you didn't tell me sooner, and I already know why. I know you don't want to burden me with it, but everything that concerns you and LJ concerns me."

I lick my lips, and his eyes darken. My nipples harden at

the reaction, and my core throbs between my thighs. We had sex early this morning, but with Kalum, it isn't enough. It feels like the first time, every time. The memory of him between my thighs leaves a trail of delicious soreness.

"It will be taken care of. Exie and I are on it. No one is taking LJ away from you, and you sure as hell will not have to sell anything."

I trust him, and I trust Exie. A wave of relief that they're doing this gives me the courage to spill the news that he's going to be a father.

"Is there anything else you need to tell me before I ask you for a kiss and your thighs wrapped around my waist?" he asks huskily.

I bite my lip, slide my hand inside the envelope, and pull out the test, covering them. He looks at my hand and tilts his head curiously.

"What is that?" he asks.

I give him a nervous laugh and lift my head, looking at the tall ceiling in his office until my gaze lands on his. "I'm pregnant," I blurt.

His eyes widen, and his gaze falls to my stomach and then to my face. I slide the test over to him on his desk.

"I took three of them. They're all positive. I switched contraceptives, and there was a day from switching, and I guess that was all it took. I'm so sorry, Kalum."

He stares at me and doesn't say a word. His expression is blank. Maybe from the shock.

"Kalum?"

Silence.

"Kalum?" I repeat.

He doesn't move a muscle or say anything. His office door opens, and Janine walks in.

"Oh, I'm sorry," she says behind me. "I'll come back."

"That won't be necessary," I tell her. "I-I was just leaving," I stammer, looking back at Kalum, who still hasn't uttered a single word.

He looks at Janine but doesn't notice me walk out of his office, and I repeatedly jab the button on the elevator. "Stupid thing," I mutter.

I ignore the curious look from Melissa. When I turn, I see the exit sign to the stairs. I walk hurriedly to the door and open it and make my way down the stairwell. A ball is in my throat, my pulse beating rapidly in my ears as I try to go down the flights of stairs as fast as I can.

I make it to another floor and press the elevator button. The elevator opens and some random people are exiting, but I make it before the doors close.

Relieved I'm the only one inside the car, I take a deep breath and let it out slowly through my mouth. My phone vibrates. I pull it out of my coat pocket and notice it's Janine.

Great. He sent his secretary to tell me to fuck off or maybe to schedule a doctor's appointment to confirm it's true. He sends his secretary to buy me clothes and let me guess, the flowers were from his secretary. I know I'm being petty and a brat, but he said nothing. I called his name, and it was like he checked out mentally. I'm grateful for his help and all of that, but shit, he could have said something or told me to give him time to think. I'm scared shitless, and I don't know what to say, but all I know is that I'm keeping it. He can tell me he doesn't want children, but I'm keeping our baby.

The elevator doors open, and the security detail is already waiting. I nod and walk briskly with them trailing me. My phone keeps going off when I'm inside the car with Henry, but I ignore the call. It's still Janine.

Chapter 58

Kalum

"She isn't answering, Kalum. I have called her like ten times," Janine states.

"Fuck. She wasn't on the elevator, and when I went after her down the stairs, I didn't catch her."

"What happened?"

I gesture to the pregnancy tests on my desk. When I finally catch my breath, I answer, "She's pregnant."

Janine's eyes widen. "And you let her walk out?"

"I tried to catch her, genius." I wipe sweat off my brow from going down the stairs. That woman is fast for her small frame.

"What did you say when she told you that had her running like the building was on fire?"

"Nothing."

"What do you mean, nothing? Be a little more specific."

"I froze." I slam my hand on my desk. "I fucking froze, Janine! I didn't know what to say. I wanted to ask her to marry me eventually, but I wanted to do it right, not because she's having my child. I want to marry her because I love her."

"Then prove it to her and ask her like a normal man in love. Be creative. Fix it. I'm sure she's scared."

Chapter 59

Aura

"It's been three days, Judy. He hasn't come home. LJ is wondering where he is, and I told him Kalum's busy with work," I tell her, taking a sip of my chocolate shake, seated at the booth in the diner.

"Give him time, love. He'll come around. Maybe he's wrapping his heart around the idea. That man loves you. He almost killed Bradley for touching you. The man has been head over heels in love with you since he was a teenager. Has he called?"

"His personal assistant has called me, but I ignored it. I feel bad telling Exie that I fell pregnant. I was married to her brother." I shiver. "Feels weird."

Judy leans over the booth and gives me a friendly shove. "She'll be happy for you both. She's even siding with you over her evil parents, and she went to him for help. That is love, honey. Not everyone gets a second chance at love."

I trust Judy and tell her everything going on with Lane's parents. She even agreed to help me out with my jewelry business. She needs the extra money and has agreed to help me make more jewelry for the next pop-up store and orders that need to be fulfilled. I have been making them by hand, but my fingers are hurting.

I get a message from Camila that LJ is ready for his lunch. He was working on a virtual project with other kids on the computer, and I headed over to the diner to catch up with Judy and visit Nancy.

"I have to go." I grab the takeout order and head to the house.

I get in the back seat, Henry closes the door, and a text comes through.

I look at my phone, and it's from Janine.

> Janine: He doesn't know I'm sending you this text. I know you're upset with Kalum and his reaction, but something awaits you at the house. Please give him a chance.

> Aura: I'm sorry for ignoring you. I was scared, and I miss him.

> Janine: I know.

Henry parks in front of the house and heads inside with the food. I stop when I see it. The sun is high in the sky, and the blur of tears makes the light around me look like a kaleidoscope of colors.

The Jeep.

The Jeep I wanted to buy from Lane all those years ago is restored in its full glory with big mud tires and the convertible soft top. Memories from my mother telling me about her adventures in her Jeep come flooding back. Lane never told me what he did with it, and I never asked when we moved from Spencer. My fingers grip the black handle of the door, and I open it. The smell of refurbished leather hits me. I look at the note and the football jersey inside it.

I pick it up and inhale the smell. Kalum's cologne and his scent. It's a Spencer football jersey. I pick up the old notebook paper and read it.

Even through loss, there are still amazing and beautiful things in this life. The best part of mine was meeting and falling in love with you. I hope you love your gift and would love to be part of your journey. I love you, Aura. Happy eighteenth birthday.
Love,
 # 68 Kalum St. Claire

I choke on a sob as his words from the other night in the hotel room by the harbor come back to me. He bought it and kept it all this time. I take off my coat, thankful for the sun, even if the clouds cover it. I pull his jersey over my head and run into the house.

I gasp.

Tears stream down my face, and my two favorite boys wait for me, both down on one knee. LJ with flowers, and Kalum with a black velvet box. There is a huge sign made of construction paper colored with crayons that reads:

WILL YOU MARRY ME?

"Yes! Oh God. Yes!"

I run and kneel on the floor and hug and kiss them both.

Camila comes forward from the kitchen with happy tears streaming down her face. "The box." She motions toward the black box Kalum holds out in his hand.

"It's okay, Momma. It's pretty."

Kalum opens the box, and the most beautiful ring I have

ever laid eyes on sparkles in the light. It's big but delicate, with three giant stones.

"One is your past, one is your present, and one is for your future. The two woven diamond bands on the ring are for our children." He looks at LJ and then at my stomach. "LJ, are you ready to be a big brother?"

"I'm going to be the best," he says, looking at me. "I promise, Momma."

"You're already the best. Both of you," I say softly.

Kalum hugs us both. How could I be so lucky to have fallen in love with two boys who would do anything for me?

Epilogue

Aura

I watch my husband with both one-year-old Kalum Jr. and LJ as they play in the pool at our home in Spencer. We bought a new home to spend time closer to Exie and Dex. Camila is still like a mother to me, watching over our sons as if they were her own grandchildren. I don't treat her like a babysitter or housekeeper but like a mother. She helps me, and I help her, and if it wasn't for her, I would have never met the most wonderful men in my life. Kalum and Lane.

Since marrying Kalum and becoming Mrs. St. Claire, Lane's parents dismissed the case against me. Exie had the board outvote them and remove them from the company, leaving Exie as CEO, and they quietly retired. My business has taken off online, and I am happy to be married to Kalum.

You can't help falling in love.

I fell in love twice in my life.

How is that possible?

There is a time when you meet the one you're destined to be with, but sometimes, time isn't ready. You get a glimpse if you're lucky. We move on, and if that person is your true love and destined to be your last, they will love you no matter what happens. This year or the next. Five years. Even ten.

They will let you go if your happiness means more to them than their own. I'll always love Lane and will fulfill his dream. He'll always be part of me, and the best part is that his legacy will live on through our son. Our love lives through him.

"Are you ready, Mrs. St. Claire?" Kalum asks, the water sluicing down his sexy, tatted frame.

I smile. "Yes."

I grab our beautiful baby boy Kalum Jr. as his chubby arms reach out for me, wet with his swim trunks from Camila's lap.

LJ comes out of the pool, drying off.

"Are you ready?" LJ asks, his face lit up with excitement.

I smile. "Yes, baby."

Today is LJ's birthday. All of our family and friends are ready to wish him a happy seventh birthday. His first track is built to practice with his Kid Karts in the back of our property. He has a great love for race cars, like his father. Kalum caters to his every whim in both love and understanding. I look around at my family. At my husband. Our sons. LJ slides in his Kid Kart with the same look as his father.

This is us.

Now and forever.

THE END

About the Author

Carmen Rosales is an emerging Latinx author of Steamy, and Dark Romance. Join her VIP list- www.carmenrosales.com

She loves spending time with her family. When she is not writing, she is reading. She is an Army veteran and is currently completing her Doctorate Degree in Business and has the love and support of her husband and five children. She loves to interact with her readers.

Scan the QR code to follow her on Social Media and sign up for her Newsletter: